THE WHISPERS OF EDEN

THE WHISPERS OF EDEN

KURT BARNES

THE
BRANCH PRESS

For Summer, Keegan, and Kyler

Who patiently endured the rambling tales of a world before our own, and in doing so, taught me how to imagine once again. This is for you.

Contents

1

Foreword

Welcome, dear reader, to the world before the Flood—ancient, mysterious, and trembling with echoes of Paradise lost and shadows rising. The story you hold, *The Whispers of Eden*, is a journey into that shadowed dawn, an exploration born from imagination yet rooted firmly in the bedrock of revealed truth.

First and foremost, let me be clear: This is a work of fiction. While I have drawn deeply from the narratives, themes, and truths found within the Bible, the specific events, character interactions, and the unfolding plot are products of my own imaginative pondering. Like many who grew up immersed in the rich worlds crafted by C.S. Lewis and J.R.R. Tolkien, I often found myself captivated by the tantalizing gaps in the earliest chapters of human history. What might have living in those first generations after Eden been like? What struggles did the faithful face? What forms did the growing evil take? This story is my humble attempt to imagine answers.

This tale grew from years of wondering, praying, and sketching the edges of a world I longed to understand—a world where faith and imagination walk hand in hand.

The Bible itself provides the anchors for this imagined world. Scripture tells us of Enoch, the seventh from Adam, a man who walked so faithfully with God that he *"was no more, because God took him away"* (Genesis 5:24), escaping physical death. We know of his son, Methuselah, whose lifespan exceeded all others (Genesis 5:27), and his great-grandson Noah, chosen by God for preservation amidst coming judgment (Genesis 6:8-9).

These incredible figures lived in an era populated by more than just ordinary men. Genesis speaks plainly of the Nephilim, the *"heroes of old, men of renown"* (Genesis 6:4), born of an unnatural union between the "sons of God" (often understood as fallen angels) and the "daughters of humans." Scripture also hints at the earliest rebellion in Heaven (Isaiah 14, Ezekiel 28, Jude 6, 2 Peter 2:4) that introduced cosmic evil into God's perfect creation. Even after the Flood, remnants of giant peoples, like the Sons of Anak who terrified the Israelite spies (Numbers 13:33), lingered, their lineage tracing back to those pre-Flood times.

Against this backdrop—the staggering beauty of Creation (Genesis 1-2), the heartbreaking tragedy of the Fall (Genesis 3), the unwavering promise of a Redeemer who would crush the Serpent's head (Genesis 3:15), and the reality of spiritual warfare—The Whispers of Eden takes flight. It imagines the lives of Enoch and his family, their desperate quest to preserve the truth, their encounters with giants both noble and corrupt, their flight from the insidious power of the Nephilim, and their unwavering hope in the Creator's plan.

My deepest hope in sharing this story is twofold. First, it might provide an engaging adventure that stirs your heart. But more importantly, I pray it might spark your own imagination and drive you back to the source—the Bible itself. May it encourage you to ponder the richness found there, visualize the people and places described, and marvel at the depth of God's unfolding plan of redemption "between the words on the page."

May you find blessing in this fictional exploration, and may it ultimately draw you closer to the Author of the one true story.

Grace and Peace,

Kurt Barnes

2

The Glade

Enoch stood in the cool, pre-dawn stillness beside the great stone altar, its surface cold and solid beneath his weathered palms. The first light of day was a pale, hesitant promise, not yet able to pierce the dense canopy overhead. The scents of damp earth and the smoldering remnants of last night's fire mingled in the air, a familiar perfume of peace. *Another day the Creator has given,* he thought, his gaze lifting toward the interwoven branches that formed the Glades living cathedral.

This was his ritual, this solitary watch before the others stirred. It was here, in the quiet, that the weight of his calling felt most intense. He was the storyteller and knowledge keeper of his people, tasked with preserving the fragmented truths passed down through countless generations in whispered tales and chanted rhythms around flickering fires. He was the one who remembered, who kept alive the aching memory of Eden—a paradise lost—and the pervasive sorrow that had followed its fading.

A thin blue ribbon of smoke curled from the roof of his dwelling, where Elara was already tending the hearth. The thought of her brought a smile to his face. There were no grand halls of stone but huts of woven branches and leaves, their rounded shapes blending seamlessly with the natural world, as if they had sprung from the earth it-self—a testament to the life that stubbornly thrived within.

Life in the glade followed the rhythms of the sun and the moon, a steady cycle of labor and rest, of reverence and remembrance. The days began near the central clearing, with offerings of thanks laid upon the altar—the first fruits of a hunt, the best heads of grain from the harvest—acknowledging their dependence on the unseen Creator.

Then came the tasks of survival, shared by all, yet each according to their calling. The men, though skilled hunters, also tended cultivated fields stretching along the glade's sunnier edge. Giant grains, their stalks heavy as a man's fist with seed, swayed in the gentle breeze, a unique bounty found only here. Fruit-bearing vines climbed trellises of woven branches, offering sweet sustenance. They also raised livestock, unlike those found beyond the glade: herds of docile creatures such as oversized goats valued for their rich milk and thick hides, and flocks of large, flightless birds with iridescent feathers, providing meat and eggs. These were gifts, they knew, remnant blessings from the Creator in this sheltered place, for the lands beyond their hidden valley were often barren, haunted, and unforgiving.

Yet, even within this pocket of abundance, the shadow of danger never truly receded. Spears tipped with fire-hardened wood or sharpened bone, and heavy stone axes were always close at hand, stark reminders of the threats lurking in the surrounding wilderness. Ever-present were the great beasts—predators with eyes like burning coals and teeth like jagged daggers, a tangible reminder of the brokenness of the Creator's masterpiece. There were also other dangers, closer to their own kind: roving bands of men, driven by desperation or malice, their hearts twisted by the darkness that had seeped into the world since the Fall. And there were whispers, carried on the wind or by rare, fearful travelers who stumbled near the glade—whispers of giants dwelling in distant mountains, some said to be peaceful artisans, others consumed by a hunger for power and conquest.

The glade was a haven, but necessity had made it a fortress. A sturdy palisade of sharpened stakes, reinforced with intricately woven branches, encircled the clearing—a silent warning to any who might trespass. Watchtowers, cleverly built high among the branches of the giant surrounding trees, offered vantage points for spotting approaching threats long before they reached the perimeter. The people of the glade were skilled in defense, their strength matched by their cunning, their unity their greatest shield against the encroaching shadows.

It was a hard life, filled with constant toil and the low hum of awareness of peril. But it was also a good life, marked by the simple joys of family, the deep comfort of shared purpose and belonging, and the unwavering belief in the Creator's providence, even if His ways sometimes felt obscured.

They knew, from fragmented tales passed down, that all the scattered sons of Adam did not share their experience; many lived in constant fear and brutal hardship, their lives scarred by violence and despair. The glade remained a small beacon of hope, a demonstration of the possibility of a different way—a life striving for harmony with the Creator and with each other.

A steady *thump-thump* filled the air as women pounded grain into meal, mingling with the softer sounds of hide being scraped and stitched. As the sun climbed toward its zenith, burning away the morning mists, the day unfolded in its familiar rhythm, casting shorter, sharper shadows across the clearing. Children, morning lessons with the elders finished, tumbled in the grass, their laughter a bright counterpoint to the men's discussions as they returned from checking snares or tending the fields, bringing with them game or bundles of firewood.

The afternoon waned, and a sense of shared purpose settled over the glade as tools were cleaned and put away and thoughts turned toward the evening meal and the gathering fire.

As twilight deepened, painting the sky in hues of fiery orange and deep violet, the heart of the glade became the fire. It crackled merrily in the central clearing, flames leaping and dancing, casting a warm, flickering glow on the faces gathered around it. The air filled with the savory scent of roasting goat and the comforting murmur of voices settling into quiet anticipation.

Enoch sat on a large, smooth stone near the fire, its coolness grounding him as he pondered the importance of the tale he was about to tell. *How many times have I spoken these words?* He wondered, his eyes sweeping across the beloved faces illuminated by the dancing flames. *Yet each time, the sorrow feels fresh, the hope so desperately fragile.* His family surrounded him, their faces turned toward him. Elara sat close by, her hands resting in her lap, her presence a silent pillar of strength beside him. He saw the quiet pride in her eyes as she watched him, but also the shared burden of knowledge, the understanding of the vital importance, and the frustrating incompleteness of these stories. She knew, as he did, that these fragments were more than history; they were identity, warning, and a map toward a dimly remembered promise.

His children, now grown from the youths he had once taught at his knee, sat on the soft earth. There was Jareth, a young man now, his shoulders broad and his jaw set, already carrying the weight of dawning responsibility like a mantle. He rested a hand on the haft of the stone axe at his belt, his gaze fixed on the flickering flames as if discerning threats within their dance.

He feels the darkness growing, Enoch thought with a pang of pride and sorrow.

Beside him sat Adah, a young woman of striking beauty, her long red hair, a gift from her mother Elara, glowed in the firelight. With curious eyes missing nothing, she leaned forward, absorbing the atmosphere. She drank in stories like fertile ground absorbing precious rain, her brow often furrowed, always seeking the *why* behind the what.

She is in search of understanding, the reasons lost to time.

And then there was Methuselah, youngest of the three. His body had grown to the strength and breadth of a man, but his youthful energy was barely contained. He shifted restlessly, his gaze darting from his father's face to the deep shadows beyond the firelight, imagining the serpents and beasts his father spoke of lurking there.

His fire burns bright, Enoch reflected, *but must be tempered with wisdom.*

Around them sat other members of the community, faces reflecting the same blend of reverence and longing, the familiar hunger for connection to their origins, for answers held just beyond memory's reach.

Enoch drew a deep breath, the scent of pine and woodsmoke filling his lungs, centering him. *Focus. They need the truth... what precious fragments we retain, pieced together across the aching silence of generations. May the Creator grant me wisdom to share it faithfully.* He spoke, his voice a low, resonant cadence that seemed to draw the very shadows closer, quieting the last whispers. "In the beginning," a hush fell over the gathering, the crackling fire the only sound, "as the oldest chants remember it, there was only the Creator. He was alone yet complete, and within Him resided the potential for all that was and all that ever would be."

He gestured toward the towering trees that formed their natural temple, branches reaching toward the heavens like supplicating arms. "The whispers say He spoke, and the world shuddered into being. He stretched out His hand, and the land took shape, mountains rose, rivers flowed. He filled the skies with light, set the sun and moon in their courses, scattered the stars like jewels across the void—each one bearing a true name we no longer know."

His voice softened, filled with a sense of inherited awe as delicate embers were passed down through time. "He fashioned creatures of wonder, the stories tell of beasts of the earth, birds of the air, each unique, perfect in ways we can now only imagine. And then, He formed Adam, the first man, from the very dust of the ground, shaping him with unique care. He breathed into him the breath of life, and

Adam stood, a being reflecting the Creator's own light, imbued with a purpose now lost somewhere in the mists of time."

Enoch paused, his gaze sweeping over the faces of his listeners, seeing their earnest hunger for clarity. "The Creator placed Adam in the garden called Eden—a place our hearts remember though our eyes have never seen, a place of beauty and abundance beyond all telling. There, the stories insist, Adam walked with God, in perfect harmony with all creation. He had dominion, tending the garden with joy, knowing no sorrow, no pain, no fear. The fullness of that communion..." Enoch's voice faltered slightly, "it is a memory that haunts our deepest dreams, a longing woven into our very being."

A shadow crossed his face, the recognizable sorrow surfacing as he approached the heart of their fractured history. "We know the Creator saw Adam and said, 'It is not good that the man should be alone,' and so He formed Eve, the first woman, from Adam's own side, bone of his bone, flesh of his flesh. They were together then, man and woman, perfectly matched, reflecting His love in their unity."

He paused again, his voice dropping to a whisper, touching the edge of the remembered trauma that shaped their world. "And then... something entered. A shadow fell. The stories name it 'Serpent'—whether beast or fallen spirit or something more terrible, the tellings differ. But all agree it was a creature of cunning, deceit, and deep enmity toward the Creator and His creation."

A shiver ran through the gathering, an involuntary response, a collective tremor against the known darkness and the incalculable, terrifying unknowns.

"This Serpent," Enoch continued, his voice filled with inherited anger and grief, "whispered lies into Eve's ear. What lies exactly? The fragments agree on the core: temptation wrapped in promise, the allure of forbidden knowledge, the offer of power gained apart from the Giver. It tempted her to disobey the Creator's one command, the nature of which we can only guess, tied somehow to the fruit of a specific tree. The Serpent promised godhood, insight equal to the Creator's, but it offered only dust and death."

He looked at his family, his eyes filled with warning born from generations of harsh experience in a fallen world. "We are told that Eve, possibly curious, maybe deceived, perhaps seeking something she felt she lacked... listened. And she ate. Why she listened, what tilted the balance in her heart against the Creator's clear goodness... these are painful questions lost to the silence between ages. And she gave the fruit to Adam. He, though knowing better, deceived himself and ate as well."

A heavy sigh escaped Enoch's lips, carrying the weight of ages and unanswered 'whys.' "And in that moment, everything changed. The harmony shattered instantly. A wrongness—what the elders name sin—entered the world, like a subtle poison spreading through the veins of creation itself. Shame, fear, and awareness of their brokenness overwhelmed Adam and Eve, and God banished them from Eden, exiling them from His presence. Their bodies became subject to pain and suffering, their lives destined inevitably to end in death." He felt the familiar ache in his chest, the inherited grief of that separation. He saw Jareth shift uncomfortably, knuckles white where he gripped his knee, saw Adah blink rapidly, her brow deeply furrowed, the 'why' sharper, more elusive than ever. He watched as Methuselah stared into the fire, seeing not just destruction now but the mystery of that choice.

Elara reached out again, her fingers briefly brushing his arm, a silent gesture acknowledging the shared burden of not knowing, of living with the consequences.

He gestured toward the deep darkness that pressed in around their firelit circle. "The world outside the garden became harsh, resistant." *Why? As direct punishment? As the natural consequence of separation from the Source of Life?* "The ground brought forth thorns and thistles, demanding sweat and toil for sustenance. Animals, once companions Adam named, became creatures of fear and aggression, predator and prey. And the shadow of death, unknown in Eden, fell over all living things." *And it creeps closer to our own door. Even now*, the thought echoed in his mind.

His voice grew stronger, pushing back against the shadows of doubt and mystery, forcing the core of their enduring hope to the surface. "But this we know for certain: Even in their sorrow, even in banishment, the Creator did not abandon them outright! He provided their first covering. And He *promised*," the word resonated with fierce conviction, a promise whispered first through Adam's tears, remembered faithfully through the ages, "that one day, a descendant would come who would somehow confront the Serpent, crush its head, even while being wounded in the struggle. One who would bring redemption, break the curse, reopen the way to life—though how or when or even who precisely remains veiled in prophecy. And we, my children," his gaze lingered intensely on each of them, on Jareth's guarded strength, Adah's searching mind, Methuselah's restless spirit, "we cling to that promise like a tiny, precious flame in the overwhelming darkness of this world. We wait, we watch, we remember, anticipating the promised dawn to break." *May you live to see it*, he prayed inwardly, *and understand it more fully, more clearly, than I ever can.*

As Enoch finished speaking, a hush fell over the gathering, deeper than before, laced now not only with sorrow and hope but the weight of unanswered questions, of weighty mysteries barely touched upon.

The fire crackled, its flames reflecting in eyes filled with contemplation.

Jareth slowly relaxed his hand, but his gaze remained fixed on the deep shadows beyond the firelight, as if still seeking answers there.

Adah hugged her knees tighter, her brow deeply furrowed. "But, Father," she asked softly, unable to contain the question that burned within her, voicing the thought many held, "the Serpent... if the Creator is all-powerful, all-knowing... where did it come from? Why would He allow such a creature in His perfect garden, especially if He knew the harm it would cause?"

Enoch met her searching gaze, his own eyes reflecting the acute limits of his inherited knowledge. "That, my daughter," he spoke gently, his voice heavy with the admission, "is one of the deep mysteries the ages have obscured from us. The fragments we hold speak only of its cunning, its enmity toward the Creator and all He loves, and its pivotal role in the Fall. Its ultimate origin before that moment, its purpose beyond pure malice... these are truths veiled from our sight, possibly beyond our comprehension this side of eternity."

Methuselah, still staring into the fire, spoke up, his youthful voice puzzled. "And the tree... the knowledge. Why was knowing things bad? Isn't learning, understanding, good?"

"Maybe it wasn't the knowledge itself, son," Enoch replied carefully, "but how it was sought—grasping it defiantly, apart from the Giver. Perhaps one can only receive true wisdom as a gift, in relationship with Him." He sighed, the weight of these fundamental, unanswered questions pressing down on him. The story, vital as it was, felt achingly incomplete, like charting a perilous course by only a few known stars, the massive, silent darkness between them holding unknown truths and potential dangers.

As the gathering dispersed, people drifted back toward their huts, carrying the weight of the fragmented tale and the heavy questions it raised.

Enoch remained by the dying fire. Elara stayed with him, her hand resting gently on his arm now, her presence a silent, unwavering comfort in the face of the immense unknown. The peace of the glade felt real, tangible, yet undeniably shaky against the backdrop of their limited understanding and the encroaching shadows of the world beyond. He looked up, past the towering canopy reaching like praying hands toward the heavens, toward the distant stars scattered like diamond dust across the infinite dark.

So many questions, Lord, he prayed silently, the words forming in his soul. *So much lost to time, to sin, to silence. Is there more? Is there a way to truly know, to recover the fullness of what Adam lost? Guide us... show us the path... if it be Your will...*

He felt the burden of his people's history, the gaps in their understanding a tangible ache in his spirit, fueling a raring, rising yearning for clarity, for the full truth hidden somewhere beyond the glade's borders, somewhere in the deep echoes of the past. The time felt near; he sensed it like a change in the wind, when the whispers of Eden might finally call them forth into the unknown.

3

The Burden of Whispers

Night descended upon the glade, a velvet cloak studded with the cold fire of distant stars. The communal fire had dwindled to embers, their orange glow pulsing softly against the encroaching dark, casting dancing shadows that stretched and twisted like restless spirits against the woven walls of the nearby huts. Most of the community had retired, seeking the solace of sleep after the weight of Enoch's fragmented stories, but Enoch himself remained by the fading flames. He fixed his gaze not on the dying embers but upward, into the cosmic darkness between the stars.

So much unseen, he thought, *so much forgotten.*

A strange stillness had settled upon him, an inward quietness that seemed to separate him from the sleeping world around him. His breath came slow, each exhalation carrying away a layer of earthly weariness, each inhalation drawing in the cool night air and something... else, an attentiveness that went beyond mere thought. His eyes, though directed toward the heavens, seemed to see beyond them, holding a distant, almost otherworldly light.

He felt a gaze upon him and turned his head slightly. Elara stood in the shadowed doorway of their hut, her arms wrapped around herself against the night chill. He knew that posture well—the familiar mix of loving unease and deep-seated trust that always surfaced when he drifted into these deep states of listening. The unspoken question in her stance—*What will this demand of us?*—was a burden he felt as keenly as she did.

And then it came, not with a crash of thunder or a blinding flash of revelation but with a gentle, inexorable unfolding within his mind, like the slow blooming of a moonpetal flower in the quietest hour of the night. A vision, sharp-edged and undeniably real, blossomed in Enoch's inner sight.

He saw a cave, its entrance veiled by a thick curtain of clinging vines, nestled low in the rocky foothills of a mountain range whose peaks clawed at the distant sky like bony fingers reaching for answers. A sense of incalculable age emanated from the place, the very stones saturated with sorrow, yet beneath it, like a heartbeat deep within the earth, pulsed a dawning hope. *The first shelter,* the understanding resonated within him, clear as a spoken word, though soundless. *Where Adam and Eve wept their first tears outside the garden, remembering the lost light.*

Within that shadowed space, the vision focused with startling clarity. He saw scrolls, ancient and brittle-looking, bound with leather thongs, lying upon a rough-hewn stone shelf. Clay tablets were etched with rows of precise, angular symbols, the clear markings of a written language. Artifacts lay scattered nearby—a tool of unfamiliar grace and material, a shard of pottery painted with intricate, forgotten patterns. *Adam's own record. His testament,* the vision pressed upon him with undeniable force, *of Paradise, of the Fall, of the path taken... and possibly, the path back toward the Promise...*

The vision pulsed with a divine imperative, an urgent heat that kindled deep within Enoch's soul, demanding action. *It must be found. It must be preserved.*

The vision receded abruptly, leaving an imprint burning behind his eyes as he stirred. With a gasp and a sharp intake of the cool night air, his eyes snapped open, the distant, otherworldly light replaced by a sharp, immediate focus. He rose to his feet, his movements deliberate, charged now with a potent, undeniable energy. He turned, un-surprised to see his family gathering in the dim ember-glow filtering from their hut, drawn by the almost tangible shift in the surrounding atmosphere. Nearest was Elara, her face displaying loving concern. Jareth moved to her side, appearing cautious. Adah peered from behind her mother, curiosity warring with apprehension. Methuselah stepped out last, blinking sleep from his eyes, sensing the sudden tension.

"I have seen," Enoch said, his voice low but carrying the weight of the vision that still echoed within him, "a place of ageless truth. A cave hidden in a mountain," he gestured vaguely toward the east, "near the very place where our original parents wept their first tears upon being exiled from the garden."

A hush fell over the small group, thicker and colder than the night air. The stories were one thing—cherished history, foundational belief, core identity. But this... this spoke of geography, of tangible reality dangerously close to the mythic past.

Elara stepped forward, her hand instinctively reaching for his arm. "Enoch, what do you mean? Your quietness... this stillness... was it this? What did you see?"

Enoch recounted the vision, his words painting a picture not just of the cave and its precious contents but of the overwhelming certainty, the divine compulsion that accompanied it. He described the feel of sorrow and hope embedded in the stone, the urgency that burned within him.

He finished, his voice still thick with the awe of what he had witnessed. The family stood in stunned silence, trying to absorb the magnitude of what he had described. It was Elara who finally broke the quiet, her voice a fearful whisper. "So... what does this mean, Enoch?"

Enoch's gaze, which had been distant, sharpened with purpose. He looked from his wife to his children, his expression hardening with a resolve that seemed to solidify in the cool night air. "It means the Creator has answered my prayer," he stated, his voice now firm, leaving no room for doubt. "He has shown us where the full truth of our beginning is hidden. And I believe He has shown it to me for a reason. I must go. I must seek out this cave and bring back the record Adam left for us."

As he spoke, he watched reactions flicker across their faces in the dim light. Skepticism tightened Jareth's jaw almost immediately. His eldest son shifted his weight, folding his arms across his sturdy chest, his practical nature resisting the unseen. "Father," Jareth said, his voice respectful but firm, "visions are... fleeting things. We know this from the old tales. Dreams twist truth; shadows mimic substance. Will you risk your life, based on an image in the night?" He glanced worriedly toward the sturdy palisade, then the deep, protective woods beyond.

Adah, her voice trembling slightly, stepped closer to Elara, seeking her mother's reassurance. "And the journey, Father... you told us we were never to leave the glade. You told us of great beasts... and roving bands of lost men... and," her voice dropped to a fearful whisper, "the Nephilim... their influence... their patrols..." She couldn't finish, the fear evident in her wide eyes.

Her mind always leaps to the dangers, the obstacles, Enoch noted again with a pang of love and sorrow. *She feels the world's brokenness so acutely.*

Even the few others who had emerged from nearby huts, drawn by the low, urgent voices, hesitated, their faces troubled in the embers' glow. The glade was safety, precarious but known, and familiar. The Nephilim's growing power cast a shadow over the dangerous world outside. To abandon safety for a quest born of a vision seemed like madness, like walking willingly into a gathering storm.

Doubt. It is the Serpent's other, subtler weapon, Enoch thought grimly. *Fear paralyzes where force cannot reach.*

But then Methuselah stepped fully into the dim light, moving past Adah almost impatiently. His youthful face, usually alit with restless energy or quick humor, was now startlingly transformed, set with a quiet determination Enoch had rarely witnessed in him. His eyes, mirroring his father's visionary light for a moment, seemed to burn with a reflected fire.

"I believe you, Father," he said, his voice clear and unwavering, cutting through the heavy silence like a thrown spear. He looked not just at Enoch but swept his gaze deliberately across the others, challenging their fear and doubt. "The Creator speaks to those who listen. We pray daily for guidance, for hope against the encroaching dark. Why would we turn away when He answers?" He straightened his young shoulders, shedding his usual restlessness like an outgrown skin. "This vision... it is not a dream. It is a call."

A collective gasp swept through the small group. Methuselah—impulsive, sometimes reckless—stood suddenly as a beacon of unwavering, immediate faith. The very air seemed to shift, the ice of their collective fear cracking under the simple heat of his conviction.

Enoch's heart swelled with a powerful mixture of overwhelming pride, deep relief, and a dawning apprehension for the perilous path his son now so readily embraced.

He sees beyond the shadows.

"Then you will come with me, my son?" he asked, his voice regaining its strength, steady once more.

"I will," Methuselah answered without a flicker of hesitation, meeting his father's gaze squarely, his eyes alight with purpose. "Where you go, I will go. We will seek this truth together."

Hope, stronger now, blossomed in Enoch's chest, pushing back the weight of doubt, pushing back the shadows. *One voice, firm in faith, can indeed be enough to start an avalanche of purpose. It begins.*

Methuselah's unexpected faith, combined with the vision, ignited the decision; Enoch and Methuselah would undertake the journey. A flurry of quiet, urgent activity immediately followed, chasing away the night's stillness.

Elara, her face resigned to the inevitable, yet resolute, moved quickly to gather dried provisions, her practical love overriding her fear.

Jareth, his skepticism silenced by loyalty and Methuselah's conviction, began checking the condition of their best stone axes and tools, his jaw tight with worry for their safety.

Adah, her own fear pushed aside by familial duty, brought forth sturdy cloaks and waterskins, her movements precise and efficient.

Neighbors awakened by the activity whispered quiet farewells, and prayers were offered beside the now-gray ashes of the central fire. The glade, mere hours ago a haven of quiet peace and lingering questions, now thrummed with a tense sense of urgent purpose, an undercurrent of fear pulling against the undeniable tide of hope.

The whispers of Eden had called, and two of its sons would answer, their hearts filled with a daunting mixture of trepidation and unwavering faith.

4

The Untamed River

The morning dawned with a fiery brilliance, the sun a molten disc climbing above the eastern horizon, casting long, dramatic shadows from the trees across the glade floor. Enoch and Methuselah, their packs laden with provisions, tools, and the heavy weight of their mission, stood at the threshold between home and the unknown. The air itself felt thick with unspoken words, with the sheer gravity of their departure.

Elara, her eyes brimming with tears she fought to hold back, clung to Enoch tightly. "Be careful, my love," she whispered, her voice thick, muffled against the rough fabric of his shoulder.

Her strength holds this place together, Enoch thought, feeling the slight tremor in her arms despite her resolve. *Leaving her is the hardest step.*

"May the Creator watch over you both."

Enoch returned the embrace, holding her firmly for a long moment before gently setting her back. He forced his voice to be steady, a rock for her to lean on in these last moments. "Fear not, Elara. We go under His guidance. Trust in His protection. We will return." He then turned to Methuselah, whose youthful excitement warred visibly with the dawning reality of the perils ahead. Enoch placed a hand on his son's shoulder, feeling the tension beneath the rough-spun tunic. "Remember, my son," he said gravely. "Listen to the whispers of the wild, yes, but weigh them against the wisdom we carry from the Creator. And never," his gaze intensified, holding Methuselah's, "stray from the path—either the one beneath our feet or the one within our hearts."

Methuselah swallowed hard, his bravado momentarily flickering under his father's serious gaze. He straightened, meeting Enoch's eyes. "I will not fail you, Father. I understand."

Does he truly? Enoch wondered briefly, seeing the spark of adventure still warring with apprehension in his son's eyes. *Or does he merely feel the call without yet grasping the cost of answering?*

With a final, lingering glance back at Elara's lone figure standing brave at the edge of the clearing, they turned and stepped into the deep shadows of the forest. The dense canopy closed behind them like a heavy curtain, the sounds of the glade fading instantly, replaced by the whispering hush and alien calls of the wood. Nervous energy charged the initial days. Exhilaration at the unknown battled with apprehension in Methuselah's quick glances and eager strides, while Enoch felt a grim sense of purpose settling over him; the memory of the vision was a constant compass in his mind.

They followed game trails, their feet crunching on centuries of fallen leaves, the air alive with the unseen chatter of strange birds and the rustle of hidden creatures in the undergrowth. Once, a distant, guttural roar echoed through the trees, making Methuselah's hand fly instinctively to the axe at his belt, his eyes wide, until Enoch gave a shake of his head.

Not close. Not yet.

But as they journeyed farther westward, leaving the relative sanctuary of the glade's influence behind, a subtle shift occurred in the forest's very character. It seemed older here, heavier, less welcoming. The air grew thick, stagnant, filtering the sunlight through a canopy of sickly yellow leaves that cast an unsettling, jaundiced pallor on the ground. Beneath their feet, the bleached bones of long-dead creatures lay scattered like warnings amidst the roots and ferns, stark reminders of the cycle of life and, increasingly, the pervasiveness of death beyond their sheltered home.

A persistent sense of being watched prickled at Enoch's neck, though the woods remained stubbornly, unnervingly silent whenever he paused to listen intently.

Something feels wrong here, he thought. *Stale. Like breath held too long, waiting.*

Then, the sound reached them—a low, distant rumble that grew steadily, ominously, into a deafening roar. Pushing through a final, dense screen of grasping thorns that tore at their clothes, they emerged onto a crumbling bank and came upon it—the river. It was monstrous, less a river than a raw, untamed force of nature slicing through the landscape like a fresh, weeping wound. Its waters were a churning, turbulent mass of muddy brown, thick with sediment and uprooted debris, the sheer power of its current terrifyingly audible above the roar. Gigantic trees, their roots laid bare like exposed nerves by relentless erosion, clung precariously to the collapsing banks, their branches gnarled, arthritic fingers of dying old men.

The world bleeds here, Enoch thought, awestruck and disturbed by the raw violence of the scene.

Following the river's tormented edge downstream, searching desperately for any sign of a crossing, the roar intensified, becoming almost painful. They rounded a sharp bend choked with broken rock and stopped dead, silenced by a mixture of terrifying awe and fear. Before them, the river, gathering all its fury, plunged over the edge of a sheer cliff—a thunderous, ground-shaking waterfall cascading into a churning, mist-shrouded pool far below. The rising vapor clung like a spectral shroud, obscuring the far side, swallowing the light. And built into the cliffs on both banks, like barnacles clinging to a leviathan's flank, half-submerged in the raging water at the fall's edge, lay the impossible ruins of a city.

Broken walls, like the shattered teeth of some massive skull, jutted from the cliffs. Crumbling towers leaned at precarious angles, threatening to collapse into the torrent. The broken remains of grand arches and devastated plazas lined the river's violent path. It was a city of ghosts, wholly silent save for the river's deafening song, a chilling, water-scoured testament to a civilization obliterated from the world.

Enoch's brow furrowed, his mind racing, trying to reconcile this impossible, drowned city with any history or legend known to him. "This is... formidable," he breathed, the word inadequate to capture the desolation and mystery before him. *A city here? So far from any known settlement? Destroyed so completely? By what?* "But also," he added, feeling a deep chill despite the damp, heavy air, "it feels like a warning."

Methuselah, however, seemed less struck by the ominous ruin and more immediately challenged by the physical obstacle the river presented. His earlier apprehension, momentarily forgotten in the face of this tangible barrier, gave way to youthful confidence and impatience. "A warning? It's just water, Father!" he scoffed, his eyes already scanning the churning torrent, dismissing the ruins. "Fear not! I can find a way across. I am a strong swimmer!"

"Methuselah, wait!" Enoch commanded sharply, sensing the reckless surge in his son, alarmed by his dismissal of the evident danger. "The current—"

But before the words were fully out, Methuselah had shucked his pack and tunic, leaving them carelessly on the rocks. Clad only in his loincloth, he gave a defiant whoop and plunged into the raging water near the bank, striking out for the other side. His powerful young arms churned against the brown water, but the river seized him instantly, contemptuous of his strength. *Foolish boy! Reckless!* Enoch's heart leaped into his throat. The current, like an invisible hand, grabbed Methuselah and swept him downstream with terrifying speed, toward the roaring maw of the waterfall.

"Father!" Methuselah's cry was thin, frantic, almost swallowed by the river's roar as the full realization of his folly hit him. His strokes became wild, useless against the implacable, overwhelming force pulling him toward the abyss.

Horror spurred Enoch into immediate action. He scrambled along the treacherous, crumbling bank, loose rocks skittering under his feet, his eyes locked on his son's desperate struggle against the muddy torrent. The terrain was too rough, too broken to keep pace. Methuselah was being pulled closer and closer to the edge, with the heavy mist from the falls already swirling around him.

Then Enoch spotted it—a large, partially submerged tree trunk, snagged hard amongst the rocks near the precipice, its bare, bleached branches reaching out like grasping skeletal fingers. Adrenaline, cold and sharp, surged through him. He leaped onto the nearest part of the slick, waterlogged trunk, finding perilous footing on the treacherous surface. Using its branches for leverage, scrabbling desperately, ignoring scraped hands and straining muscles, he propelled himself farther out along the unstable bank. Above him, hanging down from an overhanging cliff face, was a sturdy vine, thick as his arm. *Creator, guide my hand! Give me strength!* He lunged, his fingers closing around the rough vine, felt it hold his weight, and swung himself out over the churning, muddy water just as Methuselah reached the very brink, about to be swept over the edge into the thundering chaos below. He snagged his son's outstretched arm, the force nearly tearing Enoch's own grip from the vine.

With a determined heave, fueled by terror and fierce paternal love, he hauled Methuselah back toward the relative safety of the bank, collapsing onto the muddy rocks beside him, both gasping, soaked to the bone, and trembling uncontrollably from adrenaline and cold.

"Father!" Methuselah choked out, retching muddy water, his eyes wide with remembered terror. "I... I almost..." He couldn't finish, shuddering violently with reaction.

Enoch pulled his son into a fierce embrace, relief washing over him in a wave so powerful it left him weak-kneed. "You are alive, my son," he gasped, holding him tight, feeling the frenetic beat of his heart against his own. "That is all that matters now. You are alive." *But the river nearly claimed you,* the unspoken thought echoed grimly. *A harsh lesson learned, I pray, though the price was almost unbearable.*

The adrenaline faded, leaving only the biting cold of their soaked clothes and the shuddering in their limbs. Enoch rose stiffly, his gaze finding the spot upriver where their packs lay discarded. "Come," he said, his voice quiet but firm, leaving no room for argument. "You need to get dry before the chill takes root."

Methuselah followed without a word, his eyes fixed on the ground, the earlier bravado washed away, leaving only a raw, shivering shame. They retrieved their packs and Methuselah's tunic. Enoch watched as his son wrung out the wet garment, the silence between them heavy with the unspoken lesson.

The need for a fire and shelter from the wind was now urgent. It drove them, finally, to turn their attention to the looming, silent ruins that offered the only refuge. As they sought a defensible spot to build a fire, the details of the ruins began to resolve themselves from the chaos. They could now see fragments of pottery painted with intricate, unfamiliar geometric designs; heavy stone tools carved with astonishing precision; the broken remnants of statues depicting strange, imposing beings with both human and animal features. And inscriptions etched onto pillars and foundation stones, written in angular, runic symbols belonging to no language Enoch recognized. *Knowledge... but what kind?*

The unease returned, colder than the river water.

"This was once a great city," Enoch said softly, his voice filled with wonder, shadowed by a growing dread. "A thriving place... built with immense skill... but whose?"

They explored the ruins cautiously on their side of the river first, seeking shelter as night approached. Venturing deeper into the ruined structures, the evidence of sudden, violent destruction became undeniable. Thick walls were blackened and pulverized as if by substantial force or heat. Buildings had collapsed inward, consumed by fire long ago, now washed away by the river's encroaching waters. Bones lay scattered among the debris, tangled in the rubble, many trapped where they fell, their bodies broken and twisted in unnatural ways.

"What happened here?" Methuselah whispered, his earlier bravado completely extinguished, replaced now by awe and a creeping fear as he nudged a cracked skull with his foot.

Enoch shook his head, rubbing a deep scorch mark on a massive, fused, stone block. "I do not know, my son." *But I feel it now, stronger than ever.* "I sense a great, ancient darkness here, a shadow that still lingers, woven into the very stones, into the memory of the water itself."

* * *

While Enoch pondered the grim history etched in stone, Methuselah's gaze drifted, drawn less by the grand scale of destruction and more by the smaller details scattered within it. His foot dislodged a loose rock near the outstretched skeletal hand, revealing something gleaming dully beneath the grime. Curiosity warring with revulsion, he knelt, brushing away centuries of silt. It was a dagger. Unlike any tool he had ever seen, its blade was not stone or bone but a warm, golden metal, perfectly shaped, sharp-edged, and, strangely, disturbingly untarnished by time, water, or the violence that had clearly consumed this place. The hilt felt cool in his hand, balanced with an artisan's skill far beyond the glade's simple craft.

A jolt, almost like recognition but deeper, more resonant, passed through him as he held it. *Such beauty... such power...* he thought, awe momentarily silencing his fear. *The harshness of our journey, the memory of the roaring beast, the dangers faced and those yet to come... Against the beasts, the shadows, the unknown paths ahead... we will need every advantage, every strength we can find.*

He knew instinctively that his father would disapprove vehemently, would see only the darkness clinging to this place, would counsel reliance only on the Creator's unseen hand. But the dagger felt solid, real, a tangible edge against a hostile world. With a furtive glance toward Enoch, who was still absorbed in examining inscriptions on a fallen pillar, Methuselah quickly tucked the dagger securely into the folds of his loincloth, hidden beneath his tunic. The secret weight felt cold against his skin, yet paradoxically, it banished some of his immediate fear, sparking a dangerous, newfound confidence, a feeling of tangible protection he instinctively attributed to the power held within the beautiful metal itself.

They found a relatively intact building further from the river's spray, its roof partially collapsed but offering some protection from the elements, possibly once a temple or meeting hall, judging by its size. They cleared a small space amidst the debris and built a fire, its small light pushing back weakly against the oppressive silence and gloom of the dead city.

* * *

As they sat by the fire, Enoch forced down a mouthful of tough, preserved meat. The taste was familiar, a taste of the Glade, but it did nothing to quiet the unease this dead city stirred in his soul. His gaze swept over the looming, shattered structures silhouetted against the night sky, their broken forms like the bones of some great, fallen beast. The questions that hung heavy in the oppressive air churned within him.

Who were these people? He wondered, looking at the intricate carvings on a nearby fallen stone, barely visible in the firelight. *What strange knowledge did they possess to build such a city in this desolate place? And what terrible force had brought about their utter annihilation? Did they fall to beasts? To men? Or to something else entirely... something darker?*

He looked across the fire at Methuselah, who stared into the flames, his usual youthful energy extinguished. A new and unsettling quietness had fallen over his son since his ordeal in the river, a silent chasm between them that Enoch could not yet name. The answer to the city's mystery, Enoch knew with a growing, cold certainty, was vital.

The river, initially just an impassable barrier, now seemed like a gateway into a deeper, older, more dangerous mystery, one that whispered of forgotten ages and the corruption that had taken root long before their time.

The night passed in a restless haze of deep unease. Sleep was shallow, fleeting, punctuated by the constant roar of the waterfall and the whispers of the wind sighing through desolate ruins. Enoch and Methuselah took turns tending the small fire, its flames defiant against the overwhelming darkness, each scanning the looming shadows beyond the firelight for any hint of movement. The weighty silence of the city, devoid of any life save their own, pressed in on them, more unsettling than any beast's cry, fueling their apprehension.

As the first hint of dawn painted the sky in bruised purples and pale gold, they stirred, muscles stiff, spirits heavy with the weight of the unknown. The mystery of the ruined city was a tangible presence, a puzzle demanding attention, yet every instinct screamed of danger, urging them onward.

"We must find a way across," Enoch stated, his voice hoarse from the damp night air and lack of sleep. He looked toward the thundering falls, then back at the impassable, churning torrent before them. "The path the vision showed lies beyond this water, but the river... it seeks to devour all who challenge it."

They began searching the treacherous riverbank again, eyes scanning the turbulent brown water, the crumbling ruins offering no easy answers, only reminders of destruction. Hope dwindled with the rising sun.

Then, Methuselah, wading cautiously into the shallows near where they'd collapsed the day before, testing the depth, stumbled, his foot hitting something solid but yielding beneath the shifting sand. He reached down, his hand closing around something thick and unexpectedly fibrous. He pulled. "Father!" he called out, surprise sharp in his voice, holding up his discovery. "Look! A rope!"

He hauled on it, revealing a thick, dark rope, its fibers strangely, almost supernaturally, preserved despite the water and untold years. It was stretched taut, disappearing into the churning water toward the center of the river, presumably anchored somewhere in the mist-shrouded ruins on the opposite bank.

* * *

Enoch joined him quickly, examining the rope, his brow furrowed in disbelief and suspicion. It was old yet felt incredibly strong. *Who would anchor a rope here? In a dead city scoured by floods and time? And why does it still hold fast after all these ages?* It felt like both a miracle and an obvious trap.

But the urgency of their quest, the clear memory of the vision directing him westward beyond this river, and a spark of Methuselah's youthful eagerness ignited his weary resolve, overriding his usual deep caution. He pointed toward a massive wooden beam intricately carved at one end with forgotten symbols, half-buried in the debris of a collapsed structure near the bank. It was long, thick, and clearly once designed to support a great weight.

"That," Enoch declared, his voice ringing with sudden decision, "will serve as our raft. We will use the rope to guide us across the current. Pray the Creator shields us from whatever danger awaits."

Working together, straining against the weight of the beam and the sucking mud holding it fast, they dislodged it. Pushing it into the swirling water, it floated sluggishly, its buoyancy just enough. Tying another length of salvaged rope around the beam, they looped it loosely over the main guide rope stretching across the river. Then, hearts pounding, Enoch leading, Methuselah close behind, gripping the beam tightly, they began their perilous crossing.

The current surged against the heavy beam, trying to tear it away, drenching them in cold spray. The roar of the nearby waterfall seemed to vibrate through their very bones, a constant reminder of the deadly power surrounding them. But the guide rope held taut and strong against the strain. They gave one aching hand over to the other, drawing themselves along the guide rope, sitting astride the great beam, as they advanced, across the raging torrent, toward the mist and ruins on the far side.

After a while, they reached the opposite bank, collapsing onto the muddy shore, soaked, shivering, and thoroughly exhausted, but miraculously alive. The river had been crossed. And here, the ruined city continued, a mirror image of the destruction they had left behind—shattered walls, leaning towers, debris-choked plazas. But as they cautiously explored this side, seeking a path onward and westward, they discovered something even more unsettling, confirming Enoch's darkest suspicions.

In the remnants of what looked like workshops or forges, amidst broken crucibles and colossal, fire-blackened hearths, lay tools and implements crafted from metals they had never seen before. Metal that gleamed with an unnatural, oily brilliance, appearing resistant to rust. Heavy chisels and hammer heads, perfectly balanced, stronger, and holding a sharper edge than any stone tool they possessed, despite lying exposed for ages. *How?* Enoch wondered again, picking up a massive, finely wrought hammer head, feeling its alien density. *This requires knowledge lost to our line... or feasibly deliberately withheld. Intense fire... complex skills...*

Then, on the soot-stained, crumbling walls of the great workshop, partially sheltered from the elements, they found the drawings.

Rendered with startling, confident skill in charcoal and ochre pigments that still held surprising vibrancy, they depicted scenes of industry: figures, recognizably Sons of Adam, working massive bellows, pouring molten metal into molds, shaping tools and intricate weapons with focused intensity under harsh light. But alongside them, standing taller, overseeing, guiding, stood other figures. Tall, unnaturally slender, with elongated limbs and faces depicted as strangely smooth, devoid of discernible emotion. Their eyes were rendered as empty, glowing points of light. These beings were clearly teaching the men the secrets of fire and metal, demonstrating techniques, pointing toward complex designs.

Enoch stared, his blood running cold as fragmented legends heard in the glade, whispered warnings from generations past, suddenly clicked into horrifying focus. "Tubal-Cain..." he breathed, the name tasting like ash and ruin in his mouth. He recognized the name from the oldest genealogies, a descendant of Cain known for forging instruments of bronze and iron. He pointed a trembling finger at the tall, eerie, luminous-eyed figures in the mural. "And *these*... these can only be the Nephilim. His teachers."

The drawings revealed a horrifying truth, laid bare in ochre and charcoal. This city, this monument to advanced craft and forgotten power, hadn't simply fallen to natural disaster or external conquest; it had been *seduced*.

The Nephilim, the fallen ones or their offspring, had come here, not initially as conquerors but as bringers of forbidden knowledge. They offered power—the secrets of metalworking, complex engineering, and other darker arts hinted at in the strange statues—to this isolated branch of Adam's children. And that knowledge, that power granted apart from the Creator, had inevitably led to pride and reliance on dangerous forces, ultimately culminating in this utter destruction. Had they destroyed themselves with the very power they craved? Or had their Nephilim teachers turned on them once their purpose was served, or when their creation became somehow flawed? Ultimately, the end result was identical: complete ruin, a city drowned in water and silenced by time.

The weight of the implications hit Enoch like a physical blow, exceeding even the river's strongest waves. The Nephilim were not just distant legends or boogeymen from fragmented tales. They were real, active agents of corruption in the world, their influence stretching back through ages, leaving desolation and twisted knowledge in their wake. And their gifts—the advanced knowledge, the power they of-fered—were poison, lures into the Serpent's oldest trap: the promise of godhood, of self-reliance apart from the Creator, a path that led only to ruin and death. *This,* Enoch realized with chilling certainty, *is the true enemy. Not just beasts or harsh lands or wandering tribes. This twisting of gifts, this age-old war against the Creator's design.*

As the sun began its descent again, painting the drowned ruins in hues of amber and plum, casting long, distorted shadows that seemed to writhe with unseen life in the ruins, Enoch and Methuselah knew they could not linger in this place of intense warning. They had crossed the river, but in doing so had stumbled into a deeper, darker understanding of the world they journeyed through and the powerful enemy they opposed.

This terrible truth strengthened their resolve—the record Adam left behind, the *true* history, was more vital, more precious than ever, but it also filled their hearts with a heavy, bitter sense of foreboding. The path ahead, leading away from this city of ghosts and toward the mountains that held Adam's cave, felt infinitely more treacherous than it had that morning. The whispers of Eden, calling them toward the hidden cave, now seemed less like a promise of hope and more like a desperate plea in the face of an encroaching, powerful darkness.

5

Hostile Shores

Behind them, the dead city, its silent screams and chilling warnings etched in stone, faded, finally swallowed by distance and the shimmering heat haze rising from the parched earth. The landscape shifted dramatically. The sheltering, if unsettling, forest gave way entirely to a barren, sunbaked expanse of cracked earth stretching toward a hazy, indifferent horizon. Stunted, thorny shrubs clawed stubbornly at the parched ground, offering no shade, only hazards. The air grew hotter, drier, vibrating with heat, as the wind became an enemy, carrying a gritty dust that stung their eyes and rasped in their throats.

From one desolation to another, Enoch thought grimly, adjusting the pack on his shoulders. *The whole world groans under its corruption.*

For days, they trudged onward, often wrapped in a heavy silence born of weariness and contemplation. Conversation felt difficult, dwarfed by the immensity of the wasteland and the weight of their discoveries in the ruined city. The knowledge of the Nephilim's influence, the evidence of destruction born from forbidden knowledge, had cast a pall over their spirits.

Methuselah, usually quick with observations or questions, walked mostly with his head bowed against the wind, his earlier eagerness replaced by a subdued watchfulness.

The whispers of Eden seemed fainter here, harder for Enoch himself to hear above the wind's desolate howl. *Is this what becomes of those who forget the Source?* he pondered, scanning the bleak horizon. *Emptiness within reflects the emptiness without.*

Then, one evening, as the sun bled across the western sky like a fatal wound, painting the sparse clouds in streaks of angry red and bruised purple, they saw it. A tiny flicker against the darkening land. A fire. Hope surged unexpectedly in Enoch's chest—a sharp, almost painful pulse after days of emptiness. *Others! Sons of Adam, perhaps? Maybe they know this unforgiving land, maybe they still hold to the old ways.* He quickened his pace, his weariness momentarily forgotten, Methuselah moving close behind, his own eyes fixed hopefully on the distant light.

But as they drew closer, the hope curdled into a cold, prickling unease. The figures huddled around the meager, smoky fire were starkly different from the people of their glade. Gaunt faces, hollowed by hardship and suspicion, stared out from beneath matted hair. Their eyes, reflecting the uncertain firelight, held a fierce, almost feral gleam. They carried heavy weaponry—not the tools of builders or providers but crude, brutal weapons: jagged stone axes, bone-tipped spears, and slings loaded with sharp rocks. They moved with a tense, jerky energy, their bodies taut, constantly scanning the shadows like predators expecting rivals.

These are not people of peace, Enoch realized, his hand moving subtly closer to his sturdy walking staff. *These are people shaped and broken by fear and violence.*

As Enoch and Methuselah stepped cautiously into the edge of the firelight, the group stiffened as one, a dozen pairs of eyes snapping toward them. Hands tightened on weapons. A tall, haggard figure detached himself from the others and stepped forward, blocking their path. His face was a brutal roadmap of old scars, and his voice, when he spoke, was a harsh rasp.

"Who are you?" he demanded, his eyes narrowed to suspicious slits. "What brings you prowling like night beasts into our lands?"

Enoch kept his hands open, his stance deliberately non-threatening. "We are travelers," he said, his voice steady. "Followers of the Creator, seeking passage. We mean you no harm." *May they see truth in my words, not just reflections of their own fears.*

The gaunt man spat contemptuously onto the cracked earth. "Travelers? Knowledge?" He laughed, a short, ugly bark. "Lies! We know your kind. Children of the curse!"

The accusation hung in the air, thick and poisonous. Enoch frowned. "Curse? We are Sons of Adam, like you. Blessed by the Creator—"

"Blessed?" the man sneered, his face contorting. "He banished us! He stole our rightful home! It is the Serpent who offers true wisdom! True power!"

A murmur of fervent agreement rippled through the ragged group. Their eyes burned with a disturbing, fanatical light. Enoch felt a jolt of horror colder than the desert night wind. *They've twisted everything. Inverted the entire story.* "You are deceived," he pleaded. "The Serpent brought only sorrow—"

"LIES!" the gaunt man roared, his voice cracking with fury. "He showed us the path! Freedom from the Creator's petty tyranny! We will not return to the darkness of ignorance you serve!" He raised a bony hand, pointing a trembling finger at them. "They follow the Deceiver God! They are unclean!"

At his cry, the group surged forward, weapons raised, faces masks of fanatical fury.

This is madness, Enoch thought, bracing himself. *How can truth become so fully warped?*

He saw Methuselah beside him, his face pale in the firelight, his eyes wide with a terror that threatened to paralyze him. The boy's gaze darted from the onrushing horde to his father, a silent plea for an escape that did not exist. Then, before the first blow could fall, Methuselah's hand darted beneath his tunic.

He pulled forth the bronze dagger.

Enoch saw it appear as if from nowhere, the metal gleaming with an unnatural, sickly light in the flickering fire. A relic—beautiful, deadly, Nephilim-linked. A cold dread, sharper than any spear point, lanced through him. *My son... why? Deceit born of fear? Or has the temptation of its power already taken root?*

He saw the shift in his son's posture. The raw panic in Methuselah's eyes was replaced by a brittle, false confidence as he raised the dagger, his trembling hand now steadied by its dark promise.

But the effect on the attackers was instantaneous. They froze mid-stride, their aggressive momentum spent. Eyes widened, fixing on the gleaming blade not with fear but with a concentrated, almost slavering, naked desire. A collective gasp swept through their ranks.

The haggard leader stumbled back, his harsh confidence gone. His voice trembled, no longer with rage but with something akin to reverence. "What... what is that?"

Enoch stared at his son, then at the dagger pulsing in the firelight. A whirlwind of confusion and a sharp sting of betrayal churned within him. *He kept this hidden. He brought this corruption with us.*

Methuselah stood his ground, though his confidence was now shaken by the tribe's bizarre reaction. He lifted the dagger slightly higher. "It is a dagger," he said, his voice commendably steady. "Forged by the hands of Tubal-Cain's students."

"Bronze," the leader whispered, the word drawn out with longing and worshipful hunger. His eyes devoured the blade. "The elders spoke... legends... the sky-metal... the metal of the Shining Ones... the Nephilim."

A strange energy emanated from the group, hostility forgotten, replaced by an obsessive fascination. They leaned forward as one, drawn helplessly toward the dagger as if by invisible strings. Its unnatural gleam seemed to hold them captivated.

"Give it to us," the gaunt man pleaded, his voice a raw, desperate whisper. "The bronze... give it to us, traveler, and you may pass unharmed. We will give you food, water... anything..."

Enoch's mind raced. He saw the trap inherent in the metal itself, felt the dark power humming within it, amplifying the desperation already festering in these lost people. It wasn't just metal; it was an artifact imbued with the Nephilim's influence. And beneath his fear for their safety, a colder fear settled in his spirit—a fear for Methuselah.

He took it. He hid it. He revealed it. Does he truly understand what he holds? Does he feel its seductive pull?

"We seek no bargains," Enoch said, his voice firm and clear, cutting through the leader's plea. "We wish only to continue our journey."

But the gaunt man was beyond reason. The lure of the bronze had consumed him. His eyes blazed. He lunged, not with a weapon but with his hand outstretched like a claw. "The bronze!" he shrieked, his voice thin and high-pitched. "It will be ours!"

His cry broke the spell. The tribe surged forward again, a wave of ragged figures, their crude weapons forgotten, their faces contorted now with a ravenous hunger for the gleaming metal.

Methuselah flinched back, startled by the sheer ferocity of their need.

He thought it a shield, Enoch realized grimly, *not a magnet for madness.*

Before anyone could reach Methuselah, Enoch acted. With a speed born of absolute necessity, he snatched the dagger from his son's surprised hand. The bronze felt strangely cold yet pulsed with a disturbing energy that made his spirit recoil. It flashed once, malevolently, in the firelight.

Then, putting all his strength and rejection of this dark power into the throw, Enoch hurled the dagger away from them with a sharp cry, sending it spinning end over end deep into the surrounding thorny scrubland. It vanished with a soft thud.

The effect was immediate and dramatic. The tribe's charge dissolved as if they'd run into an invisible wall. Heads snapped around, eyes straining wildly into the darkness where the dagger had fallen. A collective groan of pure, agonizing loss escaped their lips. Then, as one, they abandoned Enoch and Methuselah, surging toward the scrubland, scrambling, pushing each other aside, their mad desire for the hidden bronze overriding all else.

The gaunt leader, his face a mask of frenzied desperation, stumbled into the undergrowth first, his followers crashing blindly after him like hounds on a false scent. The sounds of their desperate search—napping branches, harsh cries, scrabbling in the dirt—faded, leaving Enoch and Methuselah standing alone in the eerie silence beside the abandoned fire.

Enoch's heart hammered against his ribs. He grabbed Methuselah's arm, his grip hard. "We must go," he commanded, his voice tight. "Now. Before they realize it's lost, or turn on each other."

Into the opposite darkness, they turned and fled, their feet pounding the hard-packed earth, never daring to look back. They ran until their lungs burned, until the empty silence of the wasteland swallowed the sounds of the desperate search, until the deep wilderness enveloped them wholly.

Gasping for breath, they eventually collapsed in a rocky depression miles away. The encounter left them shaken, adrenaline slowly draining away, leaving behind a residue of fear and unsettling disquiet. They had witnessed firsthand the seductive power of the Nephilim's legacy, how mere metal, imbued with their dark influence, could incite madness.

Harsher still for Enoch, it had revealed a dangerous crack in his trust. The secret dagger, the impulsive act born of fear reaching for forbidden power... it was a sign of a perilous susceptibility his son carried within him. The shadows of the world deepened around them, and the path ahead felt infinitely more treacherous, haunted now not just by external threats but by the seeds of corruption they carried within themselves.

6

The House of Anak

The cracked, sunbaked earth, parched and dusty, finally yielded after several days of arduous travel, its grip loosening with each labored step. The landscape began tentatively to breathe again. Rocky hills thrust themselves from the flatlands like the bones of the earth; tenacious patches of green, hardy shrubs, and wiry grasses clung stubbornly to their scorched slopes, their dry scent sharp in the air.

Life endures, Enoch thought, scanning the terrain with renewed vigilance. *But what kind of life awaits us now?*

They traveled onward for many more days, moving with a deliberate caution born of harsh experience. Their senses remained acutely alert; every distant bird call, every rustle in the sparse vegetation caused them to pause, hands moving toward staff or axe. The memory of the dagger-crazed tribe remained a raw wound, a constant reminder of the unseen currents flowing through the world, and, more troublingly for Enoch, the dangerous impulsiveness lurking even within his own son.

He found himself watching Methuselah closely during their silent marches, noting the almost unconscious way the boy's hand sometimes strayed toward his belt where the dagger had been—a phantom gesture mixing regret with the remembered false confidence of its power. They spoke little; the silence was filled mostly by the crunch of their weary footsteps and the weight of unspoken anxieties.

Then, one late afternoon, cresting a long, windswept ridge, they saw it. Nestled in a broad, sheltered valley below lay a cluster of dwellings, their sheer scale unlike anything Enoch had ever imagined. These were not the woven huts of the glade nor the shattered, drowned ruins of the river city. These were formidable structures of rough-hewn stone blocks, fitted together with surprising precision, built not merely for shelter against the elements but to dominate the landscape and withstand the passage of ages. Moving through the village were figures that made Enoch and Methuselah seem like mere children in comparison. *Giants.*

A sharp gasp beside him made Enoch turn. Methuselah had stepped back abruptly, his hand flying to the axe at his belt.

"Father..." Methuselah breathed, his voice tight.

Enoch knew the source of that terror; the fearful whispers of the Glade had just taken solid form before them. *Giants,* the firelit stories warned, *brutal, descended from the Nephilim...*

Enoch placed a calming hand on his son's shoulder, though his own heart hammered against his ribs like a trapped bird. He squinted, studying the distant figures below. They moved with purpose, with deliberation, not the anxious, jerky energy of the hostile tribe. *Caution, yes,* he thought, steadying his breathing, *but despair gains us nothing. Remember the fragmented legends—some spoke of cruelty, yes, but others of wisdom. Could there be truth in those other, less fearful tales?*

A flicker of hope ignited within him against the backdrop of their desolate journey. "Hold, Methuselah," he murmured. "Observe first. Let us not condemn an entire people before we know their hearts."

They descended the ridge slowly, openly, making no attempt to hide, wanting their approach to be seen as honest, not stealthy. As they neared the valley floor, a group of giants emerged from the settlement's wide, stone-arched entrance, their approach equally deliberate, watchful. They were an imposing sight indeed. Most stood as

tall as two men, one standing upon the other's shoulders, their powerful limbs thick with muscle, casting long shadows in the dipping
afternoon sun. Their faces were stern, broad, carved as if from the surrounding rock by wind and time. Yet, as they drew closer, Enoch noted
again the distinct lack of feral hunger, the desperate madness they had
witnessed in the dagger tribe. Instead, he saw deep-set eyes holding a
wary curiosity, a watchful intelligence that assessed them without immediate malice.

One giant, whose frame seemed even larger, broader than the others, towering to a height that would equal two men with half another
man stood upon their shoulders, stepped forward from the group. He
carried an air of quiet authority that reminded Enoch distantly of the
oldest, most resilient trees in the glade, and his voice was a deep, resonant rumble that vibrated not just in the air but through the very
earth beneath Enoch's feet, yet somehow held none of the harshness he
might have expected. There was a surprising, world-weary gentleness
beneath the undeniable power.

"Who are you, small ones?" he boomed, though the volume seemed
effortless for him, his gaze sweeping over them, taking in their travel-
worn clothes, their human stature, their cautious, weaponless stance.
"What brings you, unlooked for, to the House of Anak?"

Enoch met the giant's gaze directly, forcing his own voice to remain
steady despite the tremor deep inside his chest. *Speak truth,* he reminded himself. *It is our only real shield.*

"We are travelers," he said, projecting his voice clearly. "Sons of
Adam, from a hidden glade far to the east. We seek knowledge and
guidance on our path through these lands."

The leader studied them for a long, silent moment. His gaze was intense, a weight that seemed to peer into the very intentions of Enoch's
heart.

Methuselah shifted, uneasy under the scrutiny.

Then, a slow smile spread across the giant's massive face, crinkling
the weathered corners of his deep eyes. The expression transformed

his stern, formidable features, revealing an underlying warmth and a deep-seated kindness.

"Sons of Adam," the giant repeated, the name thoughtful, almost wondering, on his tongue. "From the line of Seth, then? You have journeyed far indeed, and into dangerous lands." He nodded slowly. "I am Anak. You are welcome to our home," he said, his voice softening, the intimidating rumble lessening. "We offer shelter and hospitality to those who seek it with honest hearts and peaceful intent. Enter and rest."

Relief washed over Enoch, so potent it almost buckled his knees. He heard Methuselah let out a shaky breath, and their awe grew with every step as they entered the settlement.

The giants' dwellings were indeed fortresses, built of massive stone to endure, yet inside the rough-hewn walls, they found surprising ingenuity and signs of settled life. Workshops hummed with activity—they saw giants hammering glowing iron at great forges, shaping sturdy tools and functional weapons with a skill far surpassing the glade folks' stone and bone craft, though lacking the disturbing, unnatural perfection of the Nephilim bronze.

Intricate, deeply carved patterns adorned stone lintels and massive support pillars, depicting scenes from what was clearly a long and complex giant history—great hunts of monstrous beasts, vast migrations across changing landscapes, figures locked in solemn council or solitary struggle. *They build, they create, they remember,* Enoch observed with growing hope. *Not just destroy.*

The giants of Anak's tribe treated them with a cautious, reserved respect. Their initial suspicion seemed tempered, then replaced by a genuine, almost childlike curiosity about these rare human visitors. They shared food generously—huge portions of roasted meat from an unrecognizable but savory beast, large, sweet fruits Enoch had never seen before, and dense loaves of a thick, nutty bread. They spoke readily once their reserve thawed, their voices rumbling like summer thunder or the shifting of deep earth, telling stories of their lineage tracing back centuries, of other scattered giant clans and their differing cultures and beliefs.

And there, over days spent recovering their strength under Anak's protection, Enoch and Methuselah learned a weighty, complex truth. The giants—the Anakim, as they called their specific people—were not a monolithic race, as the fearful whispers in the glade implied. They were, as Anak explained one evening, the varied descendants of a fraught, ancient union—the offspring of the Nephilim and the daughters of Adam from ages past, when darkness first spread aggressively. Some giant clans, Anak confirmed, had embraced the cold power and arrogant pride of their celestial fathers, becoming tyrants who enslaved men and ravaged the lands, allies of the Serpent City. But others, like Anak's own tribe, descendants from unions where human love or faithfulness held stronger sway, wrestled constantly with their volatile dual heritage. They revered their human ancestry, cherishing fragmented stories passed down through maternal lines, striving consciously to resist the cold influence they felt stirring like a shadow within their own blood.

"You see, Son of Adam," Anak explained with his massive form slightly slumped on a stone bench beside the flickering light of a central fire pit, his voice heavy with ancestral sorrow, "we are torn. We carry both fire and water within us. The shadow of the Shining Ones grants us great strength, unnaturally long lives, an affinity for stone and metal... but it whispers constantly of dominance, of pride that curdles the heart, of contempt for fragility." He sighed, a sound like wind through mountain passes. "The blood of your mothers, the daughters of Eve, gives us the capacity for empathy, for loyalty, for deep sorrow and sudden joy... but it also brings vulnerability, fear, the knowledge of mortality. It is," he concluded wearily, "a constant battle for the soul of our people, generation after generation."

Listening, Enoch felt a deep, sorrowful resonance. *The struggle against darkness, against the whispers of the Serpent, is not unique to Adam's direct line. It is the curse of the Fall itself, echoing even here, in these mighty forms.*

Enoch watched his son as Anak spoke of his people's torn heritage. He saw the tight, fearful grip Methuselah had kept on his axe handle slowly relax. The boy leaned forward slightly, his young face, once pale with apprehension, now filled with a profound, almost scholarly fascination. *He sees them now,* Enoch realized with a wave of relief, *not as the monsters of legend, but as they truly are: complex beings, caught in their own struggle between shadow and light.* The boy was learning, not just with his ears, but with his heart.

Later, as trust deepened between hosts and guests, the giants shared their knowledge of the wider world—tales of other giant strongholds, both friendly and hostile, descriptions of ruined cities older than even their long memories, accounts of migrations forced by changing lands or devastating wars, and grim, firsthand accounts of the Nephilim's pursuit of power and influence, their spread across the known territories.

But as they spoke, Enoch noticed a surprising, significant gap in their knowledge. Their recorded history and deepest legends appeared to begin after the world's formation and after the Fall had already broken it. They knew little of the true beginning, of the Creator's original intent, the specific beauty of Eden, or the precise details of Adam and Eve's transgression and the subsequent Promise. Their understanding of these foundational truths was fragmented, mythologized, and inevitably viewed through the complex, sorrowful lens of their own mixed origins.

A sense of quiet purpose stirred powerfully in Enoch's heart. He carried something precious, something vital they lacked—the core truth, passed down, however imperfectly, unbroken through Seth's line in his hidden glade. He began to speak, hesitantly at first, feeling the weight of the responsibility, then with growing confidence as he saw the giants' earnest attention. He shared the stories as his people remembered them: the staggering beauty of the unmarred Creation, the perfect harmony of Eden, the deceit of the Serpent, the tragic, world-altering choice of Adam and Eve, the pain of exile, and, crucially, the Creator's enduring promise of redemption through the Seed of the woman.

The giants listened in utter silence, their usual rumbles of conversation ceasing entirely. Their massive, weathered faces, lit by the flickering firelight, were filled with a weighty, almost childlike awe mixed with a deep, resonant sorrow as the pieces of their own fragmented understanding clicked into place. These were foundational truths that vibrated deep within the human part of their souls. In the tragedy of the Fall, they heard the painful echoes of their own human mothers' lost heritage, their vulnerability exploited by powerful, fallen beings. In the description of Eden's perfect harmony, they felt an instinctive, almost unbearable longing for a peace their own conflicted natures constantly warred against.

As he spoke, Enoch felt a powerful connection being formed in the firelit hall. He saw Methuselah, spellbound, and realized his quiet, steady words were weaving an unexpected, powerful bridge of shared understanding between these drastically different peoples. Enoch continued through the long evening, sharing both hope and sorrow, an unexpected kinship was forged in a shared, though differently understood, history, and a powerful, common yearning for wholeness, truth, and restoration.

In the House of Anak, amidst these complex, striving, sorrowful giants, Enoch and Methuselah found not just temporary shelter from the harsh land but a surprising, vital alliance of the spirit that transcended all the vast, intimidating differences in their physical forms. And Enoch knew then, with a growing, unshakeable certainty that settled deep in his bones like the very foundations of the mountains surrounding them, that their journey was indeed far more than a personal quest for a lost record; it was an integral, vital part of a far larger cosmic struggle. A spiritual battle whose outcome would shape the destiny of all creation.

Enoch watched his son closely as the evening ended. He saw the tension that had kept Methuselah's shoulders perpetually tight since the river city finally eased in the warmth of the fire. A simple weariness replaced the haunted, watchful look in the boy's eyes. Later that night, looking over at the furs where Methuselah lay, Enoch saw not the fitful, shallow sleep of a hunted traveler, but a deep and sound slumber, his son's face finally relaxed in true rest. *The kinship of these Giants,* Enoch realized with a surge of gratitude, *has offered my son a healing no poultice could ever provide.*

Later that night, long after the great hall had fallen silent and the last of the giants had retired to their stone dwellings, Enoch found he could not sleep. He churned with the weight of all that had been shared—the giants' sorrowful history, his own people's delicate hope. He rose from the warm furs and tiptoed out of the grand house, into the cool, crisp mountain air.

Silver moonlight bathed the valley. The stars here, far from the oppressive haze of the blighted lands, were impossibly bright. He stood for a long time, just looking up, feeling the silent turning of the cosmos.

A soft footfall announced he wasn't alone. Anak emerged from the shadows of his own great dwelling. He came to stand beside Enoch, the two of them—man and giant, so different in form yet so similar in spirit—gazing up into the same celestial expanse.

"My people call that one 'Haran's Spear'," Anak rumbled, his voice a low vibration in the stillness, pointing a massive finger toward a familiar constellation. "He cast it into the heavens to mark the path for our people when he led them from the pride of the Mountain-Kings."

Enoch followed his gaze. "We know it as the 'Shepherd's Staff'," he replied softly. "A reminder that the Creator guides His flock, even when they wander in darkness."

A long silence settled between them. It was Anak who broke it, his voice heavy with a new understanding. "Your story... it begins with Light. With a Garden. With the Creator walking among His creation."

He sighed. "Our story... it begins with a shadow. With a sundering. With a war in our own blood before we ever drew breath. We have remembered the sorrow, Son of Adam, but we had forgotten the reason for it. We remembered the wound but not the world before the wound."

"The memory is a heavy burden," Enoch said quietly, his own heart aching with the weight of it. "But the promise it carries... that is the only thing that makes the burden bearable."

"This promise..." Anak murmured, his gaze still fixed on the heavens. "Of a Seed who will crush the Serpent's head. It is a hope greater than any giant's strength, a truth more enduring than any mountain." He turned his eyes to meet Enoch's. "You carry the memory of the beginning. You seek the fullness of that memory, the record left by the First Man himself. This is not a quest for your people alone."

Enoch met the giant's gaze, seeing not just a king or a warrior but a fellow keeper of history, a soul yearning for the wholeness his own people had lost. In that moment, under the silent, watching stars, a bond deeper than words was created between them—a shared understanding of their sacred duty to remember, to preserve, and to fight for the truth in a world determined to forget.

"The path is perilous," Enoch stated, not as a warning but as a simple fact.

"The path has always been perilous for my people," Anak replied, a new resolve hardening his voice. "But for the first time in uncounted generations... I believe I can see where it leads."

With that shared understanding settling between them, the two men parted for the night.

When Methuselah and Enoch awoke the next day, the sun was already high in the sky, casting golden light through the open doorways of Anak's dwelling. They stirred slowly, their limbs heavy but their spirits remarkably refreshed, feeling more rested than they had in longer than they could recall. They found themselves in beds that could easily have accommodated Enoch's entire family back in the glade, crafted from thick layers of soft, warm furs and resilient woven reeds, a far cry indeed from the hard, cold ground they had grown so accustomed to.

The inviting scent of roasting meat and sweet, baked fruits filled the air, a tempting invitation to join the giants for their morning meal. They found Anak and many of his tribe already gathered in a large, high-roofed, central hall, their voices a low, companionable rumble of conversation. They greeted Enoch and Methuselah with warm, genuine smiles and gestures of welcome, their earlier wariness replaced by open curiosity and respect.

As they ate—immense portions again, which the giants seemed to find amusingly small for their human guests—sharing more stories and even occasional, surprising bursts of rough laughter, a comfortable sense of genuine camaraderie grew between the Sons of Adam and the Giants of Anak. The differences in their size and physical stature seemed to fade in importance, replaced by a growing recognition of shared humanity, faith in the Creator, and a dawning sense of common purpose in a world increasingly threatened by darkness.

The meal ended, and a hush fell over the hall as Anak rose, his imposing stature filling the space, silencing the lingering murmur of conversation. His gaze swept over Enoch and Methuselah, who sat before him. His face was solemn, his deep voice now filled with a quiet, powerful determination.

"We have listened carefully to your stories, Enoch, Son of Adam," he said, his words echoing slightly in the great hall. "We have heard of the Garden, of the Fall, of the Serpent's deceit, and of the encroaching darkness that has spread its shadow across the world. And we believe now that your quest, this search for Adam's true record, is important—not just for the surviving Sons of Adam but for all who dwell in this land and seek the Creator's light."

He paused, his eyes meeting Enoch's, holding a new depth of understanding. "Therefore, after counsel with our elders, I have decided that the House of Anak will aid you. I myself and two of my strongest sons, Kael and Ronan, will accompany you on your journey."

A murmur of surprised but widespread approval rippled through the assembled giants. This was a significant decision, a solemn commitment to a dangerous, uncertain path beyond their own protected valley.

"We will guide you," Anak continued, his voice resonating with authority and promise, "through the treacherous, unfamiliar lands that lie ahead. We will protect you from the dangers that will attempt to harm you. And we will help you find the truth you seek, the record left by the First Man. For his story, we now see, is our story too."

Enoch was speechless for a long moment, his heart overflowing with thankfulness so deep it brought tears to his eyes. He had hoped, prayed for assistance, but he had never expected such an all-encompassing, self-sacrificial commitment from these mighty beings.

"Anak," he said, his voice thick with emotion he couldn't quite control, "your generosity... your courage... your faith... I do not know how to thank you."

Anak placed a massive hand on Enoch's shoulder, his touch surprisingly gentle. "There is no need for thanks, little brother. We are bound now by a common destiny, a shared hope in the Creator's promise. And we will face whatever lies ahead together, as kin."

Methuselah, his eyes shining with rekindled excitement and the thrill of this unexpected, powerful alliance, stepped forward impulsively. "Then let us depart soon, Father!" he said, his youthful eagerness bubbling to the surface once more. "Let us find this cave and uncover the secrets it holds!"

Anak chuckled, a deep, rumbling sound like distant summer thunder. "Patience, young one," he said, his eyes twinkling with amusement. "There is much to prepare for such a journey. We must gather supplies and consider the paths. But fear not." His gaze grew serious again, sweeping from Methuselah to Enoch. "The path forward is clearer now than it has been for many generations. And we *will* walk it together—Sons of Adam and Sons of Anak—united in purpose, under the Creator's guiding hand."

As the sun climbed higher in the sky, casting its bright, hopeful light on the determined faces of the newly formed fellowship of travelers, a new chapter in their perilous journey began—a chapter filled with both renewed hope and the ever-present, looming shadow of the unknown dangers awaiting them in the west.

7

The Daughter of Eve

Hope, tenuous yet tenacious, had taken root in the House of Anak, nurtured by shared stories and unexpected kinship. Yet the wilderness cared little for the tender shoots of camaraderie. It demanded respect, vigilance, and sometimes, a steep and sudden price for passage through its domain. The peace found in the giants' valley was real, but like all things in a fallen world marred by shadow, it was destined to be tested.

The first days of their journey after departing from the stone dwellings of Anak felt surprisingly light, almost hopeful. Escorted through unfamiliar wildflowers bursting in vibrant color, streams that sparkled clear and sang over smooth stones. The giants, with their long, ground-eating strides and innate knowledge of the land, guided them along hidden paths less traveled, their sheer, quiet presence a silent deterrent against unseen watchers or wandering beasts.

It's like the glade is in high summer, before the shadows lengthen, Enoch thought, a wave of bittersweet nostalgia washing over him as he watched Methuselah walking comfortably beside Ronan, listening to some giantish tale.

A camaraderie had blossomed between them. Laughter, seldom heard thus far on their journey, now echoed through the open valleys as they exchanged stories—the giants shared legends of their ancestors, while Enoch recounted tales of the glade's quiet rhythms and the lost memories of Eden.

Methuselah, his earlier recklessness tempered by the near-disaster at the river and the sobering encounter with the hostile tribe, attached himself to Kael and Ronan, eager to learn from their experience. Enoch watched him, relieved to see his son's energy channeled into learning, observing how the giants read the subtle signs of the terrain, their effortless strength in clearing obstacles, their quiet wisdom regarding the ways of the wild.

He sees true strength now, Enoch hoped, *the strength of stewardship and wisdom, not just the brittle power offered by forbidden knowledge or brute force.*

But the wilderness remained untamed, its beauty often masking sharp teeth and sudden violence. The ease of their passage was not destined to last.

One sultry afternoon, while traversing a narrow, sun-drenched canyon flanked by high, sheer rock walls that amplified every sound, a noise cut through the peaceful quiet. The canyon's acoustics caught and magnified a distant roar, low and guttural at first, until it echoed like rolling thunder all around them. Every member of the party froze, heads snapping up, hands reaching for weapons or staff.

"That is no common beast," Anak rumbled, his voice tight, his hand already clamped firmly around the haft of the massive, iron-headed hammer slung at his side.

Hearts pounded in chests like frenetic drums. They turned as one to see a creature of nightmare emerge with terrifying suddenness from a dense thicket of thorny brush clogging the canyon's mouth ahead. It was enormous, its shaggy, earth-colored bulk dwarfing even Anak himself. A behemoth born from forgotten ages, radiating primal power. Thick, matted fur, caked with mud and snagged with burrs, covered a body rippling with corded muscle. Its legs were like tree trunks, ending in broad, splayed feet armed with heavy claws that tore at the earth. A crown of massive, wickedly curved horns adorned its broad, low-slung head, and its small, beady eyes, sunk deep beneath bony ridges, glowed with a disturbing, unnatural intensity. Foam dripped from a wide mouth filled with teeth like jagged daggers. It was pure, unadulterated force, an apex predator that had likely claimed this canyon as its territory for centuries, unchallenged.

The giants reacted instantly, their newfound camaraderie vanishing, replaced by the focused, deadly efficiency of seasoned protectors facing mortal threat. "Form circle!" Anak commanded, his voice sharp, cutting through the sudden fear. He, Kael, and Ronan moved with smooth, practiced speed, forming a living wall of muscle and determination around the smaller figures of Enoch and Methuselah, their heavy weapons—Anak's hammer, Kael's axe, Ronan's thick-shafted spear—raised and ready. Their faces were grim, set lines of absolute resolve, replacing their earlier relaxed expressions.

The behemoth, sensing the challenge to its domain, lowered its massive horned head and let out another earsplitting, furious roar, a sound so powerful it seemed to shake the very stones beneath their feet. Dust puffed from fissures in the canyon walls. Then it charged. The ground trembled as its body crashed through the undergrowth like an avalanche, horns aimed low like battering rams, teeth bared in a terrifying snarl that promised annihilation.

The impact when it hit the giants' makeshift line was brutal, a sickening collision of flesh, bone, and weapon. Iron and stone clashed against thick hide and horn with heavy thuds, yet the beast barely seemed to notice blows that would have felled lesser creatures. It fought with relentless, primal fury, its sheer strength and surprising agility overwhelming.

Kael roared in pain and anger as a horn tip tore a deep gash in his arm, forcing him back a step. Ronan's heavy spear shaft snapped like a twig against the creature's armored shoulder plates. The behemoth tore through their frantically held line, massive claws raking, horns tossing, its powerful jaws seeking purchase.

Enoch and Methuselah, suddenly exposed within the breaking circle, reacted with the courage of desperation. Enoch jabbed upward with his sturdy staff, aiming for the eyes, but the blow glanced off thick, bony ridges. Methuselah swung his axe with all his might, managing to chip the tip of one great horn but eliciting only an enraged bellow in response. Their efforts were pitifully inadequate against such raw power.

We are nothing against such fury! Enoch realized, his breath catching in his throat, desperately searching for any weakness or strategy. *Creator, shield us!*

The beast was too powerful, too driven by territorial rage. It was only a matter of moments before they would be overwhelmed.

It knocked Ronan aside with a contemptuous sweep of its head, then turned its terrifying focus and hate-filled glowing eyes onto Enoch, its foul, hot breath washing over his face. Enoch stumbled back, instinctively raising his staff, knowing with chilling certainty it was useless against the coming charge. The creature reared, gathering its enormous power for a final, crushing blow...

From above, a hiss sounded through the air as arrows, trailing sparks like fiery comets, whistled down from the canyon rim high above. They struck the dry grass and thorny brush around the behemoth with uncanny accuracy. Flames erupted instantly, consuming the tinder-dry vegetation, exploding into a rapidly spreading wall of fire.

Shouts echoed from above. Figures moved along the ridge—three women, bows pulled tight again without delay. The leader, a woman whose weathered face bore the harsh lines of survival but whose eyes held a fierce, unwavering command, notched another flaming arrow.

Enoch thought with a jolt of disbelief, *"A Daughter of Eve!"* His silent prayer had been answered.

The behemoth, roaring in confusion at the unexpected inferno, backed away, shaking its head, unwilling to brave the heat and choking smoke. The women didn't relent, continuing to rain down flaming arrows, not at the beast itself but strategically placed to fuel the flames, expertly guiding the fire, forcing the creature farther back. Their aim was precise, their teamwork seamless—a testament to long, hard years of practice born from bitter necessity.

As the behemoth crashed away into the undergrowth, its panicked bellows fading, the lead woman lowered her bow. Her chest heaved with exertion, but her gaze, sweeping over the scene below, was steady, assessing. She gestured toward the canyon walls opposite their position. "Quickly!" she called down, her voice echoing against the walls. "Before it thinks of returning or other scavengers arrive! Our refuge is near!"

Even as she spoke, the women were already scrambling down a steep but manageable path on the canyon side with surprising agility.

Anak, Kael, and Ronan, leaning on their weapons and bleeding from numerous wounds, looked up, nodding their weary gratitude.

"Come," the lead woman urged again as she joined them, her voice firm but not unkind. "You're injured. You need rest."

The women guided the weary party through a concealed opening in the canyon wall, masked by thorny bushes and what looked like a natural rockfall. The path led into a narrow, winding passage that soon opened into a verdant, hidden hollow, protected on all sides by sheer rock. Here, nestled against the cliff face, was their dwelling—not a grand structure but a series of interconnected natural caves, expanded and improved over time with rough stonework. Sturdy hide coverings hung over the entrances, smoke curling from a hidden chimney vent high above. Pens held a few watchful livestock, and small, terraced plots showed signs of careful cultivation. It was a hidden sanctuary carved out of the wilderness, radiating self-sufficiency.

Resilience, Enoch thought again, deeply impressed. *Life finds a way, even in the deepest shadows.*

Inside, the main cave was no mere hollow but an extensive natural chamber, its ceiling soaring high into the darkness beyond the reach of their torchlight. The space was wide enough for all three Giants to stand abreast with room to spare, and a large fire pit in the center burned without making the air feel close. The air was cool, smelling of woodsmoke, drying herbs, and roasting meat.

Woven mats covered the smooth stone floor, and niches carved into the walls held clay pots, tools, and neatly folded hides. While one of the younger women set about tending the giants' deeper gashes and bruises, grinding herbs into fragrant poultices with practiced hands, the leader offered the others cool water from a skin, pieces of dried fruit, and tough, smoked meat. The hospitality was simple, unadorned, but genuine.

As the injured giants rested, Anak looked toward the lead woman, his form slumped onto a sturdy stone ledge. "You have saved us, Daughter of Eve," he whispered. "We owe you our lives. I am Anak, and these are my sons, Kael and Ronan."

The woman nodded. "Survival teaches us to aid others when we can," she said simply. "Few enough travel these harsh lands with honest hearts. I am Selah. This is my daughter Tirzah," she gestured to the young woman tending Kael's arm, "and my other daughter, Naamah." She paused, her keen gaze lingering on Enoch. "You are their leader?"

"I am Enoch," he confirmed, meeting her direct gaze. "And this is my son, Methuselah."

At the mention of his name, the cautious warmth in the cave seemed to vanish. Selah stiffened, an almost imperceptible movement, but one that radiated a sudden chill. Her eyes narrowed, the welcome in them extinguished, replaced by a flicker of deep-seated suspicion. Her hand drifted, almost unconsciously, towards the worn handle of the knife at her belt.

"Enoch..." she repeated, her voice now flat and cold, devoid of its earlier kindness. "That is a name known in these parts. A name of ill omen."

Enoch frowned, sensing the shift in her demeanor, the air suddenly thick with distrust. "Known? How so?"

Selah hesitated, glancing toward her daughters, then the words poured out, bitterness sharpening her tone like a honed blade. She spoke of her tribe, once many, living in these now-empty valleys. She described the brutal raid years past—savage warriors bearing cruel, serpent-like sigils, wielding weapons of dark metal, overwhelming their simple defenses. "They took our men," she said, her voice trembling with remembered grief and rage. "My husband... my sons... dragged away in chains like cattle." Her gaze hardened, becoming chips of flint. "Taken eastward, toward the darkness. Taken to the great city built at the foot of Serpent Mountain. The slave city *they* call Enoch."

She locked eyes with Enoch, her suspicion now a palpable force in the quiet cave. "Named, the survivors whisper, after the first murderer's own son, Cain's progeny. A place of darkness, of crushing slavery, where they practice the Serpent's forbidden arts and wield the terrible power of the Nephilim."

Her hand, which had been resting near the knife at her belt, now closed around its worn handle, her knuckles whitening. She took a small, almost imperceptible step back, subtly positioning herself between Enoch and her daughters. The shift was not lost on Enoch; the cautious survivor had vanished, replaced by a cornered protector ready to strike. He saw the conclusion she had leaped to in her cold, narrowed eyes: he was not a fellow traveler, but a spy from that wicked place, his name an impossible coincidence.

"Why do you bear such a name, traveler?" Her voice now a low and dangerous growl, "If you truly follow the Creator?"

Enoch experienced a cold dread seep into him, understanding her fear instantly, horrified by the blasphemous association. "Selah," he said, holding her suspicious gaze, keeping his voice calm, truthful. "The city you speak of, the city of Cain's line, has stolen and twisted a holy name. My name comes not from that darkness but from the light. I am Enoch, of the line of Seth."

He saw disbelief warring with a flicker of hope in her guarded eyes. He spoke then, earnestly, sharing the known history of his people—the faithful remnants who held fast to the Creator's ways in their hidden glade, preserving the memory of Eden, rejecting the Serpent's lies, clinging to the promise of redemption. He spoke of his vision, the quest for Adam's true record, a mission to preserve the Creator's truth, not embrace the darkness that had stolen her family.

She must understand, he prayed. *Let her see we are not the enemy she rightly fears.*

As Enoch spoke, sharing the pure lineage and purpose passed down through generations who walked with God, he watched Selah intently. He saw her rigid, hostile stance begin to soften almost imperceptibly. The hand that had rested on the hilt of her knife now fell limp to her side. The hard suspicion in her eyes faded, replaced by something he had not expected to see: raw astonishment, then a dawning, hesitant recognition. The harsh lines of bitterness around her mouth seemed to dissolve, and her shoulders slumped, not in weariness, but as if a great weight had finally been lifted. "You... you truly follow Him?" she whispered, the question filled with disbelief and wonder. "We thought... We believed that all others had fallen away or that the growing darkness had destroyed them. We thought only scattered remnants like ourselves remained, clinging to survival, the memory of truth fading..." The news that some Sons of Adam still followed the light, and that the Creator was neither forgotten nor scorned, revealed a truth that cracked open her hardened heart.

"We endure," Enoch confirmed gently, his gaze filled with shared understanding. "As you endure, Selah. We hold to the light as best we can in a world that embraces the shadows."

A new understanding bloomed in the quiet intimacy of the firelit cave. The grief over the world's brokenness, the collective but varied memory of a better past, created a link more potent than mistrust.

It was into this newly established trust that Naamah stepped forward. Enoch watched as the young woman straightened, and her sorrowful expression coalesced into a sharp, clear resolve. The pain was still there, visible in the depths of her dark eyes, but it was now overshadowed by a fierce determination. *Her grief has found its purpose,* Enoch realized. She looked first at Enoch, then at Anak. "My mother speaks truth," she said, her voice low but clear and firm. "The city called Enoch is a pit of despair and lies. But they took my father and my brothers there. If your path leads near that darkness," she squared her shoulders, meeting Enoch's gaze, "then I *will* accompany you. I must seek them. I must know their fate."

Her decision, born now not just of grief but of a shared purpose illuminated by Enoch's revealed faith and quest, hung in the air. Anak looked toward Selah, who met his gaze and gave a slow, resigned nod, understanding her daughter's heart, seeing a reflection of her own lost hope rekindled into action. The path was dangerous beyond telling, but the need to know, the refusal to surrender kin to the darkness, could not be denied.

Enoch met Naamah's determined gaze, seeing the pain flickering beneath the strength. "Your courage is a testament to your family, Naamah," he said. "And your hope is a powerful witness to the Creator, who plants resilience in wounded hearts. We would be blessed to have such spirit join our journey. We walk toward peril, yes, but perhaps, together, guided by the Creator, we can bring some small light into that great darkness."

And so, the fellowship, tested by violence and suspicion, transformed by shared truth and newfound purpose, grew once more. They would rest here, heal their wounds, gather strength in Selah's hidden refuge, preparing now for the next stage of their journey—a path leading toward the brooding shadow of Serpent Mountain, guided now by a Daughter of Eve seeking lost kin, united by a common enemy and a renewed faith in the enduring promise of the Creator.

8

Serpent Mountain's Shadow

Gratitude mingled with grim purpose as they departed the hidden refuge of Selah and her daughters. The days spent recuperating under Selah's watchful care had been a necessary balm, but the weight of their quest, now intertwined with Naamah's search, a painful pilgrimage born of both deep sorrow and a stubborn, resilient hope, pressed heavily upon them. They knew that this next leg of the journey, leading them deliberately into the territory of the enemy, would be the longest and most perilous yet. Selah's warning echoed in their minds: The journey would last for weeks, perhaps longer, taking them through a landscape twisted both in body and spirit by the power emanating from Serpent Mountain.

They moved out with renewed caution, the memory of the behemoth attack and Selah's chilling tales of raiders fresh in their minds, acutely aware that the peace they had found was now behind them. The ominous, jagged peaks on the western horizon loomed closer each day.

Naamah led them on a hidden path, often barely more than a winding game trail twisting through stark rocky defiles choked with thorny trees, and across shadowed woodlands where sickly sunlight struggled to penetrate the dense canopy.

Days bled into weeks, marked only by the moon's slow cycle overhead. The initial cautious optimism faded, replaced by the monotonous rhythm of hard travel and constant, nerve-wracking vigilance. Anak, Kael, and Ronan, despite their mammoth size, moved with the surprising quietness of creatures long accustomed to wilderness, their deep knowledge of reading terrain—a broken twig here, the faint imprint of disturbed earth there—complementing Naamah's specific familiarity with this region's secret ways.

Enoch often watched Naamah navigate, her focus absolute, unwavering. She moved with a grace born of necessity, her dark eyes scanning, interpreting the subtle language of the earth and wind. *Her sorrow does not weigh her down,* he observed silently during one long twilight march. *It has become the very fire that drives her forward.*

Serpent Mountain became a constant, oppressive presence in their westward view. Some days, shrouded in an unnatural, swirling haze, it seemed no closer than the day before, a frustrating optical illusion across the intervening, desolate distance. On other days, after cresting a high, windswept ridge, it would loom menacingly close, its jagged peaks clawing at the bruised sky like blasphemous fingers pointed toward heaven. Bizarre yellow-gray clouds loomed ominously at the heights, their swirling forms appearing to writhe with a slow, malevolent awareness. Despite the fierce winds that swept across the lower slopes, the clouds stubbornly refused to disperse, hanging in the sky like a dark, brooding presence, intensifying the eerie atmosphere that enveloped the landscape. The mountain radiated a clear wrongness, a heaviness that settled on their minds, causing dull headaches and a low, constant thrum of anxiety. Unlike the weathered peaks they had known before, worn smooth by centuries of weather, these mountains felt sharp-edged, aggressive, shrouded in shadow regardless of the sun's arc.

Enoch noticed a change in his son. Methuselah now avoided looking at the mountain, keeping his gaze fixed firmly on the treacherous path beneath his feet. He saw the boy focusing with an intense, almost desperate concentration on learning the faint tracking signs Naamah pointed out, or pausing often to check the edge of his axe. *He seeks refuge in the tangible,* Enoch realized, *a young man's way of battling an unseen fear, a dread too large to name.*

As the first week bled into the second, then the third, step by step, the land itself testified to the mountain's corrupting influence. The vibrant greens and hardy resilience of the wilderness nearer Selah's valley surrendered entirely to decay and distortion. They were forced to pass through groves where gnarled trees stood twisted into unnatural shapes, their branches contorted like arthritic fingers clawing at the oppressive sky, their bark weeping a black, foul-smelling, tar-like substance. The air beneath their canopy was still and chillingly cold, and the silence was complete—no birdsong, no insect hum, only the soft, unsettling crunch of their own footsteps on the brittle, blighted leaf litter.

Even the trees feel its presence, Enoch thought, touching a warped trunk that was disturbingly clammy and diseased. *The very lifeblood of the land is poisoned here.*

Water became a constant, pressing concern. The streams they crossed grew sluggish; their banks lined with a sickly gray slime that clung to their boots. The water itself often ran cloudy or held unnatural colors, carrying an acrid metallic tang that scraped the back of the throat and left an oily residue on their waterskins. Kael, using his deep knowledge of herbs and nature, would often test the water, dipping a finger, smelling it intently, sometimes tasting a minuscule drop before grimly shaking his head. Their dwindling water supply forced them to rely on their carefully rationed stores, as thirst became a nagging companion under the often oppressive, hazy sky.

Hunting proved equally fruitless; the few animals they spotted seemed diseased or deformed, unfit to eat, their eyes holding a dull sickness or crazed aggression. A deep fatigue settled into their bones, a constant companion fueled by meager rations and fitful sleep. They subsisted on the last of Selah's dried provisions and whatever tough, unappetizing roots Naamah could find, leaving them perpetually hungry.

The need for vigilance was a constant tension that frayed their nerves. Naamah's warning about patrols from the city of Enoch proved accurate. Midway through the third week, Kael's sharp eyes spotted movement high on a distant ridge against the skyline—the unmistakable glint of dark metal reflecting the harsh sun.

"Down!" he hissed urgently.

They scrambled for cover, melting into a cluster of jagged rocks and thorny, diseased bushes, hearts pounding, holding their breath as a patrol marched into view on the ridgeline above. Not giants this time, nor Nephilim themselves, but a dozen armed men clad in black scaled armor, marching with disciplined efficiency. They scanned the terrain below with cold, dismissive eyes, their progress marked by casual cruelty—one soldier set fire to a patch of struggling dry grass with a small torch, laughing as it flared briefly then died; another kicked aside the bleached skull of some unfortunate creature lying near their path. One carried a long, cruel-looking whip coiled at his belt, its tip stained dark.

The Serpent's enforcers, Enoch thought, his heart aching with a mixture of anger and pity. *Men trading their souls, their very humanity, for scraps of power under his shadow.*

Enoch lay flat, his face pressed into the dusty earth, trying not to breathe, the image of Selah's captured husband and sons superimposed onto these emotionless figures. They waited, muscles aching, cramped and stiff, long after the patrol disappeared over the next rise, the heavy silence they left behind feeling somehow more threatening, more watchful, than their actual presence.

The creatures inhabiting this blighted region were another distinct threat—tortured, corrupted, twisted reflections of natural life, or perhaps things that had crawled from deeper, darker shadows under the mountain's noxious influence. They spent hours one tense, humid afternoon cutting their way through thick, sticky gray webs that draped between gnarled trees, occasionally glimpsing the spiders that spun them—bloated, multi-eyed, leg-jointed horrors the size of Enoch's head, skittering away with unnerving speed into dark crevices when disturbed. They learned to skirt fetid, bubbling swamps where snakes, marked with disturbing, angular, unnatural patterns, slithered through the foul, sulfurous water, their unblinking eyes glowing with a faint luminescence in the gloom.

One evening, as they sought shelter for the night near a protective rocky overhang, danger struck with lethal speed. From the shadowed gloom high above, a massive serpent, thick around as a man's waist and five times a man's length, launched itself downward at Kael, who was weary and less alert than usual. Its green-and-black scales, disturbingly slick-looking even in the dim twilight, blurred as it uncoiled from the darkness like a released spring of primeval malice. Its gaping maw, lined with rows of backward-curving fangs dripping a dark fluid, opened wide as a venomous hiss filled with explosive rage echoed off the cold stone walls. Before Kael could comprehend the lethal threat dropping upon him, Ronan moved like lightning. His heavy, iron-headed hammer, always ready in his grip, swung in a powerful, precise arc born of countless battles. The hardened hammerhead impacted the serpent's skull with a sickening crunch of bone and sinew. The massive, muscular body slammed onto the path between them, its powerful coils thrashing violently for a heart-stopping moment before lying still, its deadly attack cut short by the swift, brutal intervention. Shaken by the encounter, they were reminded once more of the ever-present dangers in this cursed land.

Each near-miss with patrols, each unsettling encounter with poisoned nature, each narrow escape from monstrous creatures demanded constant stealth, quick thinking, and the combined strengths of their weary group—Naamah's agility and knowledge of evasion, the giants' raw power and unwavering resilience, Enoch's steadying presence and wisdom, and Methuselah's growing courage and developing skill with his axe.

The long journey, stretching now into what felt like an eternity under the mountain's oppressive, watchful gaze, forged their camaraderie into something harder, more essential, tempered by shared danger and grim determination. The easy laughter shared in the first days after leaving Anak's home was gone, replaced by economical communication—essential hand signals, hushed whispers when speech was necessary, or shared glances that spoke volumes of fear, resolve, or warning.

Sleep remained fitful at best, haunted by the heavy, threatening atmosphere, the memory of horrors seen, and the gnawing anxiety of what lay ahead under the mountain's shadow. Watches were kept, each member taking their turn scanning the darkness for threats both seen and unseen, listening for any sound that broke the unnatural quiet.

Eventually, after many weeks, going over areas that seemed antagonistic to the idea of life, they stopped at the edge of the blighted, rocky foothills. Serpent Mountain loomed directly before them, huge, terrifyingly close, its highest, jagged peak lost in the unnatural, churning gray clouds that perpetually hid its summit. The air itself seemed to thrum here with a low, almost sub-audible vibration that resonated deep in their bones, setting Enoch's teeth on edge, a feeling of incalculable *bound* power emanating from the dark rock. Somewhere in those foreboding mountains lay the city called Enoch, the dark heart of the distortion they had witnessed bleeding out across the land for leagues. They had survived the approach, navigated the treacherous wilds, evaded the patrols, and either bypassed or overcome the monstrous guardians. They had reached the threshold of the enemy's domain. The shadow of Serpent Mountain now lay upon them, cold and heavy as a burial shroud, and the city of Enoch, nestled in its malevolent embrace, awaited their desperate gamble.

9

The Serpent's Jewel

T he shadow of Serpent Mountain consumed the land completely
now, a palpable, chilling presence that muted the light and
seemed to deaden the very air. Guided by Naamah's grim knowledge
of the region's edge and Anak's unwavering strength, they emerged
from the last of the blighted foothills onto a wide, smooth road paved
with seamless, dark, fused stone that remained cold even under the afternoon sun. In the distance, rising from the shimmering heat haze
like a disturbing mirage, stood the city called Enoch. And it was,
against all expectations, breathtakingly magnificent.

Unlike the organic strength of Anak's home, built with the mountains, or the honest simplicity of the glade woven *from* the forest,
this city glittered with defiance against nature itself. Towers of polished obsidian, white alabaster, and strange, iridescent metals soared
toward the heavens, their impossible, needle-sharp spires seeming to
pierce the very clouds that clung to the mountain peaks behind them,
rivaling those peaks in height and sheer audacity. Intricate, almost
feverish carvings snaked across every visible surface, depicting stylized scenes of triumph, discovery, and raw power—giants and men
portrayed as equals, working together under the guidance of taller,
luminous figures, mastering fire, metal, stone, raising mighty, geomet-
rically perfect structures, their carved faces alight with fierce, almost

arrogant intelligence. Colossal statues of beings both vaguely human-like and angelic, undeniably Nephilim in their cold, alien perfection, stood sentinel at crossroads and adorned great plazas. Enormous murals, painted with pigments of startling, almost painful vibrancy, showcased epic, self-aggrandizing narratives—a fiery being descending like a star, gifting forbidden knowledge to awestruck humans; figures wrangling enormous, nightmarish beasts into submission; architects drafting intricate plans for impossible, logic-defying structures that seemed to reshape reality itself.

Walls, impossibly high and smooth as polished glass, without seam or joint, encircled the city, radiating an aura of unbreachable power and absolute, chilling order. Within those walls, the very environment felt controlled, artificial.

The road beneath their feet remained flawless, without dust or cracks. When evening arrived, crystals embedded in elaborate, unrecognizable metal pillars pulsed with rhythmic, cold light, removing shadows entirely, producing a continuous, sterile twilight.

Fountains of intricate design sprayed water that shimmered with shifting colors into tiered, black stone basins. Music—complex, repetitive, and strangely hypnotic—drifted from high, unseen balconies, played on instruments whose tones slid dissonantly against Enoch's memory of natural harmony.

The air itself lacked the wild scents of nature, of earth. Instead, it reeked of heavy, exotic perfumes mingled with the tang of ozone and hot metal. *It is a jewel,* Enoch thought again, his spirit recoiling from the cold perfection even as a part of him couldn't deny the sheer, breathtaking, unnatural artistry. *But forged in what unseen fire? Polished with the tears of how many forgotten souls?*

As they approached the massive gates—themselves flawless masterpieces of interlocking black metalwork flanked by colossal statues of Nephilim figures, stern and watchful—Enoch heard Methuselah's sharp intake of breath beside him. He turned to see his son stopped in his tracks. His shoulders, once set with grim purpose, had slackened.

His eyes were wide, tracing the intricate, alien beauty of the metal-work with a dangerous mixture of wonder and confusion. *He is not seeing a fortress,* Enoch realized with a jolt of alarm; *he is seeing a marvel. The power of this place... it intoxicates him.* "Father," he murmured, "look at the detail... the precision... How could such things be entirely evil?" Even Naamah, though her eyes still darted amongst the passing figures, searching every downcast human face near the gate for a spark of recognition, seemed stunned into silence by the sheer, imposing grandeur, a stark, painful contrast to the simple, lost life of her captured kin.

Anak and his sons, however, radiated visible unease, their connection to the earth and stone sensing the deep discord beneath the surface. Their experience allowed them to sense the wrongness masked by perfection. "Too perfect," Kael rumbled, his hand resting on the haft of his honest iron axe. "Stone should breathe, show its age. Metal should yield to time, bear the marks of its making. This... this feels forced, held against its nature by some unseen will. Like a beautiful corpse."

They slipped into the city not as guests but as shadows, merging with the weary evening crowds returned from unseen labors beyond the walls—mostly humans, faces etched with fatigue, their eyes blank, avoiding contact, moving with listless obedience alongside hulking, brutish giants unlike Anak's kin, whose features lacked thought or nobility, only dull strength. Overseers, both human and giant, clad in dark livery, directed the flow with curt gestures and harsh glares, their authority absolute and unquestioned. And then there were the true masters, glimpsed occasionally like apparitions. Striding through crowds that parted before them, with an effortless, predatory grace that belied incalculable power, were the Nephilim themselves, or their closest, purest descendants. Tall, often clad in fabrics that seemed woven from light, their beauty was cold, flawless, lacking any trace of human warmth or frailty. Their eyes, dark voids, held calculating intelligence and a chilling lack of empathy that made Enoch's soul shrink back. Power radiated from them like heat from a forge. As they passed, the diverse populace—human slaves shuffling in chains, giant over-seers standing rigidly, artisans hurrying by, strangely clad priests with shaved heads—bowed low as one, a wave of reverence washing through the crowded streets.

They rule by power, yes, Enoch thought, observing the fear in the averted eyes, the trembling hands, *but also by this... overwhelming, soul-crushing presence. They present themselves as gods and demand the worship due only to the Creator.*

The city pulsed with a strange energy, a seductive blend of luxury and oppression. Markets overflowed with exotic foods whose origins Enoch couldn't guess, luxurious fabrics in impossible colors, intricate mechanical contraptions whirring and clicking with unknown pur-pose. Public squares featured large, shimmering displays—conceivably illusions, possibly some other craft—depicting stirring, false scenes: the 'Bearer of Light' descending heroically from the heavens, ethereal chains shattering from grateful human wrists, reverent crowds receiv-ing scrolls of forbidden knowledge. Orators stood on high platforms, their voices magically amplified, echoing through the plazas as they proclaimed the glory of Enoch, a city of enlightenment, a haven from the jealous rage and stifling ignorance imposed by the 'Old God.' They spoke of the 'Great Sacrifice' made by the 'Shining Ones' who left celestial perfection to guide struggling mankind, led by the benevo-lent, misunderstood 'Light-Bearer'—Lucifer, they named him without shame—who battled the tyrannical Creator not for malice but for hu-manity's essential freedom to know, to grasp power, to become gods themselves.

Enoch listened, his heart growing colder, heavier with each blas-phemous, prideful twist of truth. They had inverted everything. The Creator, the infinite source of all life and love, painted as a restrictive, jealous tyrant. The Serpent, the very author of lies and death, hailed as a heroic, self-sacrificing liberator. He saw Methuselah listening in-tently to one particularly charismatic orator, his brow furrowed, a flicker of troubled confusion, even fascination, in his young eyes. *The lies are potent*, Enoch realized with sharp alarm. *They offer pride, power, knowledge seemingly without cost—appealing directly to the weaknesses born of the Fall.* He felt the city's cunning allure himself, a constant, subliminal pressure to accept this dazzling, ordered reality, to forget the hardship, the struggle, the 'inefficiency' of faith, and embrace the ease offered by this tangible power. The sheer order, the apparent control over nature and man, was seductive after the chaos and peril of the wilderness. *Is the glade's simple faith, its reliance on the unseen, truly enough against this level of power and deception?* He clung desperately to the memory of Eden's true harmony, to the Creator's gentle presence felt even in exile, to the deep sorrow of the Fall—anchors against this glittering, treacherous tide.

He knew he needed to see the heart of this blasphemy, the focal point of their worship, to fully understand the enemy. The crowd propelled them forward, a wave of bodies drawn to the opulent, towering structure at the city's heart; intricate carvings gleamed under the sun as they neared. It dwarfed everything else, a temple of staggering proportions, constructed seemingly of solid, seamless, gleaming gold, its surface reflecting the cold crystalline lights in blinding, almost painful fashion. Intricate, spiraling reliefs climbed its impossibly high walls, telling the Serpent's story in horrifying detail, culminating near the top where stylized Nephilim figures seemed to commune with dark stars. The sheer weight of arrogant power emanating from the structure made Enoch's spirit quail.

"The Temple of the Light-Bearer," a nearby woman whispered reverently to her wide-eyed child, bowing her head low as they passed its enormous gates.

Hesitantly, feeling both overpowering repulsion and grim necessity, Enoch led his companions inside. The interior was cavernous. The air tasted metallic on the tongue. But it was the murals dominating the polished walls that seized their attention, holding them frozen in horrified fascination. Painted with breathtaking beauty and a technical skill that spoke of mastery, they depicted the Nephilim's twisted version of history.

One large panel showed the Garden of Eden—not as a paradise of life but a stagnant, unchanging, gilded cage. The painting showed Adam and Eve as beautiful but vacant, doll-like figures kneeling passively before a huge, shadowy, glowing entity labeled 'The Jealous One,' forever forbidden from reaching a luminous tree prominently labeled 'Wisdom.' Another panel showed the Serpent—depicted as a glorious, winged being of pure light and beauty—offering the glowing fruit gently to Eve, whispering secrets of liberation into her ear. Eve's face as she accepted transformed from blank obedience to ecstatic enlightenment. Adam, receiving the fruit from her hand, stood suddenly tall, powerful, his eyes alight with newfound freedom and intelligence.

The next mural showed the 'Jealous One' roaring in impotent fury, casting Adam and Eve out—not into hardship but directly toward the waiting, welcoming arms of the 'Light-Bearer,' who offered them tools, fire, and the promise of *real* power. And then, the most jarring, most blasphemous panel: It showed Cain, depicted as a heroic, muscular, Promethean figure, illuminated and guided by the 'Light-Bearer' and other 'Shining Ones,' justly striking down a cowering, ignorant Abel who clung foolishly to the 'Old Ways.' The mural then triumphantly showed Cain laying the foundation stones of a glorious, towering city—this very city of Enoch—a testament to liberated mankind's potential, while, in a small, dark, insignificant corner of the mural, the artist portrayed Adam and Eve shivering miserably in a cold, primitive cave, clinging pathetically to superstition, abandoned by their failed 'tyrant' God.

Like a physical blow, the hatefully twisted image slammed into Enoch's consciousness. The cave from his divine vision—Adam's first shelter after exile, the place of deep sorrow but also enduring hope, the sacred repository of true history—perverted here into a symbol of ignorance, fear, and despair. The blasphemy was absolute; sickeningly complete. This entire city and belief system, built by the Deceiver, rested on a foundation of deliberate, malevolent inversion of truth, designed to steal mankind's true heritage and enslave them body and soul.

Enoch's perception of the temple's overwhelming beauty instantly shifted to ash and perversion. The power humming in the air felt like the oppressive vibration of an extensive, soul-crushing machine, fueled by lies and misery. He saw Methuselah staring at the heroic depiction of Cain, his expression deeply confused, troubled, still half-awed by the sheer artistic power but clearly disturbed by the message. He saw Naamah physically recoil from the image of the radiant Serpent, her hand going to her belt knife, the memory of her family's destruction giving her clarity. He saw Anak and his sons looking at the idealized Nephilim figures in the murals with intense disgust.

"Enough," Enoch choked out, his voice hoarse with revulsion and cold, righteous anger. He grabbed Methuselah's arm, pulling him away from the mural's seductive artistry. "We must leave this place. Now. It is all lies. A beautiful, glittering cage built upon damned souls and forgotten truth."

He turned, pushing through the throng of silent worshippers who knelt before a massive, beautiful golden statue of the 'Light-Bearer' enthroned at the temple's far end.

His companions followed without question now, Methuselah looking back one last time with lingering confusion quickly fading into dawning horror, Naamah stumbling in her haste to escape the suffocating presence, the giants forming a protective, grim-faced wedge around them. They fled the golden temple, bursting back out onto the city's main thoroughfare, the crushing weight of the revealed deception heavy upon them. Without pausing, they plunged into the shadowed backstreets, seeking the anonymity of darkness, seeking the enslaved, seeking any flicker of truth that might still survive amongst the oppressed in the rotten heart of the Serpent's Jewel.

10

Cain's Lament

Bursting from the overwhelming, blasphemous grandeur of the golden temple, the group plunged into the relative darkness and filth of the city's backstreets. The air here, thick with coal smoke, sweat, and refuse, felt almost cleansing after the cloying perfumes and humming, oppressive power of the Nephilim sanctuary. Enoch, his face pale but his eyes blazing with righteous fire, pulled them into a shadowed alcove between leaning, crumbling structures.

"Did you see?" he demanded, his voice low and urgent, trembling with revulsion. "Did you understand the depth of the lie? The Serpent hailed as savior! They scorn the Creator as a jealous tyrant! Our entire history, Adam's legacy, twisted into a weapon against us! Even the cave—the sacred place from my vision, Adam's first sorrow, his first hope outside Eden—perverted into a symbol of ignorance!" He shook his head, shuddering with a spiritual sickness. "This entire city is built upon lies that seek to usurp Heaven itself. We cannot linger where such blasphemy reigns."

Methuselah looked deeply shaken, the dazzling allure of the temple's artistry now thoroughly tainted by his father's horror and the undeniable wrongness that had settled cold in his own gut. Naamah clung unconsciously to his arm, not for support but as if needing a physical anchor against the tide of spiritual poison they had just witnessed. Anak and his sons grunted guttural agreement, their faces masks of grim understanding and disgust. "We felt it," Anak rumbled, his voice vibrating with suppressed anger. "The cold pride. The power built on suffering. It resonates with the worst parts of our own Nephilim blood—the parts we fight daily to deny."

Their purpose clarified, unified now in shared revulsion, they moved with renewed urgency deeper into the shadowed network of alleys, heading toward the sounds of heavy labor they had noted earlier. They sought the hidden truth, the counter-narrative, amidst the city's most blatant display of oppression. Here, in the slave quarters and work sites, the glittering mask of prosperity was fully discarded. Enslaved Sons of Adam, their bodies showing the cruel ravages of endless, brutal labor, toiled under the watchful, indifferent gaze of hulking overseers—both giant and human. Their eyes were mostly empty, holding only dull exhaustion save for occasional flickers of deeply ingrained fear.

Naamah, moving like a ghost beside Enoch, suddenly froze. Her gaze locked onto a single figure in the distance—a gaunt slave hauling stones, his back bent in defeat. Her breath hitched in a sharp, audible gasp. The mask of weary grief she had worn for weeks shattered, replaced by a look of stunned, impossible hope. Before Enoch could ask what she saw, before he could caution her against breaking their stealthy cover, she was moving. Forgetting all danger, she rushed forward, crying a name he had only heard her speak in stories of loss: "Malachi!"

The overseer nearest them—a large, cruel-faced giant hybrid with scarred knuckles—bellowed in rage at the disruption, striding forward, a thick whip cracking menacingly in the air. Malachi flinched violently at the sound, dropping the heavy ropes he was hauling, stumbling back as he turned. His eyes widened first in terror of the whip, then in stunned, disbelieving recognition as he saw Naamah running toward him. "Naamah?" His voice was a dry, broken rasp, cracked with disuse and disbelief. "Little sister? Is it... Truly, you?"

Tears streamed down Naamah's face, cutting paths through the dust as she threw her arms around his thin, frail frame. "Malachi! Oh, Malachi! I thought... we all thought you were gone..."

He clung to her, his own eyes filling with tears, the sudden shock of impossible reunion overwhelming years of hopeless despair. "Naamah... alive..." He pulled back, his gaze searching her face, then darting with ingrained fear toward the overseer who was now almost upon them, whip raised high.

Before the blow could fall, Anak moved with deceptive speed for his size, interposing his massive form in the overseer's path. There was no prolonged struggle, no warning. A single, swift, brutally efficient blow from Anak's stony fist connected with the overseer's temple. The brute crumpled instantly, unconscious before he hit the packed earth. Kael and Ronan moved quickly, dragging the heavy, inert form into the deep shadows behind a pile of discarded stone blocks, ensuring he wouldn't be found immediately. *Speed is essential now*, Enoch thought, his heart pounding, knowing their time here was perilously limited.

The tearful reunion between Naamah and Malachi unfolded in hushed, urgent whispers, tragically punctuated by the harsh reality Malachi delivered—their father dead from the brutal labor years ago, broken by the stones; their brothers, Jared and Caleb, taken for the Nephilim's 'Great Work' deep beneath the mountain, a dark, sacrificial fate from which none ever returned. "I am... I am all that is left of us, little sister," he choked out, his voice thick with survivor's guilt and overwhelming grief.

Naamah's renewed anguish was a raw wound in the oppressive atmosphere of the slave yards. Enoch watched as Naamah, through her tears, quickly explained who he was, their quest for truth, and their hope in the Creator. As she spoke, Enoch saw a subtle shift in Malachi. The defeated slump of his shoulders seemed to lessen, as if an invisible weight had been lifted. His gaze, which had been darting fearfully towards the shadows, now fixed on Enoch with a new, searching intensity. *It is not just recognition*, Enoch realized, *it is hope. A flicker of something long dormant, something beyond mere survival, returning to a man who thought all was lost.* "There is a place," Malachi whispered, glancing around, keenly aware of the watchful eyes of other slaves and the potential for unseen watchers. "They call it the 'Founder's Tomb,' though they mock Cain even as they claim his twisted legacy. It lies in the oldest, most neglected part of the city, near the mountain's base. Few go there; it's deemed unimportant, cursed." He hesitated, his gaze fixed on Enoch's expression. "Maybe... maybe truth lingers there, untouched by their gilded lies?" He then spoke of the tunnels beneath that sector, an escape route known only to a few of the longest surviving slaves. "I can show you the way out," he offered, his voice strained. "But you must go *now!*"

But Enoch, his spirit still reeling from the temple's polished deception, now ignited by Malachi's words confirming a real tomb of Cain, felt an overwhelming conviction, a divine insistence that pulsed like a second heartbeat. The temple showed the Lie; they *had* to see the Truth, however grim, before fleeing. And his companions needed to see it too, to arm their souls against the Serpent City's lingering, poisonous allure before they risked the unknown dangers outside. "Before the tunnels, Malachi," Enoch stated, his voice carrying quiet authority that allowed no argument. He met his companions' eyes. "Take us to this tomb. All of us. We must face the true foundation of this city and understand the authentic story of the first murderer before we turn our backs on this place forever. It is necessary."

Methuselah looked uncertain but nodded, his trust in his father absolute now after the temple. Naamah, numb with grief but clinging to Malachi, followed his lead. Anak exchanged a brief look with Kael and Ronan, then gave a slow nod. "Quickly, then. Show us."

Though fearful of lingering, Malachi understood the deep spiritual need driving Enoch. He led them away from the slave yards, deeper into derelict sectors where the city's glittering facade had crumbled into decay. As they navigated a dark, refuse-choked alley, a hunched figure emerged from a hovel made of scrap refuse and cracked stone.

The man was impossibly old, his skin like dried leather stretched over bone, his eyes holding a cunning, watery light. He looked past the humans and fixed his gaze on Anak.

"A son of Haran's line," the old man rasped. "You are far from your valley. What brings you to this pit?" His eyes then shifted to Enoch, a flicker of curiosity in their depths. "And you, little man. You carry a different air about you. Not the stench of this city."

Enoch, his heart filled with pity for the wretched state of the old man, stopped. "We are but travelers, old father."

"Travelers have names," the man pressed, a sly look entering his eyes.

"I am Enoch," Enoch replied.

The old man's eyes widened. "Enoch," he repeated, "A name of power here. The Founder's son. Have you returned to claim your father Cain's legacy?"

The innocent mistake, born of this city's twisted history, gave Enoch an opportunity to clarify, to bear witness. "No, old one," he said gently. "My name is Enoch, but I am of Seth's line, not Cain's."

The old man froze. The vacant dullness in his eyes vanished, replaced for a heartbeat by a sharp, calculating glint that made Enoch's skin crawl. The shift was so quick Enoch might have doubted it, but the old man's entire demeanor had changed. He bowed low, a gesture of deference so deep, so sudden, it felt mocking. "Of course, of course. Forgive an old man's ramblings." He shuffled back into the shadows of his hovel, his eyes darting away, refusing to meet theirs again. *I have made a mistake,* Enoch realized with a jolt of cold certainty. *A terrible, unseen error.*

* * *

In a high chamber of polished obsidian, where the air hummed with power, two luminous figures sat across from each other, a board of intricately carved stone between them. Their beauty was cold and perfect. Their game was interrupted by the hurried entrance of a dark-armored guard, who fell to one knee, averting his eyes from their faces.

"Lord Jotunn, Lord Gilga," the guard said, his voice tight with fear and urgency. "Forgive this intrusion. The old one, Mehujael, from the lower sectors. He claims to have news of the highest importance."

"Let him enter," Jotunn commanded, his voice devoid of emotion, not looking up from the game.

The old man was brought in, trembling, falling prostrate. "Lords of Light! I have seen them! The renegade giants of Anak's line... and with them... a man who calls himself Enoch, of *Seth's* line! The bounty... You promised a bounty for any word of the Sethites!"

The air in the chamber grew instantly colder. Jotunn and Gilga exchanged a long, silent look. The game on the table was forgotten. For centuries, their hunters had scoured the known world, extinguishing every settlement, every family that carried the blood of Seth. They had believed them all gone, the threat neutralized.

"The Seed of Seth," Gilga whispered, the words like chips of ice. "Here. In our city."

Jotunn rose, his form radiating coiled power. "It seems the Creator's last, flickering hope has wandered foolishly into the very heart of the flame." He looked down at the groveling Mehujael. "Your prize for this news is that your miserable life will be permitted to continue... for now. Guards, remove him. Let him toil with the others until he expires." As the old man was dragged away, his pleas for his reward ignored, Jotunn turned to his commander. "Alert the hunt masters. Make ready the beasts. They will not leave this mountain alive."

* * *

At last, dominated by the dark mass of Serpent Mountain towering above them, the fellowship arrived at its location—a low, square mausoleum of pitted black basalt, old and crumbling, oddly lacking the city's pervasive, arrogant ornamentation. It appeared extremely old, alone, and heavy, with an atmosphere of deep sorrow and extended neglect that contrasted sharply with the energetic, almost frantic energy of the golden temple.

Torches were lit as they entered the dusty, silent interior. The air was cold, tasting of centuries of undisturbed dust. In the center stood a single, unadorned sarcophagus of the same black stone. There were no blasphemous murals here, no gilded statues, only this silent, brooding presence demanding acknowledgment. Enoch moved forward as if drawn by an invisible current, the others following closely, their torchlight casting uneasy shadows. He reached the sarcophagus and brushed away the thick mantle of dust from its heavy lid. Etched there, crudely but deeply, in primitive, angular letters—an early form of Adam's own tongue—was an inscription.

Enoch traced the letters with a trembling finger, reading the words aloud. His voice echoed eerily in the dead, silent space, each word falling like a heavy stone into the stillness:

"I AM CAIN, SON OF ADAM, SLAYER OF MY BROTHER." A collective intake of breath from the group. No heroic founder here, only a stark, terrible confession.

"THE SERPENT PROMISED KNOWLEDGE, I FOUND ONLY ASHES."

Methuselah's eyes widened in the torchlight, the memory of the golden temple's seductive lies shattering completely against this raw admission of deceit.

"HIS MARK IS MY CURSE, THIS CITY MY MONUMENT TO FOLLY."

Anak grunted, a deep sound of unhappy recognition. He and his sons understood monuments built in pride, and the heavy, enduring bitterness of regret that often followed.

"CREATOR, THOUGH I AM BANISHED, LET TRUTH ENDURE."

Naamah looked up, tears still tracking pathways through the dirt on her face, but a different light—fierce, understanding—now dawning in her eyes. The echo of the faith her mother clung to resonated with Cain's dying acknowledgment.

"MERCY..."

The final, unfinished word hung in the air, raw, desperate—a plea cutting through millennia of silence and exile. Here, forgotten in this neglected corner of the city, lay the unvarnished, agonizing truth, stripped bare of all Nephilim propaganda. Not a defiant rebel seizing power but a broken man, cursed by his own murderous actions, admitting the Serpent's ultimate deceit, acknowledging the Creator even in his banishment, and begging for the mercy the golden temple arrogantly proclaimed unnecessary.

The contrast was absolute. The temple screamed lies in gold and dazzling light; the tomb whispered unbearable truth in dust and darkness.

Their shared experience solidified their resolve beyond doubt, uniting them in a deep, visceral understanding of the evil they fought. The city's seductive allure was gone entirely, replaced by cold horror and righteous, determined purpose.

The heavy quiet of the tomb was broken by a distant horn, its urgent notes echoing oddly in the derelict sector. Shouts followed, seeming to come from the direction of the slave yards. "They found the overseer!" Malachi gasped, his face paling, eyes wide with terror. "Or watchers saw us come here! We lingered for too long! We must go—NOW!"

The spell of the tomb broke instantly, replaced by immediate, pressing danger. "Malachi," Enoch said, his voice ringing now with conviction and urgency, gripping the man's thin arm. "The tunnels. Guide us. Now!"

Malachi nodded, his weariness momentarily forgotten in the face of imminent peril. He led them from the tomb, plunging back into the labyrinthine, refuse-choked alleys just as the sounds of alarm—harsh horns, running feet, distant shouts—grew undeniably closer, echoing unnervingly through the derelict sector. With the desperate cunning of a long-term captive, he navigated the maze of shadows, avoiding the patrols whose hurried footsteps they could now hear approaching. Finally, in a forgotten, trash-strewn corner near the outer city limits, he brought them to a heavy iron grate buried beneath loose debris. "Here," he rasped, straining with a rusted metal bar he produced from his rags to pry the heavy grate open. "The waste tunnels. Filth runs deep, but they empty beyond the walls. Go, quickly! There is no other way now!"

"You come with us, Malachi!" Naamah pleaded desperately, grabbing his thin arm.

He detached her hand, his face etched with a loving resolve that tore at her heart. "No, sister," he said softly but firmly. "My body and spirit have been broken by this place. I would only slow you down." He looked at Enoch, his eyes holding a spark of the hope Enoch represented. "They carry the light. They must escape. I... I can help ensure it. Buy you time."

Before they could argue further, Anak shoved the heavy grate open with a groan of stressed metal, revealing a dark, foul-smelling abyss. "He speaks truth, Naamah!" the giant urged, his voice grim. "We must hurry!"

Heartbroken, tears streaming, but knowing Malachi was right, Naamah scrambled into the stinking darkness after Enoch and Methuselah. Kael and Ronan followed immediately, pulling the heavy grate closed behind them, hoping to obscure it. Malachi gave Naamah one last look, filled with unbearable sorrow and fierce love, then melted back into the alleys just as the harsh shouts of the first pursuers echoed nearby. An alarm horn blared again, closer this time. They had lingered too long at the tomb.

They plunged into the tunnel's filth. Enoch glanced back at Naamah and saw the image of her brother's determined, sacrificial face seared into her wide, unblinking eyes. The weight of Malachi's choice fell heavily upon them all as the escape became a desperate flight through suffocating darkness, stench, and unseen obstacles. Behind them, they soon heard the clang of the grate being thrown open again, followed by the angry shouts of pursuers entering the tunnel system. Torches flared far behind them, casting long, dancing, menacing shadows down the passageways. They scrambled onward, slipping on slime-covered stones, splashing through ankle-deep foul water, guided only by Malachi's hurried directions echoing in Enoch's mind. The pursuit was relentless, their heavy footsteps gaining ground.

At a junction of several dark, converging tunnels, the sounds from behind grew alarmingly close. Suddenly, seemingly from nowhere, appearing from a narrow side passage ahead, Malachi stood before them again, his face grim, resolute. "This way! Quickly!" He called them into a narrower, steeper passage they hadn't noticed. "Keep going! Don't stop for anything!"

"Malachi, come with us!" Naamah cried again, reaching for him as Kael pushed her forward into the cramped passage.

"No time! Go!" he yelled back, turning his back on them. He braced himself in the center of the main tunnel junction they had just left, placing his hands against a heavy, crumbling central support beam, clearly weakened by age and neglect. "They chose the wrong path following you..." he shouted toward the approaching torchlight, his voice echoing defiantly, "I will make sure they cannot follow *this* one either!" With a tremendous, desperate heave born of ultimate sacrifice, he threw his entire weight against the beam. Rocks groaned overhead. Dust billowed thick and choking.

"Malachi! NO!" Naamah screamed, trying to fight her way back to him, but Kael's hand grabbed her arm, pulling her firmly down the narrow escape tunnel after the others.

From behind them came a deafening, grinding roar as the tunnel junction's ceiling collapsed in a cascade of rock, earth, and darkness. The sounds of pursuit, the shouts, the torchlight—all were abruptly cut off. Silence, save for their own ragged, panicked breathing and Naamah's heartbroken sobs, filled the narrow passage. Malachi was gone, buried instantly under his final act of defiant love, buying their freedom with his last breath.

Grief tore through Naamah, a raw, silent scream trapped in her chest, threatening to consume her, but Kael's firm grip hauled her onward, following the others down the narrow, descending passage left open by her brother's sacrifice.

The roar of the collapse behind them was horrifically final.

They stumbled forward through the suffocating darkness, the air thick with choking rock dust, driven now only by raw survival instinct and the echoing weight of Malachi's final, selfless act.

Gasping, near collapse, they emerged from the tunnel's low opening—not onto a gentle slope but a narrow, frighteningly unstable rock ledge clinging dangerously to a cliff's sheer face. Beneath, far down, the blighted river snaked through the gorge. There was no path forward or back along the cliff, only empty air and jagged rock dropping away into impenetrable shadow. Above, the impossibly high, smooth, uncaring walls of the Serpent City loomed, effectively sealing them onto this sliver of crumbling rock.

Trapped, the thought slammed into Enoch with sickening force. *Malachi saved us from pursuit from behind only for us to be trapped here.*

Before panic could set in, Naamah's sharp eyes, honed by a lifetime of vigilance, scanned the cliff edge far above. "We are not alone!" she hissed, pointing. Silhouetted against the city's faint glow were dark figures, preparing ropes. "They're coming down!"

Without a moment's hesitation, she shrugged the bow from her shoulder. Her movements were fluid, her grief momentarily burned away by the cold focus of a hunter. She nocked an arrow, drew the string to her cheek, and loosed. The bowstring sang a sharp, deadly note in the night air. High above, a cry echoed as one figure preparing for descent stumbled back from the edge and disappeared.

"They cannot see us well in this darkness," Enoch said, hope warring with terror in his voice.

"But I can see them," Naamah replied grimly, her eyes fixed on the glint of moonlight off a helmet above. She nocked, drew, and loosed another arrow. Another faint cry. Her focus was absolute, a shield against the pursuers above. It was this focus on the distant threat that kept her from seeing the silent danger much closer.

A shadow detached itself from the darkness just above them. With terrifying speed, a figure who must have already been descending when the tunnel collapsed rappelled down, landing as light as a cat on the ledge mere feet from Enoch. Clad in segmented black armor that seemed to drink the faint starlight, the figure rose swiftly, drawing a wicked-looking blade, short and dark as solidified night.

The attacker lunged, not with a shout but with chilling, focused intent, aiming for Enoch. Enoch reacted instinctively, raising his staff, but the assailant moved with unnatural speed. The black blade slipped past his defense, slicing deeply into his left arm. A searing, unnatural cold shot through him, stealing his breath. He cried out, stumbling back against the cliff face, his staff clattering uselessly. The attacker pivoted instantly toward Naamah, whose attention was still fixed on the clifftop above.

"Naamah!" Methuselah roared. Moving with a speed Enoch had never witnessed in him before, fueled by pure adrenaline, he launched himself forward, slamming shoulder-first into the black-armored attacker and driving them both dangerously toward the ledge's crumbling edge. Methuselah's axe, drawn in the same desperate motion, swung wildly but connected. The figure shrieked, a thin, grating sound, losing its balance. Methuselah shoved hard, and the attacker tumbled backward over the precipice, vanishing into the black abyss below with a final, fading cry.

Methuselah stood panting, axe dripping with dark fluid, his body trembling. He turned immediately to Naamah, grabbing her shoulders, his eyes blazing in the dim light. "Naamah! Are you hurt?" His voice was rough, ragged with adrenaline.

From a few feet away, clutching his own wounded arm, Enoch saw Naamah shake her head. She stared up at his son, her eyes wide not just with shock and terror, but with a dawning awe. The look that passed between them was no longer just that of companions in hardship; it was something new, something more. In that desperate, life-or-death moment, Enoch witnessed the forging of a bond deeper than friendship, born of selfless action and fierce gratitude.

"No," Naamah finally whispered, her voice shaky. "Thank you, Methuselah. You saved..."

The moment was shattered as shouts echoed from above. More dark figures appeared at the cliff edge. Torches flared, their light beginning to probe down the cliff face. Arrows hissed down around them, striking sparks off the rock.

"The rope!" Enoch gasped, clutching his bleeding arm. "It's our only way down!"

Anak surged forward and grasped the dangling rope. He tested it with his weight—it was strong, well-anchored somewhere far above. But one rope wasn't enough for all of them to descend quickly, and more attackers were already beginning to rappel down toward them.

"We need more ropes!" Anak bellowed, ducking as a spear thrown from above exploded on the rock near his head.

Chaos erupted on the narrow, treacherous ledge. The giants became a whirlwind of desperate, close-quarters defense. Naamah loosed her last arrow at a figure beginning a descent, before returning her now-useless bow to her back. Anak, using his incredible reach and strength, grabbed the next rappelling guard mid-air, yanking him brutally from his rope with a roar and sending him plummeting into the darkness. Ronan used his heavy hammer to smash a third guard who landed on the ledge, dispatching him before seizing the fallen guard's line. Methuselah, heart pounding, found himself fighting almost back-to-back with Naamah near the tunnel mouth, using his axe to fend off grasping hands or thrown rocks, while Naamah used loose stones and her small, sharp knife with surprising, vicious effectiveness. With each downed attacker, another precious line was secured.

"Enough! We go NOW!" Anak roared over the chaos. "Naamah! Methuselah—you first! Your weight is less! Go now!"

The descent was terrifying, a frenzied flight into the black abyss. Swinging out from the relative safety of the ledge, trusting the captured ropes of their enemies, they lowered themselves hand over aching hand down the sheer cliff face. The night wind tugged at them, threatening to spin them around. Loose rocks, dislodged by the fighting above or deliberately sent down, skittered past them in the darkness. Arrows still occasionally struck the cliff near them with sharp pings.

Naamah, nimble and light despite her terror, moved with surprising speed, finding footholds where none seemed to exist. Methuselah followed, his muscles burning, glancing up occasionally to see Kael and Ronan begin their descent, covering each other, while Anak prepared to come last, the heaviest and most vital anchor for their escape. Enoch, hampered significantly by his wounded arm, descended painfully, the black blade's sinister cold seeming to seep deeper into his bones, making his grip feel treacherous. He gritted his teeth against the waves of pain and dizziness, focusing only on the next handhold below, his faith a burning ember against the encroaching chill and the emptiness beneath.

They reached the bottom in ragged succession, collapsing onto the sharp, rocky scree near the blighted river's edge, lungs searing, hands raw and bleeding, bodies bruised and trembling. Looking up, they saw Anak begin his final, perilous descent just as more figures swarmed the ledge far above, cutting the anchor ropes one by one. With a final, powerful leap, Anak slid the last few dozen feet, landing safely among them as the final rope was cut high above, severing their last connection to the hateful city.

They were down. They were alive. They were free.

Without pausing, knowing pursuit might still find another way down, they scrambled away from the base of the cliff, putting as much distance as possible between themselves and the accursed city clinging like a leech to Serpent Mountain. They moved westward through the deepening night, exhaustion warring fiercely now with adrenaline, the giants crashing through the unfamiliar blighted undergrowth while Naamah and Methuselah helped the weakening Enoch keep pace.

Hours later, as the land flattened into desolate foothills, Naamah stopped, peering into the impenetrable darkness ahead, a new uncertainty etching itself onto her face. "I... I do not know this place," she admitted, her voice strained with fatigue. "My people never ventured beyond the mountain's shadow. We are in uncharted territory now." Her role as guide, tenuous as it had been, had ended, leaving them truly adrift in an unknown world.

They collapsed near a cluster of dark boulders that offered meager shelter, the relief of escape finally giving way to chilling uncertainty and overwhelming weariness. Naamah sank to the ground, the dam of her control finally breaking, tears tracing paths through the grime on her face as the full weight of Malachi's sacrifice crashed down upon her. Methuselah knelt beside her again, saying nothing, simply offering his waterskin, his presence a small, solid anchor in her sea of grief. Enoch watched his son, and in the boy's unwavering gaze as it rested on the grieving young woman, he saw something new take root. The shared horror of their flight had burned away the last of the boy, leaving in its place a man's fierce, aching resolve to protect what little good was left in their broken world.

Anak, Kael, and Ronan slumped nearby like fallen mountains, their massive forms radiating exhaustion. Enoch saw the brief flicker of relief for their own survival in their weary eyes, but it was quickly overshadowed as their gazes converged on him, heavy with a shared, unspoken concern for his worsening condition. Kael moved to Enoch's side, carefully examining his arm under the starlight. The wound, inflicted hours ago by the black blade, was deep, bleeding sluggishly still, the surrounding flesh unnaturally cold to the touch and darkening to a bruised, unhealthy purple. It emanated a wrongness, a chill, that troubled the giant healer greatly. "This is no common steel, Enoch," Kael rumbled, his brow furrowed with worry. "There is venom in this wound, or some other darkness... a chill that fights the body's natural warmth. It deepens." Enoch nodded grimly, feeling the cold seeping further into his bones, an acute weakness battling against the fire of his spirit. He looked back in the direction they had come, though the Serpent City was invisible now, its oppressive presence still felt like physical pressure against his soul. Wounded, adrift in an unknown land, yet the longing for the truth concealed in Adam's cave burned brighter than ever within him. The glimmering deception was behind them; the long, hard path of resistance lay ahead.

As they rested there, huddled together against the unknown terrors of the night and the encroaching cold from Enoch's wound, Ronan, who had been staring intently toward the west, suddenly pointed. "Look."

Against the star-dusted blackness of the western horizon, long after the sun had plunged below the world's rim, a faint but steady light glowed softly. It wasn't the moon, which was only a thin, waning sliver elsewhere in the sky, nor was it the flickering uncertainty of a distant fire. It was a soft, constant beacon. Hope? A warning? Another, more subtle deception? In their extreme exhaustion and uncertainty, adrift without a map or known guide, they could not know. But the distant light offered the one thing they desperately needed: a direction.

Enoch met Anak's weary gaze across the small space, then looked toward Naamah and Methuselah. A silent understanding passed between them all. Despite the pain, the overwhelming grief, the unknown dangers ahead, they could not stay here.

Pushing themselves to their feet, leaning heavily on each other for support, they turned their faces toward the inexplicable glow on the far horizon. Drawn by mystery, compelled by the fundamental need to move forward, away from the darkness behind, they began walking into the unexplored darkness, toward the distant, unknown light.

11

Echoes of the Past

The darkness yielded no solace, only a gnawing ache of uncertainty and deep physical exhaustion. Guided by the inexplicable, steady glow on the far western horizon—a delicate beacon in the oppressive night—they pressed onward. Each step was an effort, draining their already depleted strength. The land beyond Serpent Mountain remained brutally scarred, a broken, tormented aftermath of forgotten cataclysms or, more likely, the deliberate, poisoned wreckage left by pitiless wars. Jagged ravines, invisible until they nearly stumbled into them, forced long, wearying detours. Fields of jagged rock made footing treacherous even for the sure-footed giants. Thorny, gnarled thickets clawed at their clothes and skin like grasping hands. Progress was agonizing.

Enoch leaned heavily on his staff, fighting waves of dizziness as the cold venom from the black blade continued its work in his wounded arm. Kael had bound it tightly again, applying what meager poultices he could scrape together from the scarce, often blighted flora, but the unnatural chill persisted, a constant drain on Enoch's vital strength.

Just keep moving, he told himself repeatedly, his gaze fixed on the distant, unwavering light. *It led us from the shadow... it must lead somewhere of consequence.*

Enoch watched Naamah and Methuselah walk just ahead of him. They moved now with a new synchronicity, a quiet awareness of each other's presence. When Methuselah stumbled on a loose rock, her hand was there to steady him before he could fall; when a thorny branch snagged her cloak, his axe cleared the path without a word passing between them. *The shared horror of the escape,* Enoch realized, *the crucible of the cliff face, has formed a bond between them deeper than words.* Her grief was still a palpable presence, a shadow in her eyes, yet she moved with the unwavering determination of one who had nothing left to lose but the truth itself, her eyes fixed on the distant light as if it were a personal promise. Anak and his sons pushed ahead whenever the terrain allowed, scouting the broken landscape, their forms radiating a weary but unbroken protectiveness, constantly scanning for threats.

* * *

One evening, as the others rested, Methuselah saw Naamah sitting apart, her back to the small fire. She held the two halves of a broken arrow shaft in her hands, running a thumb over the intricate thread bindings of the fletching. She had gathered a pile of gnarled, dead branches, but as she tested each piece, it would snap, brittle and useless. With a sigh of frustration, she cast the last branch aside.

Methuselah moved to sit near her. "No luck?" he asked quietly.

She shook her head, not looking up. "The wood here is poisoned, like the rest of this land. It has no heart, no straightness. An arrow made from this would shatter on the string or fly wild. My bow is useless without arrows." Her voice was flat, heavy with the weight of her own perceived failure.

He watched her fingers trace the pattern on the broken shaft. The fletching was bound with threads of white and a deep, vibrant blue. "I have never seen such work," he said, trying to draw her out of her despair. "The bindings are a craft of their own."

A sad smile touched her lips. "It is my family's mark," she explained, her voice a whisper. "Each family in our tribe has its own, so we know whose arrow found its mark in the hunt... or in a fight. This blue thread... it was my father's color. The white was my mother's prayer for peace." She looked at the broken shaft, her eyes glistening. "Malachi and I... We shared the same mark. He was a better fletcher than I. His were always straighter, stronger." She finally looked at Methuselah, her gaze holding the full, raw depth of her loss. "I have none left. I cannot even make more. I am defenseless."

A fierce disagreement rose in him, a need to refute the lie her grief was telling her. She felt defenseless, but he had seen her stand on a cliff edge against the darkness, a warrior in her own right. "You are not defenseless, Naamah," he said, his voice low and certain. "You saved us all on that ledge. Your eyes and your bow bought the moments we needed to escape. And when you could no longer shoot, you fought with a knife and stones. Your strength is not just in your arrows."

For the first time since the escape, a tiny measure of warmth touched the cold grief in Naamah's heart. She gave a small, almost imperceptible nod, a silent acceptance of his comfort.

Many days later, dawn crept upon them, revealing the source of the light they had followed. The glow pulsed one last time, emanating from deep within sprawling ruins that littered the landscape before them. These were the remains of an ancient city, entirely different in style and spirit from the dark, arrogant towers of the Serpent's stronghold. The sun rose above the scarred eastern horizon, bathing the scene in golden light, leaving them staring, breathless, at the silent yet broken majesty of this once-great city.

These ruins spoke not of cold, calculated power but of immeasurable age, of a grandeur worn down by centuries of sorrow and struggle. Huge cyclopean blocks of weathered granite formed crumbling walls and plazas wider than any space within the glade. Graceful arches, a testament to a forgotten mastery of stonework, lay broken before them. The stumps of what must have been soaring towers, rivaling those of the Serpent City in height but not in menace, stood guard.

Unlike the unnatural, sterile perfection of the Nephilim city, the stones here bore the honorable marks of wind and time, the scars of seasons, but also something far more violent—deep scorch marks blackened mighty blocks, walls were breached as if by terrible siege engines or unnatural forces, suggesting not slow decay but brutal warfare. Yet, amidst the destruction, life stubbornly persisted. Hardy green vines clung to the stones, and resilient wildflowers in hues of defiant purple and yellow pushed up between cracked flagstones, whispers of enduring life against overwhelming odds. There was deep melancholy here, but not the active, suffocating malevolence they had fled. This felt like a place of tragedy, not intrinsic evil.

Readying their weapons, they entered the quiet city. No figures emerged to greet or challenge them; no voices called out in welcome or warning. The only sounds were the sighs of the wind through empty doorways and the crunch of their footsteps on debris-strewn avenues. They searched for any sign of recent life, for potable water, for defensible shelter, for answers to the questions pounding in their hearts. The scale was breathtaking, hinting at a once-thriving civilization that must have numbered in the thousands, but the silence now was absolute, chilling.

Who lived here? Enoch wondered again, touching a weathered carving on a fallen pillar depicting families gathered under bright stars. *And what monstrous force extinguished them so completely, leaving only stones and silence?*

Near the city's heart, beside the dark, still waters of a large lake, stood the remnants of what looked unmistakably like a great library or repository of records. Although its roof had long since crumbled due to attack or age, one part, constructed against a sheer rock surface, remained wonderfully whole, its entry blocked by huge, intricately fitted stone doors, nearly concealed behind collapsed stonework and tangled vines. Anak, examining the stonework with the expert eye of his people, recognized complex locking mechanisms. Working together, hearts pounding with anticipation, the giants exerted their great strength, groaning with effort, breaching the doors just enough to squeeze through, revealing a dark chamber within.

Torches were lit, the flames pushing back centuries of darkness. They stood in a repository of knowledge that was beyond imagination. From floor to ceiling, stone-hewn shelves lined the walls, holding rows of brittle, decaying scrolls crafted from processed bark or animal hides alongside stacks of heavy, inscribed clay and stone tablets. The air was thick, almost unbreathable, with the scent of extreme age, dry decay, and forgotten secrets. This was no mere collection; it was a deliberate archive, painstakingly assembled and miraculously preserved through ages of ruin.

With trembling hands, Enoch lifted one of the more intact scrolls, Methuselah holding a torch close. The flickering light danced across the angular, faded letters. It was the language of his people, yet in a form so old and poetic that he had to sound out the words slowly, piecing together their meaning. He read aloud, his voice hushed with awe that slowly turned to dawning horror as the story unfolded.

The scrolls named this city Shem, founded by the direct descendants of Enosh, son of Seth, after the Fall. According to the records, it was founded in a time when men first called upon the name of the Lord. They intended it to be a center of true faith and preserved knowledge, a bulwark against the growing darkness spreading from other lands.

But the darkness, inevitably, had encroached. Other scrolls, cracked tablets, detailed a long, brutal history—centuries of relentless warfare against the expanding power of the Nephilim based at Serpent Mountain and their growing armies of corrupted human and giant allies. They read harrowing accounts of other Sethite cities, sister settlements to Shem, falling one by one under the shadow's assault, their inhabitants scattered, enslaved, or annihilated, their histories deliberately erased. Shem had become the last bastion of Seth's line in these lands, fighting desperately, generation after generation, to preserve the true lineage and the Creator's ways against overwhelming odds.

The records chronicled the Nephilim's malicious, patient tactics, confirming Enoch's darkest fears gleaned from the river city. It wasn't just open warfare; they employed brutal, scorched-earth strategies, deliberately poisoning the surrounding lands beyond the valley they now stood in—burning vast forests, destroying wells with dark magic, rendering enormous tracts barren and lifeless with curses that lingered for centuries... the very desolation the group had just struggled through.

It was all purposeful, Enoch realized, sickness coiling like a cold serpent in his stomach. *Not just conquest but erasure. To isolate, to starve, to drive any survivors into dependence or despair. To erase the very memory of the Creator's bounty and replace it with the Serpent's cold, sterile 'order.'*

The scrolls told of Shem's last days—the city besieged, starving, its defenders dwindling under constant assault and sinister plagues. They recorded the heart-wrenching, debated decision to send a small, chosen remnant—carrying the very seed of their faith—eastward, on a perilous journey over the treacherous, unknown mountains, praying for preservation even as the city prepared for its final, hopeless stand against the inevitable tide. Enoch's breath hitched in his throat, tears blurring the script. *My ancestors... the first founders of the glade... they came from here? This unimaginable loss... this is our hidden history.* The glade's isolation, its fierce preservation of ancient ways and fragmented truths, suddenly clicked into sharp, poignant focus. It was not an accident of geography but the hard-won result of this desperate flight from annihilation.

Amidst these heartbreaking histories, carefully wrapped in preserved hides and sealed within stone cylinders, they found them—the detailed star charts Enoch recognized instantly from his guiding vision, maps of constellations as seen by the earliest patriarchs, clearer and more complete than any held in the glade. And with them, stone tablets described key landmarks along the westward path toward Eden's borderlands—the 'Peak of Weeping,' the 'River of Exile,' the 'Guardian Stones' marking the entrance to the First Rampart range—cryptic clues but ones that resonated with Enoch's divinely given knowledge of the 'Cave of Sorrows,' Adam's repository. Here, preserved through loss and sacrifice by his own distant kin, was the key to fulfilling his sacred quest.

They spent hours in the silent, dust-filled chamber, Enoch and Anak selecting and packing the most vital scrolls and tablets, their hearts heavy with the weight of the history they had uncovered.

Naamah wept silently for this vanished family of faith, their fate mirroring the destruction of her own people.

Methuselah was humbled into silence, the dazzling, arrogant grandeur of the Serpent City seeming hollow, brittle, and pathetic compared to the enduring, sacrificial faith recorded in these dusty, crumbling relics.

Emerging back into the harsh light of late afternoon, blinking in the relative brightness, the need for water and rest pressed upon them before they could decide their next move based on the new charts. The lake beside the ruins looked calm, peaceful, its dark surface reflecting the cloudless sky like a mirror. While Enoch and Anak conferred over the precious charts, Kael, Ronan, and Methuselah took the waterskins down to the shore to refill them. Naamah accompanied them, and Enoch watched her go, hoping the quiet tranquility of the water would be a balm for her spirit after the emotional turmoil of the repository.

* * *

Ronan was jesting with Kael about the sheer weight of the scrolls compared to their weapons when the water fifty yards out began to churn violently, breaking the lake's placid surface. The water heaved upward, and then, with terrifying, explosive speed, an enormous creature surged from the depths. Its long, thick, serpentine neck, easily as thick as a tree trunk, supported a massive, heavily armored, crocodilian head bristling with teeth like shards of black obsidian. Its gigantic, barrel-shaped body, propelled by four powerful, clawed and webbed limbs, was covered in glistening, dark green scales that seemed to absorb the light like polished jade. Cold, lidless eyes, devoid of reason or mercy, fixed upon them with absolute predatory intensity.

"BEAST!" Kael roared, instinctively shoving Methuselah and Naamah back toward the ruins as he and Ronan charged forward, Kael's axe and Ronan's heavy hammer flashing in the sun.

The creature hit the shore like a living battering ram, water cascading from its immense form, the ground shuddering under its impact. It moved with deceptive, terrifying speed on land, its powerful, ridge-backed tail whipping lethally back and forth. Kael's axe glanced off the thick, armored scales of its neck with a jarring clang. Ronan's hammer blow landed heavily on one of its powerful forelimbs, eliciting an enraged, deafening hiss but failing to stop its forward momentum.

A surge of adrenaline and terror propelled Methuselah forward, and he scrambled to join the fray. His axe felt impossibly light as he swung, finding a momentary purchase under the creature's massive jaw. Scales chipped like shale, but the blow did little more than enrage the beast further. He risked a desperate glance towards Naamah and saw her hand fly to the quiver on her back, only to find it empty. He saw the flicker of shock on her face, the warrior's raw frustration of being disarmed in the heat of battle, replaced instantly by a look of sheer, terrible helplessness. Her bow was useless, her small knife a mere pinprick against such a monster. As she was forced to scramble back toward the relative safety of the repository entrance, her eyes wide with fear, Methuselah felt a fresh wave of despair. They were all outmatched. The battle was horrifyingly short, brutal, and tragically one-sided. The creature's hide was too thick, seemingly impenetrable. Its strength was overwhelming, its rage absolute. With a sickening crunch that echoed across the water, its massive jaws clamped down on Ronan's shield arm—shattering bone and tossing the giant aside like a broken doll, his cry of agony cut short as he hit the ground. As Kael turned, roaring his brother's name, momentarily distracted, the creature's whip-like tail lashed out with incredible speed, catching the mighty giant across the back and sending him sprawling onto the stones, stunned and breathless.

Before Methuselah could react, before he could even register Kael falling, the long, serpentine neck darted forward with blinding speed. He felt excruciating, white-hot pain as huge jaws closed around his leg below the knee, teeth sinking deep into flesh and muscle. He was lifted effortlessly off the ground like a child's toy. He cried out, scrabbling uselessly, flailing helplessly as he was dragged toward the dark, waiting water.

* * *

From the repository entrance, a roar of pure, desperate fury erupted from Anak beside him, but it was too late. Enoch's own cry was a choked, soundless gasp. His gaze snapped to the shore, a tableau of horror unfolding with impossible speed: Kael struggling weakly to rise, his movements sluggish; Ronan lying still and broken near the water's edge. But his eyes were drawn, helplessly, magnetically, to the beast's true prize. He saw Methuselah, his son, eyes wide with terror and agony, being dragged without effort into the lake. The dark water erupted in a furious froth around him for one terrible, eternal moment. Then, abruptly, it grew chillingly still, the surface broken only by slowly spreading, concentric ripples that lapped silently, indifferently, against the shore. The ripples vanished. There was nothing. *Methuselah was gone.* The thought was a silent, soul-shattering scream. A terrifying silence fell, a void that seemed to hang heavy over the ruins of the city that first remembered the Name.

12

Beneath the Still Water

The surface of the lake settled with horrifying speed. The violent froth dissipated into a mocking stillness, indifferent to the tragedy it represented. Silence descended, vast and absolute, amplifying the sudden, terrible emptiness left in the creature's wake.

It was Enoch's cry that broke it, a raw, ragged sound torn from the depths of his soul, echoing the anguish of countless fathers since the Fall. "Methuselah! My son! MY SON!"

He stumbled toward the water's edge, heedless of his own throbbing wound, his eyes scanning the dark surface for any sign, any movement, any impossible hope.

There was nothing.

Anak reached him, his hand gripping Enoch's shoulder with firm empathy, though the giant's own face was a mask of grim sorrow and barely contained fury. "He is gone, Enoch," Anak stated, his voice rough but heavy with the certainty of loss. "The beast has taken him beneath. There is nothing..." His voice trailed off, unable to offer false comfort.

Naamah stood frozen a few feet away, her hand pressed hard against her mouth, her eyes wide with a shared, vicarious horror. The fresh grief for her father and brothers merged with the shock of witnessing Methuselah's violent end. *So quickly,* she thought, numbly, the world tilting slightly. *Life is so fragile, so easily extinguished.*

The immediate crisis of the living pulled them back from the brink of despair. Ronan groaned from his position close to the water, making a terrible, wet sound while trying unsuccessfully to move. His face was ashen, slick with the sweat of agony. Kael coughed, pushing himself up on his elbows from where the beast's tail had slammed him down, his movements sluggish, his eyes still unfocused from the stunning blow. "Ronan...? Methuselah...?" Kael mumbled, shaking his head as if trying to clear the fog of impact.

"Ronan lives," Anak reported, already kneeling beside his grievously injured son, his voice tight with concern. "Kael, you took a heavy blow to the back. Be still for a moment." He turned his gaze toward the still, dark lake, his eyes burning with cold hatred for the creature lurking somewhere beneath its surface. *Our priority now must be the living.*

"We must get them to shelter. Now."

* * *

Darkness. Total, disorienting darkness. And cold—a bone-deep chill that seeped through Methuselah instantly. Crushing pressure squeezed the air from his lungs, replaced by the horrifying rush of icy water flooding his mouth and his nose. The agony in his leg, where the beast's teeth remained clamped like iron bands, was a blinding counterpoint to the desperate, fading struggle for air. He felt himself being dragged deeper, ever deeper, into the black, frigid depths, the memory of sunlight on the surface shrinking quickly to a distant, unattainable star.

Creator! His soul cried out in silent terror, frantically, though no sound could possibly escape his water-filled lungs. *Have mercy!*

Then, the pressure became absolute, the lack of air complete. Consciousness dissolved into suffocating black oblivion.

* * *

Moving Kael and Ronan back to the relative safety of the repository was a slow, agonizing, blood-soaked process.

Kael, though severely bruised and moving with painful stiffness, could eventually support some of his own weight, leaning heavily on Anak's strength. But Ronan... Ronan was a ruin of flesh and bone. His entire left arm, from shoulder to fingertips, was a mangled, pulverized horror, hanging sickly by mere shreds of torn flesh and sinew. Jagged shards of crushed bone, white and glistening, protruded gruesomely from the mauled muscle in multiple places. The damage extended deep into his shoulder and upper torso, the creature's bite having crushed part of his chest as well, leaving a gaping, bloody wound that wheezed with every shallow breath he took. He was delirious with unimaginable pain, barely conscious, and needed to be carried with agonizing care, like a broken child, in Anak's powerful, trembling arms.

Enoch followed numbly, the physical throb of his own arm feeling dull and distant compared to the gaping wound ripped open in his heart by Methuselah's loss and the horrific sight of Ronan's injuries.

Naamah hurried ahead, her practical survival instincts taking over where conscious thought failed, gathering the softest mosses from damp stones and tearing strips from spare cloaks to make crude padding and bandages, her face pale and set.

Inside the dusty, torch-lit chamber that held the weight of Shem's lost history, the grim reality of their situation settled upon them like a suffocating shroud. Kael, after catching his breath and forcing down his own pain, immediately began to assess Ronan's catastrophic injuries. His face grew grimmer with each passing moment. "Father... his arm... it is beyond setting," Kael reported, his voice strained, choked with grief and stoic despair. "The bones are not merely broken, they are... pulverized. Like stone ground to dust. The flesh... it is shredded beyond repair, clear into the shoulder, the chest. I can see the cavity of his ribs through the wound." He looked up at Anak, his eyes filled with anguish. "Without the most potent healing—something far beyond my skill, beyond any herb we possess, and a miracle of the Creator Himself... I do not see how he can survive this. The water of this lake may be pure, but the beast's maw was not. Its venom, its filth... infection will be swift and deadly."

As Kael spoke, Ronan let out a low, gurgling moan, his body attempting to arch against the agony. Naamah rushed to his side, trying to gently clean the edges of the horrific wounds with water from a skin, but even her light touch elicited a fresh wave of pain that made Ronan's eyes roll back. His breathing, already shallow, hitched, then stopped. His head lolled.

"He's gone!" Naamah cried, her voice sharp with fresh terror.

Kael, his own face ashen, moved her aside and placed a massive hand on his brother's chest, pushing down hard, rhythmically, his expression a mask of desperate concentration. "Breathe, Ronan! Breathe!" He grunted with each compression. Anak watched, his great fists clenched. After what felt like too many minutes, Ronan gave a ragged, shuddering gasp, then another. He was alive, but barely.

"The bleeding..." Kael gasped, looking at the dark blood still welling from several points in his brother's mangled shoulder and chest. "The main vessels are torn. We must seal them, or he bleeds out before the infection even takes hold." He grabbed a clean knife from his belt and thrust its tip into the heart of the small fire they had managed to kindle, the metal quickly heating. While the blade heated, Anak ran to search the ruined city for a safer water source.

While Ronan remained unconscious, mercifully oblivious to the next brutal necessity, Kael worked with grim precision, Naamah assisting, her face pale but resolute. Using the glowing knife, they quickly cauterized the most significant arterial bleeders in the gaping wounds of Ronan's shoulder and chest. Anak returned moments later, his face grim, carrying a waterskin filled with surprisingly clear water from a long-forgotten cistern he'd discovered deep within the ruins. He also bore several large fragments of antique woven textiles; their patterns faded, but the fibers still held some strength. Naamah seized them gratefully. After a quick, desperate washing in the cistern water, she tore the cloth and a large piece of her own undertunic—the cleanest, softest material they possessed—into strips. With Kael still fighting to stabilize Ronan after the cauterization, Naamah worked with fierce concentration, using the cleanest fabric and gathered moss to pack the most gruesome parts of the wounds and then bind them with the textile tightly, trying to stop any remaining bleeding and offer some small measure of protection against the filth of their surroundings. Kael, meanwhile, moved with painful stiffness, deep, blooming bruises already darkening across his back and ribs from the force of the beast's tail, each breath a careful, shallow effort as he assisted his father in supporting Ronan.

Only when Ronan's breathing had steadied did Enoch become aware of a gentle pressure on his wounded arm. He looked down and saw Naamah, her face a mask of concentration, carefully cleaning the torn flesh. He watched her work as if from a great distance, distantly aware of the dark, unhealthy bruising that now spread from the cut, and the unnatural cold that emanated from deep within the limb, a chill her touch could not warm. He barely registered her careful binding, his gaze already distant, lost again in the gaping void left by his son. He fumbled blindly for the scrolls they had rescued, unrolling one numbly, staring down at the intricate script as if hoping to find an answer, a solace, a reason for this fresh horror that wasn't there.

Why? his heart cried out silently, a prayer of raw, breaking anguish. *Why lead us here, show us this hope, unveil this sacred history, only to tear my son away in such violence and leave another to such suffering?*

Faith felt like a flickering candle flame against the overwhelming, suffocating darkness of his loss.

* * *

Methuselah gasped, a violent, shuddering inhalation that miraculously brought not water but thick, damp, breathable air into his starved lungs. He coughed uncontrollably, retching foul lake water, his body convulsing on a cold, slick, uneven surface beneath him. Pain flared in his leg as he moved, sharp and sickening. Disoriented, vision swimming, he blinked, trying to make sense of his surroundings through the haze of pain and near-drowning. He was in darkness, but not the absolute crushing blackness of the deep lake. Faint, ghostly phosphorescent light emanated from strange, pale fungi clinging to the damp rock walls all around.him, casting an eerie, unsettling greenish glow over the scene.

He pushed himself up onto his elbows, crying out again as his injured leg protested violently. He was in a cave—a large, dripping, high-ceilinged cavern extending back into darkness. And as his eyes adjusted to the spectral green light, a wave of pure horror crawled up his spine, colder than the lake water.

The floor... the floor was littered, inches deep in many places, with bones. Countless bones glistening in the fungal light. Bones of fish, massive prehistoric-looking animals, giants... and humans. Empty skulls stared blankly from shadowed niches. This was the beast's larder. It had dragged him here, likely assuming him dead or incapacitated by the crushing depths and vicious bite, leaving him amongst its previous victims, a meal to be consumed later. A wave of violent nausea washed over him, followed by a surge of raw adrenaline. He was alive. Against all odds, he was alive. But he was trapped, wounded, in the belly of the beast's subterranean den.

* * *

Hours crawled by on the surface. Night fell again outside the repository. Anak stood sentinel at the entrance like a granite statue, watching the dark, silent lake, his heavy hammer in his grip.

Kael, after doing all he could do for Ronan with their limited supplies, finally succumbed to his own bone-deep exhaustion, drifting into a pained, uneasy sleep propped against the wall.

Ronan moaned in his feverish delirium, despite the cavern's cool air.

As Naamah rechecked his binding, her voice cut through his grief. "Enoch..."

He did not react, lost in the hollow ache of his loss.

"Enoch," the voice came again, a little firmer, compelling his attention. He slowly lifted his head and saw Naamah kneeling before him. Her face was young but etched with her own recent, terrible losses, yet her eyes held a quiet, fierce strength that resonated with his shattered faith.

"My mother taught us," she said, her voice trembling slightly but holding steady, "even in the darkest night, when all hope seems lost, the Creator watches. Malachi believed... he gave his life believing you carried a light worth dying for." Her voice cracked on her brother's name, but she pressed on, her gaze unwavering. "Do not let the darkness quench that light now. For Malachi's sake. For... for Methuselah's memory."

The names, spoken aloud in the quiet chamber, struck him with the force of a physical blow. *Malachi. Methuselah.* The weight of their sacrifices, the purpose for which they had fallen, suddenly became a sharp, clarifying pain. *The light they died for.* Her words were not a gentle comfort; they were a righteous call to duty. Despair, he realized, was a luxury he could not afford, an indulgence that dishonored the dead. He drew a long, ragged breath and felt the fire of his own resolve, so recently reduced to cold ashes, begin to faintly, painfully, rekindle. "You speak wisdom learned through hardship, Naamah," he whispered hoarsely, his voice rough with unshed tears. "Thank you."

* * *

Panic threatened to overwhelm Methuselah again as he stood amongst the bones, the silence broken only by dripping water and his own ragged breathing. He fought it down, forcing his battered mind to work.

Think. Survive.

The cave floor sloped downward toward the back, where dark water pooled—clearly the beast's entrance from the lake. Attempting to swim out that way with his mangled leg seemed like certain death. He needed another way. Dragging his injured limb, ignoring the waves of nausea and pain, he began to explore the edges of the eerie cavern, searching by the fungal glow. The air felt heavy, damp, thick with the stench of decay, but breathable—there had to be an air source, another connection to the outside world somewhere. The phosphorescent fungi cast just enough light to illuminate the rough rock walls, water weeping down their surfaces; the high ceiling was lost in impenetrable darkness above. Bones crunched sickeningly under his good foot. He found complete skeletal remains wedged in crevices, some still clad in scraps of armor, a rusted sword hilt clutched in bony fingers—victims from ages past, dragged here to this same end. He picked up a sharp shard of bone, testing its edge against his palm. A poor weapon against the behemoth that brought him here, but better than bare hands.

Then, near the back of the cavern, partly hidden behind a jumble of larger, moss-covered bones, he saw it—a narrow, dark fissure snaking upward in the rock face, barely wide enough for him to squeeze his shoulders through.

Is it just a dead-end crack? Or does it lead... somewhere? Anywhere?

Hope, sharp and almost painful, pierced through his fear. It was a chance. Perhaps his only chance. He *had* to try.

Using rough ledges and small outcrops as precarious handholds, ignoring the searing agony in his leg with every upward pull, Methuselah began to climb. He pulled himself laboriously, inch by excruciating inch, upward into the tight, claustrophobic darkness of the fissure, away from the stagnant water and the ghastly graveyard of bones below, praying with every fiber of his being that this narrow crack led not to further entrapment but, somehow, impossibly, back toward the world of the living, toward the air, toward the light.

The climb was tormenting, each movement sending fresh jolts of pain through his body, the darkness absolute beyond the greenish glow fading rapidly from the cavern far below. He didn't know if he was climbing toward air and freedom or simply deeper into the mountain's cold, uncaring heart, but it was the only chance the Creator seemed to have offered.

13

Fissures of Hope

Darkness pressed in on Methuselah, absolute and suffocating, tasting of damp stone and decay. The fissure was barely wider than his shoulders, the rock cold and unnervingly slick against his skin, offering treacherous purchase. Every upward movement, every desperate pull with his arms and push with his one good leg sent waves of nauseating agony through his mangled lower leg, threatening his unstable grip. He climbed by touch alone, scraped fingers searching anxiously for cracks and ledges in the unseen rock face, his good leg trembling with strain against the unyielding stone, the injured one dragging almost uselessly behind, catching occasionally with bolts of fresh pain. His breath came in ragged, tearing gasps, echoing in the confined space.

Time lost all meaning. Hours melted together in a timeless agony of determined effort, burning muscles, and blinding pain. Doubt, cold and persistent as the water weeping down the rock, whispered in the darkness. *It's hopeless. The fissure will surely narrow. You'll become wedged, trapped. You'll die here in the suffocating dark, another set of forgotten bones deep in the mountain's heart.*

He squeezed his eyes shut against the despair, fighting back tears of pain and exhaustion, clinging fiercely to the fading image of his father's face alight with faith, the memory of Naamah's shocked, wide eyes meeting his after he dispatched the dark attacker.

No! The word was a silent scream in his soul. *I will not end here. I will not.*

* * *

On the surface, under the cold indifference of the stars, the long night dragged on within the dusty repository. Enoch watched as Kael, moving with a stiffness that betrayed his own considerable injuries, worked tirelessly over Ronan. He saw Kael clean the brutally crushed arm again as best he could, reapplying poultices that seemed pitifully inadequate against such a grievous wound. But Ronan's breathing only grew shallower throughout the night, his skin radiating a dangerous heat despite the cavern's coolness. The young Giant tossed restlessly on the makeshift bed of ferns, lost in fevers' tightening grasp.

But it was the sight of Anak that struck Enoch most deeply. The great king sat hunched near his youngest son, his earlier fury toward the lake beast completely extinguished. In its place, Enoch saw something far more terrible: the raw, helpless anguish of a father. The stoic lines of Anak's face were etched with worry; his eyes, which had burned with rage, were now filled with a desperate, paternal fear as he watched his son struggle, a powerful being rendered utterly vulnerable by love and the stark awareness of his own limitations against this creeping death.

Enoch sat near the flickering torchlight, the scrolls spread before him on a flat stone, though his eyes often strayed toward the repository entrance, toward the dark, silent lake beyond that had swallowed his son. He forced himself to focus, tracing the star charts with a trembling finger, comparing the cryptic landmark descriptions—'Peak of Weeping,' 'River of Exile'—to the fragmented memories of his guiding vision. The mission, the preservation of Adam's testimony, seemed impossibly heavy now, shadowed irrevocably by the loss of Methuselah, tainted by the persistent, venomous cold still seeping from his own wound. Yet Naamah's quiet words resonated deep within him. He couldn't surrender to despair. He owed it to Methuselah's memory, to Malachi's sacrifice, to the countless generations of his kin who had fought and died preserving fragments of this truth to see the quest through. He prayed silently, not for ease or comfort but simply for strength, for clarity, for the will to take the next necessary step.

Enoch watched Naamah keep her vigil near the entrance, a lone figure wrapped tightly in a cloak against the pre-dawn chill that had settled deep into the stones. He knew she had not slept; how could she? Her gaze was fixed on the lake, its surface like polished obsidian under the sliver of a waning moon. He could only imagine the horrors that replayed behind her wide, unblinking eyes: her brother Malachi turning back into the city's darkness; his own son's final, desperate struggle before disappearing beneath the water. She stared out at the lake as if searching for what he, too, longed for—some impossible sign, some ripple against the current, some desperate hope to cling to. But the only answer was the lake's crushing silence, a final, terrible verdict.

* * *

Methuselah's fingers slipped suddenly on an unexpected patch of greasy slime. He gasped, scrabbling wildly in the darkness, his injured leg scraping unbearably against the sharp rock edge. He found a hold—a tiny nubbin of rock, his body trembling violently with exhaustion and panic. He hung there for long moments, pressing his forehead against the cold, damp stone, willing his racing heart to slow, fighting the black spots dancing before his eyes.

I'm losing strength. How long have I been climbing? Hours? A lifetime? Am I any closer to the surface or just deeper within the earth's suffocating embrace?

He felt a single hot tear escape, tracing a path through the grime on his cheek.

Father... Creator... help me... please...

Then, through the roaring in his ears, through the haze of pain and fatigue, he felt it. Faint, almost imperceptible at first, easily dismissed as a trick of his grieving mind but undeniably there—a cool whisper of moving air against his face. He tilted his head back, straining his senses, scarcely daring to breathe.

Yes!

A draft, light but distinct, cool and carrying the clean scent of damp earth.

Could it be... fresh air? Hope surged through him, sharp and potent, pushing back the suffocating despair like dawn breaking. He looked up into the impenetrable darkness above. He couldn't see anything, not even a glimmer, but the slight current of air against his cheek was real, a tangible promise.

Renewed determination, born of desperation and that flicker of possibility, flooded his limbs. He tested the rock above, found a better handhold, and began to climb again, pulling himself painfully upward toward that strength-giving hope.

*   *   *

Dawn painted the eastern sky with pale, hesitant streaks of gray and rose, but the light brought no warmth to Enoch's spirit. His gaze fell upon the scene by the dying fire, a tableau of weary suffering. He watched as Kael gently bathed his brother's face with cool water from their dwindling supply, his expression grim, etched with a healer's helplessness. Ronan's skin, even in the dim light, seemed to radiate a dangerous heat, and he tossed feverishly, muttering incoherent fragments of the giantish tongue, lost in worsening delirium.

Enoch heard Kael's low, strained murmur to Anak, who stood watching over them like a mountain of sorrow. "His spirit fights, Father," Kael said. "But the poison from the beast's bite runs deep in the wound, a darkness beyond my simple skills or herbs."

Enoch saw Anak place a massive hand on Ronan's forehead, the touch surprisingly gentle. The great king's voice was a low rumble of comfort meant only for his son. "Rest, my son," he whispered softly, though Ronan likely didn't hear. "We will find stronger remedies soon." But when Anak's eyes met Kael's, Enoch saw the facade of strength crumble, revealing a deep, shared helplessness that needed no words.

The Giant king's unspoken fear resonated with the dread coiling in Enoch's own gut. They couldn't stay here indefinitely. Ronan needed aid beyond what they could provide in these desolate ruins. But where could they possibly go? The mysterious guiding light on the horizon had vanished with the coming of day, leaving them blind. *Do we risk traveling westward, towards a memory of light?* Enoch thought desperately. *Or do we try to find a more defensible position deeper within this sprawling, unknown city of the dead?*

It was then that Enoch rose stiffly, the cold in his arm making every movement an effort. He had spent the latter part of the night meticulously comparing the star charts to his memory of the heavens above the Glade, trying to orient himself in this unfamiliar hemisphere. He believed he had found a tentative direction, a possible bearing towards the 'First Rampart' mountains described in Shem's record, but the journey would be long, arduous, and fraught with unknown dangers, especially with two grievously wounded travelers. "We must trust the path shown in the scrolls," he said, his voice hoarse but firm, looking towards Anak. "The Creator preserved them for a reason. They give us a way forward, though it will undoubtedly be hard."

Just as Anak was about to reply, Naamah, who kept her weary vigil near the entrance, suddenly went rigid. Her hand shot out, palm flat, a silent, urgent command for stillness that made Enoch's own heart freeze in his chest. Her head was tilted, her expression taut with the intense concentration of a hunter sensing a predator.

"Did you hear that?" she whispered, her voice barely a breath.

Anak and Enoch froze, straining their ears. At first, only the mournful sigh of the morning wind through the empty doorways of the ruins reached them. But then, beneath the wind, they heard it too... faint, muffled, almost lost... a scrape of stone on stone. A dislodged pebble rolling down loose scree. It seemed to come from within the ruins themselves, somewhere not far from their repository, perhaps from within a collapsed structure.

They looked at each other, not puzzled, but instantly, grimly alert. *Another creature, a scavenger, drawn by the scent of Ronan's blood? Or something else that lairs in these ruins?*

Naamah melted back from the entrance, gesturing for them to take cover behind the massive stone doorframe. Enoch followed, his heart pounding now not with impossible hope, but with cold, weary dread. The sound came again, slightly louder this time—a distinct *scraping*, followed by what might have been a muffled, pained groan of effort. It wasn't the heavy, earth-shaking sound of the lake beast moving on land. It sounded smaller. It sounded like something wounded, struggling. *Cornered animals are the most dangerous,* Enoch knew. It came from the direction of a partially collapsed section of wall near the repository, where the ground was disturbed near a shadowed fissure in the rock face.

Naamah met Enoch's gaze, her own eyes wide, but with guarded apprehension, not hope. Her hand rested on the hilt of her knife. The question in her eyes was a silent one: *What new danger have we found now?*

14

From the Depths

A cold dread, sharp and immediate, cut through Enoch's grief. He exchanged a grim, silent look with Naamah, who was already moving with a hunter's lethal quiet towards the source of the sound: the collapsed section of wall near the repository entrance. Anak's command to his son was a low rumble, barely disturbing the tense air. "Kael, guard Ronan. Do not leave his side." The massive giant then followed Enoch and Naamah, moving with surprising stealth across the debris-strewn earth. The tension in the cool morning air was thick enough to taste, a shared, weary vigilance against whatever new horror now crept towards their camp.

The sounds came again, clearer now as they drew closer – a rhythmic scraping of stone on stone, punctuated by a low grunt of exertion, undeniably human-like, but in this desolate place, that was no comfort. Naamah pinpointed the source: a narrow, dark fissure snaking up the cliff face behind the collapsed wall, its opening partially obscured by fallen blocks of weathered granite. A trickle of fresh dust spilled from the opening. Something was digging or climbing its way out from below.

Enoch gripped his staff, bracing for another fight. But the sound, a pained cry of strain, held no malice, only struggle. A wild, illogical thought, a spark so improbable it was almost madness, ignited in his heart. He knew what he had seen—his son dragged into the dark, still water, lost to the depths. He knew this sound came from the stone of the earth. The two could not connect.

Yet... *the beast's lair was an underwater cave,* the thought raced, desperate and sharp. *It dragged him under the water... into the mountain's root. This sound comes from the mountain's root.* His grief warred fiercely with a sudden, wild prayer taking shape in his soul: *Creator, after all this, could Your mercy extend even here? Could You bring life not just from an empty sky, but from the very belly of the beast's den?*

The possibility, however remote, was too powerful to suppress. It clawed its way through his sorrow. He looked at Naamah and saw only her guarded, fearful focus on the new threat. But when he spoke, the name was a choked, half-strangled prayer, a question posed to God Himself.

"Methuselah?"

He breathed the name, hardly daring to speak it aloud lest it shatter the blossoming, impossible hope. Naamah turned to him, her eyes wide with confusion, then saw the blazing, irrational certainty on his face. Seeing this man of faith, who had just lost his son, suddenly ignite with this wild hope was a powerful catalyst. Her own desperate heart dared to follow his. He saw her own expression shift from grim readiness to a fierce, terrible hope. He scrambled over loose rocks towards the opening, Naamah right beside him.

"Stand back," Anak rumbled, his voice low, gently moving them aside, his own face a mask of confusion and deep skepticism. He examined the rubble blocking the fissure's upper reaches, testing the stability of the fallen stones. With great, controlled strength that contrasted sharply with the hope pounding in Enoch's chest, Anak began shifting the heavy granite blocks, mindful not to cause a further collapse into the narrow shaft below. More dust billowed out, carrying the earthy scent of the deep rock, along with the distinct sound of someone coughing weakly within the darkness.

Finally, with a great heave, Anak pulled away a last, large, wedged block. A hand, coated in mud and grime, scrabbled through the opening, seeking purchase. Then another appeared beside it. Enoch fell to his knees at the edge, his impossible prayer answered, reaching down. "Methuselah! Son! Grab my hand!"

A familiar face, deathly pale beneath layers of filth and dried blood, appeared in the opening, framed by tangled, muddy hair. Methuselah blinked against the unexpected, blinding daylight, his eyes struggling to focus after hours in darkness. He seemed utterly exhausted, his frame trembling severely with weariness and cold, but, miraculously, astonishingly alive. He saw his father's outstretched hand, and his own weak, muddy fingers grasped Enoch's desperately.

"Father..." he choked out, a universe of relief and exhaustion flooding his features.

"My son! Oh, my son!" Enoch's composure, maintained through grief and despair, fell away completely. Tears streamed down his face as he pulled, Anak adding his strength, lifting Methuselah the final few feet out of the dark fissure and onto the solid, sunlit ground of the ruins.

Enoch gathered his returned son into a fierce, crushing embrace, heedless of the grime, the smell of the cave, or Methuselah's obviously injured leg. He felt Naamah rush forward to kneel beside them, her whole body shaking with relieved sobs. He saw her reach out, her trembling hand touching Methuselah's mud-caked arm as if to confirm for herself that he was truly, impossibly, back among them. "Methuselah," she whispered, her voice thick with tears and wonder, "we thought... the lake... we thought you were lost forever."

Enoch held his son, watching him turn his gaze from his own tear-streaked face to Naamah's. A dazed, weak smile touched Methuselah's cracked lips, a valiant effort against the agony that was still plain on his face. "Not... not yet," he managed, his voice barely a rasp.

The hard, stoic lines of Anak's face softened, and the deep sorrow in his eyes was momentarily replaced by a powerful, soul-deep relief.

He placed a heavy, comforting hand on Methuselah's shoulder. "The Creator is merciful," he rumbled, his voice thick with emotion. He then turned automatically to scan their surroundings, his relief tempered by the constant need for vigilance in this dangerous place.

Anak gently lifted the wounded Methuselah as if he weighed nothing, carrying him the short distance back to the repository shelter, while Enoch hurried alongside. Kael looked up from Ronan's side as they entered, his jaw dropping in stunned astonishment, then breaking into a rare, wide, relieved grin that lit up his rugged face.

They settled Methuselah gently onto a bed of gathered moss beside Ronan. Kael immediately began examining the injured leg. The sight was grim. The beast's teeth had torn deep, ragged gashes into the flesh below the knee, exposing muscle and sinew. Dark, severe bruising was already spreading rapidly. Kael let out a low grunt, his brow furrowed in concentration as he gently probed the wound.

"The bone seems to hold," he announced, a small mercy. His expression hardened as he looked closer at the grime caked deep within the torn flesh. "But this is the danger," he said, his deep voice low and serious. "It is packed with the filth of that cavern, the foulness of the creature's bite. If we do not cleanse it, a deadly fever is certain."

He looked at Methuselah, his expression compassionate but resolute. "This will be painful, Son of Enoch. Possibly more painful than the bite itself."

Naamah brought fresh water gathered from the cistern and textile fragments. While Anak firmly held Methuselah's shoulders, Kael, with Naamah assisting, began the excruciating process of scrubbing the deep, ragged wounds. Methuselah clenched his teeth, stifling cries as Kael worked to remove every speck of grime, every fragment of embedded debris from the torn flesh. The pain was blinding, and despite their efforts to be gentle, the wounds, which had begun to clot, tore open anew, fresh, bright blood welling up copiously, soaking the bedding almost immediately. Methuselah's face was slick with sweat, his knuckles white where he gripped the moss.

"The bleeding must be stopped," Kael stated gravely, his gaze meeting Enoch's, the brief moment of joy from Methuselah's return now overshadowed by urgent concern. He gestured again toward the small fire. "There is only one way to be certain against such festering and filth, especially now with this fresh bleeding. Fire." He knew the agony it would inflict, the brutality of the remedy, but infection in such a wound, in this desolate place, would mean certain, agonizing death. "We must close the flesh now, then pray the Creator spares him from the fever that holds Ronan."

There was a heavy silence as the weight of Kael's words settled upon them. Anak moved again to Methuselah's side, his expression grim but filled with deep compassion. "Son of Enoch," the giant spoke softly, "this will be harder still, after the cleaning. But it must be done. Hold fast. Your spirit has proven strong. I will help you." With a steadying strength, Anak positioned himself again to hold Methuselah's shoulders and torso against the ground, preventing involuntary movement. Kael, meanwhile, took his knife again and thrust its tip into the heart of the small fire, waiting, his face set, until the metal glowed a fierce, intimidating orange-red. Methuselah watched, his face pale beneath the streaks of drying mud and fresh blood, his knuckles still white where he gripped the mossy bedding beneath him. He instinctively tried to pull away as Kael approached with the heated blade, the primitive fear of burning overriding reason for a moment, but Anak's steady presence held him firm. He clenched his jaw until it ached, squeezed his eyes shut, bracing for the inevitable pain. Then, desperately seeking an anchor, he forced his eyes open, searching, and found Naamah kneeling nearby, her face mirroring his own apprehension but also filled with shared empathy that flowed toward him like a tangible force. Her eyes didn't look away; they held his gaze steadily, offering silent strength, a single tear tracing a path through the grime on her cheek, not in pity but fierce, shared endurance. He focused entirely on her eyes, drawing strength from that unexpected, unwavering connection.

Kael was swift, his movements precise. There was a sharp, sickening hiss as the glowing metal met torn, wet flesh, the acrid odor of searing tissue filling the air, mingling with the scent of dust and herbs. Methuselah cried out, a sharp, choked sound muffled against his own forearm as his body arched violently against Anak's unyielding hold.

Kael worked quickly, pressing the heated blade against the worst of the ragged edges, sealing torn vessels with brutal efficiency, creating a harsh, blackened barrier against the poisons of the lake and the beast's bite. Each searing application sent fresh jolts of agony through Methuselah, threatening to pull him under into blackness, but his eyes remained locked with Naamah's, finding in her steady, compassionate gaze an anchor against the overwhelming, consuming pain.

When it was finally done, sweat beaded heavily on Methuselah's forehead, his breathing shallow and ragged, hovering on the very edge of consciousness, but the bleeding had stopped, the grievous wounds effectively sealed.

While Kael applied soothing wet moss over the burns and began binding the leg with clean strips of cloth, Methuselah lay trembling uncontrollably, adrift in the gray aftermath of agony but dimly aware that the ordeal was over.

After taking several long, slow sips of cool water offered by Naamah, his voice weak but steadying, he began to recount his ordeal—being dragged down into the cold, crushing darkness, the impossible awakening in the horrifying bone-littered cavern, the dark, hopeless climb through the narrow fissure, drawn ever upward by the promise of fresh air.

Hearing it, seeing him lying there, wounded but undeniably present, they all understood the sheer, breathtaking miracle of his survival, the incredible tenacity of his young spirit, and the undeniable providence of the Creator.

His return dramatically shifted the atmosphere in the hidden chamber. The oppressive weight of grief lifted like a physical burden, replaced by a surge of overwhelming relief and powerfully reaffirmed

faith. Methuselah's survival felt like a direct, tangible answer to despair, a sign that even in the deepest darkness, the Creator had not
abandoned them.

Enoch felt his faith, so recently shaken by loss, rekindle with
new, brighter fervor. They had faced the Serpent's city, plumbed the
depths of loss and despair, and yet, here was life returned, hope resurrected, fragile but undeniably resilient as the wildflowers pushing
stubbornly through the ruins outside, blooming anew in their weary
hearts. Enoch watched as Naamah stayed near Methuselah's side, her
earlier silent grief now channeled into a quiet, focused purpose. Her
hands, which had trembled with sorrow only hours before, were now
steady as she helped Kael organize their meager medical supplies or
offered Methuselah sips of cool water. But the undeniable joy of the
reunion could not entirely banish the harsh realities that still con-
fronted them. Kael's expression grew grave again as he finished splint-
ing Methuselah's leg to immobilize it. "Three seriously wounded now,"
he stated, looking from his father to Enoch. "Ronan's fever still climbs;
the infection fights my remedies, strengthened by the beast's taint in
the wound. Your arm, Enoch, carries an evil chill that does not yield.
And Methuselah..." he gestured to the newly bound leg, "his leg is
deeply wounded, though the bone holds. None of you can travel easily
or swiftly."

Anak nodded grimly, his gaze sweeping over his depleted company.
"We cannot stay here long," he agreed, his voice a low rumble. "This
place offers temporary shelter but no true safety. The lake beast may
return, or patrols from Serpent City might eventually search this far
west, drawn by the crystal light we saw or by Shem's lingering reputa-
tion."

Enoch looked at the scrolls laid out beside him, then at his injured
son resting fitfully now, at Ronan tossing in feverish delirium, at
Kael's weary, determined face, at Anak's worried vigilance, at
Naamah's quiet strength. The path forward, shown in the texts, was
clear in destination but fraught with daunting peril. They desperately

needed time to heal, time they did not have. Yet, looking at Methuselah, miraculously returned from the very depths of death's grasp, Enoch felt his resolve harden into certainty. They would endure. They would heal as best they could, trusting Kael's skill and the Creator's mercy. And then, leaning on each other, trusting in the Creator's providence that had brought them this far, they would follow the path laid out, starting toward the remembered direction of the mysterious light, seeking answers and ultimate safety in the vast, unexplored lands ahead.

The cost had been terribly high, the dangers remained foreboding, but hope, rekindled against all odds, burned steady and warm once more in the heart of the ruins.

15

Altar in the Ruins

Sometime in the deep, still hours before dawn, the heat radiating from Ronan's injured body finally began to recede. Kael, keeping a weary vigil beside his brother, felt the shift first—the burning skin grew damp with cleansing sweat, the shallow, rapid breathing eased, deepening into a more regular, restorative rhythm. With great relief, Kael gently wiped Ronan's brow with a cool, damp cloth. Hope stirred in the giant healer's chest.

As the first true rays of sunlight pierced the gloom of the dusty repository, Ronan stirred, his eyelids fluttering open. He blinked, his gaze hazy at first, then slowly clearing, becoming lucid for the first time in what felt like many days. He looked at Kael, then his gaze found Anak, who had moved closer at the first sign of consciousness.

"Water..." Ronan rasped, his throat dry and cracked. Then, after Kael helped him drink from a waterskin, a sincere smile touched the young giant's lips. "And... food?" he asked, his voice barely a whisper but clear. "I am... empty."

Relief, potent and cleansing, flooded the chamber, washing away some of the tension that had held them captive since the lake beast attack. Hunger, after such a debilitating fever, was the surest sign of life returning, of the body beginning its long mend. Anak clasped his son's uninjured hand, his great shoulders slumping in a wave of pure relief. The stern lines of his face broke into a broad, genuine smile that crinkled the corners of his eyes. Even Enoch felt a measure of lightness pierce the constant throb of his wounded arm and the heavy weight of their journey. After the miracle of Methuselah's return, Ronan's recovery felt like a second, defiant spark of hope against the overwhelming darkness.

While Kael fussed over Ronan, he offered him the last few precious drops of a potent herbal broth. He had brewed it from a cluster of hardy, fragrant herbs discovered growing miraculously in the sheltered corner of a ruined plaza—a small, miraculous inheritance from the city's long-vanished temple gardens. Methuselah rested quietly nearby, his splinted leg elevated. Enoch felt an undeniable pull, a spiritual restlessness. The discovery of his people's history here in Shem, their long faithfulness against encroaching evil, resonated deeply within him. He needed to walk these streets, alone, to seek clearer guidance beyond the cryptic words of the scrolls.

Leaving Anak on watchful guard at the repository entrance, he took his staff and walked slowly out into the morning light.

He wandered through deserted plazas paved with massive, time-worn flagstones and down wide avenues now choked with debris, the sheer scale of the ruins attesting to the city's former glory.

Hardy vines crawled over magnificent columns like green shrouds; wind whispered through empty window arches like forgotten prayers or sorrowful sighs. His heart ached for this lost civilization, his distant kin, who had held fast to the Creator for so long only to be extinguished by the tide of darkness. Yet beneath the sorrow, there was also a lingering sense of holiness clinging to the stones, an aura of defiant faith that stood in stark contrast to the cold, arrogant, sterile power of the Serpent City.

This place was consecrated by generations calling upon the true Name, Enoch realized. *And that sanctity endures even in ruin.*

In the heart of what seemed to have been a temple complex, now open to the sky, its mighty roof long since collapsed or destroyed, he found it. Standing alone amidst crumbling pillars and weathered flag-stones, half-buried in wind-blown soil, was an altar. It wasn't ornate like the blasphemous structures in the Serpent City, not built of glittering gold or polished obsidian. It was crafted from simple, massive blocks of unadorned native granite, worn smooth by the passage of centuries and by the touch of countless faithful hands laid upon it in prayer and offering. Its design—sturdy, central, open to the heavens—was achingly familiar, echoing the form and spirit of the central altar in his own hidden glade, the place where his people offered their first fruits and gave daily thanks to the Creator.

A jolt of recognition shot through him like lightning. He knelt, laying a trembling hand upon the cool stone. The rock seemed to come alive under his touch, a conduit across the gulf of time and the ruins of history, connecting him to his ancestors, his home, and his God. He knew, with sudden, absolute certainty, what the Creator required of them now, in this place.

He returned to the repository, and though his arm still pained him, a new energy quickened his steps. The look on his face—calm, certain, unwavering—silenced any questions before they could be formed. He gathered the small group—Anak, Kael, Naamah, and Methuselah (Ronan, though awake, was still far too weak to move far). "My friends," he said, his voice gentle but carrying an undeniable firmness that commanded their attention, "bring forth everything we have left for sustenance. All of it."

Puzzled but obedient, trusting the conviction they saw in his eyes, they retrieved their dwindling supplies from packs and pouches. The collection laid out on a spread cloak before them was pitifully small: a few handfuls of dried, leathery meat strips, a scattering of nuts and shriveled berries gathered on the journey, the last hard half of a dry flatbread. It was barely enough for one meager meal for one person, let alone their entire hungry group for an unknown duration in this desolate land.

Seeing the provisions gathered together, Methuselah's eyes lit up momentarily with raring hope, a reaction echoed by a weak but hopeful look from Ronan nearby.

"Are we... are we finally going to eat, Father?" Methuselah asked, his voice betraying the gnawing hunger that had plagued them all for weeks. Naamah, too, looked on with quiet anticipation, the prospect of even a small, shared meal a desperately needed comfort amidst their hardship.

Enoch looked at the meager pile of food—their last hedge against starvation—then met their expectant gazes. He nodded slowly, but his eyes held a meaning they didn't immediately grasp. "Yes," he said softly. "We will partake now in a meal of faith." He carefully gathered the precious scraps—the meat, the nuts, the bread—folding them securely into the cloak. "Follow me."

Confusion rippled through the group—Kael exchanged a worried glance with Anak—but they followed without question as Enoch led them back through the silent ruins to the open-air temple complex and the stone altar he had discovered. Hope turned swiftly to bewilderment, then dawning horror, as Enoch walked directly to the altar and began carefully arranging the pitiful amount of food upon its broad, weathered surface.

"Father, what are you doing?" Methuselah cried out, taking an instinctive step forward, his voice sharp with disbelief and rising panic. "That's all the food we have! We'll starve out here!"

"Enoch, this is madness!" Kael protested, his practical healer's mind aghast, glancing anxiously back toward the repository where his brother lay weak and needing nourishment. "Ronan needs sustenance! We *all* do! Rationed carefully, this might last us a few more days..."

Naamah simply stared, her face pale. Remembering meager times in her own valley, the act of deliberately destroying their last hope seemed incomprehensible, terrifying.

"Silence." Anak's deep voice cut through the rising panic like a thunderclap. He stepped forward, placing a heavy, restraining hand on Kael's tense shoulder, his own gaze fixed on Enoch not with un-understanding but unwavering trust earned through shared peril and revealed truth. Though the giant didn't comprehend Enoch's purpose, he recognized the look of divine conviction burning in his eyes. "Let him speak."

The group fell silent, waiting for an explanation that could possibly justify this seemingly insane act.

Enoch turned from the altar to face them, his expression serene, his eyes holding a deep, burning certainty that calmed their immediate panic.

"In the city ruled by the Serpent," he began, his voice clear and steady, resonating in the quiet ruins of the temple, "we saw the very pinnacle of his lie. The lie that whispers we are masters of our own destiny. That strength, knowledge, and provision come only from our own clever hands, our own hoarded resources, or from the dark gifts of fallen powers." He met their eyes. "The lie that insists we are alone in a hostile universe, abandoned by a distant or uncaring Creator, responsible solely for ourselves."

He gestured toward the meager offering laid out upon the altar. "This," he said, his voice ringing with conviction, "is the sum total of all *our* strength can now provide. A few more days of gnawing hunger, of dwindling hope, of eventual despair when it runs out. If we cling to this, if we place our trust in these last crumbs, then we cling to the Serpent's foundational lie—the lie that our survival depends only upon ourselves."

His gaze swept over their faces—Methuselah's confusion, Naamah's fear, Kael's doubt, Anak's trust. "But my ancestors who built this city, who laid their hands upon this very altar—children of Adam, Daughters of Eve—they knew the deeper truth! The Creator is the source! He *is* the Provider! He gives the dewfall, the sun's warmth, the fruit of the earth, the strength in our limbs, the very breath in our lungs! Our survival, our *true* provision, comes not from hoarding scraps in fear but from trusting the infinite source of all abundance!"

He turned back to the altar, his movements deliberate, filled with purpose. "This act is not madness. It is faith manifest. It is a declaration against the darkness we fled, against the self-reliance preached in that city of lies. We declare today that we trust not in dried meat or hoarded nuts, but in the living Creator who guided our steps here, who returned Methuselah miraculously from the depths, who even now sustains Ronan's life against fever and injury! We give back to Him these first fruits of our deliverance, even though they are also our last fruits, acknowledging Him as the sole Author and Sustainer of our provision. We trust Him completely for what comes next."

With steady hands, Enoch gathered dry moss and brittle twigs from the base of the altar where they had collected over the ages. Using a shard of flint and a chunk of pyrite saved from his pack, he struck them together, showering sparks into the tinder until a small flame took hold. Then, with quiet reverence, he touched the small flame to the offering laid upon the stone. The dry provisions—the leathery meat, the nuts, the hard bread—caught quickly. Smoke began to curl upward into the clear, silent morning sky—the fragrant smoke of their last tangible hope, transformed into an offering of absolute, terrifying, liberating dependence.

They watched in silence as the small fire consumed the food, the unexpected aroma of roasting meat and burning bread mingling strangely with the scent of weathered stone and wild thyme carried on the breeze. They were completely vulnerable now, their survival stripped bare of any pretense of human self-sufficiency. Yet, standing before that altar, under the silent sky, in this place consecrated by generations of faith, there was also a sincere, undeniable sense of *rightness*. A release from the burden of their own limitations. They had defied the Serpent's core lie not with weapons or cunning but with an act of radical, trusting faith. They stood empty-handed, waiting, their future entirely, irrevocably in the hands of the One who had promised, long ago in the shadow of Eden's loss, never to abandon His creation.

16

The Creator Provides

Silence settled heavily over the small group gathered around the stone altar. The last ember of their sacrificial fire glowed softly, sending a final, thin ribbon of smoke spiraling up into the clear, silent morning sky—the tangible evidence of their last earthly provisions offered up in faith.

They stood empty-handed, hearts pounding in the aftermath, their future hanging precariously on the radical act they had just committed. Fear warred with the fragile hope Enoch's words had kindled. Had they been utter fools? Or had they at last put their trust fully in the only hands that could rescue them?

While the smoke still rose, painting a line against the vast blue expanse, something shifted in the quiet air. Not a sound at first, but a *feeling*, a delicate change in the pressure against their skin. Then, a soft flutter of wings, startlingly close in the stillness. A single white dove, plump and impossibly pristine, landed on the edge of the now-empty altar, seemingly unafraid, its small head cocked as if observing them with calm curiosity.

Enoch stared, his breath catching in his throat. *Doves? Here?* They had seen no birds of any kind, heard no birdsong at all since entering the blighted shadow of Serpent Mountain many weeks ago. The silence of this ruined city had been absolute.

Then another dove landed beside the first, just as silent, just as calm. And another. Within moments, the air filled with the gentle, whispering rush of countless wings. Doves—dozens, then scores, then hundreds upon hundreds—descended into the open-air temple like a soft, living snowfall. They landed all around the astonished, frozen group—on the crumbling tops of pillars, on the cracked flagstones littered with debris, even settling near their worn boots, entirely devoid of fear. A peace settled with the doves, their only sounds the soft, collective whirring of their wings and occasional low, contented coos. They moved without fear, their sudden presence an overwhelming tide of gentle, pure life that washed over the desolate ruins.

For a long, breathless moment, the travelers could only stare, stunned into silence by the sheer, quiet impossibility of it.

Then Naamah let out a choked sob, tears streaming unchecked down her face, tears born not of grief this time but of overwhelming relief and awe. Methuselah looked from the impossible flock of birds back to his father, his eyes wide with wonder. Anak and Kael exchanged a look of astonishment, their pragmatism silenced, humbled by the undeniable miracle.

Enoch knelt slowly, his knees weak, tears blurring his own vision, his heart overflowing with a wave of gratitude. "He provides," he whispered, the words catching in his throat, thick with emotion. "The Creator *always* provides."

The message was unmistakable, undeniable. This was no natural occurrence, no mere flock taking shelter. This was a direct, tangible answer to their offering, a sign as clear and irrefutable as if spoken aloud from Heaven. The doves showed no fear, milled around them gently, almost seeming to offer themselves with quiet trust. Their stunned stillness gave way to reverent movement. With murmurs of wonder and hearts full of gratitude, they gathered the birds, each soft, warm touch a tangible confirmation of the Creator's miraculous provision. They filled their cloaks until they could hold no more, then wove quick, rough baskets from pliable vines growing nearby, their arms soon overflowing with this sudden, unexpected, life-saving bounty.

Soon, the fire in the repository roared back to life. The room filled quickly with the rich, almost forgotten, savory scent of roasting meat—a smell none of them had experienced in months of scarcity. They worked together seamlessly, plucking and preparing the birds, their earlier bone-deep weariness miraculously replaced by a joyful, grateful energy. Even Ronan, propped up carefully against the repository wall, managed a genuine, broad smile, his eyes following the bustling activity, the aroma clearly stirring his returning appetite and spirit.

And then, they ate. Not carefully rationed scraps but a true, unrestrained feast. They tore into the plump, roasted doves with a gusto born of long-denied hunger, savoring the tender, juicy meat down to the bone. For a time, the only sounds in the repository were the crackle of the fire and the low groans of sheer pleasure, the simple act of eating their fill feeling like the greatest, most unbelievable luxury imaginable.

It was Methuselah who broke the reverent silence, his face greasy and shining in the firelight. He shook his head in lingering disbelief. "I can still smell the beast's breath," he said, a shudder running through him. "Foul as a stagnant swamp. I think I much prefer this aroma." He took another large bite of roasted meat, and a choked, slightly hysterical laugh escaped him.

Kael, watching Ronan already reaching with his good hand for a third portion, let out a deep chuckle that rumbled in his chest. "Careful, brother," he jested, his eyes twinkling. "Your arm may be mending, but your belly might not survive such a sudden assault after weeks of roots and hope."

Ronan, his mouth full, could only manage a weak glare and a dismissive wave of his hand, which only made the others laugh harder.

Naamah's own quiet, weary smile finally broke into genuine laughter, a sound of pure relief that seemed to surprise even her. The laughter was infectious, and soon it was genuine and unrestrained, bubbling up and spilling out into the chamber. It culminated in Anak, who threw his great head back and let out a deep, booming laugh of pure, unburdened joy. The sound echoed strangely, wonderfully, in the silent ruins, chasing away the lingering shadows of fear and despair. For the first time since leaving Anak's distant home, their bellies were truly full, their immediate needs met not by their own striving but by sheer, unearned grace.

The provision was truly abundant, far more than they could possibly eat before it spoiled. Recognizing this gift was meant not just for this moment but for the arduous journey still ahead, they spent the rest of the day and into the evening carefully preserving the bounty. Thin strips of dove meat were hung on racks fashioned from branches over the smoky fire, curing and drying in the steady heat. They worked together, shoulder to shoulder, a renewed sense of purpose and unity flowing between them—giant, man, and woman, resurrected from despair, united by shared hardship, and now, undeniably, by shared miracle. Enough meat was prepared and carefully packed to last them for many weeks without rationing, a visible and tangible reminder of the lesson learned so powerfully at the altar.

That night, they rested differently. Bellies full, the immediate, gnawing anxiety silenced, a deep, quiet peace settled over the small group within the firelit repository. The flickering light played on the rows of drying meat hanging like promises from the makeshift racks—a comforting, reassuring sight.

Enoch watched his companions, his own heart full to bursting. He saw Ronan sleeping soundly beside the fire, his fever finally broken, his breathing deep and even for the first time since the beast's attack. Kael rested nearby, the tense lines of worry finally eased from his rugged face. He watched Methuselah, whose splinted leg was propped carefully on a bundle of furs. The boy's face, even in sleep, held a quiet confidence that had not been there before, the lingering fear in his eyes seemingly replaced by a newfound trust. And he saw Naamah, curled near the fire, finally surrendering to a peaceful, unguarded sleep, her own face, so often a mask of controlled grief, now softened and at rest in the warm glow.

The miracle was a soothing balm on their spirits, Enoch realized. They had faced the Serpent's lies in its very stronghold, they had been stripped bare of their own resources, offered their last measure of control at the altar, and in that absolute vulnerability, they had found the Creator's unwavering faithfulness made manifest. The path ahead remained dangerous, their wounds were real, and the enemy still loomed. But they would face it differently now—not alone, not reliant solely on their own dwindling strength, but as children provided for, seen, and answered by a Father who held the universe in His hands. The echo of thankful laughter still lingered amongst the stones, a testament to the enduring power of trust over fear.

17

The Light of Eden

The morning after the miracle of the doves dawned bright and clear, carrying a measure of peace that settled deep into their weary souls. The comforting aroma of smoked meat hung in the repository.

Ronan, though still weak, had retained his lucidity through the night, the fever's grip finally broken.

Methuselah rested near the entrance, his splinted leg propped up. Gone was the frantic, pain-driven energy from his ordeal, replaced now by a quiet stillness that, while born of exhaustion, no longer spoke of agony. Kael moved between the wounded, tending their injuries with renewed hope, while Anak stood as a watchful guard.

Naamah organized the precious dried meat for the journey ahead. The gnawing despair had lifted, replaced by gratitude and the strength drawn from full bellies and answered prayer.

But Enoch knew they could not linger. While the others recovered their physical strength, his mind remained restless, driven by the truths held within the scrolls. He returned to them that morning, unrolling a delicate section, scanning the texts. He sought not just confirmation of the path to Adam's cave but answers about the ruined city of Shem and the mysterious light that had guided them across the wastes. His fingers traced the archaic script on one well-preserved scroll detailing the city's central structures. It spoke of a great tower, built to overlook the temple courtyard where the altar stood.

According to the text, the tower's now-shattered pinnacle had once housed a marvel of sacred craft: a massive, perfectly formed crystal described with reverence as the 'Heartstone Lens.' Its purpose, the scroll stated, was to capture the light visible only at night on the western horizon—a light the scroll named 'Edenfire.' The patriarchs of Shem believed it emanated from the unquenchable glory of the Tree of Life itself, still burning like an eternal star within the inaccessible Garden of Eden. The great lens focused this captured light into a concentrated beam, directed downward to illuminate the high altar, a tangible connection to the Creator's original blessing. The scroll lamented the Heartstone's shattering during the city's final long siege, noting with sorrow that only a small fragment remained embedded in the ruined tower's peak, still catching a faint echo of that distant, holy light—the very glow that had guided their steps.

Enoch's fingers, tracing the archaic script, suddenly stilled. He drew in a sharp, audible breath, his eyes widening as he stared at the brittle scroll. The others, resting nearby, looked up, sensing the sudden shift in his demeanor.

"Father? What is it?" Methuselah asked, his voice hushed.

Enoch glanced up from the text, his face showing deep awe. He seemed to be looking right through them, toward the unseen west. "The light," he whispered, his voice trembling slightly. "The light we followed..." He cleared his throat, his gaze returning to the words, and began to read aloud, his voice filled with a reverence that commanded their absolute attention.

"'...and though the way is barred to us, the Light of the Garden remains, a steadfast beacon against the long night, a promise of what was, and what will be again.'"

He lowered the scroll, his hands shaking. "Do you understand?" he asked, his voice thick with emotion as he looked at his companions. "The light that guided us across the wastes... it wasn't a star. It wasn't some Nephilim trick." He stared at them, the staggering implication dawning on his own face as he spoke it aloud. "It was Eden. The Garden, lost to us since the Fall, still exists."

A stunned silence fell over the group.

"The Garden isn't just a story," Enoch continued, his voice rising with a passion born of revelation. "It's not just a memory on a cave wall. Its light, its very essence, still touches our world." He looked at Anak, then at Methuselah and Naamah, a sense of connection washing over him. "We weren't just following a light. We were following a promise home."

Driven by this revelation, he left the repository. Ignoring the pain in his arm, he climbed the crumbling ruins of the Great Tower's base, scrambling high enough to gaze westward over the unexplored lands. It was broad daylight, the distant Edenfire invisible, but he knew the direction. He stared to the west, toward that distant point where Paradise lay hidden, his soul reaching out across the intervening wilderness.

And as he clung there, gazing westward with prayerful intensity, the world around him shimmered. The familiar sense of spiritual detachment washed over him, the sounds of the wind sighing through the ruins fading, replaced by a vision, stark and terrifyingly clear. He saw the dark, arrogant battlements of the Serpent City far behind him to the east. But movement caught his inner eye, pouring forth not from the main gates but from hidden posterns carved into the mountain's base, opening directly toward the west. A legion issued forth—ranks of dark-armored soldiers marching with inhuman tread, hulking corrupted giants moving with brutal purpose, shadowy forms flitting at their flanks like hounds loosed from shadow. They moved not with the arrogance of conquerors but with the grim focus of hunters entering new territory on a vital mission.

Leading the vanguard, already leagues ahead of the main host, was the hunting party itself. Giant, low-slung reptilian beasts strained against chains of black iron, their multi-faceted eyes scanning, their forked tongues tasting the air, their snouts pressed to the ground, following a scent invisible to Enoch but horrifyingly clear to them. The chains were held tight in the fists of brutish handler giants, their faces set in masks of grim concentration as they were pulled along by the creatures' savage eagerness. They were tracking, relentlessly following the trail left by Enoch's small company.

Overseeing this deadly vanguard were two commanding figures, their dark cloaks hiding their forms as they rode their huge, nightmare steeds. They radiated a darkness that marked them as the Nephilim commanders. Their reptilian mounts seemed to absorb the light, their eyes like malevolent embers. The chilling presence of these riders, their mounts, and the straining beasts froze the marrow in Enoch's bones. He understood with a jolt of sickening terror that shook him to his core. The quarry these beasts strained so eagerly to find was them. Their escape, their very existence, had alerted their enemies. The Nephilim knew they sought the path westward and were now unleashing their full power to hunt them down and extinguish the light they carried.

He gasped as if physically struck, the vision vanishing. He was left trembling on the ruins of the tower, the bright sunlight feeling suddenly cold and inadequate against the encroaching shadow he had just witnessed. Danger—immediate and moving with unnatural speed—was no longer a distant threat but a tangible pursuit, closing the distance with every passing moment.

He scrambled down from the ruins, his injured arm forgotten in the surge of adrenaline, and burst back into the repository. The others looked up in surprise at his panicked return, his face pale and strained.

"They know!" Enoch cried out, his voice hoarse with dread. "An army marches from the Serpent City—westward! They have tracking beasts! We must leave this place! NOW!"

This time, there were no questions, no hesitant doubts. The memory of the miracle was too fresh, the confirmation of Enoch's leadership too absolute, the stark terror in his voice too undeniable. It was enough.

Instantly, the repository sprang into frantic, unified action. Anak bellowed sharp orders, his voice galvanizing them. Kael swiftly checked the bindings on Ronan and Methuselah, ensuring they were secure for a desperate flight. Naamah, her movements swift and economical, rapidly bundled the precious dried meat. Amidst this chaos, Enoch's gaze fell upon the priceless scrolls lining the stone shelves. A fresh wave of agony washed over him—to have found their entire history only to leave it to be consumed by the enemy. He knew he could not save it all; the weight was impossible, the time non-existent.

With a choked cry of despair for what must be left behind to the flames, he lunged towards the shelves and grabbed only the most vital records—the star charts from his vision and the key scrolls detailing Adam's testimony and the promise of the Seed. He shoved them deep into his own worn pack as Methuselah pushed himself upright, grabbing his axe, his face set, ready to move despite the pain.

They worked with silent efficiency, fueled by the adrenaline of renewed danger and the strength gained from their brief respite. The small hearth fire was doused, meager belongings packed in seconds, weapons secured. The injured would simply have to endure; speed was paramount.

Within minutes, they were leaving the silent ruins of Shem behind, abandoning the repository that had offered both revelation and, now, imminent mortal danger. They moved quickly westward, plunging into unknown territory, following the remembered direction of the now-invisible Edenfire light.

Hope for reaching Adam's cave still burned within Enoch, a desperate ember against the wind, but it was now overshadowed by the terrifying reality of the hunt.

As the sun began its descent once more, casting long, pursuing shadows behind them, they plunged deeper into the wilderness, the memory of safety fading, the knowledge that they were actively pursued a cold spur driving them onward.

The hunt was on.

18

The Sunken Path

They fled westward through the remainder of that day and deep into the following night, a flight driven by the terrifying clarity of Enoch's vision. Every unexpected rustle in the darkness, every distant, unknown animal cry, sent jolts of raw fear through them, their imaginations painting Nephilim hunters in every shadow.

They pushed their weary bodies, knowing the hunting party was already driving hard onto their trail from the east.

Enoch leaned heavily on his staff, fighting the creeping cold in his arm that seemed to worsen with fatigue.

Methuselah gritted his teeth against the constant, jarring pain in his splinted leg, his endurance fueled by adrenaline and Naamah's steadying presence beside him.

Even the mighty giants, though their endurance was vast, showed growing signs of strain, burdened by Ronan's weakness and the punishing pace.

Just before the first hint of the next dawn, as the stars began to fade in a paling sky, they reached the edge of it—a massive, dismal marshland stretching southward and westward as far as the eye could penetrate the pre-dawn gloom, its sluggish waters shimmering like obsidian under the last starlight.

Twisted trees, choked by decay, rose like grasping claws from stagnant, black pools, draped in thick shrouds of pale, weeping moss. Heavy banks of mist clung to the water's surface, swirling sluggishly, obscuring whatever lay within or beyond. The air hung heavy, still, thick with the cloying, gagging stench of decay, putrid water, and rotting vegetation. It presented itself as a formidable, deeply repellent barrier.

Anak surveyed the mire, his nostrils flaring in distaste. "This will slow us terribly," he rumbled, his voice low. "The footing will be treacherous, perhaps impossible, especially for Ronan and Methuselah in their weakness." He looked back toward the east, where the sky was beginning to blush. "But..." he added, "the hunting beasts... their weight, their nature... they would likely be forced to go far around this mire. It would cost our pursuers days, possibly many days."

Enoch looked at the stinking swamp, then toward the west, where Eden's light, invisible now, still beckoned in his memory. He felt the crushing weight of their pursuers and recalled the unnatural speed of the tracking beasts. Going around the marsh, exposing themselves on open ground for days, felt like suicide. Then, quieter but more insistent than the fear, he felt it again—that inner prompting, a sense not of logical certainty but of stark necessity. A definite pull toward this treacherous, sunken path. "We go through," he stated, his voice carrying absolute conviction, meeting Anak's gaze directly. "It is perilous beyond measure, yes. But it may be the only way to blind the hunters, to truly break the trail, to gain the time we desperately need." He knew the terrible risks—becoming hopelessly lost, the foul water aggravating wounds past healing, unknown venomous creatures lurking beneath the surface—but the alternative felt like certain capture and death.

Trust, hard-won through shared miracle and sacrifice, held.

Anak studied Enoch's face for a long moment, then gave a single, solemn nod. "As the Creator guides you, Enoch. We follow."

The decision was made.

Entering the marsh was like stepping off the edge of the living world into a realm of decay and suffocation. The ground immediately softened beneath their feet, giving way to thick, greedy, black mud that sucked at their boots, trying to pull them down. Tangled, unseen roots lay hidden beneath the murky, tea-colored water, tripping the unwary, sending jolts of pain through injured limbs.

The air grew thick, humid, buzzing with clouds of biting insects that swarmed around their faces, finding every inch of exposed skin. Within minutes, the memory of firm ground behind them vanished, completely swallowed by the swirling mist and the dense curtain of tangled, rotting vegetation. The horizon disappeared. Soon, even the sky above became obscured by the dripping canopy of tortured trees and low-hanging fog. They were enveloped, directionless, the memory of Eden's guiding light and even the guiding stars lost to them in this suffocating haze.

The passage became a grueling, timeless ordeal. Each step forward was a victory hard-won against the clinging, sucking mire. They waded for hours through waist-deep, foul-smelling water that chilled them to the bone and seeped into bandages, prompting Kael's worried glances toward Ronan and Methuselah.

The giants struggled mightily, their great weight causing them to sink alarmingly deep, forcing them to use depleting strength just to pull their feet free with loud, sucking sounds. Often, Kael or Anak had to heave aside rotting logs or clear paths through knotted thickets of razor-sharp reeds with their hammer or axe, or use their sheer bulk to steady the smaller members across treacherous patches of black water.

Methuselah leaned heavily on the sturdy branch Kael had fashioned into a crutch, his face pale and strained with constant pain, Naamah often beside him, her lighter weight allowing her slightly easier passage, offering him a steadying hand or finding firmer footing he couldn't sense.

Darkness, when it fell within the marsh, was absolute, pressing in on them, thicker even than the fog. They could risk no fire; the damp wood wouldn't catch, and any smoke or light would be an immediate beacon in this desolate, disorienting place. The swamp's unsettling symphony filled the night: the maddening drone of insects, the guttural croaking of unseen things, and the sudden splash of something large moving in the black water nearby.

Worse still were the periods of absolute silence that fell, heavy and watchful. Huddled on small, muddy islands, they chewed grimly on smoked dove meat. Sleep was a fleeting luxury, constantly disturbed by the penetrating cold, the relentless damp, and the sharp awareness of danger lurking inches away in the dark. Disgusting leeches attached themselves unnoticed in the murky water, discovered only later as thin trails of blood when they made brief halts. Swarms of biting flies left painful, itching welts on any exposed skin.

Once, during a rest, a large, pale, multi-eyed serpent slithered silently from the black water onto their small islet, its disturbing eyes gleaming in the ambient light before Anak sent it sliding back into the depths with a swift, powerful kick.

Disorientation became their constant, tormenting companion. With no sun visible by day, no stars by night, no discernible landmarks in the repetitive, fog-shrouded landscape of twisted trees and stagnant pools, their sense of direction completely frayed. Panic, cold and corrosive, began to set in after what felt like days adrift, moving seemingly in circles. They stopped one bleak afternoon on a slightly raised hummock of mud and tangled roots, outright exhausted, the oppressive grey fog sealing them in. Ronan, shivering despite Kael's attempts to shield him, looked at his father, his face pale with more than just physical weakness.

"Father, stop," Ronan rasped, his voice cracking with pain and effort. The desperate conviction in his tone made them all freeze. "Listen to me. Please." He looked at Kael, then Enoch, his eyes hollow with exhaustion. "We are lost. Every step you take carrying me... every time you help Methuselah... you grow weaker. The hunters don't weaken." His gaze, filled with a terrible, resolute sorrow, found Anak's. "Don't let everyone die because of us. Leave us here. We will face our end to-gether. But you... you can still escape. You can save the story. It's the only way that makes sense."

A horrified silence met his words. Methuselah started to protest, "Ronan, no! We stay together!" Kael looked stricken, shaking his mas-sive head vehemently. Naamah reached out instinctively toward Ro-nan, her eyes filled with compassion and dismay. Enoch watched Anak, sensing the deep pain Ronan's words, born of despair and a warped sense of sacrifice, caused the giant patriarch.

Anak knelt beside his son, ignoring the mud that oozed around his knees. He placed a hand on Ronan's uninjured shoulder. His voice, when he spoke, was a low rumble, thick with emotion but absolutely firm, leaving no room for argument. "Ronan, my son. Listen to me." He waited until Ronan met his gaze. "There is no path forward that leaves you behind. None." He shook his head slowly. "The strength of our fellowship, the bond we share... these are not burdens that slow us. They are the very heart of our strength. To abandon family, to aban-don hope, that is the path of the enemy we fled. That is the logic of darkness." His grip tightened on Ronan's shoulder. "You are my son. Methuselah is as my son now. We started this journey together, bound by the Creator's purpose. We will finish it together or fall defending each other. If need be," his voice softened further, filled with unwa-vering paternal love, "I will carry you on my back through this entire cursed swamp to the ends of the earth. But I will never leave you be-hind. Do you understand me, Ronan? Never."

Ronan stared up at his father, tears welling in his eyes. He managed a weak nod, unable to speak. The heavy silence returned, but it was different now, charged not with despair but with the fierce, quiet power of Anak's unwavering loyalty, his absolute refusal to break faith.

It was into this renewed, albeit grim, resolve that Kael finally asked, his voice still heavy with exhaustion, "Which way, then, Enoch?

I cannot find a bearing. Even the moss seems to grow thick on all sides of these cursed trees!"

Enoch closed his eyes, shutting out the disorienting grey swirl, drawing strength from Anak's powerful declaration of faith and love. He focused his inner senses, reaching for the guidance that had led them here. He remembered the faint but steady wind they had felt upon entering the marsh, blowing gently but persistently from the west. It was subtle, almost nonexistent within the tangled vegetation, but it was their only potential guide. "The wind," he said, lifting his face, turning slowly, straining to feel the slightest movement of air against his damp skin. "There. Do you feel it? Barely a breath, but steady. From the west." He pointed into the grey void. "We must keep it upon our faces, trust it. It is all we have now." He took a cautious step in that direction, testing the ground with his staff, and gestured for the others to follow his lead.

They moved forward again, Anak probing ahead now with his heavy hammer haft. For a few yards, the ground seemed firmer, the mud less deep. Then, without warning, Anak let out a startled grunt as the earth beneath his feet gave way with a soft, sickening *slurp*. He sank instantly to his waist in thick, black, putrid mud that seemed to grasp and pull with terrifying strength. "Quicksand!" he bellowed, his voice tight with sudden alarm, struggling against the powerful suction.

Kael lunged forward to grab his father's outstretched arm, but the ground near Anak was equally treacherous. Kael too plunged in with a startled roar, sinking rapidly due to his weight. Ronan, weaker and less steady, trying to move back, stumbled nearby and also found himself caught fast, letting out a pained cry as the foul mud engulfed his injured arm up to the shoulder. Within moments, the three mighty giants were hopelessly bogged down, their strength useless against the mire's grip, their struggles only seeming to pull them deeper.

Enoch and Methuselah, trying desperately to circle on what looked like firmer tufts of grass near the edge, found their footing fatally compromised by the disturbed mud. Methuselah's injured leg couldn't support a sudden sideways shift, and he cried out as he slid into the cold, viscous muck up to his chest. Enoch, reaching desperately for his son, felt the ground dissolve entirely beneath him as well, his injured arm sending waves of fresh agony through him as he fought uselessly against the downward pull. The cold, sucking mud grasped them all, pulling them down into the marsh's unforgiving embrace.

Only Naamah, lighter, more agile, instinctively more wary, had hesitated near the solid roots at the very edge as the chaos erupted. She scrambled back onto the patch of relatively firm ground dominated by the gnarled roots of a large, long-dead cypress tree, watching in wide-eyed horror as her companions thrashed futilely, sinking deeper with every desperate movement.

Panic seized her for a terrifying moment—they were all going to die here, swallowed whole by the indifferent swamp. Then, seeing Methuselah's pale face strained with pain and effort, seeing Enoch struggling weakly, the mighty giants trapped and slowly disappearing, a fierce, protective resolve surged through her, ignited by desperation.

Malachi didn't sacrifice himself for us to perish like this!

Her eyes fell on Kael's heavy iron axe, dropped near the edge of the mire as the giant sank. Adrenaline lent her a strength she didn't know she possessed. She lunged for it, hefting the weapon—it felt brutally heavy, almost unmanageable in her smaller hands. Nearby stood the dead cypress, its massive trunk thick but visibly brittle with advanced decay.

Sobbing with effort and desperation, ignoring the insects swarming her face, she began hacking furiously at its base, the heavy axe biting deep into the pulpy, dead wood. Chips flew like startled birds. Her arms burned, her lungs screamed for air, her breath came in ragged gasps, but she didn't stop, didn't dare stop, fueled by the terrifying image of her friends sinking before her eyes.

"Naamah! Careful!" Anak roared, seeing her intent even as he fought the mud.

The tree groaned and leaned dangerously. With a final, desperate, two-handed swing that took all her remaining strength, Naamah struck deep into the heartwood. There was a loud, tearing *crack*, and the massive trunk began to topple directly toward the trapped group. A collective cry of alarm went up from those still able to draw breath. For one heart-stopping, terrifying second, it seemed destined to crush them all beneath its colossal weight. But it fell with a thunderous crash all around them, its heavy upper branches landing across the mire, miraculously within reach of their mud-coated hands.

Muddy arms grabbed hold of the branches, the rough bark a solid, blessed anchor in the unyielding ooze. "Hold fast!" Anak bellowed again. Planting his feet against the submerged part of the trunk below the mudline, he used his incredible strength, combined with the leverage offered by the branches, to begin the agonizing, muscle-shredding process of hauling his frame upward, fighting the mud's greedy suction. With a final heave that sprayed black mud wide, he pulled himself free, collapsing onto the relatively stable trunk of the fallen tree, gasping for air like a landed fish.

Without pausing to rest, he reached back into the mire for his sons. Kael, then Ronan, were hauled from the quicksand's grip, their weight testing even Anak's tremendous strength. Then came Enoch, who was pulled free with surprising ease due to his lighter weight but was hampered significantly by his useless, throbbing arm. Finally, Anak and Kael painstakingly extricated Methuselah, trying desperately not to worsen the already severe injury to his leg.

They lay sprawled in sheer exhaustion on the muddy trunk and the small patch of firmer ground around its base, covered head to foot in black, stinking mud, shivering uncontrollably with cold and exertion, gasping for breath.

They were safe from the sinking mud thanks entirely to Naamah's quick thinking and courageous effort. But the ordeal had required the remainder of their already meager reserves. The little strength they had regained after the miracle of the doves, the energy carefully gathered over days of rest and rationing, now completely stripped away, leaving them exposed, weakened, and vulnerable in the heart of the disorienting, hostile marsh, the faint westward wind feeling colder, more mocking than ever against their damp skin.

The breeze became their only guide. They learned to trust its subtle pressure against their faces, a compass in the disorienting mist. Their progress slowed to a painstaking crawl, each step deliberate, and they paused whenever the current of air died, leaving them blind and uncertain once more.

Yet, somehow, they endured. They helped each other without question.

Anak often carried Ronan across the deepest sections, shielding his injured arm.

Kael tended wounds constantly, using the last dregs of his herbal knowledge against the swamp's dampness and filth.

Naamah's agility proved invaluable, scouting ahead mere yards at a time, finding slightly firmer paths through the mire, warning of sudden drops or hidden roots.

Methuselah, driven by grim determination and a refusal to be seen as the weakest link, pushed himself through the constant agony in his leg, leaning heavily on his staff and often, gratefully, on Naamah's offered arm.

Enoch, despite his own worsening wound making him increasingly weak and burdened by the heavy responsibility of leadership, provided quiet words of encouragement when spirits flagged, reminding them constantly of the Creator's providence, of the purpose that drove them onward through this seemingly endless trial.

After what felt like an eternity trapped in that grey, stinking twilight—four days, possibly six—time itself seemed to lose all meaning in the oppressive gloom of the marsh.

Naamah, scouting slightly ahead as usual, gave a low, choked cry, different from her usual warnings. "Firm ground! I see... I see light!"

Stumbling like drunken men, they pushed through a final, heavy curtain of weeping moss and grasping, thorny roots, emerging suddenly from the swamp's suffocating embrace onto solid, dry earth.

They collapsed as one, gasping, covered head to foot in mud and slime, scratched and bitten, absolutely, bone-deeply exhausted. But above them, the sky was clear, dotted with high, white, afternoon clouds. The air smelled fresh and clean again, carrying the welcome scent of pine and dry earth from the woods ahead. They had made it. They were through.

Looking back, the great marsh stretched behind them, a foreboding barrier of mist and mangled trees. They could see no sign of pursuit on its bleak expanse. They had bought themselves precious time.

They rested there, at the edge of the sunken path, letting the welcome sunlight warm their chilled, weary bodies, too tired initially even to feel true relief, only a hollowed-out weariness.

The cost of passage had been great. Ronan was weak, his breathing still shallow. Methuselah's leg was swollen and angry-looking around Kael's bindings. Enoch's arm throbbed relentlessly. But they were through. The Nephilim army, especially the tracking beasts, would be forced to go the long way around this natural barrier.

As dusk began to fall again, Enoch painfully pushed himself up and looked westward. There, low on the darkening horizon, faint but steady, the mysterious Edenfire light glowed once more, a distant promise.

Their ordeal in the marsh was finally over; the long journey toward the light, and whatever dangers it held, continued.

19

The River of Life

They dragged themselves away from the cloying edge of the stinking marsh, each step onto solid, blessedly dry ground feeling like a minor miracle. Behind them lay the oppressive gloom, the sucking mud that had nearly claimed them, the unseen terrors, and the stark memory of near-fatal entrapment.

Ahead, the land began to change with almost startling, welcome rapidity. The sickly trees of the swamp gave way to hardy grasses, sparse at first, then growing thicker, greener with every westward stride. The air lost its heavy, stagnant quality, replaced by a fresh, clean breeze carrying the scent of damp earth, growing things, and distant water—scents they hadn't realized they had missed so desperately.

As they pressed onward, pushing through the exhaustion left by the marsh ordeal, true life returned to the land in glorious abundance. Patches of vibrant wildflowers erupted in unexpected splashes of color—deep blues like twilight skies, sunny yellows, startling reds like drops of blood on the green—scattered like forgotten jewels across rolling meadows. Healthy trees—sturdy oaks, graceful maples, and unfamiliar species with broad, luxuriant green leaves—formed welcoming groves, their branches reaching toward the clear sky in praise, not contorted agony. And then came the sound, almost forgotten, washing over them like a balm—birdsong. Tentative at first, a single flute-like call, then swelling into a joyous, intricate chorus that filled the air, chasing away the oppressive, watchful silence that had haunted them since nearing Serpent Mountain. Small animals—nimble rabbits, furry rodents darting through the grass, and graceful deer with soft, curious eyes—moved through the undergrowth, watching the travelers with wariness yet also with a clear, healthy curiosity, unlike the feral madness or diseased state of the creatures in the blighted lands.

The sheer normalcy, the vibrant, uncorrupted health of this land, was almost overwhelming after the long weeks of desolation and perversion they had endured.

Naamah stopped, tears welling in her eyes again, this time not born of sorrow but of intense relief. She knelt, gently touching the velvety petals of a bright blue flower as if needing physical proof of its simple, perfect reality.

Methuselah leaned heavily on his staff, breathing in the clean air, a slow, wondering smile spreading across his face despite the lingering ache in his leg.

Even Anak and his sons seemed to relax their shoulders as they surveyed the thriving, peaceful landscape. The urge to stop, to shed their burdens, lie down in the soft, sun-warmed grass, and truly rest was almost overpowering. But the sharp memory of Enoch's vision, the knowledge of the hunters inevitably circling the marsh far behind them, spurred them onward. They could appreciate this beauty, draw strength and hope from its very existence, but they could not afford to linger.

Soon, another sound joined the swelling birdsong—the unmistakable, musical murmur, growing louder, of swiftly running water. Following the sound through a stand of tall Willow trees whose leaves shimmered in the breeze, they emerged onto the banks of a magnificent river. It was wide, powerful, its waters running startlingly clear and swift over a bed of smooth, multi-colored stones, sparkling brilliantly in the midday sunlight. Large fish darted in the transparent depths. The banks were lush and green, lined with graceful willows trailing their leaves in the current and thick stands of healthy reeds humming with insects. Life teemed here—bees buzzed among wild-flowers, waterfowl called from hidden inlets, the very air felt vibrant, clean, charged with vitality. It was a stark, breathtaking contrast to the sluggish, oily streams near the city of Enoch or the black, fetid waters of the marsh they had just escaped. Kael knelt at the water's edge, scooping some into his hand, examining it closely, then tasting it before nodding to the others. "Clean," he pronounced, relief evident in his deep voice. "Pure."

The word hung in the air, a promise of restoration. Covered head to foot in the stinking, clinging mud and slime of the marsh, scratched and bitten, weary beyond measure, the sight and scent of the pure, flowing water was an irresistible invitation.

Without words, drawn by a fundamental need for cleansing, they moved toward the river's edge. Anak carefully helped Ronan ease himself down into the shallows, the cool water swirling around his injured arm. Kael knelt beside his brother, gently washing away the filth near the bandages, his large hands surprisingly tender as he ensured no foul marsh water contaminated the slowly healing wound.

Ronan sighed in relief, the clean coolness a stark contrast to the feverish heat that had plagued him.

Methuselah, wincing as he lowered himself into the current, struggled to clean the mud caked around the bandages on his injured leg without putting weight on it. Naamah, having rinsed the worst of the filth from her face and arms, saw his difficulty. Hesitantly at first, then with quiet, natural tenderness, she knelt beside him in the flowing water. "Let me," she said softly. Gently, she began washing the mud from his lower leg, her touch light, her movements efficient yet filled with unspoken care. The sharp throb in his leg faded to a dull echo as he watched Naamah's hands, so steady and gentle as she worked. In that moment, she wasn't just a fellow survivor but a point of stillness in the chaos, a quiet strength that seemed to anchor his own weary spirit.

Enoch, too, gratefully submerged his wounded arm, feeling the pure water wash away the grime, though the unnatural chill from the Nephilim blade remained stubbornly beneath the surface.

For a few precious moments, they simply existed in the cool embrace of the river, the clean water washing not just mud from their skin but seeming to soothe the deeper weariness in their bones, cleansing some of the clinging taint of the marsh from their spirits.

A collective sigh of relief seemed to rise from the group, a shared moment of quiet restoration, of simple physical comfort intensely felt after so much hardship.

The river felt alive, benevolent, a tangible blessing against the harshness they had endured.

As they refilled their waterskins and drank deeply of its purity, Enoch stood gazing at the powerful eastward flow, a sense of dawning recognition stirring within him. Its clarity, its untainted vitality, the sheer abundance of healthy life it supported... it resonated with the descriptions preserved in the scrolls from Shem and with the oldest legends spoken of in the glade. He remembered the lore passed down by generations before him: four mighty rivers flowed out of Eden, the source of all life-giving water on Earth. The Pishon. The Gihon. The Tigris. The Euphrates. Knowing they traveled westward, toward the remembered direction of the Edenfire light, toward the hidden Garden itself... this *had* to be one of them. *The Gihon*, the name came to him with sudden, intuitive certainty, the river said to flow eastward from the lands bordering Eden.

He turned to the others, his weary face alight now with awe and renewed, fervent purpose. "This river," he announced, his voice filled with reverence that made them all look up from their drinking, "this is no ordinary stream we have found! Look at the life it carries! This flows from the very springs of the world, born near the garden itself! The scrolls of Shem spoke of it—this is the Gihon!"

He explained the staggering significance, his words painting a picture drawn from lore and the texts they had rescued. This great river flowed from the west, originating in the sacred region where Eden lay hidden, the region where Adam's Cave of Sorrows must surely be found. By following this river upstream, fighting against its powerful current, they would be traveling toward their ultimate goal. It was a living map, provided by the Creator Himself —a pathway of pure water leading back to its source.

The hope kindled by Enoch's revelation was tempered by the enormous challenge it presented. Standing by the vibrant, mighty river, they felt its powerful eastward flow—a current they now had to overcome. Traveling upstream, even along clear banks, would be difficult, especially with their still-mending injuries. And on foot, they would leave some trace for the Nephilim's tracking beasts.

It was Anak who broke the silence, his practical giant mind focusing on the challenge, his gaze resolute. He swept his eyes over his sons—Ronan still needing support, Kael strong but weary—then toward Methuselah leaning on his staff, and Enoch, whose arm bore the mark of the Nephilim blade. "The river is the path," he stated, his deep voice firm, echoing Enoch's conviction. "And it must also be our shield. We will travel *on* it, not merely beside it. The water will hide our passage completely, and defying the current's speed will hinder any who pursue." He turned to Kael. "We build a raft."

Under Anak's experienced direction, they began the arduous task, their movements now dictated by an urgent need for silence. The powerful, ringing blows of their axes were a luxury they could not afford, a sound that would echo through the valley and serve as a clear beacon to their pursuers. Instead, the Giants sought out massive, storm-felled trees near the riverbank, their wood sound and cured by time.

With quiet commands and immense, coordinated effort, Anak and Kael used their strength to haul the heavy timbers from the undergrowth to the water's edge. Ronan, despite his weakness, used his warrior's eye to direct the selection of the best logs for buoyancy and the strongest lashing points, his practical experience proving invaluable.

Methuselah and Naamah worked together, gathering tough, pliable vines. While Methuselah, with his strong hands, twisted and braided the vines into sturdy ropes for lashing the main logs, Naamah moved through the nearby thickets, carefully selecting the straightest, strongest branches she could find. She gathered a precious bundle of these straight shafts, her heart lifting with the prospect of crafting new arrows.

Enoch, though his arm throbbed, used his good hand to help trim smaller branches, his presence a quiet encouragement to their shared labor.

It took the better part of a full day of strenuous work, under the warm sun filtering through the healthy leaves, but by evening, a sturdy raft lay ready near the water's edge—thick logs lashed side-by-side with layers of interwoven vines and bark rope, wide enough and buoyant enough to carry them all, with a raised, drier section carefully constructed for Ronan.

Launching it onto the powerful Gihon required the giants' full, coordinated strength, pushing and levering the heavy structure into the water until it floated freely, tugging against the restraining ropes tied ashore. As the new dawn broke, painting the pure water with strokes of gold and rose, they embarked on the next phase of their journey.

Where the riverbanks were clear and the water shallow enough near the edge, Anak and Kael employed sheer brute force. Securing the ropes to the raft's front, they slung the lines over their shoulders like harnesses and stepped into the cold, rushing water, sometimes wading up to their chests, sometimes finding purchase on the bank itself. They leaned into the mammoth task like beasts of burden, muscles straining visibly, feet finding purchase on slippery rocks, digging deep into the mud of the bank, slowly, painstakingly hauling the heavy raft against the Gihon's powerful current.

Progress was a grueling battle. An hour of agonizing effort might gain them only a stone's throw of ground. Yet each pace was a victory—a step westward, upstream toward Eden's hidden border, putting tangible distance between them and the horrors left behind.

On the raft, Enoch, Naamah, Methuselah, and Ronan kept vigilant watch for submerged rocks or floating debris, fended off low-hanging willow branches with poles, and managed the tow lines, conserving their precious strength.

Naamah, however, found her purpose renewed. With her quiver slowly being refilled with arrows she painstakingly fletched and tipped with sharp stone flakes during their brief rests, she often stood near the front of the raft, her bow in hand. Her keen eyes would scan the lush riverbanks, and more than once, the sharp *twang* of her bowstring would break the silence, bringing down a deer or large bird that had come to the water's edge to drink, providing them with fresh, vital sustenance for their grueling journey.

But the banks were not always forgiving. Sheer cliffs often plunged directly into the swift water, or impenetrable thickets of thorns grew to the river's very edge, making towing impossible. When the shore offered no path forward, Anak resorted to a laborious technique of his people: kedging.

He would take Kael's heavy axe—its weight and edge perfect for the task—to which their longest, strongest rope was securely fastened. Bracing himself firmly on the front of the raft, or sometimes wading into the powerful current for a better angle, Anak would whirl the axe and rope around his head like a mighty sling, building incredible momentum, then launch it with focused, explosive force far upstream. The axe head would fly through the air, trailing the rope like a comet's tail, aimed with uncanny accuracy toward visible rock crevices on the far bank or sturdy-looking boulders breaking the river's surface midstream. Often it took several throws, the axe clanging uselessly off smooth rocks, forcing them to haul the heavy, dripping rope back in for another attempt. But eventually, their persistence would be rewarded, the axe head lodging fast with a solid *thunk*, wedging securely between boulders. With the axe serving as a temporary anchor far ahead, Anak, Kael, would haul hand over fist on the taut rope. Arduously, straining against the river's power, they would winch the heavy raft upstream toward the lodged axe.

As they drew alongside the lodged axe, Kael would roar, "Hold her! Now!"

Instantly, Methuselah and Naamah would throw their full weight against the two long poles lashed to the stern of the raft. Using them like giant levers, they would drive the sharpened tips deep into the rocky riverbed, their muscles straining, knuckles white. The poles would groan and vibrate under the strain as the river's full power fought to tear the raft away, the crude levers pinned between the heavy raft and the river bottom holding them precariously in place. This crucial, desperate pause gave Anak the precious seconds he needed to retrieve the axe, quickly coil the wet, heavy rope, and prepare the next throw, seeking another anchor point further up the demanding river.

Throw, lodge, pull. Retrieve. Throw, lodge, pull. Retrieve. The process was mind-numbingly exhausting, repeated countless times each day under the watchful sun. Yet they moved steadily westward, deeper into the unknown lands bordering Eden, following the living water toward its sacred source. The Gihon, the River of Life, though demanding great effort and unwavering resolve, was bearing them onward, a pathway of hope carved through a world still groaning under the weight of the Fall, leaving the poisoned lands and the haunting shadows farther behind with every hard-won cycle.

20

Where Rivers Meet

D ay after weary day, they fought their way upstream against the Gihon's unyielding current. The journey became a testament to sheer endurance, a slow, grinding battle measured in painstakingly gained raft lengths against the living water flowing from Eden's border.

The sun rose and set, but the days bled one into the next, a blur of exertion and exhaustion. Their only true calendar was the slow mending of their wounds under Kael's diligent care. Ronan's fever vanished, and though his crushed arm remained bound and useless, strength began to return to his weary frame.

Methuselah, graduating from a crutch to a staff, tested his leg with each step, the sharp agony of the wound dulling to a persistent throb. Enoch's arm remained a source of deep concern; an unnatural cold lingered in the flesh, a constant reminder of the Nephilim's touch, but he focused instead on the westward pull in his spirit and the guidance of the scrolls.

With Anak and Kael consumed by the effort of towing the raft and the others focused on healing, it was Naamah who sustained them. Her skills in hunting and foraging, once used for her own small family, now proved vital for the entire fellowship.

The grueling pace was a constant source of anxiety, yet the river remained their only viable path. For long stretches, the Gihon carved its way through deep, echoing canyons where sheer cliffs plunged directly into the swift water, offering no foothold for man or beast. Elsewhere, impenetrable thickets, dense as a woven wall, choked the shoreline for miles. Enoch knew any hunting party, even one as relentless as the Nephilim's, would be forced to navigate the same impossible terrain, making long, arduous detours inland that would cost them precious time and risk losing their scent completely. The river, for all its hostility, was a shield. It washed away their tracks and offered a single, direct path westward where the land offered none. Though days passed with no sign of the hunt, Anak remained a vigilant guardian, his eyes constantly scanning the banks for any unnatural disturbance. Hope grew not from the quiet behind them but from the land ahead. With every league gained westward, the landscape grew more vibrant and the air felt purer, reinforcing Enoch's certainty that they were drawing closer to the sacred borders of Eden.

One morning, ahead, through a lifting mist, the Gihon widened. Its powerful current calmed as it was joined by two other mighty rivers flowing from the north and south, converging into a single, colossal waterway. It was purer and more alive than anything Enoch had ever conceived, radiating a deep, primal power. The confluence itself was a place of staggering power and serene beauty, the distinct currents mingling in slow, deep, swirling eddies of impossible, crystalline clarity.

As they navigated the raft into this majestic expanse, the landscape transformed dramatically around them. The steep banks and dense forests they had struggled against gave way to a broad, impossibly beautiful valley stretching westward before them as far as the eye could see. Lush meadows, greener and softer than any spring pasture in the glade, rolled toward distant, welcoming foothills. Trees of unfamiliar grace and perfect form dotted the landscape, some laden with intricate blossoms of extraordinary color, others bearing strange, softly luminous fruit. Crystal-clear streams, tributaries born in the valley itself, meandered through the meadows like silver ribbons, feeding into the great river. The air here was soft, warm, fragrant, filled with the harmonious chime of birdsong more complex and lovely than any earthly melody Enoch had ever heard.

Herds of peaceful, uniquely beautiful animals—some recognizable in shape but possessing an unknown gentleness, others entirely new—grazed undisturbed in the meadows, lifting their heads to watch them pass with calm curiosity. It was a land overflowing with vibrant life, seemingly untouched by blight or corruption, radiating an almost palpable aura of deep peace and hallowed blessing.

The group poled the raft ashore onto a grassy bank, and as they did, a creature emerged from a grove of silvery trees nearby, more magnificent than any they had yet seen. It was a great stag, taller at the shoulder than a man, its coat the color of rich, dark earth. But its antlers seemed crafted from polished pearl, catching the valley's golden light in an iridescent sheen. It stood and watched them, its gaze direct and unnervingly intelligent.

Instinct, honed by a lifetime of hunting to survive, took over Naamah. Before a conscious thought could form, her bow was in her hand, an arrow nocked and drawn.

Such a beast... its hide, its meat, the sheer prize of it... It would be a trophy unlike any her people had ever claimed, a story for generations. But as she aimed, her breath held tight, she locked eyes with the creature. What she saw there shattered her focus. There was no fear in those large eyes. No animal panic. There was only a deep, familiar sorrow. She saw a creature that had witnessed unimaginable loss, a being that carried the grief of a broken world in its very posture. In its sorrowful gaze, with a jolt that nearly made her drop the bow, she saw a reflection of her own pain, her own loss.

Slowly, her arms trembling, she lowered her bow, the unloosed arrow suddenly feeling heavy and foolish in her hand. The great stag didn't bolt. It simply watched her, its head lowering slightly in acknowledgment.

Hesitantly, moved by an impulse she didn't understand, Naamah took a step forward, then another, her companions watching in silent astonishment. She reached the magnificent creature and, with a trembling hand, reached out and placed her palm gently on its broad, lowered head, between the pearlescent antlers. The stag's hide was warm and soft. It leaned into her touch for a brief moment, a silent communion of shared grief passing between the Daughter of Eve and a creature of the fallen world. In that moment of connection, Naamah's understanding of the world, of the Creator's love for *all* His creation, and the depth of the tragedy that had wounded it, shifted irrevocably.

Enoch stared, tears filling his eyes and spilling unheeded down his weathered cheeks, the open scrolls from Shem forgotten in his lap.

The confluence of the great rivers, this specific, sheltered valley nestled before the distant 'First Rampart' mountains—now clearly visible on the western horizon—matched precisely the descriptions from the scrolls.

"We are here," he whispered, his voice thick with overwhelming emotion and reverence. "This is the land just beyond Eden's sacred edge. The valley where Adam and Eve first settled after leaving the Garden. The place that witnessed the births of Cain and Abel and later, the profound hope brought by the arrival of Seth."

The realization washed over the others like a wave. Methuselah looked around, mouth agape in awe, the memory of the long, painful journey momentarily forgotten in the face of this breathtaking beauty. Anak and his sons surveyed the valley, recognizing instinctively the deep sanctity of this place.

Yet the valley, for all its abundant life and beauty, held no sign of human habitation. The deep peace was also the crushing peace of abandonment.

As they eased the raft ashore onto a grassy bank, the unspoken question hung heavy in the suddenly quiet air. Enoch voiced the grim answer he had gleaned from the scrolls of Shem and his growing understanding of their ancient enemy. "The Nephilim," he whispered, his voice filled with sorrow, gesturing toward the pristine valley that contrasted so sharply with the scarred lands they had passed through further east. "They could not abide this place. This living reminder of the Creator's goodness, this echo of Eden's harmony stands as a testament against their lies. Over centuries, they waged war, drove our ancestors slowly eastward, poisoned the surrounding lands," he indicated the direction they had come, "creating a desolate buffer zone, isolating this sacred valley, hoping its memory, its very existence, would be forgotten. They seek always to erase the memory of the world as it *should* be, as the Creator intended it."

The sheer normalcy, the vibrant health of this land, felt almost overwhelming now, charged with significance. It resonated with purity, a rightness that echoed in their souls, like a half-remembered dream of the world before the Fall, preserved here like a jewel.

Amidst groves of oaks and graceful willows stood other trees unlike any they had ever encountered before. Their bark seemed to shimmer with an inner light, and their leaves displayed impossible hues of living silver and warm gold alongside the deepest emerald green. Most astonishingly, they bore fruit that glowed softly with gentle luminescence—some were heavy clusters of purple spheres the size of a fist, others resembled teardrops hanging delicately from slender branches, still more were shaped like intricate, multi-faceted jewels pulsing with soft, shifting colors.

It was Methuselah who, his youthful hunger finally outweighing his caution, tentatively reached out and plucked one of the teardrop fruits. Enoch watched him lift it to his nose, inhaling deeply. A look of pure astonishment crossed Methuselah's face before he had even taken a bite. Emboldened, he bit into it.

The effect was instantaneous and startling. Methuselah's eyes widened in stunned delight, and a choked sound of pure, unadulterated pleasure escaped his lips. The deep weariness that had hunched his shoulders seemed to simply fall away, replaced by a sudden, vibrant energy. Color flooded his face.

"Father! Everyone!" he exclaimed, his voice no longer weary but filled with a new, powerful energy. He held out the half-eaten fruit, his hand steady. "You must taste this! It's... it's like eating sunlight!"

Seeing no ill effect, only radiant, joyous surprise on Methuselah's face, the others cautiously followed suit. Enoch chose a deep purple sphere, its skin cool and smooth to the touch. He took a bite. The taste was beyond description—not just delicious in an earthly sense, but somehow *complete*, nourishing his very spirit, seeming to wash away layers of ingrained weariness and sorrow. More than that, a tangible warmth spread through his own limbs, an invigorating energy that pushed back weeks of accumulated exhaustion in a single moment.

He looked up, breathless, and saw the same miracle reflected in the faces of his companions. He saw Naamah, her eyes wide, a genuine, wondrous smile spreading across her face, the deep shadow of her grief momentarily erased by a wave of pure, unburdened joy. He saw Anak straighten his weary shoulders, his great back no longer slumped with the weight of their journey, a low rumble of pure astonishment escaping his lips. It was more than food. It was a gift of life itself, a taste of the world's original goodness, miraculously preserved here on Eden's very threshold.

Enoch looked down at his injured arm in astonishment. The unnatural cold that had seeped into his flesh from the Nephilim black blade seemed to recede, replaced by a comforting, healing warmth flowing outward from his core. The edges of the wound, previously dark and sluggish despite Kael's care, now looked cleaner, tinged with a healthy pink.

Suddenly, Methuselah gasped, his hand flying to his splinted leg. Naamah, beside him, asked quickly, "Methuselah? Is it the pain?"

He shook his head, his eyes wide with utter disbelief as he looked up at his father. "My leg," he said, his voice filled with awe. "The ache...

It's not just better, it's *gone*. I can almost feel it mending beneath the skin."

But the most dramatic change was in Ronan. The weakened giant, who had been leaning heavily against Kael, pushed himself straighter, true color returning rapidly to his face, his eyes clearing completely of any lingering delirium. He reached out eagerly, without prompting, for another piece of fruit Kael offered him, chewing it with surprising, rediscovered strength.

Kael examined Ronan's arm with disbelief, then looked again at Enoch's rapidly improving wound, then stared at the glowing fruit remaining in his massive hand with amazement. "Creator's Breath!" He gave a slow shake of his head. "This is... this is beyond any herb, any healing art I have ever known or heard of. The life force concentrated in this fruit... it heals almost as you eat it! Ronan's strength has returned! And the venom... Enoch, the darkness, seems to be retreating from your arm!"

Overcome with bewildered wonder, they feasted. They ate until they were truly full, the miraculous fruit satisfying their deep hunger completely, leaving them feeling not heavy or sluggish but energized, vibrant, clear-headed, their bodies humming with renewed strength and vitality they hadn't felt since childhood. Laughter echoed again amongst them, lighter this time, freer, tinged with awe, as the sheer relief and unexpected, potent blessing washed over their weary souls. They understood now, without doubt, that this was a direct gift of this sacred place, a tangible taste of the world's original goodness, miraculously preserved here on Eden's very threshold.

Strengthened and revitalized in a way they hadn't thought possible just hours before, a deeper sense of awe and purpose settled upon them. This valley was indeed special, protected, and imbued with a life force that actively defied the corruption staining the rest of the fallen world. Now possessing renewed energy and clarity of mind, the desire to explore further, to understand the history held within this cradle of humanity before making the final ascent, burned even brighter.

They made a simple, temporary camp near the riverbank, intending only a brief rest to fully absorb the fruit's effects before pushing onward toward the mountains.

While exploring the immediate area for easily gathered firewood, they found the tangible echoes of the past Enoch had spoken of. Half-hidden beneath flowering vines near the stream, Naamah uncovered the foundation stones of simple, circular dwellings, impossibly old, radiating peace.

Further along, Methuselah's foot struck something hard buried in the rich earth—a beautifully crafted hand-plow blade, worn smooth by generations of use, a testament to peaceful cultivation.

And Enoch himself, drawn toward a shallow cave sheltered in the nearby hillside, discovered delicate carvings upon the inner wall—simple, moving figures planting grain, children playing freely, families gathered around depicted fires, hands raised toward the Creator. Simple scenes of life, faith, and family from the very dawn of time outside the lost Garden.

Touching the faded carvings, Enoch felt an almost unbearable connection across the centuries to these first children of Adam and Eve, his distant kin, who had lived here in the shadow of Eden. Here, they had loved, worked, farmed, and worshipped, clinging faithfully to the Creator's promise even in their exile, before the shadows lengthened further and the Nephilim's long war against truth began in earnest.

As dusk painted the sky in soft, peaceful pastels over the valley, they gathered by their small, smokeless fire, the dry wood burning clean and bright. They were closer than ever now to their final goal, standing in the very lands walked by the first men. The breathtaking beauty of the valley offered great solace, the miraculous fruit offered physical restoration, and the relics offered a tangible connection to their sacred past.

But the knowledge of why this place now lay empty and the ever-present memory of the hunt behind them served as potent reminders of the ongoing struggle. They looked westward, toward the majestic peaks of the First Rampart, silhouetted sharply now against the dying light. Somewhere within those looming mountains lay Adam's legacy, the Cave of Sorrows. They would rest this night, gather their renewed strength on this sacred ground, and prepare for the final ascent into the heart of the mystery, carrying the hope of Eden and the heavy burden of ages with them.

21

Creatures of Innocence

Revitalized by the miraculous fruit, the small company resumed its westward journey toward the serene peaks of the First Rampart. They moved through the Land of First Steps not as desperate fugitives but as pilgrims treading on sacred ground. Their steps were lighter, their spirits imbued with the valley's unique, lingering peace, though the knowledge of the hunters following them remained a sharp spur driving them onward.

The beauty intensified as they traveled deeper into the valley, following the course of a crystal-clear tributary stream toward the rising foothills. Lush meadows gave way to open woodlands where golden sunlight streamed through leaves of emerald and shimmering gold, illuminating mossy banks soft as velvet and carpets of unknown, star-like flowers that seemed to glow from within. The air itself was cleaner, purer than any they had ever breathed, humming with a gentle vitality and carrying harmonious scents that were both alien and deeply familiar. But it was the valley's inhabitants, the animals they encountered with increasing frequency, that captured their hearts and filled them with breathless wonder.

Creatures grazed peacefully in the meadows or rested beneath the perfect trees, often lifting their heads to watch the travelers pass, not with panic but with large, intelligent eyes holding no trace of fear, only a calm, insightful curiosity. There were herds of graceful deer, and flocks of birds with plumage like wildflowers landed on nearby branches without alarm, trilling complex, interwoven melodies that felt more like purposeful communication than simple calls. They saw creatures resembling the cattle and sheep known in other lands, but these were sleeker, healthier, gentler in aspect, their forms possessing an elegance, an inherent *rightness*, that spoke of an unmarred, original lineage. Once, startlingly, they came upon a great cat—built like a powerful lion but larger, sleeker, with a flowing mane like spun sunlight—resting on a sun-warmed rock. It opened great golden eyes, regarded them with a steady gaze that held no predatory hunger, only a kind of quiet dignity, before yawning and turning its magnificent head away with serene indifference.

These were animals behaving as Enoch had only heard described in the tales of Eden passed down in the glade—peaceful, trusting, living in effortless harmony. There was an undeniable awareness in their eyes, a depth of seeming understanding that startled the companions. They felt less like mere beasts driven by instinct and more like fellow inhabitants of a world operating under different, older rules.

Looking into the soft eyes of a young deer that allowed Naamah to gently stroke its muzzle, Enoch saw not just a startling innocence but also a deep, inexplicable sorrow—as if these creatures, too, somehow felt the grief of the Fall echoing through creation. The sight triggered a memory, a fragment from a scroll he had copied in Shem. He paused, closing his eyes, recalling the words of the ancient scribe: *"And the Enemy, in his long war against the Light, could not unmake what the Creator had wrought, so he sought instead to defile it. He taught his children to twist the beasts of the field, to breed them for savagery and malice, to poison the streams where they drank and salt the earth where they grazed, so that all creation would bear the scar of his hatred and forget the memory of its true Master."*

Enoch opened his eyes, his throat tightening with the clarity of it. These creatures were not perfect as they were in Eden; they were still subject to the sorrow of the Fall. But they were *unbroken*. They had been preserved here, on the very border of Eden's influence, spared the deliberate, systematic corruption and poisoning the Nephilim had unleashed upon the lands to the east. They were a living echo of the world as it was meant to be, a stark and painful contrast to the snarling, diseased beasts near Serpent Mountain. This inherent goodness, this quiet dignity, was what the Nephilim sought to erase from the world.

Following a clear stream, they began the gentle climb out of the valley. Guided by Enoch's meticulous deciphering of the scrolls—matching rock formations and tributary junctions from the ancient texts—they entered the foothills of the First Rampart.

The ascent grew steeper, the air cooler, scented now with pine and cedar. Here, they walked through a forest of a different order. These were trees of a scale that dwarfed the woods of their memory; cedars so large in girth that it would have taken their entire fellowship, human and giant, holding hands in a great circle to embrace just one. The lush valley floor gave way to rocky slopes covered in this primeval forest, a place untouched by time or axe.

A few nights later, as they camped in a sheltered ravine, the duty of tending the wounds fell to Kael. Ronan now slept soundly, his recovery slow but steady. Kael, however, was focused on Enoch's arm, which remained a deep concern. The cold, though held at bay by the Edenic fruit, still lingered, a dark stain beneath the skin. Kael worked with a quiet focus as he cleaned the wound and applied a fresh poultice of herbs and leaves.

Naamah, watching him, was struck again by the contrast. "Your hands know healing as well as they know the axe," she observed softly. "Among my people, that is a skill held by the women."

Kael paused, his work finished, looking at his own hands in the firelight. They were calloused and scarred from both the forge and the haft of his axe. "Among my people as well," he admitted. "The setting of bones, the knowledge of herbs, the stitching of wounds... this is the domain of the giantesses. My mother, Mara... she is the chief healer of the House of Anak. Her hands can coax life back from the very edge of the shadow."

He looked over at Ronan, who slept peacefully. "When we were boys, the other giantlings would gather around my father to learn the hammer and the spear. Ronan was always there, his heart eager for the warrior's path. He learned the songs of battle, the ways of breaking and felling." A faint, sad smile touched Kael's lips. "My own heart was rarely there. I was often found at my mother's side, watching her grind herbs, learning which roots drew out poison and which leaves cooled a fever. She taught me that a giant's strength is not only for breaking things."

He picked up a piece of wood, his thumb testing the grain. "My father taught us to shape iron with fire and hammer. I loved the craft of it, the way something new could be brought forth. But Ronan saw a weapon. I saw a tool to build a stronger home. He saw a shield to deflect a blow; I saw the curve of a plow that could turn the earth."

He met Naamah's curious gaze, his own eyes holding a deep, quiet conviction. "Our sires, the Shining Ones, they only knew how to unmake, to twist what the Creator had formed. Our mothers, the Daughters of Eve, knew how to nurture, to mend, to bring forth life. Ronan... he has always wrestled with the fire of our sires. I have always felt the pull of the earth from our mothers." He flexed his powerful hands. "It is a greater challenge to mend a broken bone than to break it. It takes more strength to build a wall that protects families than to tear one down."

With the first light of day, the fellowship continued their climb out of the valley floor. The stunning views across the valley spurred them onward despite their fatigue.

Finally, as the sun began its descent toward the western peaks, Enoch stopped, his breath catching. They stood on a high, sheltered plateau, surrounded by towering, weathered granite peaks that seemed to scrape the heavens. Below them, nestled in the plateau's heart, lay a hidden, bowl-shaped inner valley, perfectly shielded from winds. Standing sentinel across this inner valley rose a unique rock formation—a natural archway of stone, worn smooth by ages, draped with teeming, flowering vines.

"There," Enoch breathed, pointing with a trembling hand, his voice thick with overwhelming emotion. "The Guardian Stones... described in the record of Shem. The entrance... it must be near."

They descended into the inner valley. The air here felt still, quiet, imbued with a sense of antiquity, of sacredness that made them instinctively lower their voices.

Following a faint path that led toward the great stone arch, they found it. Set deep into the sheer cliff face beneath the arch's protective span, obscured by heavy curtains of flowering vines, was an opening. It wasn't large or imposing, just a dark, natural cleft in the rock, sealed not by doors or stonework but by time and divine will itself. Etched onto the stone lintel above the opening, almost eroded away but still visible to Enoch's searching eyes, was a simple symbol he recognized instantly—a mark representing Adam, the First Man.

They stood before it, the entire company silent, motionless, gazing into the dark opening.

Methuselah leaned on his staff, his youthful face filled with a mixture of awe and nervous trepidation. Naamah stood close beside him, her hand resting lightly, unconsciously, on his arm, her expression reflecting both deep reverence and anxious anticipation.

Anak, Kael, and Ronan formed a silent, protective semicircle behind them, their usual stoicism tinged now with deep, quiet respect for this sacred place. Enoch felt the crushing weight of centuries settle upon him, the culmination of generations of faith, sorrow, and hope. They had journeyed through corruption and desolation, faced monsters and madness, followed signs both divine and ancient, guided by faith, loss, and rediscovered words. And now, finally, they stood at the threshold—The Cave of Sorrows, Adam's repository, the place where the First Man, mourning the terrible loss of Paradise, had recorded the unvarnished truth of their beginning. The sacred legacy entrusted now to their keeping.

Before anyone could take another step toward the opening, Enoch raised his hand, palm outward. "Wait," he said, his voice quiet but firm, cutting through the heavy silence. He looked around the small, sheltered plateau before the cave entrance, his gaze settling on a large, naturally flat-topped boulder nearby, weathered smooth by time and elements. "Before we enter this most sacred place, before we seek the knowledge Adam left for us, we must first give thanks to the One Who guided us here."

He turned to the group, his eyes meeting each of theirs. "Bring forth the fruit we gathered in the valley below. What remains of the Creator's miraculous provision."

Hesitantly, understanding flickering in their eyes, they unslung their packs. The fruit, though diminished in quantity from their journey up the foothills, still glowed with its soft internal light, a stark, vibrant contrast to the gathering twilight settling over the high peaks.

As Enoch motioned for them to place it upon the flat boulder he had indicated as a makeshift altar, Kael spoke again, his voice troubled. "Enoch," the giant healer said, gesturing toward the precious, glowing fruit, "this is potent medicine, as we witnessed. It speeds our healing greatly—Ronan rallies still because of it, your own arm resists the chill far better, and Methuselah walks sooner than he should by rights. Should we not preserve what little we have left? This cave is unknown. We may face new dangers within, feasibly new wounds."

Anak nodded slow agreement, adding respectfully, "And an offering here... are you considering fire? At this height? As dusk falls? A flame will be a beacon visible across the entire valley below."

Enoch looked at the concerned faces of his companions, acknowledging the truth and practicality of their fears. He picked up one of the glowing fruits, feeling its gentle warmth, its vibrant pulse of life force. "Your wisdom is sound, Kael," he said softly. "This fruit *is* a wondrous gift, a powerful tool for the body. And your caution is wise, Anak."

He met Kael's eyes, his gaze clear and steady. "But *who* gave the fruit its power? Who wove such potent healing into its very flesh? The Creator is the Healer. This fruit," he held it up, its gentle light illuminating his face, "is merely His instrument, a tangible sign of the pure life that flows ultimately from Him, the same life that still touches and blesses the land near Eden's edge."

His gaze swept over all of them, earnest and clear, compelling. "The Deceiver's most potent lie, the one we saw enshrined in arrogance in the Serpent City, is that we are alone, adrift, that we must rely solely on our own strength, our own cunning, our own hoarded resources. That we must trust the *gifts*—be it miraculous fruit, forbidden knowledge, or brute power—more than the eternal Giver. That is the devious path to enslavement of the soul."

He placed the fruit back onto the rock with the others. "We need not light a fire, but we *will* make this offering. We lay down this precious gift, this potent tool of healing, acknowledging before we enter Adam's resting place that our life, our healing, our protection comes not from what we hold in our trembling hands but from the One who holds all creation in His." He gestured toward the softly glowing pile. "We thank Him for bringing us safely, miraculously, to this sacred place. We place our trust entirely in Him for the strength to enter, for the wisdom to understand what we find within, and for His continued provision for whatever comes next."

Enoch bowed his head, and after only a moment's hesitation this time, moved by his conviction and the memory of the doves, the others followed suit, bowing their heads around the makeshift altar.

No fire was lit by human hands, yet the pile of otherworldly fruit glowed gently on the stone in the fading twilight, a small, luminous beacon of pure faith against the encroaching night.

Enoch offered a simple, heartfelt prayer aloud, his voice resonating with quiet power in the stillness of the high plateau, filled with gratitude for their deliverance through countless perils, for the revealed history of Shem that connected them to this place, for Methuselah's impossible return, for the clear guidance that had brought them, finally, to this sacred threshold. He asked for wisdom, humility, and protection as they prepared to enter the cave, placing their trust, their lives, their future entirely, unreservedly, into the Creator's loving hands, acknowledging Him as the sole source of their hope and survival.

He finished speaking, the final "Amen" hanging heavy, expectant, in the sudden silence of the high plateau.

For a heartbeat, nothing happened, only the whisper of the wind around the peaks. Then, the very air itself seemed to crackle with unseen energy. A sound began, seemingly not from any direction but originating *everywhere* at once—a low, resonant hum that rapidly escalated into a deafening, terrifying roar like a thousand mighty winds converging precisely upon them. Simultaneously, a blinding, unbearable light flashed directly above the makeshift altar.

With cries of shock and pure terror, the entire party threw themselves flat on the ground, shielding their faces, pressing themselves against the cold earth. A pillar of fire, impossibly white-hot, swirling like a tornado, descended from the heavens with unimaginable speed, striking the flat boulder where the fruit lay. The heat was instantaneous and immense, washing over them even yards away, stealing the very breath from their lungs. The roaring wind generated by the vortex buffeted them, threatening to tear them from the ground and hurl them into the abyss.

Through squeezed eyelids, shielding hands, or moments when sheer terror forced their eyes open, they glimpsed the impossible: the fire consumed not only the glowing fruit but the massive granite boulder itself. The rock glowed for a fraction of a second, then seemed to dissolve, pulled upward into the heart of the fiery vortex. The pillar of fire burned with an intensity that seemed to purify the very air around them, a terrifying and awesome display of raw, untamed, and unbearable holiness.

And then, as suddenly as it had begun, it was over. The roar ceased. The blinding light vanished. The intense heat dissipated, leaving the twilight air feeling unnaturally cold by comparison.

A stunned silence fell, broken only by the pounding of their hearts and their ragged, trembling breaths. Slowly, one by one, they pushed themselves up from the ground. They stared, wide-eyed at the spot where the makeshift altar, the massive granite boulder, had stood only moments before.

There was *nothing*. No smoke lingered, no residual heat warmed the air, no scorch marks marred the surrounding earth or sparse grass, no fragments of melted rock, no lingering ash from the consumed fruit. The ground was simply... empty, undisturbed, as if the massive boulder and the offering had never existed.

The Creator had not just accepted their offering of trust; He had consumed it wholly, leaving behind undeniable, terrifying proof of His presence, His power, and His acceptance of their faith.

They looked at each other then, faces pale and awestruck in the fading light. The arguments about practicality, the fear of discovery, the reliance on earthly remedies—all seemed laughably insignificant now. They had stood, however briefly, however terrifyingly, in the consuming power of the Almighty Himself, and the experience had shaken them to their core, stripping away any lingering reliance on their own frail understanding or limited strength.

Humbled beyond measure, trembling still but filled now with a certainty that transcended all logic and fear, they turned together toward the dark, silent entrance of Adam's cave.

The path forward remained unknown, the hunters inevitably still pursued, but they would face whatever lay within, whatever lay ahead, knowing now, without a single shadow of a doubt, that they did not walk alone.

22

Adam's Testimony

Humbled and awestruck by the consuming fire on the makeshift altar outside, the companions turned toward the dark opening of the cave. The divine affirmation, terrifying as it was in its raw power, had also banished their practical fears, replacing them with a solemn, almost trembling sense of sacred purpose.

With Anak leading the way, his massive form moving with new-found reverence, carefully testing the ground, they lit torches. The flickering flames seemed inadequate against the darkness after the celestial fire outside. Taking deep breaths, they stepped together across the threshold into the Cave of Sorrows.

The air inside was cool and still, thick with the scent of dust and cold stone. A sorrow clung to the very atmosphere, the weight of the world's first heartbreak.

Deeper in, the darkness drank their torchlight, the flickering flames only hinting at vast, unseen chambers extending into the mountain's root.

As their eyes slowly adjusted, they saw that the smooth walls near the entrance were covered not with natural formations but with intricate paintings, rendered in a style utterly different from the cold, alien perfection of the Nephilim city or the stark, brutal simplicity of Cain's tomb. These images felt... human. Made with hands that knew love and sorrow, depicting essential truths remembered with aching clarity across lost ages.

The first great panel unfolded the story of Creation, breathtaking in its scope and beauty. Here was the Creator, depicted not as the shadowy tyrant of Nephilim lies but as a swirling vortex of cosmic, generative light and love, shaping swirling nebulae with outstretched hands, calling forth land and sea, tenderly crafting teeming varieties of animals and birds with infinite, joyful detail. Then, Man—Adam—formed from the dust, receiving the breath of life directly from the Creator, depicted standing tall and radiant with innocent wonder in a world bursting with vibrant, newly formed life.

Enoch felt tears spring to his eyes, blurring the pigments; it was the core story cherished in the glade, the foundation of all hope, brought vividly to life before him.

Further in, the cave walls opened onto a breathtaking panorama of the Garden itself—Eden as it truly was, painted with pigments derived from flowers and minerals unknown since that first age, still holding a vibrancy that defied the passage of time. It was depicted as a realm of impossible beauty and perfect, effortless peace. Crystal-clear rivers, four great streams originating from a central point of light, flowed through landscapes bursting with unimaginable life. Trees heavy with glowing fruit grew beside flowers that seemed to hum with soft, gentle light. Animals of all kinds imaginable moved through the scenes—majestic, golden-maned lions rested peacefully beside gentle lambs, great iridescent birds perched calmly near playful, silvery monkeys, even enormous, wise-looking serpents walked with graceful majesty through tall, flowering grasses—all dwelling together without fear, without predation, in perfect harmony. Adam and Eve walked through this paradise, their forms radiant with shared innocence and joy, tending the Garden not as a chore demanding sweat but as a delightful, interactive partnership with a world that yielded its abundance freely, joyfully.

They were shown naming the animals who approached without fear, laughing with pure delight, resting together under flowering bowers, their loving connection one of perfect trust and effortless companionship.

And permeating every scene, the Creator's tangible presence infused the very light, depicted as a warm, gentle, golden radiance that enveloped them, walked beside them, communed directly, intimately, with them in the cool of the day. This was not the gilded cage the Nephilim portrayed but a world brimming with boundless freedom, perfect love, and open, joyous fellowship with God.

The sheer, aching beauty of what was lost pierced Enoch's heart, and he saw the same sorrow reflected on the faces of his companions. Their torchlight seemed to illuminate not just pigments, but the deep, hidden wounds each of them carried.

He watched Methuselah stare, transfixed, at a panel showing Adam easily plucking radiant fruit from a low-hanging branch. He saw the wonder on his son's face, quickly followed by a shadow of confusion and longing. *He sees a world without the curse,* Enoch understood. *A life without the toil, the thorns, the constant struggle that has defined every moment of his own.*

His gaze shifted to Anak. The great Giant stood before a mural of the peaceful assembly of creatures, his massive shoulders slumped in a way Enoch had never seen before. The warrior's hands, which had so recently wielded a war hammer with devastating force, hung limp at his sides. He was not looking at the strength of the great beasts, but at their harmony—the lion resting with the lamb, the serpent gliding harmlessly through the grass. Enoch knew Anak was seeing a perfect natural order that stood as a stark, painful contrast to the brutal realities and internal, blood-born conflict of the corrupted world he knew so well.

Enoch's own heart ached with an almost unbearable longing as he looked upon the depiction of Adam and Eve walking and talking freely with the Creator's light, a yearning for that lost, effortless intimacy that was the very purpose of their creation.

* * *

Standing beside Naamah amidst the silent awe of the group, Methuselah found his own gaze drawn from the vibrant, painted scenes to the quiet depth of emotion on her face. He saw fresh tears tracking silently through the grime on her cheeks as she absorbed the depiction of perfect, innocent safety. A profound empathy, a recognition of their shared longing for a world without loss, moved him more than simple comfort. Hesitantly, he reached out and gently took her hand.

The contact was tentative, yet felt warm and firm in the cool cave air. He felt her hand tense in his, saw her flinch—a barely perceptible tensing of her shoulders as a lifetime of ingrained caution flared. For a heartbeat, he feared he had trespassed, but then she turned to meet his eyes in the flickering torchlight.

He held her gaze, trying to pour all the unspoken understanding, all the shared sorrow and newfound hope of their journey into that single look. He saw the sharp, defensive readiness in her eyes soften, replaced by a flicker of surprise, then a quiet, questioning trust that made his own heart ache with a gentle warmth.

That connection seemed to be what she needed. She turned her gaze from him back to the central mural, and he followed her line of sight to the portrayal of Adam and Eve walking hand-in-hand through luminous flowers, looking at each other with expressions of pure, unguarded love. And then, he understood. He saw the new tears that streamed down her face. He understood then that her grief was not just for her own lost father and brothers, but for the loss of this original design—a world of perfect love and absolute safety she had never known. The piercing beauty on the walls, he realized, was also a testament to all that had been so tragically thrown away.

Moving deeper into the cave system, the tone of the murals shifted dramatically, darkening. A new chamber opened, the paintings here taking on a more somber quality. One section depicted the heavens, hinting at discord amongst radiant beings—a central figure, Lucifer, depicted as breathtakingly beautiful but with eyes burning with fierce pride, subtly whispering dissent, turning other angelic beings away from the Creator's light, toward himself.

Then, the tragedy of the Fall unfolded with heartbreaking clarity. The Serpent—depicted here explicitly as Lucifer having taken the form of a powerful, beautiful, winged serpent, cunning and mesmerizingly deceptive—was shown speaking with Eve beside the forbidden Tree. The mural captured Eve's hesitation, the allure of the whispered lies, her eventual yielding, and the subsequent sharing with Adam. The very next scene was one of crushing shame: Adam and Eve huddled together beneath dark leaves, suddenly aware of their nakedness, their innocence shattered, hiding amidst the trees like frightened animals, their faces masks of terror and guilt as the Creator's light sought them out.

Methuselah stared, the heroic narrative peddled in the Serpent City temple revealed now as the hollow, blasphemous mockery it truly was.

The following panel depicted the Judgment, rendered with stark honesty but, crucially, interwoven with unmistakable threads of mercy. It depicted the Creator confronting the Serpent, promising his ultimate doom at the hands of the 'seed of the woman,' a promise of hope even as judgment fell.

They saw Adam and Eve, weeping before their Maker, receiving garments of skin—a covering provided by the very One they had disobeyed, requiring the shedding of innocent blood, the first death, a tangible sign of His sorrowful provision and the cost of sin, even as He banished them.

Adam and Eve were shown turning, leaving the Garden, looking back one last time with expressions of unbearable loss, shame, and dawning understanding of the magnitude of what their choice had cost not just themselves but all creation yet unborn.

And in the final, stark panel of this sequence, the way back was barred forever. Towering, impassive, awe-inspiring Cherubim, angelic beings radiating tremendous power and divine authority stood sentinel at the now-closed gate of Eden. In their hands, they wielded great swords that blazed with consuming, restless fire, turning every way like vortexes of light and heat, guarding the Tree of Life, sealing the path back to Paradise under the undeniable weight of righteous judgment. The depiction left no doubt: The break was complete, the loss absolute, the way back barred by Heaven's own power.

They moved silently onward, torches held low, drawn deeper still into the cave and into history. Another cavern opened, its walls telling the story of those first difficult years outside Eden, likely depicting the beautiful valley they had just discovered.

Life here was undeniably hard. Adam was shown sweating profusely, straining with unfamiliar tools to till resistant soil that now yielded sharp thorns alongside sparse grain. Eve was depicted enduring the sharp pains of childbirth yet holding her firstborn son, Cain, with fierce, protective love. Abel followed soon after, shown peacefully tending sheep in the valley's meadows.

The paintings showed the construction of simple shelters against the elements, families working together, offering the first animal sacrifices on rough stone altars, seeking communion with the Creator. His presence was still felt—shown as sunlight breaking dramatically through storm clouds—but the easy, walking-together companionship of the Garden was clearly gone, replaced by a more distant, sought-after, ritualized communion. There was joy here, love, the goodness of family establishing itself anew, but always shadowed by the memory of Eden's loss and the constant hardship of life in a fallen world.

The next chamber plunged into darker themes, depicting the first fruits of the Fall blossoming into deeper tragedy. It showed the growing discord between brothers: Cain's jealous, angry glare as his offering of earthly toil was rejected, while Abel's offering of blood sacrifice was accepted by a sign of fire from the Creator. Then, the brutal, heartbreaking depiction of the first murder—Cain striking down his trusting brother in the field, the very ground itself seeming to recoil, stained dark.

Following this, Cain was shown wandering alone, marked by the Creator for protection yet still an exile, being approached then by shadowy, persuasive figures—the fallen ones, followers of Lucifer already spreading their influence, offering Cain forbidden knowledge, occult power, promises of security apart from God. Cain was shown accepting their tutelage, turning his back fully on the Creator's way, guiding the building of his own city—a place of defiant self-reliance, dedicated to his name and the Serpent's glory.

Adjacent panels expanded on this growing corruption spreading through Cain's line and beyond. Ethereal, beautiful, but cold figures, the fallen 'sons of God,' were depicted descending from the heavens, captivating the 'daughters of Adam and Eve' with their displays of power and forbidden beauty. The murals depicted their unnatural, unholy union, leading to the birth of monstrous, powerful offspring—the first Nephilim, towering figures radiating dark strength and arcane power but entirely lacking the Creator's light in their eyes. These beings, alongside their fallen angelic fathers, were shown spreading violence, perversion, and tyranny across the land, teaching mankind warfare, sorcery, idolatry, and the worship of created things instead of the Creator.

Creation itself was shown groaning under this weight—animals turned unnaturally savage, plants grew twisted and poisonous, fear and death reigned, the very air seemed to thicken with spiritual darkness. It was Lucifer's shadow lengthening horrifically across the earth, attempting to twist and remake the world entirely into his own dark, tormented image.

Anak stared at these panels, recognizing the terrible source of the destructive pride and power that warred within his own lineage.

Finally, torches held high, trembling slightly now, they reached what seemed to be the cave's innermost, largest chamber. The murals here were epic, scaled beyond anything before, devastating in their scope. They depicted titanic, cosmic conflict—armies of brilliant light, radiant heavenly warriors wielding swords of flame, descending from the heavens to wage open war against the amassed, grotesque forces of Lucifer, his primary fallen angelic host, and their monstrous Nephilim offspring. The battle raged across the heavens and the face of the earth, depicted with terrifying power and celestial violence that dwarfed any earthly conflict.

Ultimately, inevitably, the forces of light prevailed. The climactic mural showed Lucifer himself, depicted now not as a radiant being but as a figure of terrible, consuming, shadowy power, being overcome by a figure of even greater light, bound in shimmering chains along with his lieutenants. They were then shown being cast down violently, physically imprisoned deep within the bowels of the earth—specifically, the murals indicated, beneath the jagged, shadowed peaks of Serpent Mountain, their ability to manifest tangible forms upon the earth decisively curtailed by divine judgment.

Accompanying text, painstakingly carved, explained that while these prime movers, the original rebels, were now bound and no longer permitted to take direct physical form to walk among or war against mankind as they once had, their evil influence was far from extinguished. Their spiritual darkness, their capacity to tempt, deceive, possess, and corrupt from their prison, remained potent. Furthermore, their offspring—the Nephilim and their children, the giants, alongside humans who willingly embraced the darkness—continued their imprisoned masters' work on the physical plane. Most chillingly, the final images showed these descendants, generations upon generations of them, tirelessly, obsessively digging into Serpent Mountain, chipping away endlessly at the living rock, seeking to breach the ancient prison and unleash their bound masters upon the world once more.

Malachi's words about the 'Great Work' beneath the mountain echoed with horrifying, sickening clarity. The Serpent City wasn't just a seat of corrupt power; it was an engine fueled by stolen lives, relentlessly dedicated to freeing, or at least re-empowering, the ultimate source of cosmic evil.

They stood in stunned, breathless silence, torchlight casting flickering shadows on the final, terrible images. They had found Adam's testimony, etched not just in sorrow and hope but in the stark, terrifying reality of a cosmic war still raging. They now understood the true nature of the enemy, the source of the corruption they had witnessed, the dark purpose of Serpent City, the tragic origins of the Nephilim and the giants, and the world-altering stakes involved. The knowledge was overwhelming, clarifying the vital importance of their quest while simultaneously revealing the terrifying power they stood against.

Beyond the final, chilling mural depicting the endless digging, Enoch noticed faint markings low on the far wall—not paint but carefully carved lines indicating a hidden recess, almost overlooked in the chamber's immensity. He traced them, recognizing symbols for 'Preserve' and 'Remember.'

With Anak's strength, they dislodged a section of rock that blended seamlessly with the cave wall, revealing a dry, cool, sealed chamber within. The air inside smelled incredibly still, as if time itself were held captive. Here, protected from the centuries of dampness and decay, lay carefully on stone shelves covered in preserved hides, scrolls crafted from some enduring, unknown material, and stacks of heavy clay tablets, covered end-to-end in the precise, deliberate, angular script of the First Man. Here was not just history painted on cave walls for remembrance but Adam's own words, his detailed account of life in Eden, the full tragedy of the Fall, his personal laments and confessions, his understanding of the prophecies, his unwavering, enduring hope in the Creator's ultimate promise—the tangible, written record they had crossed a broken world to find.

Enoch stood before the shelves, the sheer weight of recovered history, of answered prayer, pressing down on him. He reached out a trembling hand, his fingers brushing the edge of a brittle-looking scroll. He felt the burden settle fully onto his soul—not just to preserve this priceless knowledge but somehow to act upon it, to understand its whole meaning for his people, for the future, and to stand firm against the darkness still digging mercilessly from its prison far to the east.

They stood in stunned silence within the heart of the cave, torchlight flickering on murals depicting cosmic war and on the priceless, newly uncovered records of humanity's dawn.

They now understood the full scope of the conflict, the origins of their enemies, the true significance of Serpent Mountain, and the extreme, almost unbearable weight of the truth they now possessed. Adam's testimony, in both image and text, lay before them. The cave had yielded its deepest secrets; the terrifying question now was how to carry that truth, and these precious records, safely back into a world besieged by lies and rapidly succumbing to darkness.

23

The Seed of Seth

Surrounded by the silent, painted history of the world, Enoch felt inexplicably drawn to one particular scroll amongst the priceless records they had uncovered in the hidden chamber. Its polished hide casing felt different, smoother to the touch, possibly handled more often, more reverently, by the First Man himself. Unrolling it, Enoch felt it resonate with a familiar echo of the very vision that had first sent him out from the glade on this perilous quest.

With meticulous care, using fingers surprisingly steady despite the thrumming cold still present in his arm, he unrolled the brittle hide across a flat stone slab that might once have served Adam as a table.

Kael brought a torch closer, its warm light illuminating the dense, precise, archaic script. The others gathered around, sensing the importance of this particular document, listening intently as Enoch began to read aloud.

This was it. Not merely history but prophecy interwoven with it. Adam's own hand recounted the birth of Seth, born after Abel's tragic murder, described with sincere relief. Not just a replacement son but the *appointed seed*, the beginning of the chosen lineage through which God's promise—whispered in judgment upon the Serpent even as the sentence fell in the Garden—would find its ultimate fulfillment. Adam wrote, with humbling clarity, of the Creator's assurance: that from Seth's descendants, down through the ages, would one day arise the One—the Seed of the Woman—who would suffer in the conflict but ultimately crush the Serpent's head, breaking the curse of death, healing the deep wound of the Fall, and reopening the way to true, eternal life with the Creator, though the path back to the physical Garden itself remained barred by the Cherubim's flaming swords.

As Enoch read the final words, his voice trembling with the sheer weight of revelation, the ultimate purpose of their entire, hard-fought journey slammed into him with blinding, breathtaking clarity. It wasn't just about preserving history for its own sake. It wasn't merely about finding a lost cave filled with relics. It was about understanding, protecting, and ensuring the continuation of the sacred lineage itself—the thread of hope woven through fallen history, culminating in the promised Redeemer who alone could defeat their ancient enemy. The Nephilim, the Serpent's servants, sought to corrupt or destroy that specific line, to prevent the prophecy's fulfillment at all costs. The isolation of the glade, the faithfulness of lost Shem, their own desperate flight and miraculous survival—all were integral parts of this cosmic, ongoing struggle to preserve the Seed of Seth until the appointed time.

This, Enoch realized with growing awe, *this is why my ancestors fled. This is why we were preserved in secret. This is why I was sent.*

In that very moment of world-altering understanding, as his soul grappled with the immensity of the revelation, the vision seized him again—sudden, sharp, terrifyingly immediate.

He saw the valley below—the beautiful Land of First Steps—no longer peaceful. Invaded. The dark host from the Serpent City poured into it from the east, spreading out, searching. The reptilian hunting beasts strained violently at their chains, pulling their brutish giant handlers up the foothills, directly toward *this* mountain range, *this* hidden plateau. Below them, on their nightmare steeds, the Nephilim commanders directed the search with cold precision, their eyes sweeping upward, radiating imminent discovery.

They are here. The thought was a jolt of pure ice through Enoch's veins.

He gasped, stumbling back from the scroll, the vision vanishing, leaving icy terror and absolute urgency in its wake.

"They are here!" he cried out, his voice sharp, cutting through the cave's silence. "The hunters are in the valley! They ascend the foothills now! We have no time left!"

He turned, his gaze sweeping fiercely over his beloved companions, his decision made in that instant, swift and absolute, born of immediate necessity. "Methuselah! Naamah! Kael! Ronan!" he commanded, his voice leaving no room for argument or delay. "You must leave. *Now.* Flee eastward, back the way you came! You carry the truth of what you have seen and heard here—the story on these walls, the history confirmed by Adam's scroll, the Creator's promise, the Serpent's lies. This knowledge cannot die with us! You are the living witnesses! You must escape, tell the story, and keep the true hope alive in the hearts of men! That is your sacred burden now!"

Anak immediately grasped the terrible necessity, his face grim, nodding once to Enoch. "Kael! Ronan! Your duty is clear," he commanded his sons, his voice a deep rumble of authority. "Protect the Son of Enoch—he carries the Seedline. Protect the Daughter of Eve—she carries the memory. They *are* the future."

"No!" Methuselah cried out, stepping toward his father, his face stricken, aghast. "Father, I will not leave you! Never! We fight together, as we always have!"

"He's right!" Naamah pleaded, moving to stand beside Methuselah, her eyes darting between Enoch and Anak, fear warring with fierce loyalty. "We cannot abandon you! We face them with you!"

Kael and Ronan looked torn, glancing at their father with anguished eyes, then at Enoch, their faces etched with the terrible conflict of duty versus love. "Father," Kael protested, his voice rough, "we cannot leave you alone against such overwhelming force—"

"Silence!" Anak's voice boomed, the command echoing off the cave walls, cutting them off mid-protest. Yet his eyes, when he looked at his sons, at Methuselah, at Naamah, softened with a surfacing emotion none of them had witnessed in him before. He stepped forward, placing a massive, steadying hand on Kael's shoulder, another on Ronan's. "Listen to me," he said, his voice dropping lower, filled now not just with authority but with the quiet power of transformed faith. "Before this journey began, my life... the life of our people... was bound by pride, by brute strength, by the ever-present shadow of our Nephilim blood. We fought. We endured. We survived. But we served no purpose greater than ourselves, living only under the shadow of our cursed heritage."

He looked toward Enoch then, his gaze filled with deep, unwavering respect. "Learning from Enoch, hearing the Creator's truth echoed in Adam's own words in this sacred place... it has broken chains within my spirit I did not even know I carried. It has shown me a life, a hope, a purpose beyond anything my ancestors conceived or desired." His gaze returned to the young people. "This promise," he gestured toward Methuselah and Naamah, encompassing the lineage and the testimony they represented, "the hope for *all* peoples, carried forward in the line of Seth, witnessed now by the Daughter of Eve... *that* is what truly matters. That hope is greater than my life. It is greater than Enoch's life. It is greater than any one of us."

He looked lovingly at his sons. "This truth must survive, not just on scrolls but in *living hearts* that can carry it back into the darkness. Others *must* hear it. The future of this world depends upon it. Swear to me now." His voice became a command again, imbued with patriarchal authority. "Swear you will protect the Seed of Seth in Methuselah and the witness Naamah. Swear you will carry them safely away from this mountain, guard the story they carry with your very lives, and lay down those lives without hesitation before you let that living testimony fail. Swear it!"

Tears streamed unchecked down Kael's rugged face, mingling with the dust of the cave. Ronan, weak as he was, straightened his shoulders, his jaw set with painful resolve. Together, looking into their father's unwavering eyes, understanding the finality of his command, they spoke the oath, their deep voices thick with emotion but absolute. "We swear, Father. By the Creator's eternal name, we swear."

The farewells were achingly brief, heavy with love and the bitter understanding of sacrifice. Enoch gripped Methuselah fiercely one last time, forehead pressed against forehead. "Be strong, my son. Trust always in the Creator. Remember all you have seen here. "Live," his voice broke slightly, "and tell the story." Methuselah clung to him, choking back sobs, unable to form words. Anak embraced his sons, whispering words of pride and final instruction only they could hear. Methuselah and Naamah exchanged one last, long look—terror, sorrow, determination, love, and the terrifying weight of the future settling upon their young shoulders, all passing between them in that silent gaze.

"Go! NOW!" Enoch commanded again, his voice urgent, pushing them gently but firmly toward the narrow eastern passage leading out of the cave system.

He turned back to the stone slab, carefully rolling up the most precious scrolls containing Adam's words, securing them within his own pack. "Anak and I will ensure they follow *us*," he stated, his voice grim but resolute. He held up the bundled scrolls. "We head deeper west, toward Eden's very border. The Nephilim despise the Creator's truth above all else. They *hunger* for Adam's authentic record, either to destroy it completely or twist it further for their dark purposes. They will pursue the written word, the tangible proof, above all else. We will lead them away. We carry the bait."

With one last, heartbreaking glance back toward Enoch and Anak standing resolute at the cave mouth, Methuselah, Naamah, Kael, and Ronan turned and disappeared into the narrow mountain passage leading east, compelled by duty, grief, and a sacred oath to carry the living memory of Adam's testimony back toward a world desperately in need of its light.

Enoch and Anak stood alone for a moment at the entrance to Adam's cave, listening until the sounds of the departing group faded completely. Then Anak hefted his great war hammer, its iron head seeming to absorb the torchlight.

Enoch secured the scrolls carefully within his worn pack, gripping his staff firmly in his good hand. Turning their backs on the escaping future, they faced westward, toward the unknown perils at Eden's border, preparing to become the lure, the final defense for the truth embodied in Adam's scrolls, ready to meet the oncoming storm with nothing left but courage and faith.

24

Wrath at the Threshold

With the echoes of a heartbreaking farewell still heavy in the thin mountain air, Enoch and Anak turned from the cave. They scrambled back up the steep incline of the hidden inner valley, emerging once more onto the high, windswept ridge that overlooked the Land of First Steps below. From this vantage, they spared one last glance back at the sacred plateau, then turned resolutely westward. Instead of the path they had ascended, they began a perilous descent down the ridge's opposite face, a treacherous slope of scree and rock.

The scrolls containing Adam's testimony felt like both lead and light within Enoch's worn pack. Every step downward carried the weight of their decision—to be the lure, the decoy, drawing the inevitable storm of Nephilim rage onto themselves.

Below and behind them, the pristine silence of the Land of First Steps was brutally wiped out. Harsh shouts, the discordant clang of dark armor, the heavy, earth-shaking tread of giant feet, and the low, guttural, eager growls of the tracking beasts echoed up as the Nephilim host converged violently up the foothills. Enoch spared one brief glance back, seeing the dark figures swarming like enraged insects upward toward the plateau where Adam's cave lay hidden. He quickly turned away, setting his jaw, focusing only on the perilous path ahead, his heart heavy but resolute.

Let them waste their first rage on stone and paint, he prayed silently. *Creator, shield those who carry the living word eastward.*

* * *

The Nephilim commanders, Jotunn and Gilga, reached the cave entrance first. Their cold eyes took in the scene—the faint tracks leading away east and west, and the undeniable aura of sanctity clinging to the cave mouth. To them, the holy presence was a palpable offense, a hateful light in their encroaching darkness. With impatient snarls of command, giants and dark-armored soldiers shoved their way into the narrow cave opening, torches flaring, heavy hammers and axes held ready for destruction.

What they found within drove them into a frenzy of desecration. The simple, heartfelt murals depicting the Creator's boundless love, Eden's perfect harmony, and the unvarnished, damning truth of the Fall were an intolerable offense to their very being.

Roaring in incoherent fury, the corrupted giants swung their massive hammers, pulverizing the irreplaceable paintings depicting Creation's beauty. Soldiers hacked furiously at the painted walls with swords and axes, gouging away the gentle images of Adam and Eve's innocence, the depictions of the Creator's light, the hated prophecy of the Serpent's ultimate defeat. They ripped at the very rock face with brute force, driven by a burning hatred for the truth, seeking to obliterate every last trace of Adam's testimony, defiling the sacred space with mindless violence and impotent rage.

Outside, Gilga, radiating fury at finding the cave empty of his primary quarry but filled instead with these hated truths, dismounted his steed. His eyes fell on the precise spot where the offering had been consumed only hours before, where the rock altar itself had vanished into heavenly fire. Sensing the lingering residue of Divine power that resisted his own dark essence, he drew his sword—a magnificent blade of black, rippling metal that seemed to drink the light. With a sharp cry of anger and defiance, he swung the dark sword down with colossal force, aiming to break the very ground that had dared to witness the Creator's touch.

But the blow met something impossibly unyielding. Instead of cleaving rock or tearing earth, the dark Nephilim blade itself exploded upon impact with a blinding flash of contained dark energy and a high-pitched, dissonant scream of tortured, unmade power. Black shards flew like shrapnel. Gilga staggered back, clutching his hand, letting out a strangled howl of agony and utter disbelief as searing pain shot up his arm. The hilt smoked uselessly in his grasp, his weapon of dark power destroyed against the sanctified earth where true faith had made its stand.

Humiliated before his troops, his perfect face contorted with pain and rage, the Nephilim commander lashed out blindly. He whirled and struck one of his own hulking giant overseers standing nearby, a blow of pure, misdirected spite that sent the brute crashing lifelessly to the ground, silenced forever. At that precise moment, a sharp-eyed lookout posted on the upper plateau's edge pointed down toward the valley floor far below. "My lords! On the valley floor! Two figures, moving west!"

Gilga whirled, his eyes blazing, instantly forgetting his shattered pride. With a snarl, he moved with unnatural speed, scaling the short distance from the cave's inner valley up to the windswept ridge. From that high vantage, he followed the lookout's gesture, his enhanced vision straining across the distance. There they were. He could just make out the figures of Enoch and Anak, having used the precious time afforded by the cave's desecration to descend an unseen path from the ridge's opposite face, now reaching the relative cover of the valley floor.

They carried the scrolls; Gilga could almost feel the intolerable presence of that hated, elemental truth radiating from them even leagues away.

"After them!" Jotunn shrieked from atop his mount, his voice cracking with unrestrained fury, taking command of the chase. "All forces! Bring me the records they carry! Destroy the man and the giant! Leave nothing but dust! Go!"

The hunt resumed with terrifying ferocity.

* * *

Hearing the distant roars and thunderous commands echoing from the plateau high above, knowing without doubt they had been spotted, Enoch and Anak broke into a desperate run across the valley floor. The heartbreaking beauty of the place was now merely a backdrop to a frantic race against time and overwhelming power. "The fruit, Anak!" Enoch gasped, remembering its miraculous effect, pointing toward the glowing trees nearby.

Even as they ran, they snatched the otherworldly fruit from the low-hanging branches. They ate quickly, barely tasting the explosion of flavor, focusing only on the hoped-for effect. It was almost instantaneous. Enoch felt the draining cold in his arm lessen dramatically again, pushed back by a surge of vital warmth and unnatural energy. His deep weariness vanished, replaced by a strength and speed he hadn't felt since his prime. Beside him, Anak let out a grunt of surprised satisfaction as his own massive strides lengthened, fatigue burned away by the fruit's potent, life-giving force.

Fueled by the miraculous Edenic fruit, they ran full speed westward through the valley of primordial beauty, following the great river toward its source, toward Eden's border.

But the sounds of the baying hunt—the unique, terrifying roars of the tracking beasts, the angry shouts of soldiers, the heavy tread of giants—echoed from the mountains behind them, drawing closer with terrifying speed. They had successfully drawn the entire pursuit onto themselves, buying precious time for Methuselah, Naamah, and Anak's sons far to the east.

Now, the race toward the light, toward whatever lay beyond, had begun.

25

River of Remembrance

Obeying Enoch's final, desperate command, driven by the solemn oath sworn under the weight of prophecy and imminent danger, Kael led the small, heartbroken group eastward through the high, cold mountain passages. The air grew thinner, colder, as they put distance between themselves and Adam's cave.

Ronan leaned heavily on his brother, his face pale but resolute, enduring the difficult terrain without complaint.

Methuselah, using his sturdy staff now instead of a crutch, moved with grim determination, the sharp agony in his mended leg overshadowed by the raw, tearing ache of leaving his father to face the darkness alone.

Naamah walked beside him, her face a mask of controlled grief, her silence absolute as she carried the still-fresh wound of her family's fate and now the terrible burden of being the one chosen to endure, a living witness.

Each step away from the Cave of Sorrows, away from Enoch and Anak, felt like a betrayal, yet they pressed onward, the memory of Anak and Enoch's desperate urgency echoing in their minds.

After what felt like a week descending through shadowed clefts and across windswept saddles, they emerged once more from the harshness of the high peaks, back into the astonishing, unexpected beauty of the Land of First Steps. The same vibrant meadows, crystal streams, and peacefully grazing creatures greeted them below, the valley's serenity now offering a stark contrast to the turmoil raging within their hearts. Exhaustion gnawed at them, deepened by the emotional devastation of the separation. Spotting the fruit hanging heavy on the trees, they stopped, driven by instinct and desperate physical need.

They ate, the miraculous fruit once again flooding their weary bodies with warmth and immediate strength. Color returned more fully to Ronan's face, the lines of pain easing, and the constant throb in Methuselah's leg subsided significantly, allowing him more freedom of movement.

Kael carefully examined his brother's arm and Methuselah's leg; the healing, though still requiring much time, was undeniably accelerated by the fruit's potent life force. Recognizing this vital blessing as crucial for the long, uncertain journey ahead, they carefully gathered as much fruit as they could carry, packing it gently into their satchels alongside the last of the dried dove meat.

Strengthened, they continued eastward through the valley, the memory of the towering peaks of the First Rampart, holding their loved ones and Adam's secrets, receding slowly behind them.

Soon, the powerful sound of the great river's confluence reached them, and they emerged onto the grassy banks near the spot where the Gihon joined its sister rivers flowing from the hidden west. Here, the mighty combined current surged eastward, a powerful, undeniable force. Hope mingled uneasily with sorrow—the river that promised swift passage away from immediate danger also carried them irrevocably further from Enoch and Anak with every moment. They located their old raft, pulled ashore amongst the tall reeds where they had left it weeks before, surprisingly intact, weathered but sound. Kael immediately began checking the vine lashings, preparing to reinforce them for the journey downstream on the Gihon, assuming they would follow the path Enoch had instructed, back toward familiar lands.

Ronan rested nearby on the bank, watching his brother work.

Naamah stood gazing at the swirling waters where the great rivers met, her thoughts far away.

Methuselah, leaning on his staff, also watched the confluence, his mind still replaying the overwhelming revelations of Adam's cave, the sheer weight of the story they now carried pressing down on him. As he stared at the powerful currents merging and diverging, a strange dizziness swept over him, sudden and unexpected. The roar of the nearby waters seemed to fade, replaced by an internal rushing sound, a sense of detachment. The sunlit world shimmered, wavered... just as his father had described when visions came upon him.

He saw the rivers before him not as water but as flowing pathways of light and shadow, each carrying a different destiny. He saw their intended path eastward along the bright current of the Gihon, the route toward home. But as his vision followed it downstream, a darkness coalesced over it leagues away—a sense of ambush, of waiting danger lurking on that known route. Then, his inner gaze was pulled forcefully, irresistibly, toward one of the other great rivers flowing eastward from the confluence—the mighty Euphrates, its broad current bending away toward the southeast, plunging into lands entirely unknown to them, lands uncharted on any scroll they had seen in Shem. A clear, undeniable understanding flooded his mind, as certain and solid as the ground beneath his feet: *This way. Danger lies upon the known path. Safety, and the Creator's hidden purpose, lies down this river, into the unknown.*

The vision faded as quickly as it had come, leaving Methuselah gasping, blinking against the bright sunlight, his heart pounding not with fear this time but with startling conviction. He looked toward the powerful, unknown current of the Euphrates, then back at Kael, who was expertly tightening a vine lashing on the raft destined for the Gihon. "Wait!" Methuselah cried out, his voice sharp with newfound urgency.

Kael looked up, surprised by his tone. "What is it, Methuselah?"

"We... we cannot take the Gihon," Methuselah stammered, still shaken by the vision's intensity but his voice gaining conviction with each word. "I saw... a vision. Like my father described his own. There is danger waiting for us on that path. We must follow *this* river instead." He pointed decisively toward the broad, unfamiliar course of the Euphrates heading southeast.

Kael frowned deeply, the vine lashing going still in his massive hands. Methuselah's heart sank as he saw the familiar, pragmatic skepticism settle on the Giant's face. He could almost hear the objections forming—the duty to Anak's last command, the foolhardiness of trusting an unproven vision.

"A vision?" Kael questioned, his voice heavy with doubt. "Methuselah, your father's command was clear. Follow the Gihon... This other river flows into wilderness no one has mapped in generations."

Methuselah stood his ground, forcing his voice to remain steady against the Giant's imposing doubt. "My father also told me to trust the Creator's guidance! The Gihon path leads into a trap!"

Kael's gaze fell upon him then, heavy and searching, and Methuselah felt the full weight of his responsibility. He held the Giant's stare, praying the Creator would let his conviction show in his eyes, knowing everything depended on this moment. He watched as something shifted in Kael's expression. The hard skepticism didn't vanish, but it was joined by a flicker of something else... recognition, perhaps, or a memory of Enoch's own stubborn faith.

Then Kael turned his head, his gaze locking with Ronan's across the clearing. A silent, weighty conversation passed between the two brothers, a language of shared history to which Methuselah was not privy. He held his breath. He saw Ronan give a slow, almost imperceptible nod of assent.

Relief, sharp and sudden, coursed through Methuselah. He heard Kael let out a heavy sigh, the sound of a practical warrior yielding to a faith he could not deny. "The look in your eyes... it is your father's," Kael admitted gruffly, running a hand through his thick beard. "We questioned Enoch's path into the marsh, and the Creator vindicated his trust. We will trust this vision now, son of Enoch." He turned decisively away from the raft positioned for the Gihon. "We follow the Euphrates. May the Creator continue to guide your sight, for all our sakes."

A sense of responsibility, heavier than any physical burden Methuselah had ever known, settled upon him. He had not asked for this guidance, this mantle of vision inherited from his father, but the path had been undeniably shown.

With renewed, albeit apprehensive, purpose, Kael directed the repositioning of the sturdy raft toward the wide mouth of the great Euphrates.

Soon, with heavy hearts looking westward one last time, they pushed off into its powerful, unknown current. Leaving the Gihon behind, they headed not toward the memory of home but now into uncharted territory, guided only by a young man's first, unexpected vision and the perilous hope it represented.

* * *

Naamah sat near the raft's edge as the current swiftly carried them eastward, trailing a hand in the cool, clear water, watching the banks of the beautiful valley begin to slide past. Her mind, now that the immediate crisis of choosing a path was over, drifted achingly to memories of her family, moments that now seemed more like fragments of a forgotten, impossible dream than reality. The faces of her own lost men swam before her eyes—her strong father, whose calloused hands had always felt so safe; her brothers, Jared and Caleb, their laughter silenced too soon. And Malachi. Her twin. The word, unspoken for so long, resonated in her heart with a fresh, searing pain. His absence felt like a phantom limb, an ache that mirrored her own heartbeat, a missing part of her very soul.

For the first time since the terrible raid that had traumatized her world, she allowed a specific memory, one she had fiercely walled off in the deepest part of her heart, to surface fully. It was of a sun-drenched afternoon in their old valley, years ago. Her father was laughing, his deep voice booming, as he tossed a much younger, shrieking Malachi high into the air, catching him securely. Jared and Caleb were wrestling playfully in the grass nearby, their youthful shouts echoing, while she and Tirzah helped their mother prepare the evening meal, the air filled with the scent of roasting meat and her mother's gentle singing. A simple, ordinary moment of perfect, unbroken peace, of unquestioned safety and love. The sweetness of that memory now, so long suppressed, crashed over her with the force of a physical blow, making the current desolation even more stark.

Now Enoch and Anak, the wise father-figure and the mighty protector who had shown her such unexpected kindness and represented unwavering faith, were also gone, potentially sacrificing themselves at that very moment, far behind them in the western mountains. She felt the crushing weight of the story they now carried—the breathtaking truth of Creation, the seductive lies of the Serpent City, the enduring hope of the Creator's promise. It seemed too large, too vital for just the four of them—wounded and grieving—to bear safely back to a world drowning in darkness.

Sensing the heavy despair settling over the raft like the river mist, hearing Methuselah's choked sigh beside her as he continued to gaze westward toward the receding mountains that held his father, Naamah straightened her shoulders. Her voice when she spoke was quiet yet laced with the unbending steel forged in the crucible of her own survival, cutting through their shared silence. "Do not look back," she urged softly but firmly, her gaze meeting first Methuselah's anguished eyes, then Kael's grim, troubled face. "Remember *why* we are here. Remember *who* we honor by enduring."

Her voice gained strength, fueled by conviction born of pain. "Think of my brother, my *twin* brother, Malachi. He chose his end in those dark tunnels, believing we carried a light that *needed* to escape. Think of the generations who lived and died in lost Shem, preserving the scrolls, guarding the truth your father found." She looked toward the giant brothers. "Think of Anak. Think of Enoch. They chose to stand between us and the hunters. They chose to draw the storm away, to give *us* this chance. They offer their lives, *right now*, so that the truth survives, carried forward *in us*."

She looked intently at each of them, her dark eyes compelling. "We honor their sacrifice not by drowning in grief for what we leave behind but by fulfilling the sacred charge they laid upon us. We carry the story. We *are* the story now—the living record passed through fire and water. We must survive. We must endure this journey. We must *tell* it. Looking back now will only paralyze us, drown us in a sorrow that serves the enemy."

Her words, raw with her own pain yet potent with unwavering purpose, struck home, slicing through their individual griefs to the core of their shared duty. The internal storm of guilt and sorrow didn't vanish, but it stilled slightly, channeled now into forward-facing resolve.

Methuselah turned his gaze from the west to the unknown east stretching before them down the wide river, his jaw tightening with determination.

Ronan met Naamah's eyes and, after a long moment, gave a slow, solemn nod, acknowledging the heavy weight of their shared duty, the necessity of her comfort.

The raft drifted swiftly onward in the powerful eastward current of the mighty Euphrates. The tranquil, otherworldly beauty of the Land of First Steps glided past them like a poignant, fading dream. Inside the hearts of its passengers, the peace of the landscape warred fiercely with the inescapable turmoil of sacrifice, loss, and the chilling awareness of the unseen battle likely unfolding far to the west.

The great River of Remembrance, as it would be known in their own stories hereafter, carried them onward, eastward, away from the sacred echoes of Eden, bearing the fragile, costly hope of the future, away from the long, dark shadow of the past. Their journey home had begun, but it was a journey down an unknown path, forever marked by the price paid at Eden's threshold.

26

The Hunters and the Hunted

Enoch pushed his weary body forward, but each stride sent a jolt of fire up his injured arm. The pain finally overwhelmed him; his foot caught in the thick grass, and he stumbled, falling hard. He lay gasping, the world a blur of green and blue, until a great shadow fell over him. Anak's hand enveloped his good arm, lifting him effortlessly. "Carefully, Enoch," the giant's voice rumbled from above. "We must keep moving."

"No time for care now, my friend," Enoch breathed, straightening with painful effort, his eyes already scanning westward along the great river's course. "They soon will be upon us." He pushed himself forward, breaking into the fastest pace his throbbing arm allowed. Anak matched his stride easily, his expression grim, casting wary glances back toward the cliffs that walled the valley.

The sounds confirmed Enoch's urgency, echoing ominously in the wide valley. High above, harsh, guttural commands drifted down, followed by the unmistakable, chilling roars of the hunting beasts as they were unleashed upon their scent. Then came the clatter of dislodged rocks and ringing armor mixed with the heavy tread of giants as the pursuit began its reckless spill down the mountainside.

A sharp cry, followed by the sickening sound of impact, echoed from the cliffs behind them. They risked a glance back without breaking stride. Dark-armored figures were spilling down the rock face with a reckless speed that sent men plummeting to their deaths. High on the rim, silhouetted against the sky, the two Nephilim commanders observed the deadly descent with utter indifference.

"They drive their thralls like cattle falling from a cliff," Anak growled, his voice thick with contempt.

Life, even that of their own servants, is expendable, Enoch thought, sickened. Anak's hand gripped his shoulder, a firm, urgent pressure. "Come, Enoch. Let their cruelty fuel our flight, not root us here in horror."

That grim reminder spurred them onward. They pushed their weary bodies through the almost surreal beauty of the valley, the peace of the landscape a mocking counterpoint to the terror snapping at their heels. The healing nature of the miraculous fruit still aided them, lending stamina beyond their normal reserves, but the sharp, vibrant edge was undeniably fading.

A deep, bone-weary ache settled back into Enoch's muscles. His wounded arm throbbed with a menacing cold. Even Anak's breathing grew heavier, the ground shuddering slightly less forcefully with each stride.

The gift was for escape, a moment's grace, not endless flight, Enoch realized with growing dread. *Our own frail strength, or lack thereof, returns now.*

The sounds from behind grew louder, closer, terrifyingly distinct now. The roar of the tracking beasts was a savage chorus, echoing unnervingly through the otherwise peaceful valley, filled with blood-thirsty eagerness. The sharp, angry shouts of their handlers carried clearly on the wind. And beneath it all, the heavy, rhythmic *thump-THUMP-thump-THUMP* of pursuing giants shook the very earth they ran upon, a relentless drumbeat closing the distance. Panic, cold and sharp as ice water, threatened to overwhelm Enoch's hard-won resolve. *They are too fast... we cannot outrun them for much longer...*

Just as his breath grew ragged and seemed to tear at his lungs, just as his wounded arm felt like useless lead, just as despair began to whisper that their sacrifice might ultimately be in vain, they rounded a sharp bend near the river and saw it. Standing placidly near the water's edge, lifting its great, horned head from grazing on the sweet grass, was the massive ox-like creature. It watched them approach, its gaze unnervingly calm, holding none of the instinctive fear any normal beast would show toward two figures fleeing in such obvious terror.

"Anak... look," Enoch gasped out, leaning heavily on his staff, hope warring fiercely with disbelief.

The giant slowed too, pulling up beside Enoch, his eyes fixed on the creature, a look of deep respect, almost reverence, softening his harsh, weathered features. "The Old Ones of the earth," Anak murmured, his voice hushed with awe. "They feel the Creator's touch on this land still."

As Enoch met the creature's deep gaze, he felt again that strange, powerful flicker of understanding, that sense of shared creation groaning under the weight of corruption. He saw not just an animal but a fellow being, aware in its own silent way of the encroaching darkness pursuing them, recognizing the light they carried, however faintly. The great beast lowered its horned head slightly, took a deliberate step toward them, and nudged Enoch gently with its broad, warm muzzle. Then, with deliberation, it shifted its huge weight, dipping its powerful shoulder in a clear, unmistakable invitation.

"It... it offers aid?" Enoch whispered again, tears starting in his eyes from relief and wonder.

"A gift," Anak confirmed, his voice filled with certainty, placing a hand on the creature's thick, warm fur. "From this land, blessed still by the Creator despite the Fall. Accept it, Enoch. You cannot run much further like this. We must use every blessing given."

Gratitude, fierce and overwhelming, swelled in Enoch's heart, pushing back the immediate terror. With Anak's strong, careful assistance, he painfully pulled himself onto the creature's broad, warm back, gripping its thick, earth-colored fur tightly for balance. The beast accepted his weight without protest, shifting slightly beneath him, its deep eyes fixed calmly westward. With Anak once again striding powerfully alongside, it began moving westward at a steady, ground-covering run that immediately began to put more precious distance between them and the growing cacophony behind.

This unexpected blessing, this moment of quiet grace amidst the desperate flight, lent Enoch vital respite, conserving his waning strength.

Yet, even with this aid, the sounds of the hunt were drawing closer on the evening air. The savage baying of the beasts echoed nearer now, reverberating through the trees lining the river, answered by the frustrated roars of their giant handlers. The heavy tread of the pursuing giants was a constant drumbeat on the earth behind them. Time, bought at a significant cost, was running out.

Eden's border lay somewhere ahead in the fading light, but the hunters were closing fast, their dark shadows stretching long across the beautiful valley floor, threatening to engulf the fading light of day and the light of hope itself.

27

Anak's Stand

Westward they raced, Enoch clinging low to the broad back of the gentle beast, its powerful gait eating up the ground, Anak running alongside, the great river a silver ribbon beside them in the rapidly fading light. But the sounds of the hunt swelled behind them, growing terrifyingly close. The savage, hungry noises of the tracking beasts were no longer a distant echo but a present, visceral reality, punctuated by the harsh shouts of their handlers urging them onward. The ground itself vibrated with the heavy, rhythmic tread of beast and giants closing the distance like an avalanche. Glancing back over his shoulder, Enoch saw the first dark, swift shapes emerging from the tree line barely more than a spear throw behind them, moving with the unnatural speed of creatures driven by dark power.

"They are upon us!" Enoch cried, his heart sinking like a stone. "Anak, we cannot outpace those beasts!"

He saw the look then in Anak's eyes as the giant turned his head, confirming the pursuit's proximity—a deep well of sorrow mixed with a sudden, fierce, unwavering resolve that seemed to solidify his form. The giant met Enoch's horrified gaze for a fraction of a second, and in that instant, a terrible understanding passed between them—the culmination of their shared journey, their unlikely friendship, their unified faith. *He intends to make his stand. Here. Now.*

"Anak, no! We stay together!" Enoch shouted desperately, trying futilely to rein in the ox, to turn back toward his friend.

But the giant was already moving, his decision absolute. With a tremendous roar that echoed not just grief but also fierce, protective determination, Anak slapped the flank of the ox hard. The startled creature, already sensing the imminent danger closing behind, surged forward into a sprint, carrying the protesting, heartbroken Enoch rapidly away westward down the valley, toward the unseen border of Eden.

Anak skidded to a halt on the valley floor, deliberately turning his form to face the oncoming tide of darkness. With a fluid, powerful motion born of centuries of war, he swung the massive hammer from his back, its heavy iron head gleaming menacingly in the deepening twilight. He planted his feet wide, gripping the hammer haft in both hands, a solitary, colossal, defiant figure silhouetted against the serene beauty of the valley, ready to meet the storm head-on.

The first wave hit him like a breaking tide of teeth and claws. Two massive, low-slung reptilian tracking beasts, slavering and roaring with bloodlust, leaped toward him simultaneously, urged on by their handlers and a knot of dark-armored soldiers rushing forward with heavy spears leveled. Anak met them with a bellowing war cry, a sound dredged from the depths of giantish history, that seemed to shake the very air and momentarily halted the charge.

His hammer became a blur of devastating motion. The first beast lunged, jaws wide, snapping, only to meet the crushing, irresistible force of the hammer head square on its armored skull, collapsing instantly in a heap of crushed bone and silenced snarls. The second beast swiped with massive claws aimed at Anak's legs, but the giant sidestepped with surprising agility for his size, bringing the hammer down in a devastating, two-handed overhead arc that split through the creature's spine mid-leap, its death roar choked off in a wet gurgle.

He didn't pause, didn't allow them a moment to regroup. Turning immediately on the handlers and soldiers surging around the fallen beasts, his movements became a terrifying whirlwind of destruction. The Nephilim had bred these giants for battle, but they were now facing a true ancient imbued with righteous fury. One after another fell with sickening crunches of broken limbs and crushed helms. Armored soldiers were scattered like dry leaves in a gale, their spears snapping uselessly against his might or glancing off his gauntlets or thick hide clothing, their bodies broken and tossed aside by the hammer's brutal, sweeping impacts. For those few, terrible minutes, Anak unleashed the full, untamed, terrible strength of his lineage, channeled now not by the cold pride of his fallen heritage but by fierce loyalty and sacrificial love.

The main body of the pursuit—the remaining giants, soldiers, and the two Nephilim commanders on their steeds—arrived then, halting abruptly at the edge of the horrifying carnage. Piles of dead and dying lay heaped around Anak's feet amidst broken weapons and spreading pools of dark blood. The tracking beasts were silenced, their handlers broken. The giant stood alone amidst the ruin, breathing heavily, his great chest heaving, his war hammer dripping, utterly defiant.

High on their nightmare steeds, Jotunn and Gilga surveyed the scene. Gilga, the one whose sword had shattered at the cave entrance, merely looked annoyed at the delay and the loss of assets. But Jotunn, the slayer of Anak's kin in ages past, regarded Anak with a flicker of cold, predatory amusement. This was a ghost from a war he thought long won. "Anak, son of Haran," Jotunn's voice slithered through the air, unnaturally clear. "I led three wars against your people. I broke your cities and scattered your kin to the winds until our masters turned their gaze to a greater prize—the last of Seth's pathetic children. I believed you were wise enough to remain in your little valley. To find you here, guarding *them*... it is an unexpected, final pleasure." He gestured dismissively toward the west, where Enoch had vanished. "Such strength... wasted in service to a failed Creator and His fleeting human pets. Stand aside. A place of honor awaits you in the true order we are building."

Anak straightened his weary frame, his exhaustion momentarily forgotten, his voice booming back across the twilight valley, clear, strong, filled with utter conviction. "Honor? You speak to *me* of honor, spawn of lies?" His voice dripped with contempt. "I have *seen* the 'order' you build—glittering cities built on the crushed bones of slaves! Knowledge twisted into tools of enslavement and destruction! Beauty corrupted into hollow, soul-killing deception!" He slammed the butt of his heavy hammer onto the ground, making the earth tremble. "I stand with Enoch, son of Adam, carrier of the true history! I stand for the Creator, who fashioned this beautiful world," he swept his hand toward the vibrant, living valley around them, glowing softly in the dusk, "a world *you* and your fallen, chained master seek only to defile, dominate, and devour!"

He glared toward Jotunn, his eyes blazing with righteous fire. "Your promises are *ashes*, deceitful one, just as Cain discovered too late! Your power is built *entirely* on fear and lies! The Creator offers life, truth, and redemption! I choose Him! I choose my friends! I choose hope!"

His words, raw and powerful, echoed in the sudden, stunned silence, carrying across the field of carnage. Anak saw the undeniable effect of his words on the surrounding pursuers—the remaining giants shifted uneasily on their feet, their dull eyes showing flickers of thought, of conflict; the dark-armored human soldiers looked down, pointedly avoiding the Nephilim commanders' gaze. Whispers of doubt, confusion, perhaps even a spark of reluctant admiration for the lone giant's courage warred visibly with their ingrained fear. Anak's defiant truth had struck a chord, a dangerous dissonance challenging the lies that held them captive.

Anak saw Jotunn's gaze flicker from him to the wavering soldiers, and the cold amusement on the Nephilim's face vanished, replaced instantly by a flash of pure, icy rage. The subtle shift in the ranks had not gone unnoticed. Anak understood in that moment: his defiance was no longer a simple obstacle to be overcome; it had become a dangerous contagion, seeding doubt among Jotunn's followers at a critical moment. With a fluid, serpentine grace, Jotunn dismounted his nightmare steed. In his hand, a dark blade materialized—long, slender, shimmering with a captive, internal darkness that seemed colder, more venomous, than Enoch's wound. "You have chosen poorly, relic of a failed creation," Jotunn hissed, advancing toward Anak across the blood-soaked grass. "Your Creator abandoned this world to its fate long ago. Allow me to hasten your reunion with oblivion."

The duel began—a final, desperate clash of titans beneath the darkening sky. Anak, mighty and fueled by righteous fury, swung his great war hammer with earth-shaking force, each blow whistling through the air, capable of pulverizing stone and shield. But he was weary now, bleeding from several minor wounds sustained in the first onslaught, his strength beginning to flag. His movements, while still powerful, lacked their initial explosive speed.

Jotunn, by contrast, moved like smoke and shadow given form, impossibly fast, his dark blade a flickering blur of deadly light. He didn't meet Anak's overwhelming force head-on; instead, he weaved and dodged with effortless grace, his sword darting in like a viper's strike, leaving searing, dark wounds that seemed to bleed sluggishly and radiate cold wherever they touched.

Anak roared, fighting with the fierce heart of a cornered lion, defending the truth, defending his friends' escape, with his very lifeblood. He landed blows that glanced off Jotunn's dark armor with showers of sparks, blows that would have felled any other creature instantly. But Jotunn seemed almost untouchable, his movements guided by evil power and skill, relentlessly wearing down the giant's defenses. Slowly, inexorably, Anak was driven back. A deep cut opened on his thigh, slowing him further. Another burning slash across his shoulder weakened his hammer swing. Yet he fought on, wholly defiant to the last, his eyes never leaving the Nephilim's cold face, his presence a solitary bulwark protecting the westward path.

Then, Jotunn saw his opening. Feinting with impossible speed to Anak's left, he darted to the right as the giant reacted, his dark blade flashing upward in a wicked, unstoppable arc that slipped inside Anak's weary guard. The blade struck deep, punching through hide and muscle, burying itself in the giant's mighty chest. Anak staggered back, a look of shocked, pained surprise widening his eyes. He dropped his hammer with a resounding thump. His hands went to the wound. He looked westward one last time, seeing in his mind's eye Enoch's distant, fleeing form carrying the scrolls, seeing his sons carrying the testimony eastward. Then, with a final, shuddering sigh that seemed to carry the weight of ages, the great giant, King of the Anakim, redeemed by faith, defender of the Seed of Seth, crashed heavily to the ground, silent and entirely still.

28

Night on the Euphrates

The great river bore them swiftly eastward, carrying them away from the valley that echoed both Eden's lost peace and Adam's deep sorrow. On the rough-hewn raft, a heavy silence settled as twilight deepened into night, broken only by the ceaseless rush of the powerful water against the logs and Ronan's occasional soft sigh against the pain in his mending arm. They floated onward, adrift on a current of shared grief and unwavering duty.

Methuselah watched Kael check the bindings on Ronan's arm with a gentle competence, saw the grim set of Ronan's jaw as he endured the discomfort without complaint. In the quiet strength, the steadfast loyalty of the giant brothers, their solemn commitment to the oath sworn to their father, Methuselah saw Anak's protective loyalty living on. It was a legacy that both humbled him and strengthened his own faltering resolve. They were truly adrift now, carrying a truth purchased at an unbearable price.

As darkness fell, rendering the riverbanks invisible shadows, Kael peered ahead into the blackness, his giant eyes discerning more than human sight could manage, yet still limited. "We should make shore soon," he suggested, his practical gaze scanning the unseen banks, listening intently to the river's voice. "Traveling this unknown river in absolute darkness is perilous."

"No," Methuselah interrupted, the word quiet but firm, surprising himself as much as the others with its decisiveness. He met Kael's questioning gaze across the raft. "Our fathers bought us precious time, likely costing them their lives. We must use every moment of it. The current is swift, day and night. We travel on."

Kael hesitated, his gaze shifting toward Ronan, then to Naamah, then back to Methuselah. "It is dangerous," Kael warned. "Rapids we cannot see, submerged rocks, unexpected falls... we will be blind to them until we are upon them."

"We will listen," Naamah said softly, finding her voice from the shadows, her own resilience surfacing. "We will take turns keeping watch. We have come through deeper darkness before." Her eyes met Methuselah's across the raft, and in that brief glance, she offered more than agreement. It was a clear acknowledgment of the new weight he carried, a silent affirmation of the leader he was becoming.

Kael considered their faces, their resolve, then gave a slow, reluctant nod. "Agreed. We travel through the night. Two on watch at all times, at the front. Listen," he commanded, his voice serious, "listen for *any* change in the river's voice. Any quickening, any roar."

Their only guide was a sliver of moon, just enough to distinguish the black water from the blacker shores. But as the river entered a narrow gorge, they watched the sky begin to disappear. The canyon walls rose like sheer, dark curtains, blotting out the stars one by one until finally, the moon itself was gone. The darkness that fell was absolute, leaving them blind, their world reduced to the chilling rush of the current and the feel of the raft vibrating beneath their feet. They strained their ears, listening past the river's steady roar for the telltale crescendo of rapids or the treacherous whisper of water over submerged obstacles. Kael and Methuselah had taken the first watch, peering into the impenetrable darkness ahead, gripping crude poles Kael had cut, ready to fend off unseen debris or push away from looming rocks. Naamah relieved Methuselah after many hours, her keen senses, honed by a lifetime of survival, alert to every nuance of sound and current, while Ronan rested fitfully, murmuring occasionally in his sleep.

For hours, the river flowed powerfully but, thankfully, smoothly through the gorge. Then, almost imperceptibly at first, the deep, steady murmur of the current began to change. It grew louder, sharper, taking on an angry, guttural edge. The raft began to move faster, pulled forward with increasing, alarming speed. The air was filled with fine, cold spray. "Rapids!" Kael bellowed from the front, his voice barely audible above the rising roar ahead. "Hold fast! Brace yourselves!"

Almost immediately, they were plunged into roaring, violent chaos. The river narrowed further, funneling them into a churning, boiling torrent of whitewater invisible in the blackness. The sturdy raft bucked violently beneath them, spinning like a leaf caught in a whirlpool. Cold, heavy waves crashed over the logs, soaking them and tearing at their desperate grips. Shouts were swallowed, useless, by the deafening roar. They fought blindly to keep the raft oriented, using the poles to push off jagged rocks that materialized suddenly out of the blackness. Control was terrifyingly impossible.

An unseen rock slammed into the side of the raft, lifting it high and tilting it perilously. Naamah cried out as her grip was torn loose, and she was flung sideways, vanishing into the raging, icy black water.

"Naamah!" Methuselah screamed, raw terror eclipsing his own struggle. He saw her dark shape surface, gasping, before the current seized her, pulling her down. For a single, horrifying heartbeat, he was back at the first river, a helpless boy being dragged toward the falls. Every instinct screamed at him to cling to the raft, to survive. But seeing Naamah's pale face disappear into the churning darkness ignited a different fire. This was not the impulsive leap of a boy seeking glory; it was the calculated choice of a man refusing to lose anyone else. Ignoring the searing protest from his injured leg, he lunged for the safety rope, grasped it tightly, and threw himself into the violent water after her.

The shock of the icy water was a physical blow, stealing his breath. The powerful current seized him instantly, not just pulling him under but sucking him down into a violent, churning abyss. He was spun end over end in the blackness, a helpless passenger in the river's cold fury, his limbs striking unseen rocks. He lost all sense of up or down, the rope a violent, jerking tether to a world he had left. Then, as suddenly as it had grabbed him, the river's grip seemed to lessen. He fought upward, lungs screaming for air, and burst through the surface, gasping and disoriented. His first frantic thought was for Naamah. He scanned the churning darkness and saw her—a pale face, arms struggling weakly—being pulled inexorably toward a large, jagged rock midstream. With adrenaline surging through him, born of fear and something deeper, he fought the current, hauling himself along the rope with one arm, reaching for her with the other. He grabbed a handful of her tunic, pulling her close. Ahead of them in the darkness, the raft struck a submerged rock with a sickening crack of splintering wood. Before he could brace himself, the current slammed them hard into the side of the disintegrating vessel, plunging them into the chaos of breaking logs and raging water.

Methuselah found himself clinging desperately to Naamah with one arm, the precious safety rope still miraculously clenched in the other, gasping for air as cold waves crashed over them, the submerged rock beneath his feet offering treacherous purchase. Kael roared nearby in the chaos, and Methuselah glimpsed the massive giant fighting his way through the torrent toward Ronan, who clung to a large, bobbing log Kael had managed to secure him to. He saw Kael reach his brother, lash him more securely to the log, then begin battling his own way toward a glimpse of sandy shore visible in the faint starlight just beyond the worst of the churning rapids.

Methuselah knew he couldn't hold onto the rock long against the current's power, especially with Naamah's weight relying on him. He found a better purchase on the submerged rock shelf, pulling Naamah closer, trying to shield her from the current's full, numbing force with his own body. "Hold... onto me!" he choked out over the roar of the water. Using the rope as leverage and kicking powerfully with his good leg, he began the muscle-burning process of pulling them both, inch by inch, toward the same small strip of shore Kael fought for.

Finally, muscles screaming in protest, his injured leg throbbing with fiery pain, his feet touched yielding sand and gravel. He dragged Naamah, who was coughing and sputtering water, the last few feet out of the river's greedy grasp, collapsing beside her onto the small, dark beach, utterly spent. Moments later, Kael emerged from the river nearby, half-carrying, half-dragging Ronan onto the sand before collapsing himself, great chest heaving.

They lay there for a long moment in the darkness, the terrifying roar of the rapids a constant reminder of their violent passage. Their bodies shivered uncontrollably from the cold and adrenaline's aftermath. They had lost the raft. They had lost most of their remaining, precious supplies. They had lost their swift passage east. But they were alive. Against all odds, all four of them.

Slowly, painfully, Naamah pushed herself up onto her elbows, turning toward Methuselah who lay beside her, still gasping for breath, his face pale in the dim starlight. Their eyes met across the small space separating them. The raw terror of the rapids, the shared, intimate brush with death, the instinctive, selfless nature of his immediate rescue—it stripped away all pretense, all hesitation, all the carefully constructed walls around her heart. Overcome with a wave of relief, bone-deep gratitude, and emotion too powerful and complex for words in that moment, Naamah leaned forward and pressed her cold lips against his. It was a kiss born of shared desperation and undeniable, dawning affection, surprising yet feeling wholly, fundamentally right in the deep darkness after the preceding chaos.

Methuselah froze for a second in stunned shock, then responded instinctively, the unexpected, gentle tenderness a stark, almost unbelievable contrast to the violence they had just endured. When they finally drew apart, breathless, the intensity of the moment hung palpably between them in the cool night air.

Then, a weak, rasping chuckle came from nearby. Ronan, propped up now against Kael's broad back, was watching them, a knowing smile on his pale face.

Kael, seeing the two youths staring at each other, then glancing at his brother's smile, let out a rough, sudden bark of laughter himself—the raw, hysterical sound of pure relief spilling forth. Methuselah, looking at Naamah's wide eyes in the darkness, feeling the impossible warmth spreading through him despite the cold, felt an answering bubble of laughter rise in his own chest. Soon, all four of them were laughing together, the sound echoing strangely, wonderfully, on the dark, lonely riverbank—the ragged, cathartic, slightly mad laughter of sheer survival, a desperate release of terror, a shared, binding celebration of being unexpectedly, miraculously, alive together.

The laughter slowly faded, leaving behind an exhausted, companionable silence. They huddled together on the sand for warmth, drawing strength from each other's presence, the sound of the river rushing endlessly past, the ordeal of the rapids now just a terrifying memory behind them. Stranded, battered, supplies critically low, but alive, and bound together now irrevocably by shared peril, profound loss, and something new, blossoming quietly in the darkness.

29

Before the Gate

Silence fell heavy and absolute over the battlefield in the valley, broken only by the whimpering gasps of dying servants and the harsh, ragged breathing of the two Nephilim commanders, Jotunn and Gilga. Anak, the great giant, lay still amidst the carnage he had wrought, his defiant stand ended, his lifeblood staining the otherwise pristine grass of the valley floor. Jotunn retrieved his dark blade from Anak's chest, wiping it clean on the fallen giant's hair with cold, contemptuous indifference.

The remaining pursuers—a mix of giants and dark-armored human soldiers—watched their masters, their faces pale beneath soot and sweat. Fear was etched there, yes, but also something else Jotunn recognized with icy displeasure: a flicker of doubt, a residue of the fallen giant's powerful, unexpected words about truth, sacrifice, and the Creator's goodness. Anak's defiance hadn't just cost them time; it had planted a dangerous, infectious seed.

Jotunn met Gilga's gaze, a silent, chilling understanding passing between them. Such seeds could not be allowed to sprout. Without a word, without warning, they turned on their own remaining forces. Dark energy crackled around Jotunn's free hand; Gilga drew a second blade. What followed was not battle but extermination. Cries of shock and betrayal were brutally silenced. Giants who had served them for centuries were cut down where they stood; human soldiers who had marched unquestioningly into darkness were consumed by shadow or blade. The Nephilim moved with swift, merciless efficiency, eliminating every witness, every vessel that might carry the taint of doubt or the memory of Anak's inconvenient truth away from this valley. Within moments, only the two of them remained, standing silent amidst a fresh field of slaughter, the setting sun glinting off their dark armor and the still forms of their erstwhile followers.

"The giant bought the man mere moments," Gilga commented, surveying the carnage with a hint of annoyance.

"Jotunn's eyes burned with cold fury as he looked westward. The scrolls Enoch carried, Adam's true record, were an intolerable offense, a dangerous spark of truth in the darkness they meticulously maintained. "He cannot escape us now."

With elegant ease, they climbed onto their mounts. The creatures sensed their masters' renewed focus, snorting eagerly, their eyes like embers glowing brighter in the deepening twilight. Turning their backs on the dead, Jotunn and Gilga urged their mounts westward at a terrifying speed, the only sounds now the thunder of unnatural hooves and the wind whistling past their cold faces.

* * *

Miles ahead, Enoch clung to the broad back of the gentle ox-like creature, the rhythmic sway doing little to soothe the deep ache in his wounded arm or the grief settling in his heart for Anak. He listened intently, his head turned toward the east. He had heard the echoes of Anak's final, defiant battle fade into a chilling, absolute silence. He waited, praying to hear a cry of victory from his friend, but only the vast emptiness of the valley answered. He knew with sickening certainty that Anak was gone. And he knew his enemies. Such silence didn't mean the hunt was over; it meant they had shed their slower troops, their malice now focused solely on him and the scrolls. They were coming.

He pressed onward through the darkening valley, the weight of Adam's testimony seeming to grow heavier with each stride of the beast beneath him. The land here felt holy, an echo of Paradise, yet the darkness pursued him even to its threshold. The miraculous energy of the fruit had dissipated completely, leaving only deep exhaustion and the enduring, cold seeping from his injury. His spirit could feel the pursuit now—a ripple of wrongness in the air, a cold pressure growing behind him like an impending storm front. The thundering beat of the Nephilim steeds grew louder, closer, an inescapable rhythm drumming doom. Escape was impossible; confrontation imminent. Knowing the end of this chase was near, Enoch lifted his weary face toward the softly glowing western horizon and began to pray aloud, his voice raw but carrying clearly over the rising sounds of pursuit.

"My Father! My God! Maker of all, hear Your servant now! They hunt me down, the sons of darkness close behind, but my soul looks only to You! You called me from my quiet glade, showed me visions, set my feet on this wonderful path! Thank You, Lord, for Your light in dark places! Thank You for leading us through the blighted land where even hope seemed poisoned! Thank you for revealing the lies of the Serpent City!

"Oh, God, thank you for Anak! For his friendship, his strength, his loyalty, his great heart that learned Your truth! Receive his noble spirit now, Father, reward his sacrifice! And Methuselah... my son! You pulled him from the water's depths, from the beast's very lair! Thank You for restoring his life to me, even for this short time! Thank you for the fire from Heaven that consumed our fear at Adam's cave, for the doves You sent when we offered our last crumb! Thank You for the fruit that healed, that gave us strength to flee this far!

"They hunt me for the truth, Lord—the truth You entrusted to Adam, the promise You made through Seth! The promise of the Seed who will *crush* the Serpent's head! Oh, protect them, Father! Protect my son, protect Naamah, Kael, and Ronan. Keep them safe as they travel east! Let them carry the story, the memory of Your goodness, Your power, Your enduring promise! Let the truth live on in them!

"My own strength fails now, Lord. My arm burns with their venom, my body aches... but my spirit clings to You! Into Your hands I commend my life! Do not let the darkness triumph! Let Your Light prevail! Let Your Mercy endure! Fulfill Your promise... crush the Serpent... bring forth the dawn...!"

His voice broke on that final plea. Just as he was finishing, the thundering hooves were upon him. A dark shape surged alongside, and Gilga, leaning low, struck with contemptuous force, knocking Enoch from the ox's back. He crashed into the soft earth, pain exploding in his wounded arm and shoulder. The gentle beast, startled and suddenly riderless, bolted away into the night.

Winded, gasping, Enoch pushed himself up. It was deep night now, yet the land around him was bathed in a soft, warm, ethereal glow emanating strongly from the west, growing brighter as they had neared its source. He could see clearly—the unique trees, the gentle slope of the land, and the two figures dismounting from their panting, monstrous steeds to stand over him. Jotunn and Gilga.

"The prayer of a fool," Jotunn sneered, his voice like cracking ice. The unnatural light glinted off his dark armor and the cruel lines of his perfect face. "Your giant friend died calling for the Creator too. It availed him nothing."

Gilga laughed, a cold, grating sound. "Did you truly think you could carry Adam's pathetic scrolls back into the world? They belong to oblivion, like all memory of the Creator."

Enoch looked past them, confirming the absence of the beasts, the handlers, the soldiers. "You murdered your own servants," he stated, his voice weak but clear, holding no fear now, only a weary pity.

Jotunn shrugged, a dismissive gesture. "Incompetent tools are discarded. They heard words they should not have. A necessary pruning to maintain order."

"You call *us* slaves," Enoch continued, pushing himself to his feet, clutching his wounded arm, the scrolls heavy on his back. He met their glowing eyes. "But you are the true slaves. Bound to a master who lies chained beneath a mountain, consumed by hatred, twisting all that is good into ruin. You wield power, yes, but it is the power of death, of illusion. You build nothing lasting. You only defile and destroy. You fear the light you fled, the love you cannot comprehend."

His words struck home. The Nephilim's cold arrogance fractured, revealing the ancient, burning rage beneath. "Silence, worm!" Jotunn shrieked. As his face contorted, the illusion of his perfect beauty shattered before Enoch's eyes. For a horrifying instant, he saw what lay beneath: a face twisted not just by fury but by centuries of hatred. Their features warped, their eyes empty of the Creator's light, and their façade of perfection became a grotesque mockery of the celestial beauty their fathers once held.

Jotunn raised his dark blade, its edge humming with malevolent energy. "You will die regretting that truth!"

Enoch closed his eyes and whispered a final prayer for deliverance.

A sound like mighty wings or rushing fire split the air, then a brilliance far exceeding the gentle Eden-glow erupted nearby. Enoch instinctively shielded his eyes, stumbling back. When he could see again, two figures stood between him and the Nephilim. They were immeasurable, radiant, clad in armor that shone like the sun, their faces awesome and terrible with divine power. In their hands, they wielded swords that blazed with pure, white-hot fire, casting the Nephilim's dark forms into stark relief. Cherubim. Guardians of the Way.

Jotunn and Gilga froze, their expressions of rage instantly replaced by abject terror. They recognized this power, this authority, against which their own dark might was as nothing. "No..." Gilga stammered, taking an involuntary step back. Jotunn tried to raise his blade but seemed paralyzed by overwhelming dread.

The Angels moved with blinding speed. Before a plea or curse could be uttered, the flaming swords swept down. There was a searing flash, a soundless scream swallowed by holy fire, and then... nothing. Where the two Nephilim commanders had stood, only wisps of dissipating smoke remained, their dark essence consumed, unmade by the pure light.

The immediate threat vanquished, the two mighty Cherubim turned their awesome gaze upon Enoch, who lay trembling nearby. Their faces were stern, impassive, radiating righteous judgment. One stepped toward him, the flaming sword held ready, its heat palpable even yards away. "Son of Adam," its voice resonated like deep music and rolling thunder combined, "you trespass. These are the borders of the Holy Garden. The way is barred. None born of the Fall may enter here."

Enoch felt a new wave of fear, different from the terror the Nephilim inspired. This was the fear of holiness, of righteous judgment against his own fallen nature. He had come too close. He sank to his knees, expecting the consuming fire.

But as the Angels advanced, swords raised high—a Voice spoke. It came not from the Angels but from *beyond* them, from the heart of the intense light pouring from the west, from within the hidden Garden. The Voice held infinite power, the authority that commanded galaxies, yet it was filled with a love so deep it brought tears to Enoch's eyes. It simply said, his name: "Enoch."

Instantly, the two mighty Cherubim fell face down upon the sacred ground, their flaming swords vanishing into pure light, their forms bowed in absolute reverence and obedience. Overwhelmed, Enoch did the same, pressing his face into the cool grass, trembling not with fear now but with unimaginable awe.

The Voice spoke again, gentle, intimate, filled with welcoming love. "Rise, Enoch, faithful servant. You have preserved the testimony. You have walked in truth. Enter now, and rest."

Enoch looked up. Before him, the light separating the valley from whatever lay beyond shimmered and parted, like a curtain drawing back upon reality itself. An unseen Gate opened. Light, pure and life-giving, poured forth, carrying scents of blossoms unknown since the world's dawn and harmonies that resonated deep within his soul, weaving together sound and light and peace. He saw glimpses through the opening—colors that had no earthly name, trees laden with living light, water flowing like liquid crystal, forms moving in perfect harmony, a sense of peace so perfect it was an almost unbearable joy.

Trembling, awestruck, leaning heavily on his staff for the last time, Enoch pushed himself to his feet. He took one hesitant step, then another, across the threshold, out of the fallen world, out of the reach of darkness and pain. He stepped into the light, into the Garden, welcomed home.

30

Face to Face

With a trembling breath, Enoch took a step across the unseen threshold. The world behind him—the harsh mountains, the pursuing darkness, the very memory of pain and struggle—seemed to simply fall away, silenced by an overwhelming wave of peace so profound it brought him to his knees. Light surrounded him, not the harsh glare of the sun; this was a soft, golden, life-giving radiance that emanated from the very air, the ground, the leaves on the trees. It soaked into his weary bones, and he gasped as the cold in his wounded arm vanished instantly, replaced by comforting warmth. He looked down in astonishment—the ragged wound was gone, the flesh perfectly whole, smooth, without even a scar to mark where the Nephilim blade had struck. Healing here wasn't a process; it was instantaneous restoration, a taste of creation remade.

He rose slowly, looking around, his senses reeling from the unadulterated beauty. He stood in a garden, yet the word felt completely inadequate. This was Creation as the Creator intended it, unspoiled, vibrant, overflowing with peace and infinite life.

As Enoch walked, tentatively at first, then drawn onward by insatiable wonder, the landscape unfolded in ways that defied earthly logic and limitation. Distant mountains shimmered as if carved from living crystal, catching golden light and scattering dancing colors across the valleys below. Rivers flowed with water so clear it seemed like liquid air; dipping his hand in, the water felt cool against his skin and tasted unimaginably pure, quenching a thirst deeper than physical need. Trees towered gracefully toward the heavens, their bark smooth as polished wood, bearing fragrant blossoms of unimaginable intricacy alongside clusters of ripe, softly glowing fruit—a cycle of perpetual abundance without a hint of decay. Flowers bloomed in impossible profusion along the pathways, their petals possessing colors Enoch had never conceived, seeming to shift and deepen as he watched, releasing waves of intoxicating perfumes.

The air itself was a song. It began with the gentle rustle of silver-and-gold leaves that chimed like tiny, delicate bells in a breeze that felt like a conscious caress. Beneath that, a low, resonant hum seemed to emanate from the very petals of the luminous flowers, a sound of pure, quiet life. The intricate trill of birdsong and the soft murmur of the crystal river did not compete but wove through these sounds, each finding its perfect place. All these individual melodies merged into a single, breathtaking chord that vibrated deep within Enoch's soul, quieting his grief and filling him with a peace so overwhelming it felt like joy. There were no thorns, no weeds, no sign of struggle, only effortless, vibrant life unfolding in this perfect, intricate balance.

The creatures of the Garden moved through this paradise with a trust that defied Enoch's understanding of the natural world he knew. The majestic creature resembling a great lion with a mane like threads of sunlight rose languidly as Enoch approached, stretched, and then rumbled, a deep sound that resonated not with menace, but with welcome. *"Peace to you, Son of Adam,"* the thought echoed clearly in Enoch's mind. *"You walk now where sorrow's shadow is faint."* Enoch stared, speechless, awe silencing him more effectively than fear ever could. Birds with feathers like spun jewels landed on his outstretched hand, trilling complex melodies that resolved into clear notes of greeting, their slight weight barely registering. One dropped a perfect, luminous blue berry into his palm. Enoch ate it. The taste exploded on his tongue, sweet yet refreshing, leaving him feeling lighter, clearer, somehow more *aware*.

He saw graceful, four-winged deer approach, their large, dark eyes holding not fear but a gentle empathy, even a shared sorrow for the broken world he represented. One nudged his hand, and its thoughts brushed against his own, *"The Shepherd's light rests upon you. Welcome."*

Small, playful creatures resembling monkeys with soft, silvery fur swung down from branches, chattering musically, offering him clusters of the teardrop-shaped fruit that pulsed with sunlight. He accepted one, biting into its yielding skin. It tasted like liquid warmth, like pure laughter and dawn combined. All creatures lived in harmony, their interactions filled with grace, communicating with him and each other in ways that transcended spoken language, sharing the unburdened joy of their existence.

Each new vista, each peaceful encounter, each taste of perfection overwhelmed Enoch with a sense of wonder mingled with deep, aching sorrow. This staggering beauty engaging all senses, this perfect harmony, this effortless life where even animals spoke peace—this was the Creator's original masterpiece. The contrast with the harsh, fear-driven, corrupted world beyond the Gate was a constant, painful counterpoint in his mind. He felt a grief rise within him for what Adam and Eve had forfeited, understanding the depth of the tragedy more fully now than ever before. Simultaneously, a deep sense of 'rightness' pervaded his soul; this was how life was meant to be lived, how creation was meant to praise its Maker. Yet, amidst the awe, humility remained; He was a son of the Fall, miraculously permitted to walk in a perfection he did not inherently belong to, keenly aware of the unmerited, astonishing grace that had brought him here.

He wandered, absorbing the wonders, served gently by the creatures of the Garden, losing all track of time in the eternal present bathed in the Creator's light. Had he been exploring for minutes? Hours? Days? Years? The concept seemed meaningless here. He walked beside rivers, through groves of trees whose leaves seemed to whisper praises, accepted fruit and nectar offered by creatures radiating pure innocence.

Then, the Voice that had called him across the threshold spoke again, no longer distant but intimately near, resonating not just in his ears but within his very soul, echoing through the perfect peace. "Enoch."

He stopped, turning slowly, his heart pounding not with fear but with overwhelming anticipation. Standing beneath a magnificent tree whose leaves shimmered like spun gold and whose fruit glowed with the soft light of life itself was a figure. It was the form of a Man yet clearly infinitely more—His garments were white, whiter than any earthly snow, seeming woven from pure light. His hair shone like refined wool, bright and radiant, and His face, though filled with an unbearable kindness that drew Enoch's soul toward it, radiated a brilliance, a glory, that forced Enoch to avert his gaze slightly, unworthy to look directly upon such perfection. His eyes, when Enoch dared to meet them for a fleeting moment, were like flames of compassionate fire, seeing everything, understanding everything, loving everything. This was no mere angel; this was the Ancient of Days, the Lord of Glory, the Creator Himself, manifest in a form His servant could perceive without being consumed.

Overwhelmed by awe, love, and a sudden, crushing awareness of his own mortality and inherited sinfulness before such Holiness, Enoch fell prostrate upon the soft grass, burying his face, weeping uncontrollably—tears of utter joy for this arrival, tears of release from a lifetime of struggle, and tears of deep repentance for the Fall of his first parents that had necessitated his own long, hard journey toward this Presence.

He felt a touch on his shoulder, radiating warmth and infinite tenderness. He looked up hesitantly through blurred vision and saw the luminous Man kneeling beside him, His fiery eyes now soft with measureless compassion. The radiant figure gently wiped the tears from Enoch's face with fingers that seemed made of light and warmth. The gesture conveyed more comfort, more understanding, more absolute acceptance than any words could ever hold.

After a long time, Enoch's weeping subsided, leaving only peace, a stillness of the soul, in the presence of his Maker. Emboldened by the intimacy, the overwhelming love emanating from the figure beside him, Enoch dared to speak, his voice thick but clear. "My Lord... my Creator... why?" he whispered, the question encompassing all the sorrow he had witnessed, all the pain his people endured beyond this Gate. "Why allow the Serpent such sway? Why the Fall? The long ages of darkness, the corruption, the Nephilim... this terrible war against Your goodness? Why did Adam... why did they choose...?"

The Man of Light answered, His voice like the sound of many waters, yet speaking directly to Enoch's heart, the understanding flowing into his mind like living water itself. *"Love, Enoch, cannot be compelled, only freely given. True fellowship requires freedom, the freedom to choose. I gave your first parents that freedom, the dignity of choice, for love born of freedom is the only love that truly mirrors My own heart, My own Being. The Serpent, himself fallen from light through pride, offered them lies cloaked as hidden wisdom, the illusion of godhood achieved apart from Me. They chose to listen to his voice over Mine. That single choice, born of doubt and desire, invited separation, introduced brokenness, unleashed the shadow of death into My good creation."*

"But the suffering... the endless darkness..." Enoch murmured, thinking of Anak's fall, of Malachi's sacrifice, of Naamah's deep well of grief.

The radiant figure looked at him, and in His eyes Enoch saw not only the sorrow of all history but the fierce light of unwavering purpose. *"The Serpent bruised the heel,"* He affirmed, the promise resonating with new power. *"But his head will be crushed. I declared it at the beginning, and My word does not fail. The path of redemption unfolds according to My sovereign will, My perfect timing. The line of Seth, the line you faithfully carry, bears that promise forward like a seed."* His gaze held infinite compassion. *"Suffering exists now, Enoch, because of the world's brokenness,* because of the freedom I granted, and because the enemy still prowls, raging against the light he forfeited, seeking whom he may devour before his time is complete. Yet even suffering, even darkness, I constrain and weave into My greater purpose—bringing forth resilience, forging faith, revealing the depth of sacrificial love.

"Judgment will come, Enoch," the figure stated, and the light surrounding Him seemed to pulse with righteous power, a glimpse of the consuming fire Enoch had witnessed outside. "This corrupted world, twisted into the Serpent's image by those who embrace his lies—the Nephilim, the wicked among men, all who choose darkness over light—it will not stand forever. The wickedness grows great, an affront to the life I give, a stench in My nostrils. A reckoning approaches, a cleansing. But My ultimate plan is not destruction alone, but recreation, restoration, through the Seed I promised."

Gathering all his courage, humbled beyond measure, Enoch asked the question that trembled within him. "My Lord... Master of All... Who... Who are You? Your Name... may Your servant know Your Name?"

The figure seemed to grow brighter still, the light emanating from Him intensifying, filled with an eternal, self-existent power that resonated through the very fabric of the Garden, making the leaves tremble and the light motes dance. The Voice spoke, clear, absolute, defining all existence: **"I AM WHO I AM."**

The Name. It settled upon Enoch not as sound but as reality itself. The First and the Last. The Uncaused Cause. The ground of all Being. He felt he understood only an infinitesimal fraction of its depth, yet that fraction filled him with peace that surpassed all understanding.

Then, the radiant Man leaned closer again, His voice intimate, sharing the deepest mystery of His plan. "I AM. That is My eternal Name. Yet, Enoch, to fulfill the promise, to crush the Serpent's head from within creation itself, to bridge the chasm of separation caused by the Fall... I will do a new thing." He gestured toward His own luminous, human-like form, the meeting place of the eternal and the perceivable. "The Seed promised through Seth will not merely be a Man of faith, empowered by Me. In the fullness of time, I Myself will enter into My creation. I will take on flesh, woven into the line of Adam through the woman, as promised. I will walk among men, know their sorrows, bear their burdens, My glory veiled in humility. And I will be known then by another name—a name that means 'Salvation.' Through this name, through My own sacrifice upon a tree born of the cursed ground, a sacrifice you cannot yet comprehend, I will break the power of the Serpent, conquer death itself, and make a way for all who trust in Me to return, not to this earthly Garden which has served its purpose, but to eternal fellowship with Me, face to face, forever."

Enoch absorbed the staggering, breathtaking truth, his mind reeling, his spirit soaring with revelation. The Creator Himself would come. He would become the Seed. He would share their fragile humanity, defeat their ancient enemy through His own suffering, and offer eternal life through His own resurrection. The plan was infinitely more thoughtful, more personal, more filled with sacrificial love than he could ever have conceived.

A deep, abiding peace settled over him, the peace of ultimate understanding, of purpose fulfilled. Yet, even standing on the shores of eternity, the bonds of earthly love remained. Humbly, he looked toward the Great I AM beside him.

"My Lord," Enoch began softly, "Your plan is beyond wonder. But... my heart still holds those I left behind. My son, Methuselah... the young woman Naamah... the faithful giants, Kael and Ronan... what will become of them? Will the line endure?"

The Man of Light regarded him with infinite tenderness, His fiery eyes softening into pools of starlight. "Fear not for the path I have set, Enoch. Your son carries the strength of your faith within him, now tempered and proven by hardship. He and the daughter of Selah, Naamah, will find comfort and strength in each other; their path will join, and they shall become one, reflecting the love I first ordained. From their union shall come a son, whom they will name Lamech, who will father a son named Noah." A weight, a sense of destiny, seemed to enter the name as the Creator spoke it. "And through Noah, I have plans yet unfolded, plans for preservation amidst the judgment that must soon cleanse the growing darkness you witnessed." The Creator smiled gently, a light that warmed Enoch to his core. "But enough of times yet to come. Know this: the line of Seth will endure, as I promised, until the fullness of time arrives. And the giants Kael and Ronan will honor the oath sworn to their father, fulfilling their purpose in ways you do not yet see."

The Creator gestured toward the magnificent, luminous tree under whose gentle light they sat, its leaves shimmering with soft music, its fruit glowing with pure, concentrated life. "Do you know this tree, Enoch?"

Enoch gazed at it, recognizing it now from the depictions in the cave, the centerpiece of the Garden, radiating vitality. "The Tree of Life," he whispered in awe.

"Yes," the Creator affirmed. "From which your first parents freely ate before the Serpent whispered his lies, partaking of the eternal vitality I imbued within it. Since their banishment, the way to it has been barred, lest humanity eat in their fallen state and live forever physically, yet eternally separated from Me in spirit." The Great I Am looked at Enoch, His gaze filled with encompassing love and gentle invitation. "But you, Enoch, have walked faithfully with Me. You have preserved the testimony, endured hardship for My name's sake, and sought Me with all your heart through a darkening world. The corruption of the fallen world holds no further claim on you now. You have reached the end of your earthly journey, found faithful." He gestured toward the glowing fruit. "Eat now, beloved son. Partake of My life freely given. Enter fully into My rest."

With trembling hands, filled not with fear but with gratitude and quiet joy, Enoch reached out and plucked a single fruit from the Tree of Life. It felt warm in his hand, pulsing with pure energy, smelling of dawn and eternity. He brought it to his lips and took a bite.

The taste was indescribable—not just flavor but pure being, pure life, pure joy, pure light flooding his senses, dissolving every last vestige of earthly weariness, sorrow, limitation, even the memory of pain. He felt himself becoming lighter than air, brighter, his physical form seeming too thin, becoming translucent, joyfully merging with the golden light of the Garden, drawn into the heart of the Creator's own radiance. There was no struggle, no pain, only an effortless release, a final homecoming, a sense of being fully known and completely loved. He saw Methuselah's face one last time in his mind, filled with love and blessing, saw Naamah finding peace and purpose, saw the faithful line of Seth stretching down through the turbulent ages toward the promised Seed, the Savior. Then, the Garden faded, only to become infinitely clearer, more real, as Enoch, son of Jared, descendant of Seth, son of Adam, was no more in the world of men, for God took him. He entered eternity without tasting death, resting in the unveiled glory of the I AM, awaiting the final fulfillment of the promises he had faithfully carried and now fully understood.

31

The Weight of Inheritance

The first pale light of dawn filtered down the high canyon walls, illuminating the small, sandy beach where they lay huddled together for warmth against the river's damp chill. Soaked, bruised, and exhausted after the terrifying passage through the rapids and the violent destruction of their raft, they had succumbed hours before to a sleep born of sheer physical and emotional depletion. The constant roar of the nearby whitewater served as a stark reminder of their near-demise.

Methuselah stirred first, not roused by the growing light filtering into the canyon but by a tangible, startling internal shift. In the deep stillness between sleep and waking, he felt a sudden connection flare toward his father, Enoch—an inexplicable warmth, a sense of overwhelming peace and brilliant light flooding his awareness across the leagues separating them. Then, just as suddenly, a feeling of release, of departure. It wasn't the brutal finality he felt when he thought of Anak, nor the cold dread inspired by the Nephilim pursuit. This was different. It was... a *taking*. A translation into light. He knew, with a certainty that settled deep and immovably in his soul even as tears welled hot in his eyes, that his father was gone from the world of men, but not in death. He had been taken into the very Light they had followed. Grief mingled strangely, wondrously, with comfort, a deep ache of personal loss accompanied by an overwhelming sense of his father's ultimate peace. He sat up slowly, wiping the silent tears from his face with a muddy hand, the cold morning air sharp against his skin.

His movement woke the others. Naamah stirred first, her eyes finding his in the dim light. She saw the tear tracks on his face, the strange mix of sorrow and undeniable serenity in his expression, and her breath caught in understanding. Kael, already checking on Ronan, looked over sharply, his gaze questioning. He saw the evidence of tears, the deep sorrow, but also the peculiar calm that hadn't been there before. "Methuselah...?" Kael began, his voice rough with sleep and concern.

Methuselah met Kael's gaze, then looked at Naamah, then toward Ronan. His expression held the clear certainty of their fathers' fate. He swallowed hard, his voice thick but steady in the quiet morning. "They are gone," he said softly.

Just three words. No other explanation was needed. The statement hung in the air, heavy and absolute. Kael and Ronan exchanged a look laden with grief, the certainty of their own father's fate crashing down upon them with devastating finality—Anak had stayed behind to face the enemy, and he would not be following. Naamah closed her eyes for a moment, absorbing the double blow, the loss of both wise, strong leaders who had guided and protected them. The two pillars of their hope, the two fathers who represented the bridge between past and future, were gone.

A heavy silence fell then, filled only by the ceaseless roar of the nearby rapids and the weight of the responsibility that now rested entirely upon the four survivors. Kael looked at his brother, his face etched with grief but also dawning resolve, then at the young man and woman beside him. His father's oath, sworn in Adam's cave, resonated in his mind: *Protect them. Ensure the testimony survives.*

The mantle of leadership, heavy and unwelcome but undeniably his now, settled onto Kael's massive shoulders. Beside him, Methuselah felt it too—the shift was palpable. No longer just a son following his father's lead but the inheritor of a sacred trust, the carrier of a lineage, guided now only by a fledgling vision and the vital stories held preciously in his memory. Naamah opened her eyes again, gripping the small knife at her belt, remembering the sacrifice of so many galvanized her resolve against the wave of despair. They were the ones left. The responsibility, the future, was theirs now.

As full daylight finally penetrated the deep gorge, illuminating their stark surroundings, their predicament became undeniably clear. They were trapped on a narrow strip of sand at the base of sheer, towering cliffs rising hundreds of feet above them. Upstream, the rapids churned violently over jagged rocks, barring any return that way. Downstream, the powerful Euphrates flowed swiftly eastward into the unknown, but without a raft, travel on the water was impossible. The sheer cliffs appeared to continue along the bank for some distance, offering no easy path forward. A quick search confirmed their fears: many of their supplies, including the precious dried dove meat and any remaining Edenic fruit, had been swept away when the raft disintegrated in the torrent.

"We cannot stay here," Kael stated grimly, his voice leaving no room for argument as his gaze scanned the imposing cliff face that towered over them like a prison wall. "The river offers no passage downstream from this beach. We must go up."

It looked impossible. The rock face was near vertical, slick with river spray near the bottom, offering few obvious handholds or footholds, especially daunting for the injured Ronan and Methuselah. But Kael, drawing on generations of giantish experience with impassable mountainous terrain, scanned the cliff face with intense concentration, finally spotting a potential, albeit perilous, route—a series of narrow, eroded ledges and diagonal fissures that might, just possibly, allow a skilled climber to ascend in stages. "I will climb," he declared, his voice firm with decision. He checked the length of heavy, salvaged rope they still possessed—thankfully, one of the longer pieces used for the main raft bindings had washed ashore, tangled but intact. "I will climb and secure the rope. Then haul you up, one by one."

It was their only option, a desperate gamble against the unforgiving rock. Kael, despite his own bruises and bone-deep weariness, began the ascent almost immediately. He moved with incredible power and focus, testing each precarious hold meticulously before trusting his weight to it, using his axe occasionally to chip a small, crucial purchase in the sheer rock where none existed naturally. His massive form seemed to defy gravity as he scaled the cliff face with painstaking slowness. Finally, he reached a narrow but stable-looking ledge barely wide enough for two giants to stand upon and, finding a sturdy, jutting outcrop, secured the heavy rope firmly around it.

He lowered the rope, its end coiling on the sand below. "Ronan first!" he called down, his voice echoing slightly off the rock. Getting the still-weakened, one-armed giant up was the most difficult part. It required Kael hauling with all his might from above while Methuselah and Naamah strained from below, pushing and guiding Ronan as he began his ascent. Ronan gritted his teeth against the pain, his face pale with effort, but he climbed, driven by sheer will and trust in his brother. Once Ronan was safely gasping on the narrow ledge beside Kael, the rope was lowered again. Naamah went next, lighter and more agile, moving quickly up the rope with Kael's assistance. Then came Methuselah, the climb sheer agony on his injured leg, relying on the rope and his upper body strength, Kael's steady, powerful pulling from above an essential anchor against the waves of pain.

Once they were all gathered on the first narrow ledge, Kael paused only for a moment before assessing the next section of the cliff face above. Finding another potential route, he began climbing again, upward through fissures and crumbling handholds. He reached a second, even smaller ledge, secured the rope again, and the slow, arduous, terrifying process of hauling the others up began once more. Section by perilous section, ledge by precarious ledge, Kael led them up the cliff face throughout the long morning, his strength and determination seemingly inexhaustible, fulfilling his sworn oath with every upward foot gained against the indifferent stone.

As the sun reached its zenith, burning hot in the now-clear sky, Kael pulled himself over the final lip onto the broad, windswept top of the ridge. He secured the rope one last time around a massive boulder, heart pounding with relief, and helped haul the others, one by one, over the edge onto flat, solid ground covered in sparse, hardy grasses. They collapsed, gasping for breath, muscles trembling from the exertion, hearts pounding from the dizzying height and the sheer effort of the climb. They were bruised, battered, covered in drying mud and river slime, and far from any true safety, but they were off the beach, out of the river's immediate trap, alive, and together.

They lay there for a long while, simply breathing, feeling the solid earth beneath them, the warm sun on their faces. The terrifying roar of the rapids below faded into the constant, distant murmur of the eastward-flowing Euphrates. Below them stretched a vast, unknown wilderness, following the river's meandering course into uncharted territory. Behind them lay the perilous cliffs, the memory of the rapids, and far beyond that, the unseen horrors of Serpent Mountain's domain. Ahead lay only the long, uncertain path they now knew they must forge for themselves.

Kael was the first to stir, pushing himself to his feet, his gaze already scanning the eastern horizon, assessing the terrain. "We cannot rest here long," Kael stated, his voice gruff but steady, pulling them back to harsh reality. He looked at Methuselah. "Your vision brought us to this river, Son of Enoch, and it flows east. But you said it showed no more?"

Methuselah looked eastward toward the hazy horizon, then briefly back toward the west where his father now dwelt in light, a flicker of pain crossing his face before resolve hardened it again. "The vision showed only this path, away from the danger on the Gihon," he admitted quietly. "It did not show the end of the journey, only the direction we must take."

Naamah spoke then, her voice low but firm, shaking her head decisively as she looked toward the northeast. "We cannot simply turn toward my home valley. That path passes too close to the shadow of Serpent Mountain, too near the trails the raiders used. I will not lead us back into that danger, Kael."

Kael nodded grimly, understanding her fear and the undeniable strategic sense. He pointed eastward along the river's course visible from the ridge. "Then we follow this river southeastward for a time, putting distance between us and the Serpent's lands. When the terrain allows, when these mountains finally diminish into hills, we strike out overland, northeastward. Try to find the trails our people used long ago." He looked at Naamah, his expression softening slightly. "Those trails, if we can find them, should eventually lead us back toward the region of your valley, Naamah, but approaching from the safer side, far from the Mountain's immediate reach."

"And see my mother again? My sister?" Naamah asked, an almost forgotten hope entering her voice.

"Yes," Kael confirmed, his voice gentle now. "We rest there, if Selah permits. We owe them much. Regain our full strength." He glanced meaningfully at Ronan, then back at the others. "Then... we return to the House of Anak. To see Mother, tell them what became of Father." His voice roughened on the last word, but he pushed on, "From there, Methuselah, once you are fully healed, we will see you safely to your glade."

It was a long, arduous plan, fraught with uncertainty. Before even reaching lands potentially known, they had to cross incalculable distances of unexplored territory. But it was a plan rooted in caution, necessity, and their shared purpose. They all nodded in weary agreement.

A heavy silence fell again as the weight of the journey still ahead and the fresh memories of those lost along the way settled heavily upon them. It was Ronan who broke it, his voice weak but clear, a wistful note entering it. "I look forward," he said softly, looking at his brother, "to resting by our own hearth fire again, Kael. To feel the warmth of the home stones beneath my feet."

Kael managed a smile, clapping his brother gently on his good shoulder. "Aye, brother," he rumbled. "And I look forward to seeing you fully healed, perhaps even strong enough to finally complain about my cooking again." He paused, the thought of their father, the true heart of their home, hanging heavy in the air between them, then added gruffly, "It will be good to be home when the Creator wills it."

Naamah looked down at her hands, imagining the feel of the grinding stone. "My mother's stew," she whispered, almost to herself, the memory bringing both comfort and a sharp pang of loss. "The smell of roasting herbs in our cave. Sitting with Tirzah... just sitting, in safety, without listening constantly for every unknown sound in the darkness."

Methuselah thought of the glade—the towering, protective canopy filtering the sunlight, the scent of woodsmoke and damp earth, the quiet, predictable rhythm of life lived close to the Creator. He thought of seeing Adah's bright, curious eyes again, even Jareth's rare smile of approval. He thought of the simple comfort of shared work in the fields and evening stories told around the central fire. "My father..." he began, his voice catching momentarily. He cleared his throat, looking not at the past but toward the task ahead. "I want... I *need* to tell them what my father learned, what Adam wrote. The truth. It feels... more important than anything now." He looked at Naamah, then at Kael and Ronan, his gaze steady. "And just... to be home again. Where it's safe." However, he knew, with a heavy, certain heart, that 'home' would never truly feel the same without Enoch's quiet wisdom anchoring their lives there.

Their shared hopes, poignant yet straightforward in their vulnerability, hung in the air, weaving another invisible thread of connection between them. They were an unlikely fellowship indeed—one Son of Adam bearing an ancient truth and a promised lineage, two mighty giants bound by loss and a sacred oath, one Daughter of Eve embodying resilience and displaced hope—drawn together by tragedy, providence, and shared purpose. They drew strength now from each other's presence, from the quiet understanding, the tested loyalty that passed between them without words.

Kael rose stiffly to his feet, extending his hand to help Ronan stand. "Come," he said, his voice gruff but resolute, pulling them all back to the present need. "We have rested long enough. Every step east now is a step further from the shadows behind us and a step closer, however long the path, to the homes ahead."

One last look westward, toward the unseen Garden where Enoch walked in light, toward the valley where Anak lay silent in noble sacrifice. Then, decisively, they turned their faces toward the unknown southeast. They began walking along the high ridge overlooking the great river, entering the uncharted wilderness, carrying their heavy grief and the undeniable weight of inheritance into the uncertain light of a new day.

32

Homeward Bound

The high ridge became their new path, carving its way eastward into mystery. Their long trek homeward was an arduous tapestry woven from shared hardship and quiet endurance, anchored only by the hope of Adam's testimony. Weeks bled together, their passage marked not by landmarks but by the slow turning of the moon and the gradual healing of their wounds.

They followed the great river for what seemed an age, navigating the high ground whenever possible to maintain vigilance, descending cautiously down steep embankments to its banks only when necessary for fresh water, the powerful current a constant, rushing companion far below. The vibrant, almost sacred life of the Land of First Steps gradually, painfully, faded behind them like a receding dream. It was replaced by terrain that grew wilder, more demanding, less forgiving—still blessedly free from the active, poisonous blight found nearer Serpent Mountain but possessing the familiar, challenging harshness of a fallen world. Eventually, guided by Kael's innate sense of direction, they turned away from the great river when the land finally flattened into rolling plains, striking overland northeastward across rugged, windswept hills and into dense forests, untrodden perhaps since the earliest ages, seeking the trails that lay far beyond the reach of Serpent City.

Progress remained slow, dictated always by the pace of the healing and the difficulty of the terrain. Ronan, though regaining strength daily, still leaned on Kael during arduous climbs or river crossings, his arm protected, mending slowly but cleanly.

Methuselah's leg grew stronger week by week; the limp lessened considerably, yet long marches over uneven ground still left him exhausted and aching by nightfall, a constant reminder of the beast's power. The miraculous provisions now lay at the bottom of the Euphrates, a devastating loss that forced them back to complete reliance on the land.

Naamah took up the burden without complaint, her bow rarely resting on her shoulder. She stalked the sparse game of the wilder hills from dawn until dusk, and when the hunt failed, she foraged, her knowledge of the earth yielding just enough to keep them moving. Some weeks yielded barely enough bitter roots and tough, stringy game; other times, her hunt provided welcome sustenance and a brief lift to their spirits. They endured biting winds that swept across exposed ridges, week-long spells of cold, soaking dew that chilled them to the bone and made fire-starting nearly impossible, and the constant, gnawing uncertainty of navigating an unknown path. Territorial beasts, driven by hunger in this harsher land, occasionally challenged their passage, forcing Kael into brief, decisive displays of intimidating strength to drive them off without serious conflict.

Yet, through the crucible of this prolonged, shared hardship, their bonds deepened in ways none could have anticipated, forging an unlikely but fiercely loyal family unit from the disparate survivors.

Kael, shouldering the heavy mantle of leadership with quiet competence and unwavering resolve, watched over Methuselah and Naamah with fierce, almost paternal protectiveness, fulfilling his solemn oath to Anak in every careful step, every watchful glance.

Ronan, despite his lingering weakness, offered steady encouragement to the others or sometimes a surprisingly dry jest when spirits flagged lowest, his quiet endurance becoming a different kind of strength for them all.

Naamah remained a constant source of kindness; she tended injuries with skills learned from her mother and enhanced by Kael's instruction, found hidden water sources where none seemed apparent, scouted ahead with silent agility when the way was unclear, her own grief now channeled into a fierce determination to see this vital mission, and her new companions, safely through to its end. And between her and Methuselah, the connection that started in shared hardship deepened steadily into quiet affection and sincere mutual reliance. Shared night watches under unfamiliar constellations, a hand offered and accepted gratefully, quiet words exchanged by the flickering light of meager, carefully concealed campfires. These small moments wove their hearts together, offering solace against their shared losses and building a foundation for the future neither yet fully dared to name.

Nights around those small fires, huddled together for warmth and security, became the most important time. Almost inevitably, after a sparse meal, Kael would nod toward Methuselah, his expression steady and encouraging. "Tell it again, Son of Enoch. Lest we forget what our fathers died for." And Methuselah, his voice gaining confidence and clarity with each retelling, often prompted by Naamah adding a specific detail she remembered from the murals or Enoch's explanations in the cave, would recount the story they now carried etched into the marrow of their souls—the breathtaking beauty of Creation, the perfect harmony of Eden, the poison of the Serpent's lies, the heartbreaking tragedy of the Fall, the Creator's enduring promise woven like light through judgment, the long, terrible war against the encroaching darkness, the origin of the Nephilim, Lucifer bound beneath the mountain, the sacred purpose of Seth's line, and finally, the ultimate sacrifices made by Enoch and Anak to preserve that truth. Rehearsing the testimony became their anchor, a sacred ritual keeping the vital details sharp, honoring the memory of the fallen, and steeling their own resolve for the long journey still ahead. Kael and Ronan listened intently each time, absorbing the weight of the legacy they were now sworn to protect.

The fire crackled low, a small circle of warmth against the indifferent darkness. Kael and Naamah were taking the first watch, their silhouettes pacing slowly at the edge of the camp. Ronan sat near the flames, the firelight glinting off the head of his massive war hammer as he methodically cleaned it with a piece of oiled hide. Methuselah, unable to sleep, watched him. The hammer was a fearsome weapon, but in Ronan's hands, it looked like a natural extension of himself.

"The carvings on the head," Methuselah said quietly, breaking the silence. "I have often wondered at them. They are not like the patterns in my father's scrolls."

Ronan paused, his large hands stilling. He turned the hammer over, letting the firelight catch in the deep, swirling grooves. "They tell a story," he spoke, his voice low. "Our stories are not kept on hide but in stone and iron." He traced a deep, spiraling pattern with his thumb. "This is the Great Chasm our people crossed to reach our valley. And this," he pointed to an intricate knot-like symbol near the haft, "is the mark of Haran, my ancestor, the one who turned from the pride of the Mountain-Kings and chose the path of our human mothers."

Methuselah leaned forward, fascinated. "And these?" he asked, pointing to a series of small, deliberate notches carved into the thick wooden handle, just below the iron head. There were many, worn smooth by Ronan's grip. "Great beasts you have slain? A mark for each one?"

The easy flow of conversation stopped. The fire crackled, filling the sudden silence. Ronan's gaze fell to the handle, and the light seemed to leave his eyes, replaced by a deep, shadowed weariness. He ran a thumb slowly over the notches, the gesture heavy with a meaning Methuselah didn't yet understand.

"No," Ronan said finally, his voice barely audible. "Not beasts." He looked up, their eyes meeting in the flickering light. Methuselah saw an intense sorrow there. "Men," Ronan said quietly. "And other giants from rival clans. Each mark... is a life claimed by this hammer."

Methuselah felt a chill that had nothing to do with the night air. He had always seen the notches as marks of a warrior's prowess, of great deeds. He had never considered the cost.

Ronan saw the look on his face and sighed. "I was taught to mark each victory. It was a warrior's pride, a testament to strength." He looked down at the notches again, his expression clouded. "But your father... he spoke of the Creator's love for all His creation. He spoke of mercy. My own father, Anak, died defending that truth." He shook his head slowly. "I look at these marks differently now. They feel... heavy. Each one a soul sent into darkness. Each one a story ended by my own hand." He set the hammer down beside him, the thud soft on the hard-packed earth. "I think... I will add no more marks to this handle."

In the quiet that followed, Methuselah looked at the mighty giant, no longer seeing just a powerful warrior but a soul grappling with the weight of his own past. A deep, quiet respect settled in his heart, forging a new, stronger bond between the son of Enoch and the son of Anak.

The threat from the Serpent City, though unseen now for many weeks as they skirted its territory far to the north, was never truly forgotten. Twice, Kael's keen eyes spotted disturbing signs far off on the plains—not patrols themselves but unsettling evidence of their passage: the cold ashes of a large, organized encampment where no settlement should be, distinctive tracks of heavy giant feet mixed with the prints of booted human soldiers heading eastward, suggesting Nephilim forces or their allies were still active, seeking easier routes east or methodically probing the wilderness edges for signs of Adam's descendants. Each time, the discovery sent a fresh chill through the group, forcing them into hours of breathless hiding amongst rocks or dense undergrowth or making cautious, time-consuming detours, a stark reminder that the Serpent's reach was long indeed and his memory unforgiving.

As they traveled further northeast, leaving the blessed influence of Eden's border far behind them, the land continued its disheartening shift back toward the familiar reality of the fallen world they knew. They found more ruins scattered across the landscape—smaller remnants than glorious Shem, often just lonely circles of weathered stones choked by thorns marking a forgotten village, or tumbledown watchtowers overlooking empty, windswept plains. These felt like silent, sorrowful testimony to vanished peoples, likely more distant branches of Seth's descendants, eradicated systematically in the Nephilim's long, patient war against the light. The land itself felt... diminished, less vibrant. The birdsong here seemed thinner, more wary, lacking the rich complexity they remembered from the west. The animals they glimpsed were universally skittish, melting into the shadows instantly at their approach, their eyes holding only primal fear. Plants bore sharper thorns again, the streams ran less clear, often carrying the bitter taste of alkaline earth. Having walked, however briefly, in the Land of First Steps, having tasted fruit from trees imbued with Eden's pure life force, this return to the 'normal' world felt deeply painful. They now saw, with open eyes, the brokenness everywhere—the fear woven into the very fabric of creation beyond Eden's lingering influence, the constant, weary struggle for life lived under the shadow of the curse. It made the truth they carried and the promise of eventual restoration feel even more urgent and precious.

Finally, after many months traversing vast plains, dense forests, and rugged hills under endlessly changing skies, Kael stopped atop a high ridge, his gaze fixed on the eastern horizon. He pointed a finger toward a distinctive trio of distant, weathered peaks just visible through the haze. "The Sentinel Hills," he announced, his voice thick with emotion he rarely showed. "We passed them on our journey west, long ago, before..." He didn't need to finish the thought.

Recognition dawned simultaneously on Methuselah's face. They had done it. They had navigated the uncharted wilderness, successfully bypassing the deadly reach of Serpent Mountain. A wave of bone-deep relief washed over the entire group, so potent it almost brought them to their knees.

From here, Kael knew the way. The journey was still long, but it was no longer entirely blind.

Weeks later, moving now through terrain that held distinct echoes of familiarity for Naamah, though still wild and requiring constant caution, they approached the hidden ways leading into Selah's valley. Naamah, her heart pounding with fierce anticipation, pushed ahead of the others, her usual caution momentarily overwhelmed by the hope of reunion. As Naamah climbed the final, steep path, her eyes were fixed on the concealed watch post above. A figure moved within, lean and watchful. Even from a distance, Naamah recognized the familiar, economical movements. "Tirzah!" she cried out, her voice filled with all the hope she had carried across the wilderness. The figure froze, then leaned out from the rocks, eyes widening in stunned disbelief. "Naamah? Can it really be you?" Tirzah's voice, usually so calm and steady, broke with emotion. She abandoned her post, scrambling down the rocks with reckless speed. They met in a desperate, clinging embrace, two halves of a whole reunited. Tears flowed freely, washing away some of the grime and sorrow of their long separation.

The reunion with Selah moments later, in the lamplit quiet of their cave dwelling, was equally emotional, a fierce, clinging embrace between mother and daughter, fraught with unshed tears, unspoken questions, and overwhelming relief. Selah listened, her face etched with reflective grief yet also burning with awe as Kael, Methuselah, and Naamah recounted pieces of their journey since departing her valley—the wonders and truths of Shem, the deceptive horror and blasphemy of the Serpent City, the miracle of Methuselah's survival from the lake beast, and the noble sacrifice of Anak and Enoch.

Selah's eyes shone with fierce pride for Naamah's endurance and reverence for the sacred story they brought back—the story Enoch and Anak had died to protect.

They were safe, for this precious moment, welcomed back into the hidden refuge like beloved kin returned from the dead. The longest, most perilous leg of their journey home was complete.

Exhaustion, deep and overpowering, claimed them for the following days. But beneath the weariness lay the quiet, hard-won satisfaction of survival and the shared weight of the living testimony they bore.

Adam's Cave lay far behind them now; the distant glade still awaited as the final destination. But here, in this small, resilient pocket of enduring faith, they could finally rest, heal, and gather strength before carrying the precious whispers of Eden eastward once more, toward the future.

33

Valley of Respite and Resolve

The hidden valley offered a desperately needed sanctuary, a welcome balm against the raw wounds—both physical and emotional—of their harrowing journey.

Days melted into a gentle rhythm of rest, slow healing, and quiet reflection, punctuated only by the murmur of shared stories whispered around the hearth fire in Selah's cave.

Under Selah's knowledgeable and patient care, using potent remedies gathered from the valley's bounty of herbs and mosses, Ronan's arm began to mend more surely. The deep, ever-present throb of pain receding each day, replaced by the duller, more hopeful ache of healing nerves beneath Kael's carefully maintained splints.

Methuselah exercised his injured leg as Kael instructed, slowly regaining strength and flexibility; the heavy limp faded, allowing him to graduate from the staff back to walking almost normally, though the jagged, puckered scars remained a permanent testament to the lake beast's fury.

Even the grief of Enoch's absence, a constant companion since their final embrace, seemed less sharp here, buffered by the unexpected warmth of this small community and the tangible peace emanating from the cave itself.

Selah and Tirzah listened intently, night after night, their faces illuminated by the firelight, as the travelers recounted their incredible tale—the staggering wonders and seductive horrors of the lost cities, the world-altering truth revealed in Adam's cave, the astonishing miracle of the doves, the devastating, noble sacrifices of Anak, Malachi, and Enoch himself. Hearing the full scope of the Creator's unfolding plan, the promise held within Seth's line, which now walked among them, brought a measure of solemn context, a framework of purpose to their immeasurable personal loss.

One quiet afternoon, as Naamah helped her mother grind dried roots into coarse meal using smooth stone tools passed down through generations, Selah spoke, her eyes on her daughter's lowered head, her voice soft and gentle. "The son of Enoch," she began, pausing her work. "He watches you, daughter. There is a light in his eyes when his gaze finds yours across the fire. And you... You watch him too, when you think no one sees."

Naamah's hands stilled on the grinding stone. A flush rose on her cheeks, visible even in the dim cave light. "We... we have endured much together, Mother," she murmured, the understatement heavy in the air.

"More than endurance binds you now," Selah stated, her wisdom direct but unclouded by sentimentality. Tirzah, weaving a sturdy basket nearby, paused, a quiet, knowing look passing between her and her mother. "We see the way his gaze follows you," Selah continued. "The way you found strength in each other on that dark riverbank after the rapids. It is good, Naamah. He carries his father's reflected light within him now, the strength of his sacred lineage, and a newfound humility learned through fire and loss. After so much death..." She reached out, touching Naamah's cheek. "It is right, even necessary, my child, to embrace life, to choose hope... to welcome love, when the Creator Himself so clearly clears the path for it."

Naamah looked up, meeting her mother's compassionate, knowing gaze. She thought instantly of Methuselah's fierce, unexpected protection on the cliff ledge, his quiet presence beside her as she wept for her family, the understanding that flowed so easily, so naturally between them now, stronger than any words. "Yes, Mother," she admitted, her voice barely a whisper, finally acknowledging the truth her own heart already knew. "My heart... it feels drawn to his."

Selah smiled then, a genuine expression of maternal warmth that significantly eased the deep lines of sorrow etched around her own eyes.

That evening, gathered around the fire pit, the air heavy with anticipation, the full, terrible truth of what had happened in the Serpent City was finally shared. With Kael and Ronan adding grim, firsthand accounts of the soul-crushing atmosphere of the slave pits and the chilling, arrogant power of the Nephilim, Methuselah gently, haltingly recounted Naamah's brief, heartbreaking reunion with her brother, Malachi. He described Malachi's gaunt appearance, his spirit almost broken but for the spark of recognition for his sister, and the devastating confirmation he delivered: Their father had perished years ago under the brutal forced labor, broken by the stones; their other brothers, Jared and Caleb, had been taken for the Nephilim's 'Great Work' deep beneath the mountain—a dark, likely sacrificial fate from which none ever returned.

Selah and Tirzah listened in heavy, stoic silence as this final, brutal confirmation extinguished the last, subconscious embers of hope they might have unknowingly harbored for so many lost years.

Tears carved paths down their weathered faces in the firelight. There was a grief laid bare in that silence, grief finally allowed its full measure without the shield of uncertainty. But then, as Methuselah's voice, steadied by Naamah's quiet presence beside him, moved on to describe Malachi's final hours, a different emotion began to surface. He told of Malachi's desperate courage in revealing the escape route through the tunnels, his refusal to join them, knowing his broken body would only hinder their flight. He recounted, his voice thick with remembered horror and awe, Malachi's last, defiant act—appearing again in the tunnels to ensure their escape, sacrificing his own life by deliberately causing the passage to collapse upon himself and their pursuers. "He bought our freedom with his last breath," Methuselah concluded, his gaze meeting Selah's. "He believed in the light we carried, the truth my father spoke of. He gave everything so that the story, so that *we*, might survive."

A new kind of silence fell then, filled not just with sorrow for Malachi's death but with a sacred respect for his sacrifice.

Selah closed her eyes, tears still flowing, but a look of fierce, terrible pride settled on her face. Her son had died not just as a broken slave but as a hero, a martyr for the truth. Tirzah wept openly now, but her tears held less despair and more a sorrowful understanding. For Kael, Ronan, Methuselah, and Naamah, recounting it again solidified the great debt they owed, the preciousness of the lives bought at such a cost. The grim closure regarding the other men was now framed by Malachi's ultimate act of love and defiance, a small, desperate light against the overwhelming darkness of the Serpent City. They now knew the full measure of the evil they had lived beside, hidden away for so long, and the incredible courage it took to resist it, even unto death.

Later that night, long after the others sought the solace of sleep, Selah sat with her two daughters, gazing into the dying embers, the weight of generations, of choices made and paths taken, settling upon her. "We cannot stay here," Selah said, her voice low but firm with sudden resolve. "This valley has been our refuge, our sanctuary for longer than memory records. But knowing what we know now, it is also a cage built by our sorrow and fear. Knowing the full truth—the final, hopeless fate of our men but also the great hope carried by Seth's line, the promise Enoch lived and died for—we cannot continue to hide while the world outside groans under the Serpent's growing power." She looked at her daughters, her eyes reflecting the embers' glow. "The world needs this testimony. And perhaps *we* need community again.

Real community, built on shared faith and purpose, not just isolated survival."

She looked toward the shadows where Methuselah and the giants slept. "These travelers head toward the glade where Enoch's people dwell—a people who hold fast to the Creator's ways. They follow the Creator's path, guided by vision and promise. I believe... our path now lies with them."

Tirzah met her mother's gaze and nodded a silent, resolute agreement, her own eyes reflecting a readiness for change, for purpose beyond mere endurance.

Naamah felt a surge of warmth, of overpowering relief, of belonging—she would not be separated from her mother and sister, her only remaining kin. Their futures would be woven together now, for better or worse.

The decision, once made, brought a quiet energy, a sense of forward momentum, to their remaining days in the valley. Methuselah, Kael, and Ronan readily, gratefully, welcomed Selah and Tirzah into their core fellowship; their presence added not just numbers but deep practical wisdom, resilient spirits, and survival skills honed by generations spent living on the edge of a hostile world.

The next few days were spent in focused preparation for the next long leg of their journey. Supplies were carefully gathered and packed—dried meats generously shared from Selah's hidden stores, ground meal, preserved roots, waterskins thoroughly cleaned and refilled. Belongings, few but precious—essential tools, sturdy cloaks were carefully packed for the journey ahead. Kael ensured both Ronan and Methuselah were as fit for the journey as rest and the valley's bounty could make them, assessing their healing with satisfaction. They spoke of the route ahead—eastward again, toward the lands the giants knew as home. It would be another long trek undertaken by a larger, more diverse company, bound ever tighter by shared loss and common purpose.

Leaving the hidden valley, sealing its secret entrance behind them, felt like closing a sacred book filled with pages of both deep sorrow and unexpected grace. They stepped out once more into the uncertain world, turning their faces resolutely eastward. The journey toward the lands near the House of Anak stretched over many weeks.. Their passage was marked by the steady rhythm of travel under open skies, the slow but sure strengthening of Ronan and Methuselah, the deepening bonds of their unlikely family, and the vital nightly ritual of recounting Adam's testimony around carefully concealed fires.

Kael led with quiet competence, navigating by landmarks remembered clearly from his youth. Selah and Tirzah moved with practiced ease, their wilderness skills proving invaluable time and again. Methuselah and Naamah often walked side by side, their quiet conversations and shared glances speaking volumes more than their words. They faced predictable hardships—scarcity of easily hunted game in certain regions, sudden, violent winds that forced them to seek shelter under rocky overhangs, the constant need for vigilance against natural predators—but buoyed by the memory of the Creator's past provision and the burning truth they carried within them, they persevered, their fellowship a source of constant strength.

Finally, after what felt like another lifetime of steady eastward travel, Kael stopped atop a high, windswept ridge, pointing toward a distinctive outcropping of weathered, granite peaks breaking the horizon against the afternoon sun. "The Dragon's Teeth," he announced, his deep voice thick with complex homecoming emotions. "Beyond them lies the valley of my father's house. We are close now. Only two days' journey remaining."

A wave of weary relief washed through the travel-worn group. After so long in the wilderness, the prospect of reaching the House of Anak, of knowing friendly kin was near, felt almost overwhelming. That night, they made camp in a sheltered spot screened by pines, within sight of those familiar peaks. The mood around the small fire was lighter than it had been in months, filled now with anticipation of another homecoming.

It was Ronan, leaning back comfortably against a tree, his healing arm resting across his lap now, who broke the comfortable silence, his gaze distant, troubled. He had been quiet throughout much of the journey, focused on healing but clearly observing, listening, and thinking. "Kael," he began, looking earnestly at his brother, then around at the faces of their companions illuminated by the firelight, his voice low but carrying unexpected weight. "Home... it feels good to be this near. But my heart has grown heavy with a fear these past weeks."

Kael looked at him, instantly concerned. "What troubles you now, brother? You are healing well."

"It is not my arm," Ronan said slowly. "It is the truth we carry. The story from Adam's cave, the knowledge of the scrolls Enoch pursued toward Eden, the promise through Seth's line... it is dangerous knowledge, Kael. Terribly dangerous." He paused, gathering his thoughts, the firelight reflecting in his serious eyes. "The House of Anak is strong, yes. Our people are mostly faithful, loyal to Father's memory and his ways. But..." He hesitated, the words clearly difficult for him to voice against his own kin. "Can we be *certain* of everyone? The Nephilim's influence, the Serpent's whispers, they are subtle things, playing on pride, on fear, on greed. We saw how they twist truth, how they tempt even strong hearts with promises of power. What if, even among our own people, there is just one whose heart already holds a hidden seed of corruption? Or one who could be swayed later, by fear, or by some future Nephilim offer?"

He looked directly then at Methuselah and Naamah, his gaze filled with fraternal concern. "If word of what you know—the true location of the hidden glade, the confirmed existence and nature of Adam's record, the specifics of the Seed's promise and lineage—ever reached the Serpent City... they would *never* stop hunting you. They would move mountains, unleash armies. Your people, Methuselah, would know no peace, ever again. You, Naamah," he included Selah and

Tirzah with his gaze, "and your mother and sister, having defied them once, would become primary targets. Everything our fathers sacrificed their lives for could be undone forever, by a single careless word, a single hidden traitorous heart, now or even generations from now."

A heavy, chilling silence fell over the small group, broken only by the crackle of the fire. Ronan's quiet words, spoken with such calm certainty, extinguished the last vestiges of naïve hope for a simple, open homecoming. Methuselah felt a cold dread grip him as the full weight of the permanent, ongoing danger settled upon him with terrifying clarity. He hadn't truly considered it beyond their own immediate survival—the fact that this knowledge made his home, his family, Elara, Jareth, Adah, everyone in the glade, a perpetual target. It wasn't just a burden to carry; it was a deadly secret demanding absolute protection, possibly forever. Naamah instinctively moved closer to her mother and sister, understanding all too well from bitter experience how easily peace could be shattered, how deeply betrayal could wound.

Kael stared into the fire for a long time, his brow furrowed, considering his brother's warning. He knew his people, loved them, and trusted them implicitly. But Ronan spoke a hard, undeniable truth. The risk, however small, of even one betrayal was far too great, the potential consequences too catastrophic, especially concerning the location of the glade or the exact nature of the scrolls Adam had written. "You are right, Ronan," Kael said finally, his voice grim, heavy with reluctance but firm with decision. "Your caution is wise. We cannot risk it." He looked around at the small, tight-knit fellowship that had become his family. "We cannot simply walk into the settlement and declare all we have seen and learned. Not openly. Not yet."

A new, more cautious plan formed quickly, born of necessity. "Naamah," Kael said, turning to her again, his voice low and serious. "You carry less history with our people than we do. You joined us *after* we first left my father's house. If you were seen approaching alone, carefully, no one would connect you back to Enoch, or Methuselah, or the full truth of this specific journey."

Naamah met his gaze steadily, understanding dawning again in her intelligent eyes. "You want me to go? Alone?"

"Under cover of darkness," Kael confirmed gravely. "Find my mother... her name is Mara. Her dwelling is near the eastern watchtower, slightly apart from the main family longhouses." He quickly repeated the specific directions and the childhood signal. "Tell her only this: that Kael and Ronan live, but we cannot return home yet. Tell her..." his voice thickened perceptibly, "...tell her how Father defended the truth he had come to cherish until his last breath. Tell her he died protecting the hope for the future, and that we live to honor his sacrifice."

He paused, ensuring she understood the gravity, the careful omissions required. "Explain clearly that we are bound by a solemn oath, sworn to him, to continue protecting that hope, and it requires absolute secrecy and continued travel away from home for now. Tell her we will send word again, find a way to reunite when it is truly safe, but we do not know when that day will be. Ask for her understanding, her blessing on our difficult path." He looked at her intently, acknowledging the burden he placed upon her. "Can you do this, Daughter of Eve? It carries great personal risk for you."

Naamah thought of Malachi's face in the tunnel, of Anak and Enoch leading the Nephilim's army away. Sacrifice was the price of truth in this broken world. "I can," she said simply, her voice firm with quiet resolve. "I will carry your message safely to Mara."

Under the deep cloak of the next moonless night, Naamah slipped away from their hidden camp nestled high in the concealing pines. Moving with the ingrained silence and skill honed by years of survival in perilous lands, she navigated the foothills leading down toward the valley housing the House of Anak. She bypassed the outer sentries Kael had warned her about, using shadows and the contours of the terrain to mask her solitary approach. Reaching the quiet edge of the sprawling settlement under the cover of deepest night, she located Mara's dwelling—a sturdy, large stone-and-timber longhouse, quieter, set slightly apart as Kael had described.

Taking a deep, steadying breath, she approached the heavy, closed hide door covering and scratched softly, hesitantly, upon it in the specific, rhythmic pattern Kael had taught her—a signal between mother and son since his boyhood. After a tense, heart-pounding moment where only the distant sounds of the settlement reached her, the hide flap lifted just enough for a pair of keen, weary eyes to peer out. A tall, strong giantess, her kind face deeply lined, framed by thick braids of grey-streaked dark hair, looked out into the night. Mara.

Seeing a lone, unknown human woman standing there silently in the dead of night, Mara initially looked wary, instantly suspicious, her hand reaching for a heavy club kept near the door. But Naamah spoke quickly, softly, using the specific, archaic greeting Kael had provided. "Mara, wife of Anak. I bring word from your sons, Kael and Ronan."

Mara's eyes widened in stunned disbelief, then sharp hope flared within them. She pulled Naamah swiftly inside, securing the heavy door flap behind them. In the dim, warm light of a hearth fire that filled the large dwelling with dancing shadows, Naamah delivered Kael's carefully worded message. Her voice trembled slightly as she recounted Anak's sacrifice, willingly given for a truth he had come to cherish more than life. She explained that Kael and Ronan lived, were healing, but were bound by a sacred oath sworn to their father to continue a vital, secret mission he had entrusted to them, a mission that tragically prevented their immediate return home. She spoke carefully of their deep love for their mother, their solemn promise to return or send word again only when it was truly safe to do so.

Mara listened in silence, sinking slowly onto a massive wooden bench near the hearth as the news unfolded, tears streaming unchecked down her face as she finally heard confirmation of Anak's death. She sat for a long time, her great shoulders shaking with grief for her lost husband, her partner through centuries. Yet, through the terrible sorrow, Naamah could also see a deep understanding dawning in her eyes, a deep, quiet pride. She knew her husband well, knew his great heart, and she knew, better than even Kael or Ronan, the change that had come over him after meeting Enoch and learning the Creator's truth. She understood the weight of an oath sworn. "My sons..." she whispered, wiping her eyes with the back of her hand. "They live. They are well. And they honor their father..." Her voice broke on a sob, but she quickly regained her composure, the resilience of her line asserting itself. "That is... it must be enough, for now."

She rose then, composing herself with the quiet strength and dignity that marked her noble lineage. "They cannot return yet," she stated softly, accepting the hard truth, her eyes meeting Naamah's with piercing understanding. "Then they will need this strength from home." She went to a large, intricately carved wooden chest in the corner, rummaging inside among stored furs and implements. She returned moments later with two small, simple objects held reverently in her hands.

"Give Kael this," she said, handing Naamah a small, perfectly smooth river stone, worn almost completely round by water and time, with markings barely visible, carved into it long ago. "His father found it for him on Kael's naming day, when he was just a small giantling. He claimed it held the river's endless strength and patient endurance. Kael carried it everywhere as a boy, until he thought himself too old for such things." Her lips curved in a sad smile. Then she held out a worn, thick, braided leather strap, smelling of old leather oil. "And this, for Ronan. From the haft of the very first practice hammer his father made for him when he began his warrior training. He always treasured it." Her voice broke slightly again, heavy with memory. "Tell them... tell them their mother understands their oath, their duty. Tell them their father's courage lives on in their faithfulness to his last command. Tell them... I love them beyond measure. And I will wait."

Naamah carefully took the precious, simple gifts, her own heart aching with the weight of the mother's love, sacrifice, and patient grief. Promising again to carry the message and the tokens safely back, she slipped back out into the pre-dawn darkness, leaving Mara alone in the firelit silence with her memories and her enduring hope.

Her return to the hidden camp just as the first light touched the peaks was met with anxious relief. She recounted her meeting with Mara, conveying the message of unwavering love, understanding, and patient blessing. Then, she presented the gifts. Kael took the smooth, river stone, closing his massive hand around it tightly, his expression unreadable in the dim light, but his jaw tight, his eyes glistening with unshed tears. Ronan reached out with his good hand, taking the worn leather strap, clutching it fiercely, bringing it briefly to his face, his broad shoulders shaking for a moment before he regained control.

No grand speeches were made. None were needed. In the quiet weight of those small, cherished objects, resonant with childhood memory, the enduring love of their lost father, the steadfast under-standing of their mother, and the harsh reality of their chosen exile converged. It was a moment of deep, shared emotion, strengthening their resolve even as it underscored the depth of their sorrow. They were truly cut off from home now, bound only to each other and the vital, dangerous truth they carried ever eastward into the unknown wilderness beyond the Dragon's Teeth, toward the final destination: the distant, hidden glade.

34

Echoes of Bronze

The wilderness stretched eastward before them, swallowing the days and weeks as month after weary month unfolded under their determined feet. Having bypassed the lands of the House of Anak, they traveled now bearing burdens heavier than their packs—not just the lingering grief for those lost but the constant weight of the sacred truth they carried and the solemn oaths that bound their unlikely fellowship. Every decision made, every wary campfire conversation held, every shared watch under alien constellations was underscored by the acute knowledge that their survival, and the absolute secrecy surrounding Methuselah's lineage and Adam's testimony, was paramount. Even simple tasks like gathering scarce firewood or drawing water from unfamiliar streams were done with watchful eyes constantly scanning the tree line, ears straining for sounds that didn't belong. They spoke often of the homes they journeyed toward. For Methuselah, it was the distant glade; for Selah and Tirzah, a hope for a new beginning there. For Kael and Ronan, it was the dream of an eventual, uncertain return to their kin. But a shared, unspoken understanding always tempered these conversations: the very knowledge they carried made each of those havens a potential target. Protecting the truth had become a living sacrifice, a constant vigilance woven into the fabric of their daily lives.

As they moved further east, leaving the territories known to the giants behind, the landscape shifted again, taking on contours that resonated with Methuselah's memory. He recognized the distinctive shape of distant, wind-scarred hills, the specific way a particular stream cut sharply through a rocky outcrop—landmarks from his initial, naïve journey westward with his father, long before reaching Eden's borderlands. A familiar sense of unease, mixed now with hard-won experience, settled over him as he realized exactly where their path was leading.

"The clearing..." he murmured to Kael one afternoon, his voice tight with unwelcome memory, pointing toward a line of distinctively gnarled trees ahead. "Where we met the tribe... the ones maddened by the bronze dagger my father threw away."

A shared look of grim remembrance passed through the group; Methuselah had recounted the tale often around their fires. They approached the area now with extreme caution, weapons held ready, and Kael moved ahead in silence to scout the perimeter. He signaled that it was clear— "deserted." They entered the small, sun-dappled clearing where, so many months ago, violence born of dangerous temptation had erupted so suddenly.

The old campfire was nothing but dead, grey ash, long cold, scattered by seasons and the passage of time. But the silence held a different kind of chill now, the silence of finality. Scattered amongst the overgrown grass and thorny bushes, almost hidden from view, lay the skeletal remains of a dozen or more human figures, picked clean by time and sharp-toothed scavengers. And there, clutched tightly in the bony fingers of one outstretched corpse as if in a final, desperate spasm of ownership, lay the object of their fatal obsession—the bronze dagger. It gleamed strangely beautiful in the harsh afternoon sunlight, its deadly metal seemingly untouched, untarnished by the elements or the death it had undoubtedly presided over. The scene told its own stark, silent, cautionary story: the tribe, consumed by the obsessive desire for the Nephilim-linked metal after Enoch cast it aside, had inevitably, tragically, turned on each other, fighting to the death for its sole possession.

Kael knelt beside the remains, his expression initially unreadable behind his thick beard. Carefully, he pried the gleaming dagger from the dead hands' unyielding grip. He turned it over and over in his hand, his craftsman's eye instinctively assessing its superb quality despite its grim and horrifying history. Methuselah recounted again the specific details of the tribe's sudden madness, their irrational, violent craving for the object the moment they laid eyes upon it. Yet, even hearing their words, Kael couldn't suppress a flicker of professional admiration for the artifact itself. "The balance," he murmured, testing its weight, feeling its perfect, lethal distribution in his palm. "The edge still holds true after all this time, sharper by far than our best iron. And so light... impossibly light for its strength." He ran a calloused finger along the smooth, cool metal of the intricately worked hilt, examining the unfamiliar patterns chased into it. "The skill required... the knowledge of metal... it surpasses anything our forges at home can produce." His interest was that of a master craftsman appreciating a superior skill, a smith acknowledging masterful craftsmanship, even while recognizing the darkness inherent in its origins.

Selah, having observed the grim scene and Kael's focused examination with quiet intensity, stepped forward as Kael rose, still holding the dagger almost reverently. Her gaze moved from the gleaming, deadly blade to the scattered bones, then rested with gentle understanding on Kael's face, noting the complex mixture of professional fascination and moral revulsion warring there. Her voice, when she spoke, was quiet but carried the resonant weight of wisdom earned through hardship and long reflection. "It *is* beautiful, Kael," she acknowledged. "And undeniably powerful in its craft. Tools, weapons, skills, knowledge beyond what the Creator first granted in wisdom... they hold a powerful, undeniable allure. They are not strictly evil in themselves."

She paused, allowing her words to settle into the heavy silence of the clearing. "But the Serpent," she continued, her clear eyes meeting Kael's directly, "is deeply cunning. He knows the hearts of men and giants alike—knows our deep, innate desire for power, for control over our world and our own fate, for strength that comes from our *own* hands, our *own* skill, our *own* hard-won, secret knowledge. He takes these desires, gifts implanted by the Creator and meant originally for good stewardship, and twists them into snares. He offers gifts—like this exquisite dagger, or the deep secrets of metalworking, or arts of power—not to uplift or serve but to seduce us into relying wholly on ourselves, on the *thing created*, rather than on the unseen Creator Himself. He makes us crave the *gift* with all our hearts, until we forget the Giver entirely."

She gestured sadly toward the bones bleaching in the sun. "This dagger," she said, her voice filled now with quiet sorrow, "promised power, a deadly advantage, control over rivals in this harsh world. And for that single glittering promise, these men forgot fellowship, forgot reason, forgot the value of life itself—their own and their brothers. They destroyed each other completely, each desperate to possess the very tool that symbolized their enslavement to desire, to the Serpent's oldest, most potent lie: the lie of self-reliance, of power found apart from God."

Selah looked at Kael again, her gaze kind but piercingly firm. "The path of dependence on the Creator, the simple life lived day-by-day in trust of His provision, His guidance—the life Enoch cherished and taught us all by his example—that is the only true freedom from this lie. Our real strength, Kael son of Anak, comes not from the sharpness of our blade or the cunning of our craft alone but from Him Who Holds All Things in His hand. Trusting the created thing, however beautiful, however powerful, instead of the Creator... that, Kael, is the Serpent's oldest, most enduring, and most dangerous deception."

Kael listened intently, motionless, Selah's words echoing the truths revealed in Adam's cave and resonating deeply with the memory of his own father's sacrifice—choosing faith, choosing others, over brute strength alone. He looked down at the exquisite, deadly beauty of the bronze dagger lying coolly in his massive palm, its alien craftsmanship a stark, seductive contrast to the sturdy, practical iron axe resting against his leg—a tool made honestly by giant hands, relying on known strength and earthly materials, intended for service, not dominance. He saw the allure of the bronze, felt its perfect balance, understood the tactical advantage it represented in a fight. But clearer still, starker than ever before, he saw the terrible price of possessing it etched into the scattered bones at his feet.

With a quiet reverence born of understanding, acknowledging the deep wisdom in Selah's words, Kael knelt again beside the fallen man. Gently, he placed the bronze dagger back on the earth beside the hand that had clung to it so fiercely, even in death. He would not carry such a seductive object, would not invite its poison into their fellowship. Let it remain here, lost in the wilderness, to be buried by time, a silent, forgotten testament to the Serpent's lies and the tragic, deadly cost of misplaced desire.

The others watched in silence, understanding the significance of the moment, the quiet victory over temptation Kael had just won. Without another word, they turned and left the grim clearing behind them, continuing their long journey eastward, sobered and wiser for the encounter. The echoes of bronze served as a potent, timely reminder that the enemy's influence was not always found in monstrous forms or overt, easily recognizable evil but could hide insidiously within the beautiful, the powerful, the things that promised knowledge and control achieved apart from the Creator. Their commitment to simple faith, to trusting the Giver above His gifts, felt more vital, more central to their survival and the preservation of the truth they carried, than ever as they walked toward home.

35

Testimony by the Falls

They journeyed steadily eastward through lands that resonated with echoes of familiarity, trails that Methuselah recognized with a sharp pang of memory from his journey now so long ago. Finally, guided by Methuselah's memories of these nearer lands, they stood on the banks of the great River, at the very place where the world had seemed to break open for him, revealing both terrifying danger and mystery. The thundering roar of the great waterfall filled the air, a constant, powerful bass note against the quiet murmur of the river downstream. Across the churning water lay the ruins of the city destroyed by Nephilim influence, where Methuselah had nearly lost his life, where he had secretly taken the bronze dagger.

Methuselah stood staring at the scene, the cool mist from the falls damp on his face, overwhelmed by the passage of time and the immensity of the changes wrought within him. He had arrived here as a reckless youth, full of undirected energy and blind eagerness, chasing adventure. Now, after what felt like several lifetimes packed into little more than two years, he stood as the designated carrier of his father's legacy, his body scarred and forever changed, his heart heavy with irreplaceable loss but also alight with a faith tested and tempered by fire, and filled with a love he hadn't known existed. The boy who plunged foolishly into the river was gone, replaced by a man burdened by sacred truth and bound by hope.

They made camp that evening in a sheltered spot amongst the time-worn ruins on their side of the river, within sight of the falls, the air heavy with powerful memories. They knew the morning would bring the challenge of the river crossing, relying on the rope Methuselah remembered anchoring the far bank, praying the Creator willed it still held fast. Around the flickering campfire, after a simple meal of small game meat and roots foraged by Naamah and Tirzah, a reflective silence fell, deeper than mere weariness, filled with the thoughts of all that had transpired since he last stood near this water.

It was Ronan who broke it, his deep voice gentle as he looked toward Methuselah across the flames. "Son of Enoch," he said, the title now holding both acknowledged respect and shared responsibility. "We have traveled far together. Seen wonders that defy words and endured losses that carved deep scars upon our souls. We carry a heavy burden, a sacred story, back toward your home. Tonight... before we cross this water again, before we take the final steps homeward... remind us why. Tell the story, Methuselah. All of it. From the beginning. Honor your father. Honor mine. Let us remember."

Methuselah met the giant's steady gaze, then looked slowly around the small fire at the faces illuminated by the flames—his family now, forged inseparable in peril and shared purpose. Naamah sat close beside him, her strength a constant presence, her eyes meeting his with trusting expectation. Selah and Tirzah watched him with the calm resilience of those who understand survival and sorrow. Ronan leaned back against a rock, his wounds healing well now, his eyes clear and keenly attentive. Kael, the steadfast protector who had fulfilled his oath with unwavering loyalty, waited patiently. Methuselah took a deep breath, feeling the weight of the request, the need to voice their shared journey not just as a sequence of recalled events but as a living testimony to the Creator's intricate, often painful, but ultimately faithful guidance.

"It began," Methuselah said softly, his voice husky at first, "with my father, Enoch, and a divine call to seek a truth lost to the ages." He spoke of their departure from the glade, and then of this very place, the ruined city. "Here," he said, his voice dropping, heavy with remembered shame, "is where I learned my first hard lesson. I saw only the river, a challenge for my pride to conquer. I plunged in, foolish and arrogant, and the current took me. It was my father's love and the Creator's mercy that pulled me from the brink. I thought strength was in my own arms, but my father taught me it was found in a desperate prayer."

He met Naamah's gaze, his own filled with regret. "And it was here I took the bronze dagger. I was afraid, and I chose to trust a thing of the world, a tool of the enemy, over the protection of the Unseen. That secret poisoned my spirit until Father cast it away."

His tone shifted, filling with warmth and respect as he looked to the giant brothers. "And from that lesson, the Creator led us to true strength, to the House of Anak. Who could have imagined? Finding kinship with the very giants we had been taught to fear. There, I learned from your father, from Anak, what nobility truly is. He taught me that strength is measured not by might but by the weight of the truths you are willing to bear. Only the Creator," his voice filled with remembered wonder, "could break down such walls of fear and forge an alliance of hearts."

He looked at Selah and Tirzah. "He sent help when we seemed utterly doomed, from the unlikeliest of hands—brave women hardened by sorrow but guided by immense courage. He brought us to you." His gaze found Naamah's again, holding it. "And you, Naamah... you chose to walk into the shadowlands with us, seeking your family, though it cost you dearly. Your path joined ours then, another vital thread woven by His intricate design."

He recounted the grim trek toward Serpent Mountain, not as a list of horrors but as a lesson in discernment. He spoke of the dazzling, soul-sickening Serpent City, its glittering towers built on lies, its golden temple spewing blasphemy. "There we saw the Serpent's greatest deception," he said bitterly. "Not monstrous and ugly but beautiful, seductive, and reasonable. It offered power, knowledge, enlightenment... everything a man's heart might desire, if he would only turn his back on the Creator. It was in the darkness of Cain's forgotten tomb, in his raw confession of regret—'*The Serpent promised knowledge, I found only ashes*'—that we finally saw the true ugliness behind the beauty."

His voice choked slightly as he recalled Malachi's sacrifice, a tribute to a different kind of strength. "He bought our freedom with his life," Methuselah whispered, seeing Naamah flinch beside him. "He faced the darkness he had lived in for years and chose to serve the light he had only just glimpsed in us. That is a courage I am still learning to comprehend."

He spoke of the long flight, the terror of the lake beast, and his own descent into the depths. "When the water closed over me," he said, his voice hushed, "I thought my foolishness had finally found its end. But He wasn't finished with me." He described his miraculous survival not as his own feat of endurance but as a moment of pure, unearned grace that left him humbled and breathless with gratitude.

"And the altar," he continued, his voice ringing now with firm conviction, looking at Kael. "Our last scraps of food. You thought Father mad to offer it, Kael. And I confess my own heart screamed in protest." He smiled. "But Father trusted. He had learned the lesson I was still struggling with, that our greatest strength is found in our deepest dependence. He gave back the last crumb, and the Creator answered with a feast. He showed us His faithfulness when we had nothing left but trust."

He spoke of Adam's cave, not just as a discovery but as the moment they finally understood the great war they were caught in. And then, his voice grew heavy with the weight of tribute. "And that truth... the promise carried through Seth... that is why they stayed behind." Tears welled, hot and sharp, for his father, for Anak, but his voice held firm.

"My father, and yours, Kael and Ronan, they saw the hunters coming. They looked at us, at the future, and they made their choice. They chose to become the shield. They chose to draw the storm onto themselves so that we," his voice emphasized the word, encompassing them all, "the living testimony, could survive."

He paused, looking at each companion, his gaze now holding the quiet authority he had inherited. "Kael," he said, his voice filled with deep respect, "your strength has been our unwavering shield, your wisdom our guide, your loyalty to your father's oath absolute. You have carried us all, literally and figuratively, through trials that should have broken us." He looked toward Ronan. "And you, Ronan, your quiet endurance through terrible injury... it shamed any thought of despair in the rest of us. You reminded us constantly that true strength is not just found in mighty blows but in enduring faith."

He saw Ronan look down briefly. Methuselah leaned forward earnestly, his voice firm but kind. "Do not *ever* think your injury was only a burden, Ronan. Perhaps it was necessary in the Creator's intricate plan. It forced us," he looked around the fire, his gaze including Selah and Tirzah, "to rely completely on each other, to care for each other with patience and humility. Our desperate need for one another became our greatest strength, stripping away pride, forcing us onto the Creator's path, not our own." Ronan looked up slowly, meeting Methuselah's eyes, and a measure of quiet peace settled on his features.

Methuselah then turned respectfully to Selah and Tirzah. "You welcomed us when we were broken and desperate," he said, his voice filled with gratitude. "You joined us from your own deep sorrow, yet you brought resilience and wisdom that reminded us we were not the only ones holding onto the light in a darkening world. You honored us, strengthened us, by choosing to walk this path with us."

Finally, his gaze rested on Naamah, sitting beside him, her eyes reflecting the campfire flames, holding his gaze steadily now. His voice softened, losing its oratorical quality entirely, becoming intensely personal, intimate despite the listening ears. "And Naamah... your quiet, unwavering strength has been a steady beacon through the deepest, coldest nights of this journey." He paused, finding the precise words, letting his heart speak plainly. "You reminded us all, and especially me, of the terrible cost of sacrifice, and the unwavering purpose worth fighting and living for. But more... so much more... for me... your presence beside me has been..." He struggled for a moment, the depth of his feeling difficult to articulate. He met her eyes directly then, his own gaze open, vulnerable, wholly certain. "It has been the Creator's unexpected, undeserved, most precious blessing amidst all the sorrow and loss. Your faith, your resilience, your compassionate heart... they have transformed me. Naamah, daughter of Eve... I love you. With all that I am. Whatever days the Creator grants me from this moment forward, I wish only to spend them by your side, sharing this burden, this privilege, stewarding this sacred truth together... raising a family who will remember, who will carry the light forward."

Tears welled in Naamah's eyes, shimmering in the firelight, not tears of sorrow now but of unexpected joy. The long, arduous journey, the shared terrors, the quiet comfort given and received, the unspoken feelings nurtured carefully in the crucible of their shared ordeal—all culminated in this single, heartfelt declaration under the watching stars. Slowly, gracefully, she moved from her place beside him to kneel directly in front of him on the sandy earth beside the ruins. She gently took both his hands in hers—calloused and strong from gripping his staff—and looked deeply into his eyes, her own filled with answering emotion, clear and true. "Methuselah, son of Enoch," she said, her voice trembling slightly at first but gaining strength, clear and strong. "My heart chose you long ago, on a dark riverbank, when you pulled me from the water's grasp. I will walk beside you always. I will love you alone among men. I will share the burden and the joy, the sorrow and the hope, and I will help carry this sacred truth for all the days the Creator gives us breath."

Leaning forward, she sealed her solemn oath, her heart's promise, with a kiss—tender, and hopeful, a testament to the resilient life and redeeming love found unexpectedly amidst the stark ruins of a broken, fallen world.

A low, pleased rumble of approval came from Kael's deep chest. Ronan grinned broadly, clapping his good hand softly against his knee. Selah and Tirzah watched, tears of quiet joy tracing paths through the firelight on their faces, seeing new life blossoming bravely from the ashes of their grief. The heavy tension of the long journey seemed to lift for a precious moment, replaced by the pure, defiant joy of love affirmed. Soon, soft chuckles turned into genuine, unrestrained laughter, echoing wonderfully off the stones beside the thundering falls—the ragged, cathartic laughter of survival. They were battered, scarred, bearing huge burdens, but they were together, bound now not just by oath but by deep love, unwavering faith, and the bright promise of a future worth fighting for. As the fire crackled low, they prepared with lighter hearts for the river crossing, their fellowship stronger, their path forward illuminated now by more than just the coming dawn.

36

Return to the Glade

Dawn broke clear and bright over the ruined city by the falls. After the emotional declarations and laughter shared around the campfire, a quiet, steadfast resolve had settled over the small company. It was time to make the final push toward the hidden glade that, for most of them now, would become home. Methuselah led them along the riverbank to the place where, two years before, he and his father had first seen the thick rope stretching across the river's turbulent, forbidding waters.

The crossing would demand all their remaining strength and unwavering focus, for even here, so close to the journey's end, danger felt palpably near. The roar of the falls was a constant reminder of the river's power, a place where their entire quest could still come to a tragic end if vigilance faltered.

"The rope holds fast on both sides," Kael announced after he and Methuselah had pulled hard on the ageless line. "It is old, but the craft of those who set it was sound. We will trust it, and the Creator Who preserved it for us."

While Ronan, Selah, and Tirzah began gathering suitable beams and tough, pliable green vines from the ruins and the river's edge, Kael and Methuselah worked to construct crude but sturdy rafts. They fashioned three small, rough platforms from the gathered beams, lashing them together with the green vines. One for Ronan, one for Kael, and a slightly larger one for Methuselah, Naamah, Selah, and Tirzah. These were then connected end-to-end with more stout vines, forming a linked conveyance. At the front and back of each raft, they fashioned strong vine loops that could slide along the now-secured main river rope.

"I will take the lead raft," Kael stated, his voice practical and commanding, as they maneuvered the first platform to the water's edge. "Methuselah, you take the rear. We will all use these smaller vine hitches on the main rope," he indicated loops designed to grip but also slide, "to pull our sections and keep us aligned against the current."

The crossing began. With Kael on the lead raft, his strength already straining against the initial pull of the current as he guided their entry into the water, the others took their places on the subsequent platforms. The linked rafts slowly began to move out into the main current, guided by the massive rope spanning the river. The river fought them with vicious tenacity. The rafts bucked and swayed alarmingly under the force of the water, threatening to twist apart or be swamped by the cold, drenching spray. The roar of the nearby waterfall filled their ears, a constant, deafening reminder of the dangers faced and overcome. Each yard gained felt like a monumental victory, each coordinated pull on the main rope and their individual hitches a testament to their shared will, their desperate, unified need to reach the safety of the eastern bank.

When the last of them, with Kael guiding the final raft section ashore, stood safely on the eastern bank amongst the others, soaked and gasping but triumphant, he turned back to look at the thick rope spanning the powerful river—the last tangible link connecting them to the lands west of the mountains, to the history they had unearthed, and for him and Ronan, to their ancestral home. Then, to the surprise of the humans watching, he lifted his great iron axe. With two swift, powerful blows that echoed sharply even above the waterfall's roar, he severed the thick rope near the anchor point on their side. The severed end whipped violently through the air and splashed heavily into the rushing water, seized by the powerful current, vanishing from sight. The bridge back was gone.

"Kael!" Methuselah exclaimed, startled by the abrupt, irrevocable finality of the act. "Why? How will you and Ronan ever hope to return to your kin, to your mother, now?"

Kael lowered his axe slowly, turning to face them, his expression solemn but clear, fully resolute. Ronan, standing beside him, offered a faint, understanding smile toward his brother. "Our kin?" Kael repeated, his deep voice resonating, softer now but no less firm. "Our oath, sworn to Father before Adam's cave, binds us elsewhere now. Our future, our true purpose, lies here," he gestured toward Methuselah and Naamah, acknowledging the sacred lineage and the living testimony, "with the line of Seth, with the truth we are sworn to protect." He glanced back dismissively at the wide, now impassable river. "That rope offered only a potential path for those who might someday pursue us. If it is the Creator's will that we one day see the House of Anak again, He will provide the way. But *you*," his gaze settled firmly on Methuselah and Naamah, then swept warmly to include Selah and Tirzah, "you are our kin now. This is our family. Our lives are pledged, until their end, to protecting this fellowship, this future, this hope." It was their final, chosen sacrifice, the quiet, deliberate severing of the last tie to their old life, an absolute, unwavering commitment to their new duty, their new home.

With that weighty understanding settling between them, cementing their unlikely bond, a new chapter truly beginning, they turned their faces eastward once more. The journey through lands now increasingly known to Methuselah felt strangely swift, each recognized landmark bringing them closer to the glade. Days passed, but their steps seemed lighter now, fueled by the undeniable proximity of home and the deep strength drawn from their solidified fellowship. They spoke often, softly, around their hidden fires, of Enoch and Anak, keeping their memory alive not just as heroes lost in sacrifice but as foundational pillars of the unwavering faith and purpose that now guided their own steps, reinforcing the hard-won lessons learned, reciting the sacred history revealed in Adam's cave until it was woven into the fabric of their souls.

Finally, after weeks that blurred together under sun and stars, Methuselah began to recognize the signs he had known since childhood—the specific way the light filtered through the canopy ahead, the unique scent of damp earth, pine needles, and mosses carried on the breeze. His heart pounded with growing anticipation. He led them through the final, concealed ways known only to his people, parting the last screen of thick, concealing vines, emerging at last into the soft, welcoming green light of the well-known clearing—the glade.

Figures emerged from the woven huts, alerted by the giants' unavoidable passage through the outer woods. Eyes widened in stunned disbelief. A woman's cry of pure shock, then overwhelming, unrestrained joy, broke the stillness. Elara, Methuselah's mother, rushed forward, her face alight with fierce, desperate hope that faltered painfully as her eyes scanned past him, searching for the one who was missing. Close behind her came Jareth, his usual serious features completely undone, breaking into stunned, joyous relief. And beside him, Adah, her eyes wide with astonishment and immediate, irrepressible curiosity at the sight of the giants and the unknown women.

Elara reached Methuselah first, throwing her arms around him, clinging tightly as if to reassure herself he was real, burying her face in his shoulder. "My son! My son! You live! You live!" Jareth grasped his brother's arm, his voice thick with emotion. "Methuselah! By the Creator's infinite grace, you've returned!" Adah rushed forward too, tears of pure joy spilling down her cheeks as she hugged him fiercely, babbling questions already. But even as they embraced him, their eyes searched desperately past him, past the strangers, seeking the tall, beloved figure of Enoch. Seeing only the unknown faces—a dreadful understanding dawned, chilling the warmth of the reunion like an icy wind. Elara pulled back slowly, her hopeful expression crumbling into anguished certainty, her hand flying to her mouth. "Methuselah... where... where is your father?" Jareth's hand tightened painfully on his brother's shoulder, his face paling. Adah's joyous tears turned instantly to confused sorrow, her gaze darting between Methuselah and the empty space where Enoch should have stood beside him.

Methuselah held his mother tightly, the embrace both comforting and heart-wrenching beyond words. He met the grief-stricken, questioning eyes of his mother, his brother, and his sister. "He... he walked faithfully with God, Mother," he whispered, the words tasting of both sacred sorrow and awe. "He is with the Creator now."

Over the next hours, nestled within the loving embrace of the glade community, amidst tears of deep grief for Enoch and Anak's heroic sacrifice, mingled with tears of overwhelming joy and gratitude for the returnees, the incredible story unfolded. Shared haltingly at first by a weary Methuselah, then expanded upon with quiet dignity by Naamah, Kael, and Ronan, corroborated by the quiet presence of Selah and Tirzah, the tale poured forth—the divine quest, the wonders and horrors of the lost cities, the dangers faced, the miracles witnessed, the sacrifices made, the world-altering truths revealed in Adam's cave. The people of the glade listened in hushed, rapt silence, absorbing the staggering weight of their true history, the terrifying reality of the vast, dangerous world beyond their sheltered home, and the sacred duty that had now irrevocably fallen upon Methuselah and those who had returned with him.

Elara drew back from comforting others, looking deeply into Methuselah's eyes again, searching his changed face. She saw the lingering youthfulness in his features, yes, but beneath it shone a new depth, a quiet gravity, a strength born of fire and faith that strongly reflected his father's enduring spirit, yet tempered now by experiences, by losses, she could only begin to comprehend. The eager, sometimes reckless boy who had left her side what felt like a lifetime ago had not returned; a man, carrying the heavy weight of generations, stood before her. Her heart ached with the fresh, sharp wound of losing her husband, her partner in faith and life, but it also swelled with a fierce, quiet pride for the son who had endured, learned, and returned, ready now to carry the light forward.

He gently took her hand and turned to formally introduce their companions, his voice holding warmth and deep respect. "Mother, Jareth, Adah," he said, bridging the old life of the glade and the new reality brought by their journey. "This is Kael and Ronan, noble sons of Anak, the great giant chief who gave his life protecting us, protecting the truth itself. They are bound by solemn oath, and now by deep friendship, to stay with us." Jareth and Adah stared up at the giants, no longer just with awe but with newfound respect and gratitude, offering quiet, heartfelt greetings, welcoming these powerful, unexpected allies into their midst. "And this," Methuselah continued, turning to the women whose presence felt equally significant, "is Selah, and her daughter, Tirzah. They gave us refuge and wisdom when we were wounded and lost." Selah nodded with the quiet dignity of one who had seen too much sorrow but refused to break. Then Methuselah's gaze softened unmistakably as he looked at Naamah, taking her hand gently but firmly in his own. "And this is Selah's other daughter, Naamah. Her family sheltered us first. She endured the very darkness of the Serpent City seeking her lost kin... she carries the living testimony with us now. And," his gaze met Naamah's, filled with steadfast, open love, "she has consented to join her life with mine, Mother, to build our future here together."

Elara embraced Naamah warmly then, welcoming her into the family without hesitation, her eyes holding tears but also genuine compassion, seeing another strong spirit fashioned in loss, recognizing instantly the deep, quiet, tested bond between this young woman and her son. Adah looked at Naamah and Tirzah with open curiosity and immediate empathy, already formulating questions. Jareth, after respectfully acknowledging Selah and Naamah, found his gaze drawn almost involuntarily to Tirzah. She stood quietly beside her mother, her face holding the same insightful resilience as Naamah's, her eyes observant, intelligent, missing nothing despite her obvious weariness. Jareth, usually focused entirely on duty and responsibility for the glade, felt an unexpected warmth stir within him, an immediate sense of admiration for her quiet strength and grace under pressure. He stepped forward slightly. "Tirzah," he said, offering a respectful nod and a rare, genuine smile that softened his serious features considerably. "Welcome to the glade. We are deeply honored to have you and your mother among us after all you have endured. Please, allow us to help you find rest and comfort here." Tirzah met his direct, kind gaze, surprised by the warmth, and offered a small, grateful, answered smile in return, a tiny, unexpected seed of connection planted amidst the complex emotions of homecoming.

* * *

The years that followed settled into a new, richer, more vigilant rhythm in the glade. Strengthened by the arrival of Naamah, Selah, Tirzah, Kael, and Ronan, the community adapted, absorbing the newcomers and the tangible, sometimes terrifying, world-altering knowledge they brought. Methuselah and Naamah married before the simple stone altar in the heart of the glade, their union blessed by Elara and joyfully witnessed by the entire community, a powerful symbol of continuing life, resilient hope, and the weaving together of diverse faithful lines. In time, they were blessed with a son, strong, healthy, with Naamah's dark, thoughtful eyes that already held a curious spark reminiscent of his grandfather Enoch's deep wisdom—whom they named, as the Creator had foretold, Lamech.

Life remained outwardly simple, centered always on faith, family, and the daily tasks of survival within their hidden sanctuary. They farmed the fertile glade soil, tended the shaggy kin and iridescent birds, raised their children, and worshipped the Creator Who sheltered them. But life was profoundly enriched. Kael and Ronan, honoring their oath daily and finding deep purpose in their new home, became invaluable protectors and builders. Their strength helped raise sturdier, more permanent dwellings against the forest's edge, cleared new ground for cultivation with astonishing ease, and significantly improved the glade's hidden defenses. Kael, cautiously applying lessons learned from both his people's craft and Selah's timely warnings about its potential dangers, shared limited, practical knowledge of metalworking, improving farming tools, and hunting spearheads without resorting to the forbidden arts. Ronan, his arm never regaining its original brute power, became a beloved, gentle figure among the growing number of children, sharing carefully sanitized giant tales of bravery and lessons of courage, his patience endless. Selah and Tirzah shared their deep knowledge of wild plants, potent healing remedies, and survival skills learned in harsher lands, weaving their practical resilience seamlessly into the glade's daily fabric. Laughter gradually, over time, replaced tears more often than not; children—human and, eventually, even some born with giant blood from unions blessed within the community—played under the watchful eyes of their elders, fires burned brightly and warmly in family hearths, and the community thrived in relative peace, faithfully calling upon the name of the Lord. The story of Adam's testimony, of Enoch and Anak's noble sacrifice, became a sacred history, recounted often around the fire, ensuring the truth remained vibrant, alive, and central to their identity.

Yet, they lived largely unaware, in their peaceful, blessed isolation, of the accelerating, suffocating darkness consuming the world outside their hidden borders. Beyond the glade, beyond the memory of lost Shem or the distant, fading echo of Eden's light, the ancient evil festering within Serpent Mountain grew bolder, more desperate, more demanding as the years passed. Its corrupting influence spread like an unstoppable plague across the lands, demanding ever greater, darker sacrifices, twisting minds and hearts further into unimaginable violence and depravity. The Nephilim and their human and giant servants relentlessly sought any trace, any whisper, of Adam's true records to destroy the light that challenged their dominion, to erase the memory of the Creator entirely. Fear, perversion, violence, and death became the inescapable norm across the face of the earth; the world reshaped steadily, inexorably, into the Serpent's hateful image. It was a grim, drowning reality that those dwelling faithfully in the glade, protected for now by leagues of wilderness, generations of secrecy, and the Creator's enduring grace, would inevitably, terribly, face when the final whispers of coming judgment grew into a worldwide roar.

www.ingramcontent.com/pod-product-compliance
Lightning Source LLC
Chambersburg PA
CBHW050146120726
47903CB00002B/515